PLUS
AND
MINUS

+ & -

DONALD DEWEY

MILFORD
HOUSE

an imprint of Sunbury Press, Inc.
Mechanicsburg, PA USA

MILFORD HOUSE

an imprint of Sunbury Press, Inc.
Mechanicsburg, PA USA

For information about special discounts for bulk purchases, please contact Sunbury Press Orders Dept. at (855) 338-8359 or orders@sunburypress.com.

To request one of our authors for speaking engagements or book signings, please contact Sunbury Press Publicity Dept. at publicity@sunburypress.com.

ISBN: 978-1-62006-195-4 (Trade paperback)

Library of Congress Control Number: 2018948226

FIRST MILFRED HOUSE PRESS EDITION: June 2018

Product of the United States of America
0 1 1 2 3 5 8 13 21 34 55

Set in Bookman Old Style
Designed by Crystal Devine
Cover by Lawrence Knorr
Edited by Lawrence Knorr

Continue the Enlightenment!

For Alan Willinger

CHAPTER 1

I was in one of my nothing-against moods. I had nothing against thousands of trees standing tall in the early fall as long as every hundredth one had a neon sign flashing the title of the latest Tommy Lee Jones movie. I had nothing against endless miles of antiseptic upstate highway as long as the dividing line veered occasionally into a street where garbage clogged the gutters. I especially had nothing against the Professor railing on about all the Indian tribes that had been exterminated to make room for the Burger Kings we passed as long as I could count on a Mohawk war party eventually jumping out from behind the pines, spruces, or whatever the hell they were to shut him up.

Call me Mister Tolerance.

What I could have done without, on the other hand, was the Paul Finley who had agreed to undertake a four-hour drive so the Professor could tell a lot of rhubarb growers about the 1918 flu pandemic. I had been so quick to go for that "fresh air" that's supposed to start immediately outside every city line that I hadn't even reacted to his hypocritical apologies about intruding upon my day. It had taken me to the Bruckner Boulevard's pothole attacks on my springs to realize I must have been desperate to get away from my desk if fleeing to a place called New Florence, New York seemed like a solution to something. Only crossing into Westchester had I started cringing about all the cardboard Davids and Lego Duomos I figured were waiting for us. Maybe the mayor even walked around his Main Street dressed up like

a Medici prince. *"Buon Giorno, Signor Finley. Visitors aren't allowed to ignore our one red light in New Florence. The fine will be
one hundred dollars or six thousand florins, whichever you have
handy."*

"The idea was to relax a little."

Joe Carroll, my father-in-law in our former lives, was the kind
who addressed half his remarks to the ether in front of him; market testing had proven it was the only audience up to his wit. "I'm
relaxed. If I didn't have to keep my hands on the wheel, I'd be
unconscious."

He made a sound halfway between a grunt and a bellow and
tried to be more interested in another clump of trees outside his
window. The truth was, he was as suspicious of his rural surroundings as I was. Where he lived in Garden City, Long Island
might not have been Brooklyn, but it wasn't exactly Antelopeville,
either; the place even had sidewalks. So the impulse to deliver
a little talk as a favor to one of his former students living in the
middle of the enchanted forest lacked something in the truth-
and-nothing-but-the-whole-truth department. I hoped the finish
line wasn't another of his brainstorms to keep Finley Investigations solvent.

I should explain that. In the few years of its tortured existence
Finley Investigations had taken on more than one case involving
the Professor's acquaintances. In the beginning I had thought he
was just trying to scare up work for me within our mutual misery
after a highway accident that had killed my wife and six-year-old
daughter (his daughter and grandchild); the first couple of people
he had sent me had needed little more than a witness for official
paperwork. But a couple of the others I ended up calling clients
had really needed the kind of help I was good for every so often.
Matters hadn't always ended happily, but that hadn't been his
fault and I didn't think it had been mine. Bottom line: He took
me seriously as a private investigator. Me? I had never had much
choice in taking him seriously as an historian. He had already
been the Professor when I had been dating his daughter Jennifer,
at least one family outing every year had been about some new
professional honor for him, and his retirement from his university

as chairman of the History department had been about as low-key as the abdication of a British king. Who could doubt he was as authoritative as everyone, including Joe Carroll himself, said he was? But that didn't mean I wanted to keep crossing wires with him professionally. After a little time in the business I had gotten used to finding my own clients. They might not have numbered a cast of thousands, but at least I had gotten used to the illusion that I was back to standing on my own feet after crawling around in dark caves for more time than I cared to remember. Sense or not, taking on more clients from the Professor threatened to undo the effort we had both made to establish some space between us.

"She was a brilliant student," he said, when the trees finally parted for another rest area.

"Who? This Karen Noon?"

"She should have ended up as more than a librarian in some goddamn place called New Florence."

I tried to picture Karen Noon, the reason for our little excursion, but gave it up before conflicting images of a timid librarian with chalk skin and a sassy graduate with cute bangs who had defied Joe Carroll's plans for her life. More to the point, his sullen tone was the one that usually came before an admission he didn't think the world was entitled to. "How about a coffee?" I said, already taking the cutoff.

"So I have to go to the john more?"

"You probably have to right now. Be pleasant and say 'Thank you, Paul. That's very thoughtful of you.'"

He didn't bother with further protest, and I counted that as my first victory of the morning. I wanted to be sitting directly across from him at a table or in a booth when he finally got around to telling me how Karen Noon, great disappointment that she might have been to him, had succeeded in pulling him out of his retired academician's routine on Long Island. By now I had gotten pretty good at deciphering his scowl levels, but that skill was useless as long as I had to keep my eyes on the road. As cardiac specialists were fond of saying, McDonald's to the rescue.

The roadside place's combination of a low ceiling, dark lighting and a meat freezer temperature had to be the brainchild of some franchise vice-president living in the middle of Miami Beach pastels, but at least it made the coffee feel reasonable. Once he had visited the Men's Room, the old man also acted easier about collecting a Danish and a coffee at the counter. He frowned to see that I had skipped all the empty tables to settle at the one furthest from the cashier. He hated being so obvious about wanting to talk.

"So Karen Noon hasn't lived up to all your hopes."

"Did I say that?"

"Yeah, you did."

"My short-term memory isn't what it used to be."

"Mine is great."

Watching Joe Carroll sip coffee wasn't one of life's aesthetic thrills. Because of his salmon features, he seemed to invite a fisherman's hook when he puckered his lips over the cup. Too bad for me I had once made that crack, so he didn't have any doubts about what I was thinking when he caught my eye. "Go screw yourself."

"Karen Noon?"

He settled down to it, and with more gloom than disapproval. "It's not her fault, I suppose," he said, pulling his Danish apart as if it were a chicken bone. "She married as soon as she graduated. The son of a Jersey politician who was already following in the father's footsteps. I had my suspicions soon as I got a look at his hair."

"What was wrong with his hair?"

"The part. It was so perfect you wanted to cut along the dotted line."

I gave him his laugh, but he really didn't want it.

"They moved to Hoboken. For a few years I'd hear from her only around the holidays and I'm not sure I would've heard that much if she hadn't been on Helen's Christmas card list. Never too much about herself except that she was using the considerable education I'd given her just for helping her husband become councilman of this and assemblyman of that."

"It's called public service, Joe."

"It's called wasted resources," he snapped. "But then she found that out for herself, the worst way she could. One day the politician—Andrew, Anthony, whatever—sat down at his office desk and blew his brains out."

Whatever way I'd been expecting his story to go, it hadn't been that way. Even he looked queasy for catching me so off-guard. "Why?"

He pulled at his Danish more earnestly. "As irony, it would've been too heavy-handed even for the Greeks. He'd just been voted the most honest politician in the county, some damn thing like that, and that got this eager reporter off the stick to see exactly how honest he had been."

"Not so much?"

"Not so much. The reporter turned up enough garbage to make the guy look like Boss Tweed. Don't ever get yourself voted the best private eye in Brooklyn, Finley. It'll be your finish."

"And Karen Noon?"

"She didn't take my calls when I read about it. The funeral was a family affair and I didn't butt in. I sent her a condolence card and waited to hear from her. About three months later she finally sent me a letter saying she was moving out of New Jersey and looking for a job upstate New York. Know what my first reaction was?"

I did. "You were pissed she didn't ask you for a reference."

He dropped his smile behind another puckering up for his coffee. "Of course, I was. How could she get any job at Stony Brook, Syracuse or any place else without my say-so? Had she met so many people with connections in New Jersey I'd become an afterthought?"

"But she wasn't going for a teaching job."

He shook his head. "Did the best dissertation on Lucrezia Borgia I ever read, but she sounded ready to work in a grocery store."

"So New Florence makes vague sense."

The eyes popped out of his fish face. "What sense??!! Lucrezia Borgia was Ferrara, not Florence! One has absolutely nothing to do with the other! Read that entry in your encyclopedia again!"

I sipped my own coffee until he had simmered down. A blond kid in a Phillies sweatshirt at the next table looked us over the way he might have taken in the night creatures at the Bronx Zoo. Which reminded me that both Philadelphia and the Bronx were in the opposite direction from where we were going, and that seemed worth getting annoyed about all over again. "I was talking about Italy. Flimsy connection, but a connection. Something in her genetic code that keeps reaching out to define her. Like why she has to have her old prof giving a talk in her library."

"You sound irritated."

"Gee, really?"

Then he won me over; he suddenly looked totally uncertain. "I don't know," he said. "She sounded upset. Like I could do her a big favor. And between you and me I've been wanting to do one for her ever since I heard about the suicide."

"So you really don't know why she wants to see you. I mean, the little talk in the library is there. But . . ."

"Is there something else? You may not know this with your hectic schedule running after sleazoids, but the last place that needs somebody like me coming to give talks about the pandemic is the New Florence area. The whole region was one big case of pneumonia at the height of the crisis. The kid who sells newspapers on the corner probably knows the history better than I do. So yeah, I think there's something else. But don't ask me what."

Had he said somebody might know something better than he did? He pulled apart another piece of Danish and looked almost human popping it into his mouth.

CHAPTER 2

He spent the rest of the ride correcting notes he had typed out on pink onionskins ages ago. The onionskins had faded to something like peach and the gawky type looked like it had been produced by one of those organ-sized Remingtons from the World War I era. I didn't know how he managed to read any of it; just glancing over at his concentration made my stomach flutter. Reading in moving vehicles was on the Finley Did Not Do list. If I had ever bothered to write it down, I'm sure the list would have covered several pages, but, luckily, another item in there would have been FINLEY DID NOT WRITE DOWN THINGS FINLEY DID NOT DO.

I wasn't all that surprised by how seriously he was taking a talk that was probably just a change of pace from bingo for the people waiting for us in New Florence. Nobody had ever accused Joe Carroll of mailing it in when it came to his subject, wherever and for whomever. Living alone since his wife Helen's death had only made the obsessive meticulousness worse, at least according to what Jennifer had told me. He had footnotes at the ready for when someone asked him directions to a bus.

And guess what? I liked thinking of myself as being as painstaking as the old man. In place of delving into flu epidemics, substitute tracking down deadbeat dads, getting the goods on malpractice doctors, and catching slumlords hammering boilers to pieces. One field could demand as much *t* crossing and *i* dotting as the other. Vanity? I didn't think so since private investigators didn't go around bragging about what inept businessmen they were, and meticulousness in my line was all business stupidity. The standard was in and out, open and closed, only quantity counts, time is money, here are my expenses, send all your friends around, and thank you very much. Vice versa, when you used gas without putting it on the client's bill or worked a few hours off the clock to be doubly sure about what went into a report, you did it with an edginess you might be found out as an amateur. Maybe only a gnat-sized edginess, granted, but still an edginess.

It was another threat to my MBA credentials that had made me so receptive to hitting the road for New Florence. No matter how tiring it might turn out to be, the trip put off for another day my decision about what to do about George Oswald as a client. Oswald was the perfect 10 for being dropped by Finley Investigations: He was paying almost double my customary rate, he had been paying it on time, and I didn't like him. The first thing I didn't like about him was his voice—one of those grating, high-pitched squeals that sounded like it was congratulating itself for struggling out of the larynx. This was especially unnerving in his case because he was a sportscaster whose sole claim to existence was in going on and going on and going on. As bad as that was on the radio, it was malicious across the living room desk I called an office. On the one occasion he had dropped by, I'd had the creepy feeling the curtains on the window behind me were about to float down into the courtyard in protest. I might have had to listen to him, but *they* didn't!

George Oswald's problem was his success. After years of moving from one East Coast station to another to give scores at the top of the hour, he had been offered a job as a play-by-play announcer for the minor league Brooklyn Cyclones baseball team. Wasn't that what people like George Oswald had always wanted? Well, yes, he had shrieked to me during his first visit, but he also wanted to hold on to the job once he started it. And why did he doubt he would be able to? Well, there were tapes. Tapes? Off-the-air tapes at his latest station stopover. Just guys in the studio clowning around. You know.

No, I didn't, and it had taken him a long minute to tell me what I didn't know. And while he had, I had decided he was as

close to a living Mister Potato Head as I'd ever seen. I had imagined sticking all kinds of carrot and celery stalks into his doughy
face to make him look like something else. The possibilities had
been infinite—a Picasso snowman, Dilbert from the comic strips,
George Bush. Whoever George Oswald looked like, though, he was
going to come out sounding the same, and that meant the clown
who maybe, just maybe, mind you, had said some derogatory
things about women and the handicapped in the studio between
score updates and, oh, yeah, there had been one afternoon when
everybody had been, you know, doing shtick about Filipinos. You
know how that can happen, right? Who can be seriously biased
against Filipinos? We couldn't have beaten Japan without them,
couldn't find enough nurses for the hospitals without them.
Heh, heh. None of it had meant anything. You know, just fooling
around, nothing offensive in a serious way. You know. But one of
the engineers had kept the studio recorder going through all the
hilarity, so . . .

"So?"

He had squirmed so hard across my desk chair I thought his
ass was going to tear the cushion. "This gig with the Cyclones,"
he had winced into the sun streaming through the window. "I
wasn't the only one up for it. There were a lot of candidates. One
was Bob Nelson."

"Who the hell is Bob Nelson?"

He had brightened instantly to hear that Bob Nelson's fame
hadn't penetrated my Bay Ridge apartment. "He does the news
at WBOV. Talks through his adenoids. But he really wanted this
play-by-play job and from what I hear it came down to me or him."

"Too bad for Bob Nelson."

"Yeah, but he was hanging around in the control booth a
couple of the times I was goofing off with the guys. He's not big on
small talk, always keeps his distance, you know?"

"Sounds like small talk you want to keep your distance from."

Annoyance. "Look, I'm not here for a lecture on political cor-
rectness. The point is Nelson didn't take the news about the Cyclones too well. Started badmouthing me to some people."

"So get a lawyer to write a letter."

"And what? Sue Nelson for what he might or might not have said? That'll really go over big with the Cyclones."

"What are you asking, Mr. Oswald?"

Down to it, he had heard his ridiculousness; but only for a second. "I think Nelson has some of those off-air tapes. And I wouldn't put it past him to feed them to some online blog. What do you think the Cyclones would say about hiring me then?"

I hadn't banked any checks from the Cyclones to give a damn about what they would have said. "Again: What are you asking?"

"The tapes. I want you to get those tapes."

"That all?"

"Well, it's not like I'm asking you to scale Everest."

"That's exactly what you seem to be asking or else you'd already have those tapes burning in your wastepaper basket at home."

He hadn't denied it. "Think it was easy for me to come around here? I felt beaten just opening the telephone directory and looking up your name."

"That's nice to hear."

"You don't have to take it like that. I'm talking about me. I thought I could handle it by myself. The day before yesterday I dropped over to the station. They claim not to know what I'm talking about. But they know. I think they were even waiting for me to come by."

"Who's the *they* besides this Bob Nelson?"

"An engineer named Pastore. He's been recording studio goofs for years, must have the biggest collection in the city by now. And he'd be the one to sell my clowning around to Nelson."

"And here I thought we just had to worry about the Russian mob."

"It's not funny, Finley. Once those things get online, they stay there. The worst shit follows you everywhere."

About that he had been right. All I'd had to do was tap a computer key to find years-old gibberish I'd said to reporters in my former life with Nassau County Major Cases. That little grab of my sympathy plus my latest income valley had made it seem reasonable that afternoon to accept the check George Oswald had passed over the desk to me. At first it hadn't felt like a bad move. What I said before about being as scrupulous as the Professor? Well, that didn't exclude an exception here and there, especially for the likes of a George Oswald. A call to the tapes collector Pastore would justify the retainer, I had told myself. But then I had complicated matters by looking at the check. Even as a ploy to get him out of the apartment, I wouldn't have asked for $750 as a retainer. "Not something just to fluff off," Oswald had said, beaming in on my B Effort intentions. "I know how vindictive Nelson can be. This is my whole career at stake here, Finley."

Resolved: George Oswald was entitled to a career. Sailing past all the firs and larches on the way to New Florence a week later, I could still make a case for being on either side of the debate. He *wasn't* entitled because he was a moron, he wouldn't raise the IQ level of the audience keeping score of Brooklyn Cyclones singles and strikeouts, and he shouldn't expect to get his way just by writing generous checks to a lowlife like Paul Finley. Plus, that voice, of course. Then, over at the lectern on the other side of the stage, he *was* entitled because . . . well, because Abraham Lincoln and the Bible said everybody was entitled. Or something.

First up had been Lou Pastore. His name had been vaguely familiar to me when Oswald had given it to me, but I had written that off to seeing too many installments of "The Sopranos," and that was about the extent of my background research. I was still drafting my cover story in the elevator on my way up to the WBOV studios on the seventy-something floor of the Empire State Building. I was a collector of radio studio trivia? I was a representative of the Brooklyn Cyclones who had heard rumors and wanted to dispel them? Or, most simply, I was an agent for George Oswald who just wanted to clear the terrain of any potential embarrassments for a big career move? Number three got the boot first because that was the truth, and who ever got anywhere telling the truth? But numbers one and two weren't much more appealing. Suppose Pastore asked something a collector of studio tapes would have considered the ABCs of the pastime? Or suppose he just picked up a phone to call the Cyclones? The truth might not have worked, but lies were no better. I needed something else.

Everything about WBOV had an old black-and-white movie feel, right down to the chubby blonde who answered phones at the high reception desk. It was a miracle she wasn't cracking bubblegum and polishing her fingernails ruby red. "Lou expectin' you?" she asked in perfect Flatbush. "He can't see just anybody, you know. He's workin'."

"I'm not just anybody."

"What's that mean?"

"It means it's important and Lou won't like it if you don't call inside and tell him I'm here."

Gladys, as she called herself, rolled her eyes as though she shouldn't have expected better from Pastore's circle. "Sit down. I'll call him."

Judging by the magazines on the reception area table, WBOV's only visitors were time salesmen. I hadn't known there were so many advertising magazines being published. Probably the only people who did were the time salesmen who were expected to flip through them while waiting for Gladys to wave them inside. But what sense did that make? Any salesman worth his attaché case would have already memorized the contents of every one of the glossies arrayed on the table. So what was the point of putting them there in the first place? What seemed appropriate was in fact totally inappropriate.

I could have done without that insight while waiting for Lou Pastore. In some irritating way it seemed to be an accusation against me.

Pastore was waiting for me at the end of a gray-carpeted hallway filled with framed pictures of people I'd last seen in the window of a photography store. I didn't recognize a single face, and didn't know where that left me with Arbitron demographics—too cutting edge to be familiar with talk show hosts ranting about immigrants stealing their wallets or too old to be worth a second thought? Lou Pastore, though, I recognized right away, and could only blame the loss of a few more trillion brain cells for not having the name register completely as soon as Oswald had said it. It had been a good 15 years, when I had been a cop in Nassau County. Back then he had also been an engineer, with a Long Island radio station in Mineola operating right under the nose of the county prosecutor's office. The station had specialized in golden oldies, at least when it hadn't been serving as a conduit for million-dollar drug deals. Instead of using unimaginative tools like telephones, the ring's suppliers had been alerting their salesmen of new product through a couple of announcers broadcasting coded messages. That might have belonged in the Criminal Stupidity Hall of Fame, but the head supplier had been an addict of those war movies where the BBC contacted European underground movements with short-wave announcements like "Charles Dickens needs a new hairpiece." He had adored himself for it, too, in open court thanking *Newsday* for calling his crew The Maquis Gang.

"Finley? I know you. Right?"

We had never found enough to tie Pastore to the Maquis Gang, but I had always thought that was because we hadn't worked hard enough at connecting the dots, not because he had been cleaner than the two announcers indicted. After 15 years, he still wasn't somebody you would spot on the street and go, "Hey, there's the perfect spokesman for Purity Linens!" The black mustache was grayer, the gut saggier over his cowboy buckle, but the black gumdrops he had for eyes had yet to see anything he couldn't envision stripping, selling, or both. I had to admit George Oswald might not have been exaggerating the bind he was in.

"Tell me where," he said. "Fort Lee? Danbury?"

"You get to all the best places, Lou."

He bit down on a hot pepper. "The cop! From WCHH!"

"Good memory. And I bet we didn't talk more . . ."

"Four hours," he shot back, an old contempt flushing his face. "An hour, an hour, and two hours. And I still don't know what was going on."

I nodded; I wasn't there for warming up 15-year-old cases. "We live and learn. Glad to see you made Manhattan."

He didn't know what to do with his reheated anger except shift his bulge against the wall; I wasn't going to be invited into any room. "You got something on the people around here now?"

"Not my line anymore. I'm not a cop."

He hadn't expected that. "No? What are you?"

Where had I discovered the path between the truth and the lies I had been going over in the elevator? Following Gladys's finger down the hall, that must have been where; somewhere between the talk show host with the bags under his eyes and the one with a built-in sneer in his smile. It wasn't a long path, but it was good for at least a few steps. "An agent. One of my clients is George Oswald."

He took that in as skeptically as the frog-faced disc jockey on the wall next to his shoulder. "George Oswald! Climbing that ladder of success!"

"More than he knew," I rushed in. "They also like his sense of humor. Now it's not just the play-by-play, they're thinking about something lighter before and after the games. But they'd like some samples."

I remembered the ugly laugh from Mineola, and immediately pictured the Cyclones going back to the drawing board for another announcer. "And these samples," he said, "I bet they'd be some of the routines he did around here when nobody was listening."

"When nobody was supposed to be listening."

"And he wants to buy them?"

Oswald had been clear on that point: Whatever it took. But there was no reason to go all in right away, either. "If you just have the original and you think it's worth sticking it to George. But he doesn't need the original. A copy would be just as good."

He sniffed the bluff it was, but wasn't all that sure. "He really thinks he was funny doing that shit?"

"You must have. Why else keep it?"

We both thought that was funny, but he smiled first. "Why else? And how much would a copy of some of these things be worth to George?"

"You tell me."

The office door behind him opened, and a scrawny kid with a handful of CDs came out. He smiled at Pastore, nodded to me with the stiffer respect due an elder, and kept going down the hall. The interruption gave Pastore time enough to come out with a bright proposal. "I got goddamn *shelves* of George," he grinned. "He can have them all for five thousand."

"Five thousand what? Oreos?"

"Dollars."

"I don't think so, Lou."

He shrugged. "So he can do new routines for them. I don't break up my collection for anything less."

I didn't really consider it a gamble; I knew the odds were already in favor of Pastore's having sold at least one tape to Bob Nelson and that even if I somehow got the rest of them, Oswald wouldn't be too much better off. But the guy's cockiness about being a wily negotiator was too irritating not to call for *some* kind of countermove. "Yeah, I understand," I said, turning and starting down the hall back toward Gladys. "I had baseball cards like that. You break up the set, you feel a pit in your stomach."

I made it all the way back to the picture with the sneering character before Pastore stopped me. He was all shrugs and reasonableness; he had even straightened up from the wall. "I don't have a price on them," he said. "I make them for myself. Don't really cost them out. They're a hobby. You know what I'm saying?"

"You never sold any of them?"

More shrugs. "Well, here and there. But I'm not running a store here. Give me a number and I'll see if it hits the bell."

"How many you got?"

"Of Oswald? I don't know. We could count them. I've got them all inside here. Won't take a minute."

"I'm just interested in the ones Bob Nelson is. They're probably the best ones, right?"

He showed nothing. "I told you . . ."

"Yeah, you told me. But I'm late, Lou. Late for an important date. So let's just get down to some minor league numbers for a minor league job and we'll all be happy, okay?"

He thought about it a second, then the second second where minds like Lou Pastore's started getting confused. "I haven't really considered it. I'll have to get back to you."

"No problem. But think about this. Anything that pops up in the wrong place with your fingerprints or Nelson's on it, then we *are* going to have a problem. So will Nelson."

"Oh, yeah?"

"Oh, yeah. The Cyclones aren't the only minor league team around. But who's going to hire a vindictive son of a bitch like him even on the outskirts of El Paso? Organizations don't like people like that around. They worry about him doing the same thing to them some morning."

"No sweat off my back."

"A, not true because your name would be sure to come up and your employers around here might not like your little hobby. B, certainly sweat off Nelson's and he sounds like a guy who lives for sharing. He and Oswald could have regular reunions on the unemployment line wondering where you ended up and making sure it wasn't for long. So why don't you pass along the word? You talk to him and I'll call you here same time tomorrow."

I could feel his profound thoughts pulsating behind me until I turned out of the hall back into the glare of Gladys and the reception area. I hadn't the slightest idea what I had accomplished. Had I made it better or worse for George Oswald? I really didn't know. It figured to be one or the other, and that seemed like enough for getting on with.

CHAPTER 3

At first sight the name New Florence had no more meaning than New Bucharest or Old Saigon would have had. The exit from the thruway barely forced a left turn before we were running down a sleepy avenue under a canopy of more trees; on both sides of the street large white frame houses alternated with tiny stores that would have been called *shop-pes* back in Brooklyn's tonier neighborhoods. There were antique furniture shop-pes, glassware shop-pes, and bakery shop-pes, not to mention the inevitable candle shop-pe. Window signs in a deli made bagels sound like contraband smuggled in from the Lower East Side and sausages like the last good parts of an alien who had crashed his UFO nearby. Stores in most places waited on customers, the ones in New Florence on outsiders. But that didn't make it any more Florentine than a thousand towns like it between Montauk Point and the Canadian border.

"Cutesville, USA."

"So be happy. You don't have to change your mind about how low Karen Noon's fallen."

"Just find the goddamn library."

I almost told him that would be the place with the block-long line waiting to get in to hear him. But that would have been a lot wittier if there had been enough pedestrians on the street to start a handball game. We passed two restaurants and, lunch hour or no lunch hour, the prevailing motif in both was empty tables. The gas station at what seemed to be the main intersection might have been selling kerosene for all the business it was doing. I was getting a picture of New Florence's citizens going off to work every day to offices and plants in other townships.

"What's that up there?"

That was another lesson in the dangers of jumping to conclusions. As frail as every other enterprise around seemed to be, the New Florence Public Library (that's what the cardinal red banner hanging down from the cornice said it was) was just as much a throwback to the days of musty reading rooms with decaying books and smelly farts. Unlike New York City's fad for those pocket library buildings that came with instructions for easy assembly, the structure halfway up the block to my left was undiluted Institution, down to the dirty white steps and two pillars guarding the entrance. The brass Man of Literature holding an opened book to the left of the steps might have been Daniel Webster or Mark Twain; whoever the statue represented, he had favored three-piece business suits and meals that left him with a big bulge through his vest.

"I think they built that just for you."

"Drive, drive."

It turned out not to be Daniel Webster or Mark Twain, but somebody named Claudio Mochi. Even the Professor looked stumped before he bent down to read the plate so low on the statue it might as well have been planted in the ground. "Meucci!" he exclaimed after swinging his head left to right and left again several times to pick up the brass lettering. "The guy who invented the telephone before Bell!"

"It says Mochi, not Meucci."

"Mochi was Meucci's wife's family name."

He could still surprise me. I wondered if in twenty years I would be able to remember the name of, say, Paul Finley. "That clears that up."

The long ride had made him even less ebullient than generations of students and fellow teachers would have sworn was his first trait. "This was Meucci's brother-in-law," he said, giving his grumpy report on what had been all but hidden in the statue lettering. "It says he settled here in World War I and started a fabric business. That's why it's called New Florence!"

"Why?"

"What I just said. Let's go inside."

"But why not Mochitown or something? Why New Florence?"

"Because Meucci came from around Florence. Why else?"

I didn't have the slightest idea what that answered. I knew my share of married people and I couldn't imagine any of them investing their profits from their instant lottery tickets in a town that made coy allusion to some in-law. But trooping up the steps after the Professor was less taxing than bending over and decoding the microscopic lettering on the statue. I contented myself with the idea that the town fathers had always despised Mochi for his slave-driver ways at the fabric factory so had found a tactful way to honor him: They had given him the statue he had extorted as the price for all his endowments, but had then inscribed the letters explaining his greatness so small nobody could read them.

The library interior lived up to expectations: a sprawling, dim maze of old wooden shelves, long tables, and red-visored lamps on the tables. The sunlight crashing through the gigantic uncurtained windows made the lamps look like party hats. I took it as a bad sign that two steps in from the door I could make out broken slats on one of the captain's chairs around the nearest table. Whoever had been doling out the endowment since Mochi had passed on hadn't spent too many pennies to keep the place in the 20th, let alone the 21st, century.

There were less than a dozen people at the shelves and tables, all but one of them looking eligible for Medicare. The exception was a kid closing in on voting age who was running a microfilm reader against a near wall. He was taking notes like a serious student. I wondered why I found that odd. Only because the Professor had told me there wasn't a college within 50 miles of New Florence and the kid looked too old for high school? But why did he have to be a student at all? Why couldn't he have just been looking up the criminal past of a prospective father-in-law?

I didn't know, and told my brain to shut up.

I didn't need the Professor's start at the sight of the tall, slim woman at the circulation desk to know she was Karen Noon. In her black turtleneck sweater and green slacks, she was the only likely candidate. And I had been right, right, and wrong. She had pale skin *and* bangs, but with a slouch that started from her eyes more than her shoulders. She had been waiting for more than Joe Carroll, and for such a long time she had gotten too used to it.

I stood back distrusting my instant expertise on passivity— and my Pavlovian attraction to it—while the two of them used the counter to justify their awkwardness about greeting one another after so long. Finally, the old man tugged her closer by her thin forearms and kissed both her cheeks European style. She seemed relieved. So did an older woman sitting a few feet away and check-ing the return stamps on books; in her salon-treated gray curls she had the look of the earthy aunt who had lectured Karen Noon more than once on the need to be less tentative with people. Since I had already made up my mind about Karen Noon's passivity flaw, I saw no reason not to decide to like the older woman for her no-nonsense view of the world.

We lingered at the front desk only long enough for some jokes about the sign advertising the evening lecture. Joe Carroll was billed as "eminent" twice in five sentences, and that seemed to surpass even his expectations for proper reverence. As for Karen Noon, she whispered, and not because of library etiquette. She had apparently been whispering her whole life, and had persuaded herself it hadn't worked to her detriment. Sitting behind the desk of her small office off the front door, she spoke with confidence that people eventually got over their craning forward to pick up what she was saying; after all, there was also the desk plaque saying she was the LIBRARIAN. Hard of hearing in one ear as he was, the Professor linked up to the volume much faster than I did. But then he could claim the practice from old classrooms. I was just glad they had a legion of names to run down between them without my contribution. Twice I missed what she said alto-gether, and resorted to a frozen smile that in other circumstances got people arrested.

Naturally, my first search of her fawn-like face was for SUI-CIDE. I suppose I would have been disappointed if I couldn't find hurt and pain. No matter how many years ago the politician had shot himself, the Professor's presence had to reawaken some of those nightmares, didn't it? And come to think of it, that made a lecture on any flus even stranger. Whatever else she had had in mind by inviting the old man, I realized, she had to have known his arrival would have her scratching at an ugly scab. What was worth provoking that kind of irritation? The aunt outside hadn't looked *that* formidable.

I didn't get close to answering those questions until we had all agreed that the long drive up from New York had earned us a lunch at the library's expense. We ended up in a place around the corner that proclaimed itself a *trattoria*; no Giorgio's or Mario's, just a *trattoria*. Tomato sauce and mild garlic aromas from the kitchen made it smell nice, but it was even emptier than the two restaurants we had passed on the way to the library. At one table sat a middle-aged couple who might have just gotten lukewarm news from a doctor, at a second there were two burly workers whose faces hadn't missed much weather, and at all the rest sat wine glasses and napkins. This time I had been right about something.

"The biggest employer in the area," Karen Noon nodded to me, "is the paper mill over at Stanton, about two miles away. Twelve percent of New Florence's work force is there."

"What about Mochi's fabrics?"

She came close to blushing. "Yes, there's still a factory south of town, but it isn't what it used to be. The great-grandson hasn't done much to keep it vital. He spends most of his time in the town bars. I don't think there are a hundred people employed there. All the old buyers now get the same thing from China and India for less than half the price."

"So you wouldn't call New Florence a thriving community?"

For some reason she aimed her answer exclusively at the Professor. "There's one thing we've really been great at lately."

"What's that?" he asked.

"Public opinion polls."

I would have sworn her voice had been on the verge of breaking, but the waiter came over toting *Daily News*-sized menus before I was sure. I hadn't been as hungry as I'd thought. In the interests of getting right back to what she had been about to say, I landed on the *penne all'arrabiata*, the first pasta listed. I could have saved myself the haste. She dawdled so long over her choice I could feel her telling herself to slow down, not to get so close again to blurting out something. I didn't know if the Professor sensed the same thing, but he too pored over the menu as if committing it to memory. By the time the waiter was back to take our orders and Joe was asking about the Barolo in stock, I regretted having picked the *penne*.

"So you were saying about public opinion polls?" I got in as soon as the waiter made himself scarce. "What do you mean?"

She didn't know me well enough to trust answering just me. "They came up here about a month ago," she said, struggling to keep her eyes fixed on the old man. "The Pulsar Institute. Ever hear of them?" She smiled wanly when he shook his head. "Wish I could say the same. They're the ones who came to Hoboken a few years ago and decided Andy was the most honest politician in the county."

CHAPTER 4

I've never gone out of my way to look for the ominous. When bad pennies like a Lou Pastore came back into my life, I didn't think of it as some cataclysmic sign from the skies. Good pennies, bad pennies—I had a few years on me, I was bound to run into some pennies more than once, and the odds still stayed even on the good kind or the bad kind. Where the Pulsar Institute was concerned, though, that kind of thinking left me 180 degrees away from Karen Noon and about 90 degrees away from the Professor. And his attempts to act open-minded irked me more than her paranoia.

"So what you're saying is, they're conducting another of their surveys up here, just like the one in New Jersey?"

"Not exactly the same, but close enough. Here the focus is on New Florence's most admired citizen. It's some kind of game show mentality, but they seem to have government money for it and nobody's saying just get lost. They got the town paper to go along as a gimmick for increasing circulation and the local radio station to keep throwing in plugs."

I knew what the old man's expression meant because I was just as surprised as he was that New Florence not only had a newspaper, but its own radio station. Joe Carroll being in front of a former student, though, he managed to get through it without offending her. "Sounds like the usual grant spongers," he said. "You know how that works, Karen. They phrase the questions in the right pedantic way, suddenly they're social scientists contributing to our knowledge of the nation."

"I know, I know."

"What you should be doing is getting your friends to stuff the ballot boxes so you come out the winner!"

I dove for my wine before I gave up one of a hundred winces. For the way he was patronizing her. For the way he wanted her to see through his paternalism. For the idiocy of the whole poll idea. And maybe most of all, for the suspicion she didn't have that many friends to go stuffing any ballot boxes on her behalf.

She gave him a polite smile and went back to picking at her food. "I have a feeling the winner's going to be a dead man," she said. She took in his bafflement and congratulated herself for retrieving his serious attention. "This late-night disc jockey on the radio. Randy Page. He had a lot of fun with the whole thing. Kept going on about how the winner was sure to be Mayor McCorkle or McCorkle's wife because the whole thing was fixed ahead of time. That was when he wasn't urging his listeners to vote for him so City Hall could have a conniption. Page would have had the under-25s anyway, but then the other night, after he finished his show, he was run over in the radio station parking lot. Whoever did it kept going."

I didn't know why I was staring at the Professor's blank face for a reaction. I was pretty impressed all by myself.

"The funeral's tomorrow and a lot of the town is up in arms about how the police are dragging their feet looking for the driver."

"Are they?"

It was my question, so she had to look in my vicinity. "I don't think they'd dare. They know how popular Page was. But . . ."

"What?"

She shook her head in exasperation. "You'd have to meet some of the characters at City Hall to understand completely," she said. "Everything they do is in some infernal slow motion, like they're afraid if they move too fast, something will come toppling down." She tried looking perkier. "Like in Lucrezia's court. Everybody blackmailing everybody else and afraid of being the first one to drink from the wrong goblet."

"That was then," he said, more severely than the remark called for.

"Really? And I thought you were the one who always said there was no Then in history, only earlier Nows."

He conceded the point by returning to his minestrone. She still hadn't persuaded him, though, why it had been such a good idea for him to come up for his lecture on the flu; if anything, he looked disappointed she hadn't had a better excuse. That made for enough of a chill for her to look eager to talk to me. "I know Pulsar is legitimate," she said earnestly. "I looked them up a long time ago and I did again last week. If you want to ruin your eyes, you can stay in front of your computer screen all night tracking down their on-scene surveys. They've been all over the country. I stopped at 1995. For all I know, they did polls for George Washington."

It was her first out-and-out reach for a laugh, and I liked her for it because she didn't feel it for a second. The Professor was disappointed in her Pulsar Institute story? She was just as disappointed in his reaction to her Pulsar Institute story.

"What do *you* think is going on, Karen?"

She risked raising her eyes to my whole face. "I don't know. But I get this creepy feeling sometimes it's enough to know something is."

The old man extended his ham hand across the table to her. "I think maybe you've been up in these woods too long," he said gently. "The trees and the forest, remember?"

"It's not just about Andy, Joe."

"But the same pollsters, the same . . ."

"Andy was a crook, Joe," she cut him off firmly. "He was just waiting to be found out. Nothing was ever said, but it was always in the air. The Coward and the Crook—that's what we could've entitled our joint memoir. This isn't the same thing, not that way. But I still feel something hateful in the air. And this time I'm not sure we have it coming to us."

If the workmen sitting near the window had been eavesdropping, I told myself, they would have accused her of whispering.

CHAPTER 5

The pasta and wine added so many barbells to my legs that I didn't immediately squelch Karen's hint about the spare room she had at her place for visitors. The old man covered my procrastination by making sounds about wanting to see how the talk went at the library before deciding about staying. No, I wasn't in the mood for the four-hour return drive to the city, and had thrown some things into a bag just in case, but I wasn't all that keen, either, about wandering around New Florence all evening or nodding off in the Noon living room while she and the old man went on wondering what had happened to this one and that one. Bottom line: I didn't know what the hell I wanted to do. I had gotten out of one place I didn't want to be to get to another where I didn't want to be. The entire state of New York seemed to have decided I was good only for afternoon bloat.

Since I had already visited the library once and was going to have to be there for the lecture, I decided to spend the rest of the daylight anywhere else. Besides, the old man wanted some private time with Karen, her library, or both. Figuring I had seen most of what constituted the town center in the drive past all the shop-pes, I took the car for more ambitious roaming. Thanks to Karen, I knew a little more about the place where I would be wandering. It hadn't always been known as New Florence. Its previous name had been Pinewood, fitting enough for the hundreds of caskets that had been needed when the Spanish Lady flu had dropped by in the final weeks of World War I. When Mochi had come to town, the bodies were still being buried and the pallbearers had been moping around waiting to be next. He had ignored all that and put money in their pockets by opening his factory. More important, he had spread some of his own profits around in a civic spirit, including financing the building of the library and a new city hall. His final blessing on the place had been to marry the daughter of the police chief and spring a little Mochi of each kind on the world. If his name had been Smith or Prescott, according to Karen, they would have embraced a proposal to rename the place after him as a symbol of their new beginnings. But even though everyone had had enough of the connotations of Pinewood, there had also been the need to respect the prevailing bigotry against Italians as Sacco-Vanzetti anarchists, so forget about Mochitown. After a couple of years, New Florence had won endorsement as a compromise solution. Mochi himself was said not to have been elated by the name, but he had accepted it in the generous sulking spirit he had shown about having to accept anything that was less than his original demands.

The first thing I discovered after leaving Karen and the Professor was that I had been wrong about the street with the shop-pes. A block north of the gas station that sold kerosene, there was a cluster of commercial streets that had far busier credentials as the hub of New Florence. There were bars, a luncheonette and couple of more restaurants, laundromats, a high school, two supermarkets practically side by side, and the Mochi-financed city hall with such clean brick and such a gleaming white steeple it might have been built in Disneyland. There were even people moving along the sidewalks, and so many were pushing carriages that endless generations seemed on tap for paying tribute to Claudio Mochi and wondering why they couldn't read the goddamn plaque under his statue.

There was also a funeral parlor.

At first, I thought the place was just a weird hangout for the high schoolers down the block. There must have been a dozen teenagers loitering near the entrance. Some were smoking by themselves, others were having one-word conversations with pals they weren't looking at, all of them looked bummed out. I thought of how Karen had described the people in Pinewood during the epidemic before Mochi's arrival. The scene also reminded me of the restlessness I'd felt at junior high after going to the wake for Freddy Capistrano, a goofball classmate who had ignored bad weather flags and drowned in the Long Island Sound. Except, as the announcement board on the wall of the Tebaldi Funeral Home said, the kids weren't there for a classmate, but for Randy Page, the disc jockey killed in the radio station parking lot. Karen had said the kids were going to vote for him as New Florence's most admired citizen? They looked capable of a lot more confused, pouty things than that. I guessed that was why a patrol car was doing a bad job of looking inconspicuous down the street.

I drove on. I didn't want to get mixed up with anger, especially the dazed kind. Call it more Finley vanity, but I always assumed I had adequate reserves of my own in that area.

I tried to get more interested in the signs. Who knew when someone back in my favorite Brooklyn saloon would demand specific details about the sights I'd seen in New Florence? I piled them up. I could tell the crowd at the Green Fox I'd seen the New Florence Tile Works, Clearview Realty, and a shuttered restaurant called Greek Taverna. The Taverna evidently hadn't been as popular as the Trattoria where we had had lunch. I wondered how The Place Where You Eat American Food was doing. I could also tell Cynthia and the Green Fox regulars that the New Florence town council had a stylish eye when it came to painting the litter baskets spaced every few hundred yards on the sidewalk— a glossy black with a diagonal red splash that suggested downward movement (as in THROW IT IN THIS WAY, ASSHOLE). I could also tell them I had followed my nose on a street that had probably flaunted its name when I had turned into it but didn't get around to repeating the information that it was Sloan Avenue for almost a mile. But there were compensations. Right over the street sign was another for Mochi Fabrics, said to be 1.5 miles further along. I certainly hadn't come that far to miss out on visiting the plant of the brother-in-law of the guy who invented the telephone before Bell!

Since I had worked myself up into a nice snitty mood, I glanced at the speedometer as I made for the 1.5 miles. Anything closer or farther, and the New Florence *Bugle* was going to get a letter to the editor. For musical accompaniment, I went to the dial number Karen had given me for the local station where Page had worked. At least during the day, it wasn't local at all: one of those stations that picked up impersonal network feeds from guys named Gary in an Oklahoma silo making sure they revealed no geographical secrets while introducing last year's hit single from Alanis or Beyoncé or somebody else I would never get straight until she cut a duet with a 50-year-old kinescope of Dean Martin. On the other hand, I didn't have to take out my pen to write to the *Bugle*. Just as the sign had advertised, the chain-link fence announcing itself as Mochi Fabrics appeared at the 1.5-mile mark. Who deserved credit for that kind of accuracy—some creepy old man in the town planning office or Mochi himself? I voted for Mochi. Creepy old men in planning offices didn't worry about accuracy so much as just being creepy old men in planning offices.

I kept going, telling myself I'd take the first indentation on the fence line as a sign that I had seen enough and turn back toward New Florence's bustling center. The three-floor building inside the fence looked like every medium-sized factory in the world: grimy windows, machine spars and suspension lines barely visible through the serrated glass, faded lettering in the brick facade with a boast from yesteryear (THE WORLD'S LEADING MANUFACTURER OF FABRICS WITH CLAUDIO MOCHI'S INITIALS ON THEM!). It was an eyesore that would have made any great-grandson, Mochi or non-Mochi, stick to saloons. If not for the cars in the parking lot, the sun wouldn't have had anything to glance off. The machinery's low hum from inside might have been producing a new slipcover, a new ball bearing, or a new hand grenade. My father had worked in a place like Mochi Fabrics his whole life, and the only thing he had ever admitted liking about it was a vending machine in the lunchroom because it had always dropped the perfect amount of milk into his coffee—not as much as my mother and more than the waitress at Henry's cafeteria around the corner from where we lived. I didn't think about my father all that much, but the association with the factory made me wonder what he would have said about the smaller brother of Mochi Fabrics, a few hundred yards behind the main plant.

Obviously, before the Indians and Chinese had gotten into the market, Mochi Fabrics had had its glory years. To keep two plants going every day was no modest accomplishment. Then again, if business had been so good, why hadn't they simply enlarged the original factory instead of erecting a second building next to it? Was it production tasks that had to be separated? I couldn't imagine anything like that in the curtain and drapery universe. Maybe the structure of the original plant was so weak it couldn't take any annexes? Or—once again—was it Mochi's will, condemning to eternal damnation anyone who tampered with his original one-building design? Whatever the cause, a makeshift sign said the separation had worked out to the advantage of the Pulsar Institute. Who knew how many security guards they would have had at the entrance if they had rented a building where Mochi Fabrics workers came and went during the week? As it was, the manufacturing seemed to be concentrated in the first building, while the second one, with only a dozen cars around the entrance, was for . . .? The no-neck lineman in the glass booth near the door of the annex looked like he could handle the job all by himself. Anybody who dressed in one of those green PGA sports jackets and had flattened a tablecloth of a white shirt over his body builder's pecs probably did most things alone.

I was sure he was looking in my direction as I cruised past. Why not? My Subaru was bigger than a squirrel and he needed to vary his entertainment. Since I didn't see any book or newspaper in the booth, it was me and the squirrel or nothing to get him through the day. I almost felt bad when I had gone too far for him to see me.

But he was going to get a second chance. A quarter of a mile along, there was a recess off to the right of the road with two waterlogged picnic tables. Why there was I didn't have a clue. Even if the Kingdom of Oz had once stretched over what was now a marshy field of yellowed grass, it was an odd place to put picnic tables for contemplating it. The space was barely big enough for me to turn the car without cracking one of the table seats. Throw in, say, the odd five-year-old jumping off the bench with his jelly sandwich for a better look at the traffic shooting by, and the picnic would have been over in a hurry.

My return pass down Sloan Avenue was almost wasted on the lineman. He had lifted his muscles to the front door and was leaning inside in conversation with somebody. If I hadn't been perverse enough to slow down to a near-stall, he wouldn't have had time to close the door, then turn and look out at me. It took him about three-quarters of a second to recognize my car, take the pen clipped to the handkerchief pocket of his jacket, and strain for a better look at my license plate. I liked thinking that as he went into his booth in search of a scrap of paper he felt useful, and that I was responsible for making him feel that way.

What I didn't like thinking was that he seemed to have sipped from the same paranoia well as Karen Noon had.

CHAPTER 6

The lineman's reaction to seeing me the second time nibbled at my nerves. My intestinal ferrets weren't fully awake and chomping, but they were stirring. In the lineman's place, wouldn't it have been more natural simply to assume I had taken a wrong turn and was doubling back after realizing my mistake? Where did all the suspicions of surveillance come from? What kind of government grant were Pulsar Institute employees working with? The kind that made for big movies and bad reality?

I didn't want to go down that road. It would have made me seem impressionable listening to Karen. Besides, there was so much local color yet to soak up. Even the radio broke for a distinctly New Florence plug—some loony bird named the Reverend Russell Dvorak was going to level with everyone about "Paradise and Perdition" that evening at eight o'clock as he did every evening at eight o'clock Sunday through Friday, just keep your dial where it was. There was more, much more. The newspaper wasn't called the *Bugle*, but the *Reporter*, and it was housed in a four-floor red brick building that was the closest thing New Florence had to a skyscraper. It also stood as another sign that Claudio Mochi had a competitor in somebody named Labine as the town's hovering spirit. The *Reporter* was in the Labine Building, I had crossed through a park square called Labine Plaza, and I had passed a sprawling department store called simply Labine's. Something told me there were more Labines than Mochis on the town council, too, at least of the sober kind. All things swimming in the same Sea of Finley, that hunch brought the idea that maybe one of those Labines could find a better job for George Oswald than broadcasting games for the Brooklyn Cyclones. What better use for his grating voice than standing in Labine's and yelling out "Lingerie and pajamas on Aisle Four!"?

I took that thought for a coffee in a corner pub around the corner from the *Reporter.* The place looked like it had been there since before Mochi's statue outside the library: beer fumes concentrate and a badly chinked wooden ceiling that made you want to yell "Tim-ber!" The only other customer was a porky middle-aged guy sitting in a back booth with a newspaper that looked like the *Reporter* and a drink that looked like a brandy. His out-of-season white linen jacket, green ascot, and half-assed comb-over said he had seen all the movies about Truman Capote.

I didn't really want the coffee I had come in for and the haggard redhead with the pack-a-day rasp on the bar seemed to regret advertising JUST FOR A COFFEE BREAK on a slate board outside, but I wasn't in the mood for alcohol and she let it go after one "I have beer, too, you know." I thought I was a saint for not saying, "Well, if that's all you're interested in pushing, don't put the coffee sign outside." That feeling subsided as soon as Bob Nelson started crowding me from the next stool. I blamed his presence on Truman in the back booth: The two of them went to the same barber.

George Oswald had warned me Nelson wasn't a good loser, but I hadn't paid attention because the warning had come from George Oswald. Then I had compounded my mistake by carrying through on my threat to call Lou Pastore the day after our meeting in the WBOV hallway. When Pastore had insisted I deal with Nelson directly for "the piece or two I might've let him borrow," I had little choice. That's what my client had asked me to do, wasn't it? A series of phone calls and machine messages back and forth came down to a Prospect Park bench just off Grand Army Plaza. I took that meeting spot to mean Bob Nelson lived in Brooklyn, and wished that meant something more than not having to go over to Manhattan again. When you start hanging around with the likes of George Oswald, Lou Pastore, and Bob Nelson, you need a booster shot of Far-Reaching Significance vitamins at least once a day.

The first funny was wandering into the park to find Nelson already there, and sitting with the spooked stiffness of somebody about to hand over an envelope to a blackmailer. He seemed to have forgotten *I* was the one who was there to do the paying. But I refrained from reminding him because of the second funny—a moose sitting one bench away and making a bad job of scanning the headlines in the *Post*. The guy was too fat for basketball, too tall for football, and probably too clumsy for ballet, but—I was sure—he represented Nelson's idea of a bodyguard. I suppose I should have been flattered, but I wasn't. It was such overdone dressing I had to wonder how far I had underestimated the importance of the Cyclones job to Oswald and his playmates. I didn't like having to second-guess myself with a bunch of idiots, especially when one of them was as big as an oak tree.

For sure, Oswald had been right about one thing: Nelson *did* have an adenoidal sound. I didn't find that as irritating as Oswald's shrieking, but it wasn't something I wanted to listen to at marathon lengths, either. It came out of a slight guy in his early forties with four strands of hair stretched from one side of his scalp to the other, a snub nose, and a walnut of a mole over his left ear. Radio had to be Bob Nelson's medium because so many beauty marks ruled out television.

I didn't have to waste time empathizing with him over television's biases toward the human body. No sooner did I plop down than, without possibly being a hundred percent sure who I was, he sputtered, "The only way Oswald got that job was banging somebody at the agency!"

I had to admire his baritone timbre; adenoids or not, somebody to hire if you needed to read stock prices. Better to dwell on that than on the picture of Mister Potato Head banging anybody or on the thought of Bob Nelson being so humbled on the food chain that he had to work up jealousies about George Oswald's sex life. "I'm not here to review their hiring practices, Bobby. You'll have to take that up with somebody else."

"It's Mr. Nelson to you. The question is, how is he going to make it up to me? He owes me and he knows it."

"And how would that be?"

Nelson aimed his sniff at a couple of sparrows pecking away after a cigarette butt. "He knows."

Granted I was no expert in the ins and outs of hiring sports-casters, but I was positive it didn't involve the secret rituals of being sworn in as a Knight Templar. "Okay. That makes two of you. But that's not why I'm here. I think your friend Lou told you what I'm interested in."

He shook his head at the wonder of it all. "Am I the one who's crazy, Finley? You've talked to him. Really think he deserves to be doing those games ahead of me?"

"You're asking the wrong guy."

"Yeah? Why? You don't care about play-by-play quality?"

Just like Nelson envied Oswald's sex life, I was beginning to envy the butt-hunting ways of sparrows. "Why don't we talk about that over a beer another time? Right now, I just need those tapes."

"Yeah, I'm sure you do."

I waited. The crow in the tree above us cawed a whole poem. The nanny in the lane coming toward us across the meadow bent down to tighten the blanket around the child in the stroller. The moose on the next bench seemed to work up a whole half-thought as he continued squinting at the *Post* headlines. And at the end of it all I still didn't know what I had missed with Nelson's answer. "You still here with me . . . Mr. Nelson?"

"I'm here, I'm here."

"Then could we get down to the tapes?"

He hunched his small shoulders down over the hands he kept rubbing. He might not have needed a barber for the top of his head, but somebody had left a Florida peninsula behind his left ear; I wondered if it was because he had told that somebody, too, to call him Mr. Nelson. "I could destroy him. You realize that, don't you, Finley? They hear just one minute of that tape and everybody in a bra and a wheelchair will be knocking on the door of the Cyclones to get rid of him."

"The ones who don't have anything better to do, I'm sure."

He peered around at me with a new petulance—the kind that came close to looking like contempt. "You think this is funny?"

"I haven't heard the tapes. Dynamite stuff, huh?"

"Bet your ass it is!"

"What are you going to do, Nelson?"

"Pastore says you want to buy them."

"Oswald's reasonable. He wants you to be, too."

"What's to stop Pastore from selling what *he* has?"

"Nothing, I guess."

"And you couldn't care less?"

"I'm trying to play messenger here, Bobby. Let me be a good messenger and we'll all end up with nice things."

He took a longer look at me, and decided he had been right not to like me. "Well, here's what you do, messenger," he said. "You go back and you tell Georgie he's never been in a tighter corner in his life. He drops out of that job or he drops out of the profession."

Later, I realized I had lost the grip on our meeting just by showing up for it. But then and there I backtracked over the one crack too many to a guy UPS would have marked FRAGILE. One thought was that if I were George Oswald, I would have demanded my $750 retainer back. Lucky for me, while I was drawing that conclusion, Nelson nodded over to the moose to make sure I did earn my money.

It took a good chunk of infinity for me to accept what was happening. Suddenly the *Post* was a rag best tossed on the ground for the park's trash patrol and the moose was standing up and lurching over toward us. The glint in his beady eyes had already been paid for. "You can tell him how serious I am," Nelson said, jumping clear of the bench.

I told myself nobody should have been getting physical over the likes of George Oswald and Bob Nelson. Besides, the Piltdown Man coming at me had been revealed as a hoax, hadn't it? I thought it a second time as I noticed how open the moose was keeping his crotch as he stepped up his big feet to almost a charge. I didn't get my shock out a third time because I almost severed my knee kicking up. Should I have sat more forward from the outside curved bench slat and cleared the wood all the way up to my thigh? My knee certainly thought so. That's why all its bones, tendons, sinews, ligaments, and other things crinkled back up into my throat. The moose didn't care, though. He was bent over sideways, as if his hip had gone screwy and he was trying to get it back where it belonged. He was yelling something he didn't know he was yelling. I didn't want him waking up the kid in the stroller the nanny was pushing closer. He had enough jaw clear of his flipped shirt collar to hit him hard without breaking him *or* my hand. He went down so fast in such a heap I almost lost my balance when his trembling legs reached my foot.

For some reason I still had breath to exhale. I didn't know the moose. He probably knew me only by name, if that. He would be spending the afternoon in an Emergency Room. I would be spending it keeping a cold towel around my right hand and wondering when psychopathic nerds had taken over the sportscasting market. What had I said to Oswald, the crack about the Russian mob? Standing over the moose, thinking I better not linger until he regained his strength, watching the frightened nanny hustle off toward the exit with her stroller, not seeing Bob Nelson anywhere, I agreed with him I hadn't been so funny.

Stirring the redhead's idea of coffee in the pub, I gave in to a shudder of relief that I had put so many miles between me and George Oswald's career path, at least for a day. The more I had slipped into that muck, the more the muck had expanded into more muck. Come to think of it, that had been a chronic problem with Finley Investigations. Whatever I touched had a built-in balloon attached to it and I was the helium. I should have been grateful to Karen Noon for introducing me to her self-contained little world. When New Florence's commuters returned every evening from the mill in the Stanton place she had mentioned, the town fathers probably sealed the borders for the night. No matter how big the foot that came down on the place, and apparently everything from killer flu to Claudio Mochi to cheap Asian labor had taken a stomping turn, it couldn't be squashed all over the map, become another Finley Investigations project. It had nothing to do with me. There was something reassuring about that.

CHAPTER 7

I went back out to the car just as somebody was parking a shimmering platinum Lexus in front of me. It was gratifying to see my Subaru looking as much like a ragman's cart in New Florence as on any street in New York. Then I looked at the driver locking up. My first reaction was to blame the coffee: The redhead had gotten even with me for accepting her blackboard invitation by slipping me a hallucinogen. Then I remembered the odds on running into Lou Pastore again—always 50-50. Pastore had been the bad penny showing up after so many years, now it was Jimmy Sewell the good penny reporting for duty.

But in New Florence??!!

The two of us stood 20 feet apart with our mouths open until we had to accept that nobody was going to come along and close them for us. If Pastore had been 15 years, Jimmy Sewell had been about 10, and the only difference I could see were a few more neatly combed gray hairs and the beginnings of a wattly throat. Why not? He had to be closer to 50 than 40. But in his black frame glasses, blue corduroy jacket, and white dress shirt, he was still the Long Island altar boy—football on Saturday, Mass on Sunday morning, studying on Sunday night. It had been my luck more than once that, instead of chemistry or biology, he had done all his cramming to be a newspaperman.

"I don't believe it!"

"You better, Sewell, because I'm not passing by here again."

We were already wrapped around each other before it occurred to me we had never been *that* close. When Jimmy Sewell had been working the police beat for *Newsday*, we had bought beers for each other three or four times in the middle of other people. Throw in a celebration dinner for him when he had shared in a newsroom team Pulitzer Prize and to which I had gone only reluctantly in case the source of some police department leaks to the paper would become obvious. (Since there had been six other cops at the dinner, it had been a non-problem.) Outside that it had been all business—mine to gain leverage with some investigation, his to prove repeatedly that he wouldn't hesitate to bite the hand that fed him if he felt he was being manipulated. I had gotten over the teeth marks.

He went first. He had given up chasing after police radio calls, he had his own office at the *Reporter* and an executive editor title to go with it. Big fish in small ponds, small fish in big ponds—I kept the goofy smile on my face while he danced through it all. Denise (whose name he assumed I remembered) and the two girls (I thought I remembered one of them from her kindergarten years) loved the move, loved New Florence. The house, the schools, the slower pace—it was all "civilized" and he didn't feel like apologizing for it to a city rat like me.

"So why are you?"

He laughed; a laugh without edges. It was the tradeoff for not asking him to snicker at something off-color. It wasn't that he growled at you if you said something blue, just that you learned after a while not to put the Catholic fervor of his teenage novitiate years (as he had once admitted to me) to the test. Next to the Professor, Jimmy Sewell imposed a mood on conversation faster than anyone I had ever known, and it never earned more than a PG rating. I didn't know how that had been working out in practice with Denise and the two daughters at home (and I didn't want to know), but it had always had me thinking twice about what I said to him.

Since I still had a couple of hours before the Professor's lecture, I had no reason not to see his office in the Labine Building.

"Pretend not to notice how everybody bows when I walk in the door. I don't want them to start thinking it's unnatural."

As I followed along with him, I saw a limp I hadn't seen before, and he said something about a car accident. That got me through Jennifer and Susan, or at least until he stopped in front of the entrance to the *Reporter* searching my face to see if he had said something insensitive. "Jesus, Paul. I didn't know anything about . . ."

"It's been a few years now," I said, as though that timed anything.

"Yeah, but . . ."

"Tell me about the Labine of the Labine Building."

We were both relieved to have him talking about Walter Labine as we went through the revolving door into the lobby. Not too loudly, though. Military bases didn't have as many uniformed guards screening visitors with forced smiles and suspicious squints. Two of them had the epaulets of a Fifth Avenue doorman, a third one looked like a hotel concierge, and the fourth one with the gun could have been doing Housing patrol in a Canarsie project. It felt like a close call, but none of them questioned the executive editor of the *Reporter*. "It only took them about three months not to demand my passport whenever I came in."

"All this for four floors?"

He smiled. "Labine's insurance company headquarters is on the top floor. He thinks it should symbolize the new national spirit. When you come in to buy a policy, feel secure against everything—terrorists, the ACLU, the French, steroids, you name it. Who knows? You pass enough ID checks and get the right policies, you may never even die."

"City Hall must be a fortress."

"More like just a branch of this place," he said, jabbing at the elevator button for the third floor. "We have a mayor, a police chief, a fire chief, a tax assessor, and—I think, but don't quote me on it—a dogcatcher. And all of them spend most of the year trembling about the possibility the post office will lose their Christmas card to Walter Labine."

"What makes me think he's your publisher?"

"Actually, that's his wife. He just pays the bills."

The elevator doors opened onto an airplane hangar of a floor cut into fashionable cubicles and lighted by those halogen fixtures that belonged on a spaceship. If I was looking at the *Reporter*'s staff, I was looking at about 20 to 25 people, all of whom must have been about the same age as Sewell's daughters. Probably because I'd had to mention the accident downstairs, it was the first time in a very long time that I envisioned a living Susan doing a normal grownup thing.

"Don't get the wrong impression," he said. "This is *all* of it, not just editorial. News, advertising, circulation. If they could've cut that wall out, they would've put the delivery trucks in here, too."

He led the way down a narrow aisle over a glistening wooden floor that smelled of fresh wax. There were more hellos back and forth than Joe Carroll and I exchanged in a year, and not a dutiful grunt in the bunch. The fact was, I *wouldn't* have minded Susan working in such a place.

The back of the floor was a pair of glassed off offices. A large metal box with handles on the sides and a slit on the top sat on a table between the offices. The door to the empty office on the left said PUBLISHER, the one on the right EXECUTIVE EDITOR. The box said PULSAR INSTITUTE.

"A little promotion thing we're winding up today. Instead of voting for the All-Star team, you get to vote for New Florence's Most Admired Citizen. We've been carrying the ballots."

Why didn't I tell him Karen Noon had told us about the poll? Or about the odd behavior of the lineman out on Sloan Avenue? Maybe just an old instinct to see if people would fill in the blanks with my answer. "And what happens if Walter Labine doesn't win? Insurance rates go up?"

He dropped his jacket over the back of his desk chair with a weary shake of the head. "Tell you the truth, this thing has become a pain in the ass and I'll be glad to see them get that box out of the office. They offered us the option of having all the ballots sent here or to a box at the Post Office and I did my wise Solomon act."

"Meaning?"

"I stupidly said both—send them here *or* the P.O. No question we've sold maybe 100, 150 more papers a day. Why vote once when you can vote a dozen times for your favorite bartender? But I've had to give up precious news space for the ballot, nobody wants to talk about anything else, and my copy boy has had to spend most of his time around here opening envelopes and making sure the ballots are filled out the right way."

He handed me a printed facsimile of the ballot. There were two questions on it: WHAT NEW FLORENCE RESIDENT DO YOU ADMIRE MOST? and WHY DO YOU ADMIRE THIS PERSON? "And who'll win?"

He tried to look interested in a small pile of telephone message slips while he leaned over to snap on his computer. "A dead man."

He told the same story as Karen had about Randy Page, and I told him about having seen the kids outside Tebaldi's funeral home. He wanted to check his emails more than anything, but he gave me another second of concentration. "The guy was your typical shock jock gutter mouth. Say anything if it got a rise out of people, but don't believe anything too hard because it might cost you a snappy line or two down the road. Would he have won anyway? I don't think so. The kids who listened to his show don't jump out of bed in the morning and dive into the *Reporter*. They're online or texting or on their cellphones. I would have bet on this woman who runs a soup kitchen for the church."

"What church would that be, Jimmy?"

He blushed. "Okay, okay. We do an article about her occasionally. She's probably saved more lives than all the doctors in town. Maybe I even suggested in an editorial last week . . ."

"Got you."

"My point is I would've figured Page for third or fourth, barely in the money. But after he was killed . . . Well, let's just say the local men in blue haven't tidied up the case as fast as they might have and that's created its own momentum. Page liked going after the mayor and the cops, and some kids are beginning to think the suits are getting back at him."

"What do you think?"

He glanced out the window so pensively I knew I was going to hear an opinion he hadn't shared with too many others. "You tell me, Detective Finley," he said after a moment. "The only other car in the lot when Page was run over was the engineer's. Wide open spaces. Even the disc jockey who followed Page on the air lived a block away and walked to the station. Then there was the roach, two cigarette butts and a Red Bull can, all on the lot in one neat little pile. Like somebody had been parked there for some time waiting and had done a little car-cleaning before Page came out."

I wanted to laugh, but Sewell didn't, and he had never been the slowest police reporter. "What are you saying? Somebody was sitting there waiting for Page to come out of the station?"

"You hear me say that? I didn't say that."

"No, you didn't say that. But you're measuring it out to me like you've seen some police report that hasn't been made public."

He laughed. And nobody was worse at an insincere laugh than Jimmy Sewell. "Pretty good, Paul."

"And maybe you miss the Island more than you say."

I thought that should have been worth more than another glance through the telephone slips he had already checked. I also didn't like the feeling that he had seized on me as an outsider who wouldn't cost him to erase some misgivings about what he had been doing about Page's death. I had known him enough to say as much, too, but then the telephone rang with a message from the praetorian guard in the lobby. Before he had put back the receiver, he had his jacket back on and was shooting a spray into his mouth. I was suddenly an intruder a couple of times over. "Let me guess. Mrs. Labine is here."

"Better, much better," he smiled. "The Pulsar Institute."

He hurried over to his door and shouted outside for somebody. I had seen the somebody before. It was the kid from the library who had been going through the old newspaper reels to see if he was about to marry into a family of crooks. His name was Alan Lockman and his eyes were all glaze as Sewell told him to pack up any more ballots he had on his desk and get them into the metal box. When his nod came, it seemed a fraction late, as though there had been a short between his ear and the invisible antenna on his head. I might have come up with a whole list of Alan Lockman's dork qualities if the elevator door at the end of the floor didn't open. I saw why Sewell had gone to the mouth freshener for Pulsar.

CHAPTER 8

She was in her thirties, in that glorious pocket when they were the rambunctious early thirties one second, the polished late thirties the next, then back again. The tan suit seemed to have come with the rest of the set—the long dark blonde hair from a shampoo commercial, the mischievous blue eyes, and the lanky walk that gathered more command with every step of her heels. Even the beefcake behind her—aside from the red shirt, practically a twin brother to the lineman I had seen out at the Mochi works—might have been part of her natural inheritance. She dropped, he picked up. She smiled like glass, he would never intrude upon her reflection. He simply wasn't there except for when she needed him, and she expected him to anticipate when that was rather than to have to say it.

Sewell waited for her to reach his office door. I would have gone out to meet her, but he seemed more practiced in the protocol rules about remaining on the reception line to welcome the queen. His visitor might have been the epiphany that had once persuaded him to give up the novitiate; now it was filling his head with bigger glories than being the executive editor of the New Florence *Reporter*.

Or was that just me wondering about the long-term rewards of being just the executive editor of Finley Investigations?

Her name was Pauline Shepherd, and that felt right. Somewhere back before she had taken over the planet, there had probably been Jimmy Sewell's kind of nuns in her life, too. But she had traveled a lot further from rosary beads and Clearasil than he had, and he knew it. The looks he gave her were more than lust, they were a second chance for grabbing and keeping what he had missed out on the first time around. When she shook hands with me, he was on the verge of stepping in to separate us.

"What brings you all the way up here, Mr. Finley?"

Chalk it up to Pauline Shepherd's Chanel and Sewell's panting, but I got it into my head that was the perfect small talk question for a North Pole cocktail party. When I told her that, she took a second look at me—the one where she had to see a face. "That's very amusing," she allowed. "Do you attend a lot of cocktail parties in the North Pole? You strike me more as a South Pole type."

"What's the difference?"

"The whole world, I've heard."

I remembered the problem with lame gambits: they were usually exposed as lame gambits.

"And this is Leo. He's here to help with the carrying part."

She lavished enough movement on making Leo visible behind her that Sewell had to take the cue to extend his hand to the bodyguard and say it was nice to meet him. I couldn't see too many people thinking it was nice to meet Leo and I was just as glad Lineman #2 saved himself the effort of shaking hands with me. Like the guy out at the factory, he was all neck and chest decorated with a nice Windsor knot.

"So has there been anything new on that dreadful hit-and-run business?" she asked as Sewell waved her to the chair where I had been.

"No, nothing."

"It's a horrible story."

There were ways to combine false notes. One part came when you built a bridge to your host by bringing up something that didn't interest you in the least but which had been occupying much of his time. Another part was when you pretended your experience of the "horrible" was equal to the hit-and-run of a small-town disc jockey you had never met. I felt one with Leo, who just stood with his mitts folded in front of his crotch scanning the walls as though they were an improvement on the rope cage he had been forced to stare at on the trip from the jungle to New Florence.

Sewell finally stopped clucking. "So how filled up is our box outside?" she asked, turning to something she was interested in. "We just collected a ton of them at the post office."

"Hundreds of ballots every day," he said, still undecided if her sitting entitled him to his desk chair. "I'll tell you the truth, Pauline: I'll be glad to get my copy boy back. You don't even have to bring those ballots out to your computers. Alan can probably tell you right now who's won. At least for the ones sent here."

Her frosty smile said she allowed one cheap shot at her computers, but not too many after that. "Which would represent only part of the responses. But even if they were all the votes, it would still just be what you're interested in—the poll for New Florence. We must apply the results to dozens of other grids. It's not just one for you and one for him, two for you, two for him. It's also how that compares with other places."

"Right."

The kid Alan saved Sewell from another symphony of fidgets by sticking his head in the door and waving a thick manila envelope. "This is the last of them, Jim. Should I empty them into the box?"

"Just give them to Leo," she said, cutting off Sewell. "I gather you're the one who's overseen our poll here."

Alan Lockman won his fourth dork stripe by giving her a nonchalant shrug and diverting his attention to Leo, who held his hand out for the envelope. But the kid no more wanted to give Leo the ballots than Sewell had liked me shaking hands with Shepherd. "It's okay, Jim?" he asked.

Sewell was embarrassed by the kid's reluctance to give the envelope to anyone except him. "Of course. You've gotten a little possessive, Lockman. They're the ones who must do the counting. Even though I'm sure you could give them the standings right now."

Alan Lockman reddened as Leo took the envelope from him. "I wouldn't say that. I'm guessing like everybody else."

"You say so."

She followed the kid's departure halfway through the bullpen. "I guess I came down on him a little heavy the other day," Sewell said. "About spending too much time with the votes."

It was her cue to get to her feet. "It really was never our intention to disrupt the normal activities . . ."

"Don't be silly. If he hadn't been dawdling over The Most Admired Citizen, he'd be going on about his new motorbike. For that change of pace, I and everybody else on this newspaper thank you. The main thing now is when we can publish the results."

"You still want them for the Saturday edition, don't you?"

"Don't even ask. Community Day is already well along. No results by Saturday, a lot of empty chairs at Labine Plaza on Sunday."

"Then how about Friday afternoon? Will that be enough time?"

"Friday morning, maybe? I'd open the office for them."

"You're blackmailing me."

"Absolutely."

"Friday morning, then."

Leo didn't need further prompting. Sticking the envelope under his arm, he moved outside and grabbed the side handles of the metal box. One grunt and he had the box up to his chest. The two deskmen in the nearest cubicles gave him a mock hand. Leo had no time for their clowning. He was already toting his barge up toward the elevator.

"It was nice meeting you, Mr. Finley," she said. "Even though you never really answered my question."

"Tourism." It occurred to me to add "like you," but one shot to the solar plexus seemed like enough for one five-minute meeting. She wouldn't have heard so much wit anyway. She was quickly back to flattering Sewell with her pregnant stares, and he didn't miss it. His schedule was what it was, hers was what it was, it was so hard to find a moment for oneself with so much work bearing down, etc. If I didn't know Father Sewell better, I could have sworn they were talking in code for my benefit, and the message was that they would indeed get together there and then as arranged earlier. But who could trust anything I thought? An ice cream cone in the sun had more shape than what I had been thinking since she had walked in.

And then she was walking out again, clacking back down the waxed floors, suggesting a rear end without showing one, drawing notice from every man and woman along the aisle until she reached the elevator door and good old Leo, who was holding the metal box with his arms and the elevator with his back. Then both were gone with their box and their most admired citizen.

"*She's* the Pulsar Institute?"

Sewell remembered to be disappointed I was still there instead of her. "One of them," he said, returning to his desk. "They have lots of hats out there. Sociology this, Statistics that. Your usual techno wizards."

"And she's what? Sociology?"

He gave me a cross look. And that time I hadn't even been attempting to be funny. "You have to come out to the house before you leave," he said, apropos nothing. "Denise would love to see you."

It was the kind of non-sequitur johns were good at after being nabbed in fleabag hotels. What I didn't like was that he was making me feel as awkward as he was. "I should really be pushing along," I said. "What's this Community Day thing you were talking about?"

Was there such a thing as a grateful smirk? If there hadn't been, he invented it right then and there—relieved to be off one irksome topic and on to another one in which he was less involved. "The Labines. They figure the poll's an occasion for the town to pat itself on the back. Plaques and ribbons and hot dogs. Don't miss it if you're still around."

It sounded less like an invitation than another reason to be glad I would be back in New York.

CHAPTER 9

The Professor was never going to admit it on his own, so I was amazed for both of us when a good 50 or 60 people shuffled into the library to hear about the Spanish Lady of 1918. Not only did they fill every folding chair Karen Noon had set up under the cathedral windows to supplement the reading table chairs, but they spilled over into a shoulder-to-shoulder standing room that blocked off most of the stacks. They weren't all-natural targets of AARP junk mail, either. For every listener collecting a pension, there were two others who had probably told junior to finish his homework before they had set out for Claudio Mochi's statue. There were even a couple of kids taking a break from the Randy Page wake, probably on some class assignment. And maybe the biggest surprise of all was Truman Capote from the redhead's bar. In the better light of the library he looked even more pasty-faced, but with an alertness in his eyes that should have warned the Professor not to get any dates wrong. In fact, there were few who didn't have that look. Joe had said it himself: A lot of New Florence citizens had lost grandparents, great-grandparents, or other relatives to the flu and almost as many had come to think of themselves as experts on the subject. What was this outsider from New York going to tell them they didn't already know?

Joe relished the challenge. The flip side of the plaques, medallions, and honorary degrees he had been collecting in his retirement was that he had begun to feel a little *too* historical. He had been finding fewer and fewer openings to practice his instinctive antagonism—whether against fellow professionals who had different views on the causes of the Thirty-Year War or against his Garden City deli owner Bernie who gave him a cheerful "Hey, Professor!" before he had a chance to gripe the place was selling tasteless Swedish meatballs. He wasn't about to fumble the opportunity Karen had given him. What better way to start off than by trundling out to the small circle not covered by folding chairs, take in the locals skeptically, and declare: "You all think you have some special connection to the pandemic because your Uncle Harry's third cousin died of pneumonia at the age of 12 just as he was launching his brilliant career as a choir boy. Well, that makes you about as special as 35 million people around the world times four generations of cousins, nephews, nieces, and the descendants of the in-laws of your former neighbors across the street . . ."

The vintage Carroll got their attention. A couple of old-timers in the front row were on the verge of reaching for their pills and a skinny teacher type preparing to take notes with an electronic gizmo was all smiles, but most stiffened their spines, counting on their eyes not to give away hostility, determined to show themselves as altogether reasonable folks just in case the Goodyear blimp flew by overhead and televised their expressions to the nation. I had an urge to break the fire emergency glass near the door, grab the extinguisher, and foam them all until they relaxed. They reminded me too much of me when I didn't want to listen to the old man saying something that (as could happen once a year) might be useful.

I was sitting up front between Karen and the aunt librarian Veronica Pell, feeling like one of the brass at a police academy graduation ceremony. I had intended gravitating toward my usual slinking place near the side door, but Karen wouldn't hear of it: Chauffeuring the old man from New York was worth at least a captain's chair and the captain's chairs were all at the front. Within so many fields of vision it wasn't easy to go off on my own mental wanderings while the Professor rattled on. Yes, I should have been concentrating on the millions who had keeled over from Spain to India in 1918, should have sat there as a shining example of the wisdom to be stored by paying close attention. But I had also collected a week's distractions in one afternoon. The nearest one was the thin crossed knee in black pantyhose Karen swung in accompaniment to the black suede pump she was softly clapping up and down over her heel. There was a backbeat to it I knew I could be mesmerized by if the old man would only shut up. I hadn't really foreseen any boyfriend showing up for the lecture, but I had gained something by being right . . . hadn't I? Even if it was only one night, we had the excuse of being the next best thing to ships passing in the night—ships anchored in the same graveyard waiting for a scraping.

Then there was Veronica, who seemed dedicated to unnerving me by addressing me as if I had always been in New Florence, she had always run into me in New Florence, and she was well past the point of expecting anything good from me in New Florence. I had known Veronica Pells before, plenty of them. They had only one flaw: They had me feeling as unreliable as they took it for granted I was.

But Romeo had company. There were crawly things in New Florence, New York. It was nice to romanticize the place as self-contained, as I had back at the redhead's bar, but not so nice to think of being sealed in with creatures of some slimy substance. Leo and the other lineman out at the Mochi plant had called to mind a lot of things, but not the "grant spongers" the Professor had assured Karen the Pulsar Institute represented. There hadn't been a trace of academic chalk on Pauline Shepherd's skirt. Then there had been the half-hour at the *Reporter* with Labine's praetorian guard, Shepherd, and Father Sewell's brittle defensiveness where the lady was concerned. The Randy Page thing? Who cared if he was run over by accident or not: It was already feeling like a miracle he had been on the air in New Florence in the first place.

Oh, and one more thing: None of it had anything to do with me. Yes, we could be sociable and accept Karen's guest room for the night, but exactly 24 hours after the Professor was pointing out how American soldiers in World War I had helped to export the flu all over western Europe, I would be back in my Brooklyn apartment dealing with serious dragons like George Oswald and

Bob Nelson. Life had its priorities, and if I didn't straighten out who was going to do next season's Brooklyn Cyclones games, who the hell was?

Then the Professor ruined everything. If you had to pick out something from the supermarket that resembled his head, you would most likely go to the melon bin. But when he stopped mid-sentence, it was because of a dark plum coloring that suddenly burst out over his face. Then he was raising a hand to his forehead and slowly crumbling most of the way to the floor before the old-timer in the front row (needing pills less than I'd thought) leaped up to grab him. I couldn't believe he would go so far to dramatize somebody keeling over from the flu.

CHAPTER 10

I was working up a good-sized sulk toward New Florence. A hospital Emergency Room with Muzak in the ceiling speaker and no other patients waiting for help? Instead of New York's typical glaring blood and vomit center, the subdued lighting, wide chairs, and wooden cabinets made me think of the maternity ward lounge where I'd waited to see Susan the first time. And it wasn't just the furniture. None of the white coats we had talked to were dawdling exactly, but there was also the annoying hint in all their non-chalance that Nature, too, had to have a say in the Professor's condition. (*"Hey, heart, lungs, brain—they weren't invented by medicine, were they? There's only so much you can expect when it comes to repairing them."*) Me, I thought Nature had already had enough of a say, and said so to the boss doctor on call, a pony-tailed intern named Martinelli. What this got me were rec-ommendations for patience—from Martinelli who said he under-stood my anxiety and who then sauntered off to the Professor in a curtained cubicle as if going for a nap, from Karen who had been acting as though Joe's collapse was her fault, and from the ad-missions nurse who was adamant about asking health and medi-cation questions about the old man I couldn't answer. The only good side to the endless minutes getting him out of the library, piling him into the car, and driving him to the Emergency Room, was that, minus mumblings about how perfectly all right he was, he had kept his mouth shut.

I really didn't think of that as much of a good side.

I told the nurse about his high blood pressure, the arthritis in his knees, and his constant pissing. She had a box for every item on her form. I hated thinking everybody was so predictable, so suited to a form box, but then I hated thinking lots of things, such as how the Muzak could still be droning out "Moon River" after so many years. If we waited around long enough, would we get to hear "White Christmas," too?

"Maybe if we'd scheduled it for tomorrow night, given him a night to rest after the long drive," Karen said.

I resented her pious insistence on being the chief supporting player. The way she sat on the edge of her plastic lounger, her hands in the pockets of her jacket, she looked ready to take forgiveness from anyone who passed by. That was a little too passive, even for me. "Whatever's wrong with him would've come up tomorrow or the next day wherever he was," I told her. "He just happened to be here. We both know that."

Her expression said she didn't know any such thing and neither did I. I thought she had a point, which was why I also thought she was much more appealing when I was just staring at her thin legs. Way back then in the library I hadn't been responsible for anything more than fantasizing about what she would have been like in bed. Now I was getting the panicked feeling of a juggler who was missing a plate he had thrown into the air: The only way things were likely to end was with a crash somewhere behind me.

"They'll want to keep him overnight," she said, just loud enough for the nurse to hear. "They do that as a regular procedure."

The nurse couldn't have missed it, but she didn't rise to the bait; she was too engrossed in her boxes. "It could be a thousand things," I said, giving it a second try. "The bastard probably forgot his blood pressure pill."

That didn't work, either: The nurse was evidently used to idiot ploys. "He's always been stubborn," Karen nodded.

"Dense is more like it."

"Same thing."

"Not really."

She was on the verge of correcting me, showing off the reference books behind her counter at the library, when Martinelli came out from behind the cubicle curtain. He had picked up a stethoscope since going inside, and looked a little more competent. "He's okay for the moment," he reported, "but I want to run some tests."

"So he should stay overnight?"

I wanted to clobber her for burning our best card, then wondered what was so good about it. "No question," Martinelli nodded. "He said you came up here from New York. I'm sure he'd prefer seeing his own doctor down there, but I really can't advise that. If nothing else, he could use the rest tonight and tomorrow. He won't get that on a long car ride."

"Can you at least tell me what you suspect it is?"

As tinny questions went it was probably Franklin Mint pure even for a 27ish-28ish like Martinelli, but he gave me his best reflective look. "His blood pressure is very high. Maybe that's something that's been building up for a while and maybe he just needs a higher dose from the pills he's been taking. Or the blood pressure and the blackout could be warning us it's something else. That's why I'd like him to stick around. I'm sure Dr. Mendler— he's our chief cardiologist—will recommend an angiogram when he comes in tomorrow."

What was I going to say—no? Martinelli had made sure I couldn't. The blackout had been warning *us*; not just Martinelli, but *us*. Once upon a time as a cop I had loved driving people into corners the way he had boxed me in. At least he was graceful enough not to gloat. He also had no objections to my going into the examination room for a minute. Karen was right on my heels. "I should calm him about the lecture," she said.

I knew she was right. The old man would have been fretting about the library crowd in the next world. And he wasted no time making that clear. When he saw me parting the curtain, he was all peevishness from his perch on the examining table. But then Karen came in, and his eyes immediately glassed over. "I don't know what to tell you, kid," he started. "I owe you and those people . . ."

"You owe them nothing. You gave them an exciting evening."

"I had things to say . . ."

"And you'll say them. We have time."

He didn't like the sound of that. "What's that mean?"

When I told him what Martinelli had advised, he surprised me by not protesting; more than surprised, worried me. "Has something been going on you haven't told me about?"

"What the hell should I be telling you? You in charge of me now?"

"If you've been feeling lousy lately."

"Yeah? So? You Doctor Finley now?"

It went back and forth a few times, both of us indignant about what we didn't know and weren't sure we wanted to know. Ten minutes earlier I wouldn't have thought I could be so glad to see an orderly arrive with a wheelchair for transporting the hospital's newest patient up to the second floor. The old man's parting shot about being sure to arrive early the next morning to collect him convinced nobody.

On the drive back to the library Karen said little but to wonder aloud how Veronica had dealt with our abrupt departure. She had to give a damn about that because she had a plaque on her desk that identified her as the LIBRARIAN. But even in those few words there was something new in her voice, too, and it took most of the ride to figure out what it was. *She was detached from both the library and her old teacher.* There was a Karen Noon who was more than both those things, and it was the first inkling I'd had of it.

About the library she could have spared herself. Veronica had not just cleared the premises, leaving merely two cars parked in front, but had turned the massive gray building into a brooding monument of the night. The only light came from the slit of an office window next to the main entrance. "You don't have to come in," Karen said, her hand on her handle as soon as I stopped. "Let me just make sure Veronica said all the proper things, then you can follow me home. Five minutes."

I watched her take a small jailer's ring of keys out of her shoulder bag as she hurried up the steps and let herself in through the door off to the side of the entrance. I would have liked a cigarette, but I would have liked one lots of times in two years and saw no reason not to ignore again what I would have liked. Both cars in the library's parking area were Fords. I put the modest blue Focus with Karen, the more aggressive black Taurus with Veronica. What I couldn't see was either of them coming out of the library, walking down the steps, and getting run over before reaching her car. I was hardly in Times Square, but there was enough light even to make out the Dentyne wrapper yards in front of my headlights. How much darker could the radio station lot have been the night Randy Page had been killed? And if there had been a neat pile of butts and roaches, the way Sewell had said . . .

I made a bargain with my brain cells: I would release a few billion more of them in the next few seconds if the ones that stuck around kept me bogged down in reality. And as if to formalize the deal, a squad car, blue beacon whirling but without the siren, came tearing down the street. The speed said at least a gun run. Only when the car kept going back into the night did it occur to me it could have been responding to a call about a suspicious Subaru parked in front of the library. I *really* needed a cigarette.

The light in the office window finally went off. Veronica came out first, closing the top button of a green windbreaker. That sight was about to dispatch my happy thoughts to baseball teams and the Brooklyn Cyclones when she took the entrance steps down two at a time. Not only was she a bawdy aunt, but an athletic one!

"He'll be all right," she said, leaning in the passenger window and drenching the car in orange blossoms. "He just underrated the stage fright he'd have trying to tell people something they didn't know."

I gave her the smile she wanted as Karen came down the steps behind her. "Are you one of those people?"

"Hell, no," she said, giving a comfort shake to the plastic bracelets wedged under her jacket cuff. "I never heard of New Florence before the creature calling himself my ex-husband lured me here 15 years ago. That was the biggest move of my life. His big one came three years later when he ran off to a government clerk in Albany. I can tell you plenty about government clerks in Albany, but no flu stories. Sorry."

I was right about the cars: Veronica went straight for the Taurus. She pulled out of her space like a NASCAR driver bent on making up for all the hours she had wasted reshelving books. Karen? She drove the way she spoke: an air of the painstaking, assuming those behind her would either adapt or pull away from her and get lost. She gave the lights their full due, the Stop signs an extra second they didn't deserve. The neighborhood she led us into was one of those flat featureless avenues of cardboard ranch houses that would never quite cover up the days when there had been nothing but cordoned off dirt tracts for development. Haunted houses had ghosts rattling chains, the street where we were would never shake the bulldozers of its beginnings. I wanted to think she had at least taken a house that had already been lived in by somebody else. I didn't want to think of her landing in New Florence, falling into the clutches of a real estate sharper, and being conned into becoming the first to pay for a glorified bungalow that should have been used for the A-bomb tests in Nevada.

As wide as the avenue was, she had to slow to a crawl before what looked like a convention of patrol car lights in front of one of the houses. A red ambulance beacon broke up the police blues. Then she stopped altogether and a uniform went over to her window. Half the block seemed to have gathered across the street from where the action was. The good news about that was that if the cars had really been responding to a gun run, the cops would have sent everyone back to their homes until the guns had been confiscated. So figure the guns had been confiscated. The bad news was I doubted the commotion had to do with a gun run. Especially with the ambulance, the scene reminded me of a domestic violence call. New Florence apparently wasn't used to that kind of excitement.

For some reason Karen started sliding over to the sidewalk space just shy of the police cars. For some other reason the uniform in the middle of the street liked the idea so much he waved for me to do the same thing. I had a bad feeling, and not because she had obviously told him that where she parked, I did, too. Then I saw Father Sewell standing near the house that was attracting all the attention. He was talking to a detective and didn't look like the executive editor of anything.

My next mistake was getting out of my car, starting down the street to where Karen was gazing off in the direction of Sewell and the detective, and seeing the name on the sidewalk mailbox. It said LOCKMAN.

CHAPTER 11

New Florence was a very small planet. I had told Karen about running into Sewell earlier in the day and she had told me he was on the board of the library. The Lockmans—the *Reporter* copy boy Alan and his widowed mother—lived two houses up from Karen. It might not have been Six Degrees of Separation from Finley, but it felt close enough.

With one exception Karen had known the Lockmans only casually as neighbors on the street—Hello, Nice Weather, Happy Thanksgiving. The exception had been the morning her car battery had died and Alan had given her a lift to work on his motorbike. He had been going to the library anyway, he had joked, and he really wasn't up for riding all the way down to find that the place wasn't open because the librarian hadn't shown up. It was that morning she had learned that the kid's father had died of stomach cancer and that the mother worked as a middle manager for Walter Labine's insurance company—about the only personal items she had picked up about the family during all their time as neighbors. She had liked the ride, gone so far as to indulge a thought or two about trading in her Focus for a bike of her own. But that fancy had evaporated before lunchtime the same day. She hadn't given another thought to owning a motorcycle since that morning.

The story came out in a whispered rush, then dropped back down between her bony shoulders again. She started to turn her head, to look through the blinds into the living room of the house to see Mrs. Lockman cringing within the arms of another woman on the couch, but then changed her mind. She couldn't take her eyes off the garage where, through the backs and shoulders of the medical examiner's people and a couple of detectives, Alan Lockman's boots could still be seen hanging over the motorbike she had sat on to go to work. Why the locals hadn't screened off the garage I had no idea. I hoped that was part of Sewell's anger as he gesticulated with the detective in front of the house.

"It must have been an accident," she said for the second time.

I didn't answer for the second time. The difference between her and the Professor being wheeled upstairs by the orderly was that she could see right in front of her eyes why wishing never made it so. Even from the sidewalk the noose looked like a thoughtful job.

Sewell and the plainclothes finally had enough of each other, and the cop turned and plodded back to the house where Mrs. Lockman let loose with another shriek as he opened the front door. It wasn't just the garage that should have been screened off, but the whole goddamn house.

"It's Alan Lockman," Sewell said, coming over to us with incredulous eyes. "They say he hanged himself. Came home from work, got off his bike, and just threw a rope over . . . It's ridiculous, Paul!"

I didn't answer him, either. What was to be gained by agreeing that the last thing Alan Lockman had made me think about a few hours earlier was a noose? Sewell wouldn't have heard me anyway. He was too trapped between wanting to chase after the wildness in his eyes and to give in to the slump of a beaten man. Karen broke the tie by nodding toward the detective in the house. "Brighton in charge?" she asked with an iron I hadn't heard before.

Sewell blinked back to the present—to Karen and to a skepticism that was apparently not just hers. "Brighton's all right," he said, sounding like somebody not up to reheating an old debate. "He'll do what he has to."

"Like with Randy Page?"

I had missed the depth of her bitterness completely. Maybe there had been a hint of smarting during lunch in the Italian restaurant, but nothing like the full-blown rancor she was now directing at Sewell. "He can only do so much," he said feebly. "The people around him . . ."

"I know. The politicians upstairs. The poor police. Be patient. Let them do their job and everything will come out okay in the end."

He looked at me as if I could explain her tone—or, failing that, apologize for it. I stared him down. "It isn't as cut and dried as some people would like to think, Karen," he managed.

But Karen had had it—with Father Sewell, with bodies hanging in garages, with library lectures that never got delivered. She'd had a long day. "I'm down there at number 16," she said to me, her eyes suddenly pinpricks and not sounding at all like a welcoming hostess. "Stay if there's something you haven't seen. But I've seen enough."

I didn't know why I hesitated. I had nothing to say to Sewell, and he already looked well along the road to a long night of whys; it would be up to the scotch in his liquor cabinet to catch up with him before he gave up and went to bed. But something about the back-and-forth over the detective named Brighton had sounded like a question to me. "I'll be right with you," I told her. "Two minutes."

She was already too offended to be offended by me, too. The way she stalked down the sidewalk toward her house, reaching into her bag for her ring of keys as she went, should have been warning enough for the uniforms not to intercept her. None did.

Sewell's idea of covering over his awkwardness was to take off his glasses for a wiping as he sort of followed her down the street past the cops. "Maybe they've already ruled out the sidewalk as part of the crime scene," he said. "What do you think?"

We were supposed to be the savvy experts from Long Island, and why not? "Yeah, fast workers."

"We shouldn't even be standing where we are!"

He was right. But that also seemed to make Karen more right about the cop in charge named Brighton.

"Brighton's got his faults," Sewell said, putting his glasses back on to read my face. "But not as many as some people say."

"Jimmy, I can't guess at what the hell you and Karen are talking about. Just ask me what you want to ask."

He nodded, but had to bite off something else before getting to it. "You still smoke those lousy Marlboro Lights?"

"No."

He kept his eyes on the cluster of neighborhood people being kept at a distance across the street by two uniforms. "As you probably just heard, a lot of people around here think Brighton shouldn't be running anything but a gypsy cab," he said finally. "I like the guy personally. And I know the slippery characters he must deal with down at City Hall every day. Left to his own devices, he'd do the right thing."

I was starting to get a knot in my head. It was like listening to the Professor saying blackouts were a normal part of the day. "What do you want to know, Jimmy?"

"You know. This damn mess of a crime scene. And that's what it is, Paul—a crime. Not a suicide. A crime."

"If this Brighton's making excuses to himself about how everybody's tying his hands and he's got people like you parroting . . ." I stared through the glare. "I said parroting. Because you're sure as hell sounding like somebody who's got a ton of excuses for not doing the job."

"We were talking about Brighton."

"Yeah, maybe him, too."

He really didn't want to argue with me any more than he had with Karen. "This is no suicide, Finley," he said again.

"Then what is it?"

The Jimmy Sewell of a few years back had never gone into print before nailing down every fact, corroborative or mitigating, whatever. The Jimmy Sewell in front of me looked like somebody who already knew he was never going to be allowed to go into print period. "You tell me," he said. "Better yet, tell her."

He looked in at Mrs. Lockman, now trying to compose herself for Brighton, who didn't even know enough to sit down instead of looming over her under the low ceiling. I felt inside Karen's anger. It had been a long day for me, too, and pathos didn't make it any shorter. "I'll give you a buzz tomorrow before I leave, Jimmy," I said, getting away before he could open his mouth again.

The uniforms didn't stop me walking down the sidewalk, either.

CHAPTER 12

Karen's mailbox said not just NOON, but ANTONACCI, the name of the dead husband. I wondered what government correspondence justified keeping her married name and why she hadn't phoned some friendly agency, pressed buttons with a robot operator for a few hours, and changed it.

The vestibule smelled of cherry leather jackets although there were none on the coat hooks. She left it to me to close the front door and hurried back to the kitchen in her stockinged feet. I was beginning to think she had been counting on me not showing up at all until I saw the second mug on the kitchen counter. "I'm having tea."

"Sounds good."

The only photographs I could make out on the corkboard above the counter were of a much younger Karen—a blondish seven- or eight-year-old at the beach with a goofy-looking father and then a heavier teenager sitting on a couch with two boys her age. She had the same passive expression in both pictures. There were three blinding yellow chairs around a blinding yellow table and, stuck in the tightest corner against the wall, a wooden folding chair. I thought about going for the folding chair to show her I understood my place in her universe, then decided that would be too much. I liked thinking I knew when not to exaggerate.

"I'm sorry for back there," she said, keeping her shoulder blades to me as she turned up the flame under the kettle.

"I can't say I followed much of it."

She reached into the overhead closet to a canister for teabags. "Was Jim Sewell a good reporter in New York?"

"He's got a Pulitzer Prize on his mantle."

"And he didn't mind rubbing the police the wrong way?"

"I think he got off on it. Not that he'll admit it." She shook her head: Who would have believed it possible of the same man she knew in New Florence? "Where is it you think he's coming up short?" The kettle whistled over whatever she said. "Sorry?"

"I said he works for Walter Labine. I think that covers most of it."

"Labine is like all the Labines in the world?"

She finally relented to show her face—or just to bring the cups over to the table. She had lost the pinpoints in her eyes, but the rest of her small face still seemed pouchy from a toothache. "No, it's not even that," she said. "It's not that personal. Jim Sewell's just part of it, and I guess I hoped an editor like him would be different."

"I'm still not following. Part of what, Karen?"

"The inertia," she said, as if it should have been obvious. "Things oozing out of control. One inch at a time. You want to shout each inch of the way that somebody better do something fast. Maybe you *do* shout. But the ooze covers the next inch anyway and keeps spreading. It's the feeling I had in Hoboken. Near the end."

She was braving her stare—at me, through the kitchen's bleary fluorescence, toward whatever Andy Antonacci demons had pursued her from New Jersey. But I didn't know what to say. I was more comfortable with her first theme—Father Sewell as the hired pen for Walter Labine. See no evil and hear no evil unless it boosted insurance rates.

"I know. You don't have a clue what I'm talking about. But I felt it the first time I read about Pulsar coming here. Veronica showed me the story at work about the poll and I got a chill."

"Why not? It reminded you of your husband."

"That's what Veronica said," she said, going back for the kettle. "But it wasn't just that. In the story they interviewed one of the Pulsar people. God, he was creepy!"

Sewell had been right about one thing: Pauline Shepherd didn't do all the talking for Pulsar. "What did he say?"

"It wasn't one special thing, but the assumptions behind *everything* he said. Like these are the terms of the question and let's not bother wasting time looking elsewhere. My turf, my rules, that kind of thing. Only New Florence *isn't* his turf, and God damn the people who let him think it is. I tried explaining that to Veronica, but the more I got into it, the more paranoid I sounded even to myself. She started looking at me like I had two heads. So I thought of the Professor."

"Nobody nearer you could talk to about it?"

She brought the kettle over with a pale smile. "I lived and worked with a politician for a long time, Paul. I got used to the way people sized up one another over a handshake, practically wrote biographies before they let go of each other. The one question you've been asking yourself since you came here is who's the guy? Or, is it a woman or is it nobody at all? . . . It's all right, it's all right. Minus two points in the grace department, but I don't really care. And for the record the answer is there's nobody at the moment. But what I was about to say was Randy Page was like the ooze moving forward still a little more. And now we have Alan even further along."

The only choice I had was to talk to her or to the asshole who ran Finley Investigations. Spacey as she sounded, the choice wasn't all that hard. "You mean of not having control?"

"Of *losing* it," she said, her hand completely steady as she poured the water. "Not having it—I don't know, isn't that normal? Pay your electric and cable every month and shut up? But giving away the little you have, knowing you shouldn't but doing it anyway, that's not so normal. I thought you might understand that better than most people."

I didn't know if she intended it as a compliment or not; eeriness was not usually what I lunged after as an asset. What she reminded me of, though, was that she and the Professor had spent the afternoon together. While I had been drinking coffee in a bar that didn't want to serve coffee and meeting too many people I wished I hadn't at the *Reporter,* he had been telling her about me. I wouldn't have minded knowing if she had asked first. "Joe been yacking again?"

"It's not a story he tells as a detached observer."

That was something. He had *no right* to be a detached observer. I still had moments—fewer every week, but they still popped up—when I could blame him for everything that had happened to Jennifer and Susan. And when they did pop up, like at that second, I could feel a muscle relaxing in my shoulder as I deliberately exercised opening and closing my hand.

"Milk? Lemon?"

She went to the refrigerator talking about how we hadn't had supper. She had this, she had that, the town had delivery this, delivery that. I had no doubt they did. And what? Wait for it to be cooked? Wait for it to arrive? Wait for it because it wasn't there on the table right then when it should have been? "It was his first Christmas after his wife died," I ended up telling her. "He insisted he was going to cook, wouldn't hear about going to a restaurant or coming to our house. I think we got there at one o'clock and he was still trying to figure out how to put the turkey in the oven. By the time we got food on the table I was totally blitzed on egg nog and bourbon. I couldn't taste dinner. Before I made more of a spectacle of myself in front of Susan, I went down to the basement room to take a nap. I didn't wake up until a state trooper was in the house telling us about the accident. Jennifer had gotten tired of waiting for Rip Van Winkle so said she was taking Susan home. The old man argued with her, said the roads were too icy, she should wait. That was what you never did to my wife—tell her she wasn't capable of something. They were killed about a mile away from the house."

She nodded absently, looking more fascinated by the tea she was squeezing out of the bag into her cup. I recognized the reaction—welcome to the club, sorry we had to meet under these circumstances, but don't make too much noise. "Joe hinted you had a little problem passing bars for a while," she said after a moment.

"He gave you the full rundown, didn't he?"

"I'm sorry. I shouldn't . . ."

The fact was, I *didn't* mind her eeriness; or the presumptuousness that came with it. "In for a penny in for a pound. But no, I wasn't much good as a cop after a while so I got out before I was thrown out. That's how you eventually become a brilliant private detective."

She hadn't heard anything funny. "There were times I wished I had that problem. But I can't get to a third wine without my head swimming. So instead I drank tea until my tongue felt like sandpaper."

She told me the rest before I had to ask for it. It got us away from me and from the copyboy down the street who had not seemed to me like a prime candidate for hanging himself. Which was another way of saying I was relieved to get away from things I knew less about than I wanted to admit.

"There were so many telephone calls the first morning after the poll came out. You'd think Andy had won an election. Telegrams from Trenton, Albany, even Washington. At first, he joked about it. It was all wink-wink-wink-let's-not-take-it-too-seriously. But the interviews and the pats on the back kept coming. The county prosecutor threw him a luncheon. Every day he believed in it a little more. What tore it was when he used the poll in a letter to his district. He always showed those things to me before the office printed them and sent them out. I told him not to do it, he was inviting trouble, it was like daring Zeus in the sky to say the Pulsar Institute couldn't have been more wrong. I should have known better. The one thing Andy inherited from his father besides the wrong supporters was arrogance. The Pulsar Institute said he was a saint, so he must have been a saint. It didn't have to be that reporter who discovered otherwise. Anybody with eyes in his head could have seen how he went around leading with his jaw. He really started to think he was invulnerable." She raised her gaze in embarrassment. "For a long time, *I* thought he was invulnerable."

My tea looked dark enough just in time. I tried to look as busy as possible squeezing the last drops out of the bag into the spoon. It seemed more tactful than plowing into the hundred and one holes in her story. "So it ended how it did because this reporter found out Andy had been dipping his hand in the till and . . ."

"You make it sound like taking out the garbage."

"To some people it is."

"Because all politicians are just politicians?"

That sounded right even with the one or two exceptions I could have named for her. But I still had the out of being her guest. "I was in what they called Major Cases a long time, Karen, but when there was a *really* major case, I was never invited into the room. The district attorney and the VIP and his lawyers hunkered down around a table to work out the plea deal that would save the VIP from being confused with a common criminal and the county from having to use up its trial funds for the year. How much time could Antonacci have gotten? A couple of years for a scaled down felony count at one of those farms for white-collar embezzlers? It's all in the negotiating. How does that add up to shooting yourself?"

I could have been an April's Fool gag to her. For a second I thought I was going to get her tea in my face. But then, instead, she erupted with a laugh—a little girl's giggle defying her heavy eyes. "*Add up!*"

"They never got that far negotiating?"

This time her eyes didn't have the patience for pinpoints, they were in full glare. "What in god's name was there to negotiate? People lost their life's savings, their homes! They got the commercial licenses they needed because they paid double and triple for them! They hired attorneys who worked against them instead of for them! Sometimes they fed their children meat you wouldn't give a rabid dog! People with badges lied right to their faces! They lost their sense of being able to . . . simply *trust*. Andy was responsible for a lot of that! Others may have done it, but he helped make it possible! That isn't something you negotiate, Paul!"

There weren't enough teabags in the canister to hide behind. I wasn't looking at a wife or even a widow. The red-faced grievance sitting catty-corner to me was all that trust that had been abused. But when desperate, when there was nothing more to lose, as an old sergeant named Bailey used to tell me, keep pushing forward. "And you knew it all along."

Defiance: "Yes, I suppose I did."

"So how much is on you? Fifty percent? Seventy-five? Or maybe the whole thing because you never got him on the straight and narrow? You must have considered a number at some point."

I didn't believe it came out of my mouth, either. But she hadn't known what to expect, so she got over her dismay first. "He was ashamed of what he had done to me," she said evenly. "Not what he had done to his constituents, but to me. He really meant it as a compliment and maybe I should have taken it as one, but I didn't. That was the second futility of killing himself. He couldn't even do it for the right reason."

"Wow, that's heavy baggage to carry around."

She blinked, and I knew at once she had made the "second futility" confession before, maybe to Veronica one night while approaching that third wine frontier. She was puzzled. It hadn't been easy for her to say something like that to a stranger like me so why wasn't there automatic respect for her? "You're trying to provoke me," she decided.

"If it'll get you to say something genuine, yeah."

She contemplated vicious, more vicious, most vicious, but even before she wet her thin lips with the tip of her tongue, I felt her discarding them all. I knew I still had the guest room; by myself, but still the bed. "Is that the way you talk at AA meetings?" she asked.

"Wouldn't know. I don't belong."

"I thought . . ."

"You thought wrong. Now you tell me. It's one thing being humiliated because you've been caught out by a newspaperman doing his job. You grit your teeth and get through it. Let the Sunday supplement come in and do a story about how you're spending Christmas behind bars and are determined never to have to do it again. But shooting yourself? Leaving the crushed Missus to handle it all? I think you're leaving out something."

She didn't find the answer in her cup. "You fell asleep. I didn't."

"That part I got."

"That's all there is."

"Really? And you just woke up, hallelujah, because the Pulsar Institute came along? Jesus, they sound better than AA meetings. At least you don't have to sit in damp church basements."

"You don't take people very seriously, do you?"

"Most of them, no. But you I'd take seriously if you answered one question. Why is his name still on the mailbox outside? His constituents can't still be waiting for him to get their water turned back on."

She didn't owe me an answer, but she told me anyway. "His mother writes to me every month. She still thinks he's her little Andrew, that 'bad people' made him do what he did. She's grateful I stayed by him, still have his name. He doesn't deserve that loyalty for what he put me through, she says, but she's grateful for it. I don't think putting his name on the mailbox is much of a price for letting her believe that. She needs something, even if it's an illusion."

I let it go. Some philosopher in a bar had once told me that operations were minor only when they happened to other people and self-delusions were minor only when they were your own. I wasn't there to interrogate her and I hadn't applied to be her conscience. It felt close enough that every half-assed answer she had given me sounded like something I had convinced myself of at some point somewhere along the line.

CHAPTER 13

The cops took forever to clean up at the Lockmans' place and clear off the block. Only after she had watched the tail lights of the last patrol car disappear down the street did she come away from the window in the front living room and click on the television set to have something not to watch. As she sat with her legs stretched out on the couch with her third cup of tea, I saw what she had meant about turning her tongue to sandpaper: Mine felt fizzier just watching her serial sipping. I had never read much about the Borgias, but I was starting to think Lucrezia too must have been expert at ignoring the cracks all around her by retreating to some rote habit that reassured her she was still in charge.

Despite the long day and the longer silences between us, I didn't feel even first-base tired and was in no rush to close myself into the airless guest room she had shown me. I hadn't gone to bed so early, sober and alone anyway, since I had broken my mother's favorite vase with my paddle ball. I could have gone out in search of New Florence night life, but I could have looked for a cave to capture some bats, too. I decided to kill at least a few seconds by checking the phone messages I had collected back in Brooklyn during the day. If nothing else, I thought my hostess would be impressed to see how I had conquered enough of the gizmo world to be able to activate my messages by remote control.

I was wrong twice—first because her gaze remained fixed with Alan Lockman thoughts somewhere over the TV screen and she was completely indifferent to how I had mastered pressing and beeping, second because there were only four messages and two of them were from a frantic George Oswald, hardly a reason for feeling like a conqueror of anything. To judge by the shriek level (even higher than normal), George had been meditating far too long on my little encounter with the moose in Prospect Park and had concluded (already a suspicion during our last conversation) that I had left him worse off than ever. Then again, he had been listening to Bob Nelson, who had apparently called him to say that my "attack" on the moose made for as much of a juicy item on blogs as all that hilarious studio repartee about women, cripples, and Filipinos. In short, Mister Potato Head had reached the firm opinion that in exchange for his $750 retainer I had succeeded in moving him from a blackmail world to a blackmail cosmos.

I could understand his point of view. He hadn't been there to see the moose's charge, or the choreographed way Nelson had sicked the slug on me. And now Nelson had told him the moose had needed medical attention? Considering his opinion of my gutter profession to start with, what else could a Mister Potato Head think? I thought about phoning him back then and there to straighten things out, but there seemed to be a lot of reasons against doing it. One was that I didn't have a clue about how to straighten them out. I also didn't want to stick Karen with the long-distance charges. And what about the time zone problem: How many hours later was it down in New York City? I certainly didn't want to be rude and wake up Mrs. Potato Head.

Reasons *for* telephoning him? I couldn't think of one.

I tried to follow the *Law and Order* episode everybody else in the house was ignoring. Just as Sam Waterston's latest assistant was begging a judge for a warrant, Karen stood up with her empty mug and padded into the kitchen. I took it as a good sign that she ran the faucet into the mug, that she didn't want another refill. But I also expected her to come back into the living room, if only to say goodnight. But the next sound I heard was the click from her bedroom door being closed. I hadn't even been given instructions on how to turn off the lights and the TV.

CHAPTER 14

All that clean air I'd picked up leaving New York did what it was supposed to do the next morning by not waking me up until after nine. By then Karen had gone to work, leaving me a note about where to find breakfast things and taking it for granted I would be dropping by the library with the Professor before doing anything so hasty as returning home. I couldn't make out anything between the lines except instructions about where to find breakfast things and the assumption I would be dropping by the library with the Professor before returning home. It all sounded overly optimistic on her part—that the hospital would be releasing the old man and that I would be getting out of her life sooner than later.

The main hospital lobby was almost as empty as the Emergency Room had been the night before. I was beginning to think that, just like the local shop-pes, the New Florence Medical Center existed only for outsiders from places like New York. That thought diverted me for about a second and a half, until I remembered what the town medical examiner was probably doing at the very moment with Alan Lockman's body. That in turn reminded me of Sewell's behavior in front of the Lockman house. If he had been the mayor (or Walter Labine), I thought as I took the fire stairs up to the second floor, he would have appointed me then and there to take over the investigation from the Brighton character nobody seemed to trust. There had been something odd about that besides the macho fantasy it allowed me to entertain on my way up to see the Professor, but I didn't know what.

The old man was sharing quarters with an empty bed and a curtainless window over the hospital parking lot; more than most hospital rooms, it looked like it had been abandoned by painters in the middle of the job. The patient's hospital gown was losing the fight against the chunks of fat across his shoulders, but at least he wasn't hooked up to any of the ominous cream-colored machines next to the bed. He had lost his plum color, and was back to looking like an old pale fish. As soon as I walked in, he gave a crack to the *Reporter* he was reading and pretended to bury his nose in it more deeply. "They don't like my heart beat," he said to stifle questions. "I haven't liked it for years, but they seem to believe their opinion is worth more than mine."

That struck me as shoddy. If it was his heart, why *wasn't* he hooked up to one of the machines? "Whose isn't? What tests they want to do?"

"There you go," he said, wetting his thumb and turning a page. "Soon as you get thrown into one of these hotels, it's always what do *they* want to do? What's this hanging thing about the kid on Karen's street?"

"How should I know?"

"She called this morning while you were snoozing. Said she doesn't believe it. I tried to find something about it in this rag, but they seem to avoid sordid things like news."

I pulled the visitor's chair over from under the window and told him what I had seen. He didn't look any more informed than he had from reading the newspaper. That made us even: I still didn't know what was wrong with him. The only thing I had to go on was his normal crotchetiness. Sometimes bad signs could be good signs.

"Karen says you met the kid. He seem like a suicide?"

"No, he didn't, Joe."

"What's that tone for?"

"I'm waiting to hear what the hell they told you."

"Oh."

"Oh."

"On the premise that I'm still alive and the kid isn't so that makes my news more important?"

"One difference."

"Then you'll stop evading the issue?"

"You want my two cents? All right. Nobody comes home on his bike, parks his bike, throws a rope over his garage beam, keeps the garage door open so everybody can see what he's doing, then hangs himself. A copyboy at the *Reporter* named Alan Lockman doesn't do that. You don't do that. The hamster in the pet store down the street doesn't do it."

He nodded as though hearing what he had expected to hear. But he also seemed to think there was something funny about it. "So I suppose you've already figured out . . ."

"I'm still waiting. What's the schedule around here today?"

He shrugged to the comic strip page as much as to me. "I agreed they could put some of their blue dye in me. Why not? I go back to the city to that blind man who calls himself my doctor and he'll give me orange."

"You want Sherman to look at you instead of these people, we can leave as soon as we check you out."

"Didn't I just say I trust these people to play their games more than that old fool in Garden City?"

"Something like that."

"Good. We're both speaking the English language this morning. They still run Pogo up here."

"In short, you've agreed to stay for another day."

"I didn't say that."

"What *are* you saying, Joe?"

He thought of another crack, but settled for crumpling the newspaper on his stomach and gazing past me out the window. "There's something rotten up here, Finley," he said softly, "and it isn't doing Karen any good. She's a goddamn mess."

"I've seen steadier people."

He nodded more agreeably than he should have. But then he dropped his eyes back to me. I felt some request coming a nanosecond before he said: "What's another day or two going to cost you? You got so many affairs of state waiting for you back in Brooklyn? What—those clowns who want to broadcast baseball games?"

"What're you talking about?"

"Get your hearing checked before you leave here. I think you should nose around a little into this copyboy thing, that's what I'm talking about. I know Karen, for one, would be very grateful."

"Karen . . .?"

"She says you had a heart-to-heart last night," he said, a little more strain to his casualness. "You didn't win any personality awards with her, but she'll give you a pass because you're not up the ass of this Pulsar Institute or City Hall or some of the other spooks around here."

"Spooks is right. Karen Noon has what they call issues."

"Yeah, she does. But one lie at a time. A day, two at most."

"For doing what, for Christ sake!"

"Earning your retainer," he said evenly. "From me to you."

I stared at him for what seemed like a long time, waiting for him to admit to his little joke. But when he finally did glance away, it was only to return to Pogo. "We have seen the enemy and it's us. Isn't that what one of the Pogo characters said first?"

"I don't even know the names of the streets around here!"

"There must be some travel office. They'll have maps."

"What is this? For two seconds, the truth. Okay?"

"I told you on the way up here: I'd like to do something for her."

"And?"

"And when she was telling us about that radio guy at lunch yesterday, I almost blew it again. I didn't take her seriously . . ."

I felt an itch in my throat. *Again?* There had been no first time where Karen Noon was concerned, at least that he had told me about. The only doubt I had was if he himself knew he was mixing up Karen with Jennifer in his emotional debts. But it really wasn't much of a doubt. If anything, he was waiting for me to blurt out that accusation. And I wasn't playing.

". . . but now there's this kid . . ."

"Who may have had enemies up the kazoo because they didn't like how he always strutted around talking about his bike. Who may have pissed off another copyboy at the *Reporter* by beating him to the morning coffee run for the office. Would I investigate it as a clumsy attempt to disguise homicide as suicide? Absolutely. Does it have anything to do with this Page guy? There's no reason to think that, let alone assume it."

"Karen says . . ."

"*Karen says.* Any question at all to Karen and the answer is the Pulsar Institute. You have to see where that's coming from, Joe."

"You mean Antonacci."

"Gee, did I say that?"

He looked back at his comics from a greater distance. "I told her that. You heard me. She can't see the forest for the trees."

"Good. Now who's the doctor I talk to for getting some answers?"

He shook his head to Pogo. "Some guy with attitude."

I waited for more, anything at all, but I had clearly missed what he had been conceding about Karen. I knew I was stuck in New Florence for at least another day. I also knew something else: that I didn't like the guy who, a few hours before talking about a woman "with issues," had been drooling over her legs and starring her in his sexual fantasies. Whatever New Florence's other attractions, it seemed very good at bringing out hypocrisy.

CHAPTER 15

I left the hospital room wondering if the old man hadn't staged the whole fainting scene in the library to keep us marooned. I was on the verge of escalating that suspicion into a religion in the corridor when I ran into the stern-faced cardiologist Martinelli had mentioned. Addressing me in a tone that insinuated I had caused the Professor's condition by imposing a long drive on him, John Mendler, a stocky 50ish with impeccably combed grey hair, gave me a rundown on arterial blockages and what lovely things they can do unless he was there to foil them with angiograms and the other tools he had mastered better than anybody else in the state. I knew he believed that because there wasn't a trace of humor in his steel gray eyes as he spoke. He promised to say something more definitive if I called him in the early afternoon. And make sure I did!

I took the elevator down the one floor to the lobby feeling unentitled to it. The fire stairs seemed more like my speed where acting as Joe Carroll's guardian, estate executor, and chief mourner-in-waiting was concerned. The fact of the matter was that even after years of being father-in-law and son-in-law, of living in his basement during the worst period of staggering around after Jennifer's car crash, and of then marking off our professional turfs from one another, after all that time I still wasn't sure I *liked* the guy. And that was one hypocrisy I couldn't blame on New Florence. Deep down inside all the official histories he ring-mastered there was still a demarcation line in him that said far enough,

Finley, no life here, go on to the next door because what's behind this one is no business of yours and never will be. Accept that and we'll get along almost fine.

I didn't know what Father Sewell's hours were, but I went out to the parking lot sure that if he ever arrived in his office before noon, today would be the day. All the better if he had a hangover from some sloppy drinking into the wee hours over Alan Lockman: Maybe then he would be so eager to get rid of me he would give me the footnotes to what he had been trying to say outside the Lockman house. But as I got behind the wheel, the tolling of a church bell somewhere nearby reminded me of what Karen had said about a funeral for Randy Page. Was there any reason but a funeral for a church to ring its bells at 11:23 on a weekday? Sewell would be in his office the better part of the day, but Page would be above ground only for a few more minutes. Besides, a funeral would kill some of those long minutes before I had to report to *Kommandant* Mendler.

I drove off in the general direction of the bells looking for a steeple to appear above the roofline. After a couple of one-way streets going the wrong way had forced me into a series of convoluted L turns, though, I was adding wilderness scouting to my list of questionable skills. It was in the middle of imploring the bells to ring again to guide me that I revisited a little item. I had been so quick to dismiss the tie-in between Page and Lockman with Pulsar Karen had been pushing that I had scooted past Lockman's scorekeeping on the Most Admired Citizen ballot. Tenuous or not, that *was* a link to Pulsar and to Page's lampooning of the poll. Even Sewell had thrown it in Pauline Shepherd's face. And Shepherd's reaction? She had . . . said something else patronizing to somebody.

I felt like Balboa discovering the Pacific when I turned the corner of a Maple Avenue into a street choked with cars and a cast of hundreds. The mob was spread out over the sidewalk and on the steps of a church; clearly, a service had just ended. A sign on the lawn said, "Saint Anthony of Padua, Roman Catholic." The vehicles were a hearse where the pallbearers were sliding in a gold-handled casket, two limousines with their back doors open and receiving mourners, a van from a radio station that I presumed had been Page's employer and, zigzag from sidewalk to sidewalk for blocking traffic like me, three squad cars. Many of the mourners were the age of the kids I had seen in front of the funeral home, which meant a lot of empty classroom desks in the New Florence school system. But judging by the self-important little circle standing on the church's top step with a robed priest, the kids had New Florence officialdom covering their backs.

I assumed it was Sewell's *Reporter* people pointing their cameras at the cuddly group surrounded by uniforms. The fat man with the frameless glasses bouncing nervously up and down on his feet would have certainly been the mayor of any town *I* founded; if Joe Carroll talked to the ether in front of him, this guy smiled to it on all sides of him, if with a proper trace of glumness for the occasion. Sewell had said there might be an official city dogcatcher, and that would have been the what-me-worry skinhead standing at the mayor's elbow and dressed in an identical blue suit and red tie; his boss was smiling so he better—or lose the sinecure he dreaded losing every morning if he guessed wrong on matching the day's sock color. Count Dracula couldn't manage the plastered grins of the other two; him I took for the kind of political aide who wasn't used to being allowed out of his closet before nightfall. The fourth one in the circle was everybody's favorite cop, the dour Brighton. He didn't want to be where he was any more than Dracula did, especially with cameras around, but he wasn't worried about the sun coming out to vaporize him. His vigilant eyes were for the more practical problem of some disorder breaking out on his watch. I thought they made for a comical quartet. If Randy Page had still been alive to play CDs, he might have called them The Four Intrusions.

The patrolman advancing on me saw a fifth. I nodded to him to cut off his progress, but he kept strolling forward. Not even going into Reverse impressed him except to interrupt his gum chewing.

"You got to let the hearse and them go first," he yelled. "Don't go jumping the gun."

I nodded obediently. Why he should have assumed I wanted to be part of the funeral procession I had no idea, but in less than 24 hours in New Florence I seemed to have been taking a lot of things for granted that the locals had to have spelled out for them and they had been doing the same with me. Only an outsider, for instance, could have wondered why, if the cops had wanted to keep the church block off-bounds for everybody but Page's mourners, they hadn't closed it at the corner so traffic could have kept going west and not turned into a bottleneck.

I sat like a good boy until the photographers got tired of the VIPs and a couple of tech types emerged from the church with wires and speakers in tow and went tripping down the steps to pack them into the radio van. No argument that Page was a local celebrity; maybe not worthy of television coverage from Albany or some other nearby city, but still what passed for a luminary. Finally, the hearse and limousines were filled with what they were supposed to be filled with and the gloved chauffeurs set off a volley of slammed doors. Private cars parked along the street on both sides kept the music going with their engines, then the squad cars broke up their wall, straightening out and rolling down toward the other end of the block, evidently assigned to leading the parade. When the hearse pulled out to go around the limousines, I thought that was standard practice; probably only in Latvia did the limos go ahead of the hearse. What I hadn't counted on was that, once the two limos got into gear behind the hearse, my friend with the gum would wave me on and then throw me a sad little salute.

I had no choice but to get into line behind the second limo. I didn't dare look into my rearview mirror to count the cars pulling away from the curbs and making up the cortege behind me. I had no doubt about the people in them. There was the pissed off in-law who hadn't made the cut for the limos. There were slews of second cousins who hadn't seen old Randy since some childhood Christmas. There were the colleagues from Page's radio station who weren't working from the van. Maybe there was an old high school teacher who had always warned him he would end up dead one day. Ex-lovers? There always had to be ex-lovers wondering what might have been and thanking God there hadn't been. And know what? It didn't matter who they were. I ranked ahead of them all. When we arrived at the cemetery, the parents, widow, and kids (no, no kids) who climbed out of the limos would gape at me as an undisclosed part of beautiful Randy's life.

The scant traffic there was at the early hour was sent scattering by the police sirens leading the caravan. Emboldened by how the radio van shot past me to get to the front of the line, I broke down to peek into my rearview mirror. The Audi immediately behind had grasped the protocol by turning on its headlights, and I could see a couple of other vehicles further down had done the same thing. I stopped peering to see what I was leading after the tenth car. Since it would have been so easy to declare myself as an accidental intruder by not turning on my lights, I turned them on. Why should funerals prompt thoughts only about the mysteries of death when my presence could supply mysteries about life?

As we moved along, I finally found something New Florence had in common with New York: both had planted their cemeteries just south of Saskatchewan. It was reasonable city planning, of course; who wanted a boneyard right next to Jerry's Deli? But I wouldn't have minded a landscape less relentless in its long-abandoned factories with tin sheets for windows, roadside houses that had moved a kitchen table outside to peddle apples and pumpkins, and muddy streams that looked too inert to reach bigger muddy streams. New Florence was badly in need of another Claudio Mochi to blow in and remind everybody there was more to today than yesterday. Walter Labine evidently wasn't up to the task.

My speedometer said we had covered almost eight miles when we finally slowed. I saw the railing around the cemetery, then the protesters wielding their placards in front of the main gate. There were eight or nine of them, and they had the look of skels used to closing the redhead's pub where I'd had coffee the day before. This wasn't an ACLU demo, and not even the Born Agains sounded right for one sign that said NOT HERE—GODLESS PEOPLE BELONG IN GODLESS HOLES. The Jesus freaks I'd known didn't care what hole got the unredeemed to Hell, just as long as it got them there. Watching the uniforms get out of the lead squad car and go over to the demonstrators, I had a flashback to my own patrol days on the Island. Sometimes when the marching licenses hadn't been registered and the protesting organization hadn't been smart enough to invite a few television cameras, there had been a wildcat tension in the air—the kind that kept reassuring you that you had a weapon in your holster but that simultaneously kept warning you never to put your hand anywhere near it. Even several cars away, I could smell the potential for trouble: smugness on the face of the brawny guy in the camouflage jacket who was the spokesman for the marchers and jumpiness on the part of the giraffe of a cop about having to ask what was going on. If things weren't sorted out right away, the smugness and jumpiness would be batted back and forth between them like a ping-pong ball until somebody returned a serve too soon or too late.

I did a jump of my own at a shout from the Audi behind me. I hadn't noticed before that it was filled with Page's most devoted listeners, and one of the kids had stuck his head out the front passenger window and was telling the fucking cops how to deal with the fucking demonstrators in front of the fucking cemetery. A slammed car door somewhere toward the middle of the caravan sounded like a seconding of the motion. The tall, skinny cop was pushing it by letting the camouflage jacket raise his voice like a bar drunk who wanted the jukebox louder. The cops from the other squad cars got out and made sure their nightsticks were still handy on their belts as they approached the gate. It was all beginning to look too much like *High Noon* when it really should have looked like *Going My Way*. Where the hell was the priest who had been posing for pictures with the mayor and the dogcatcher? Why wasn't he there to promise salvation for one and all if they behaved and let the rest of the burial be carried out?

But nobody seemed to have thought of anything. Even the radio van now appeared from *inside* the cemetery. The optimist at the wheel had apparently decided there would be nothing more of interest to record until Page's parents were throwing dirt on his coffin. Now he was doubling back to the gate far too fast to catch up with his oversight, and just his violent braking was enough to throw some more jangled nerves into the pot between Officer Giraffe and Camouflage Jacket. By blocking the gate entrance, the genius driving the van also made it harder for the cops to take the high road with the demonstrators and just wave the cortege inside. What was it Karen had said about watching things ooze ahead inch by inch all the while knowing somebody had to do something before matters got worse?

Then the Audi contributed the stupidity that had been missing. The shouter in the front seat had been joined by a second leaning out the back window. You wanted to start a riot, that's what you did. But instead of unleashing the two assholes from the car, the driver went for bigger prey by pulling out of the line and trying to squeeze between me and a line of trash cans set along the gravel path leading up to the gate. Too bad for me his parents had once lectured him about not littering the street and that the sermon had stuck. Seeing that he was about to topple the cans, he swerved right at the last second to catch my door handle with a sickening scrunch. For a second I didn't see the Audi braking, the shouter in the front seat who was sizing me up as maybe another one of those fucking things, or the demonstrators and cops who seemed to turn their heads with Rockettes precision to see what was trying to interrupt their pleasant conversation. All I could see was Sal from Vesuvio Auto Works on Fourth Avenue dancing up and down at the big repair job he had inherited from fucking New Florence, fucking New York.

I told myself that picturing Sal's glee was the equivalent of counting to five for maintaining calm. It even worked for a few beats: I could get my belt off and ease the door open without anything metallic clanging on the gravel. Only when I lifted myself out and got a look at the damage did I realize my fears were beside the point: The only way the handle would ever clang to the ground was with the help of a blowtorch extricating it from the nice vertical pose it had assumed from the base plaque up to the window.

I imagined a few more seconds of stillness, mainly because the driver and front seat passenger of the Audi were both staring out at me with sickly expressions. They had the right idea because I *did* hate them and *was* going to turn them into more of the gravel under my feet. But the moment passed. In the real world the cops were making a commotion by grappling with Camouflage Jacket and his friends as they descended on the Audi. I had underrated Camouflage Jacket's size: the closer he got, the more he seemed to be missing only a cork from his neck and a square hair shirt. Out of the corner of my eye I saw another squad car come up behind me. The thought flashed by that the punks in the Audi owed me for keeping them pinned inside while the placards and nightsticks started being thrashed around. I caught a glimpse of a sign that said PAGE TRASH. I admired the chauffeur of the hearse for trying to take advantage of the brawl by pushing forward through the gate; too bad the radio van blocked him. I heard a replay of all the doors being slammed in front of the church. I was just about to give more attention to the mourners charging up from the other cars when a chainsaw took a piece out of the back of my head.

I knew right away I was hurt, but that didn't mean I had to fall. If my door handle could remain vertical, I told myself, so could I. The last thing I needed was to be wheeled into Vesuvio for Sal to repair me, too. His prices on cars were bad enough. Imagine what the crook would have demanded for patching up people!

CHAPTER 16

There are various states between being conscious and unconscious. At the low end is the state where you come up into the wonton soup breath of a black cop without eyebrows who keeps telling you that you're all right and on your way to the hospital. You know that's a lie because if you were all right you wouldn't need a hospital, but you wither back into darkness before you can straighten him out. Only slightly more alert is the state where you are aware of going at breakneck speed through unfamiliar streets, but not at all from a comfortable ambulance cot snug in blankets and surrounded by oxygen tanks and other medical toys. Instead, you're sitting semi-erect in the back of a police car, your knees opening a major front of ache for being squeezed behind the partition cage and a black mass beginning to test its throbbing reach behind your right ear. You want to tell the cop driving to go faster or at least stop off at a store where they sell ice, but again you don't have the muscle to insist and you slip back into some netherworld between the strain on your knees and the numbness in your head. You really wouldn't mind staying there altogether, but the real hell of this level is that you know only too well nobody is going to allow that. You may be the victim, but all those masses known as the uninjured are intent on being *responsible*.

I figured I was halfway back when I recognized my pony-tailed friend Martinelli in the Emergency Room. He did a double-take as he intercepted the cops escorting me through the sliding doors, but I missed a few seconds of what happened next. When I blinked back to him, though, I took it as a good sign that I could reason that his biting tone to the cops was over me. The man looked exhausted after so many hours on duty so that made him even more of a hero for being furious at the cops for dragging me to him in a squad car instead of leaving me at the cemetery until an ambulance had arrived. I didn't get the answer the cops gave him. Who would have believed what they said, anyway?

The only thing that really penetrated over the next minutes was the rhino hoof that came down on my head as Martinelli, nurses, and the rest of New Florence's citizenry rolled me onto a bed in one of the ER cubicles. There was no denying that consciousness was back and determined to make up for its lost time. I wanted to plead that none of it had been my idea, but I knew that would sound ridiculous.

"Can't you find someplace else for entertainment?" Martinelli asked, trying to be funny, droll, witty, and all those things.

"I think it's a concussion."

"No shit, Sherlock!"

I wasn't up for *Can You Top This?*, especially because I could see he was. I closed my eyes, giving him permission to knead, probe, and do all the things he was supposed to do. Was it positive or negative that I felt the shot somebody gave me in my right arm? I decided it was positive; pain was evidence of being alive, my biology teacher Mr. Ruspoli had said before dropping his snails into boiling water. On the other hand, I hadn't answered any medical questions about allergies and the like, so why a shot and a shot of what? I opened my eyes again in time to see Martinelli tossing the cotton he had been swabbing my head with toward a garbage can and missing his shot. What was wrong with that picture? Instead of figuring it out, I thought about Lillian Chan, the owner of a Prospect Heights apartment building whose lawyer had hired me to get evidence that she had almost died from a nosocomial infection she had picked up in a Brooklyn hospital. For once it seemed like an advantage that New Florence wasn't New York City.

Getting clobbered put out more people than me. Martinelli excited the Professor by telling him what had happened to his friend, the Professor irked Mendler by acting more interested in

my condition than in his own, and Mendler gnashed every tooth
in his mouth having a nurse contact Karen as the price for getting the old man to lie back and submit to the angiogram that
was good for him. Karen recounted this jungle telegraph to me
as she stood next to my ER bed much as she had stood next to
the Professor's a few hours earlier. But there also seemed to be
a big difference. Maybe it was due to the boulder on the back of
my head, but I thought she was enjoying the moment. She was
certainly looser than she had been at the library and in the Italian restaurant, not to mention in her kitchen while we had been
having our little exchange of half-truths. And a looser Karen Noon
did everything for my testosterone. She was tall, almost stately, in
the tight black sweater that brought out her breasts. Her paisley
suede skirt and black boots alone were enough to consider trades
with the gods involving the lump on my head and how it might be
allowed to grow later if we could first pep up the present. I would
even throw in some perjury on what she might or might not have
known while married to Antonacci.

But just as I was giving her another chance to leap on me,
the divider curtain was swished back on its rod. I hadn't made as
much noise the morning I had torn off the shower curtain to escape a sudden eruption of steam from my hot water faucet. There
was no need for such a violent rip. Martinelli and the nurses had
been coming to see me by stepping around the flimsy material;
one of the nurses had practically walked through it, thinking
nothing of having it slap off her face. But the detective named
Brighton seemed in need of a dramatic entrance to establish his
authority. If we didn't get that by how he whisked the curtain
down the rod, we were supposed to get it by the way he studied
both our faces in disapproval of how we had disturbed his daily
routine. He didn't seem pleased I was smiling. He was not pleased
when Karen returned his condescension in full, said she would
be waiting for me outside, and stalked out to the waiting room. I
really didn't want her boots and suede skirt sashaying away.

The start of Brighton's problem with Karen might have been
his five o'clock shadow. The guy was either one of those maniac
swarthies named Al Something who shouldn't have been allowed

on commercial airliners with ticking hand luggage or he simply didn't know how to shave. "Police. My name is Brighton."

I nodded. Maybe I was expected to keel over in awe, but the nod took half my head with it and seemed like tribute enough.

"I hear it was quite a whack. You okay?"

The voice didn't belong to the body. He was easily six-two and more than 200 pounds, but the glassy, cultivated tone was that of a headwaiter. Or was that just another way of saying Brighton liked to keep people on edge with an affected politeness? "I'll survive."

It took him longer seconds than necessary to accept that opinion, but he finally broke off his brown-eyed stare and nodded. "Good. So you can tell me what you were doing in the middle of that funeral."

"You wouldn't believe me if I told you."

"I bet I would."

So I told him—and wondered what I should have wondered before. The man was a high-grade detective. An investigation like the Alan Lockman case, yes, it made sense for him to have been there. But the Randy Page funeral? Since when were detectives of his rank, in New Florence or anywhere else, involved in crowd control?

"Then it's not like you've come up from the big city to snoop around for somebody. You're just falling into things."

I had to give him one thing: His sarcasm came out sounding like the irony of folksy, small-town poetry. All that was missing was a penknife and something to whittle on. But then my eye caught my watch, and I remembered he had had plenty of time to check up on me. In fact, if I hadn't been told he was a complete incompetent, I might have gone so far as to think he had made a few inquiries overnight, as soon as he had seen me with Karen and Sewell outside the Lockman house. Sewell alone could have given him a lot of answers to his curiosity, and the two of them were certainly on speaking terms. "Mind a question of my own? Who were those guys out there?"

It took another eternity to decide an answer wouldn't compromise his authority. "They're people who didn't see Randy Page as family listening," he said. "Parents with impressionable kids who believe in Christian values and don't think verbal pornography is one of them."

He turned his head away to the medicine cabinet on the wall before I could be sure, but I would have sworn he was on the verge of a smile. "You could've fooled me. They looked more like saloon dregs. And the leader could've been Boris Karloff doing Frankenstein's monster."

"Yeah, well. You don't put on a three-piece suit to march up and down in front of a cemetery."

"Some people do. In fact, that's an important part of their image."

He nodded as though he hadn't considered that before. But I was beginning to think he had considered that and a thousand other things he didn't want to share with strangers. "If you're thinking of any legal action," he said, "your point of reference is a group calling itself The New Florence Society. That was them."

"You bag them?"

He shrugged and took a step closer to the cabinet, as if truly interested in what he was looking at. "A couple from Column A, a couple from Column B. A few bloody noses. One is three beds down from you with a broken leg, looks like. Lots of disorderly conduct charges. But Page got buried and his family has scattered to the four winds again. You might remember that if you really are thinking about a suit."

For some reason I was getting the feeling I *should* have been thinking about a lawsuit. "Thanks. I'll keep that in mind."

He finally got tired of peering into the medicine cabinet; he wasn't in any more danger of smiling when he came back to me. "But that's on your time. We were talking about you and your reasons for being in the middle of that ruckus out there."

"And I've told you all I can."

"Sure, are you?"

"As sure as I can be with this headache."

"Right." He reached into his shirt pocket for a business card. "Tell you what. You get a few hours' sleep, then give me a ring. Maybe we can go over a few more things before you leave town."

"You make this card sound like an exit visa."

He thought that was funny; so did I. I was so taken with my comedy that he was almost through the curtain and gone when it dawned on me what had been so weird about the cotton clump Martinelli had thrown toward the basket. "Notice anything unusual about this bed, Brighton?"

He was puzzled. "No."

"No blood."

"Well, I hope they change . . ."

"No, they didn't change anything because they didn't have to. Barely a trace on the cotton swabs, too."

"You got a point here, Finley?"

"I hope not. But I was thinking that the only way you can get a good shot from a sign like those clucks had would be with the edge, and that would leave a big gash. You know—as in blood gushing out all over the place? On the other hand, if this welt is because of a nightstick . . ."

He stiffened, and realized it a half-second too late.

". . . I'm not accusing anybody, mind you. Just that it's weird the skin wasn't broken. And the funny thing is, a minute before I went down, there was a squad car that pulled up right near me."

"Give me the names of the officers," he said dully. "I'll ask them if they happened to see anything."

"Sorry. Didn't catch their names."

He shrugged. "Doesn't leave me much to go on. Get yourself some rest. Clear your head."

Watching his purposeful walk through the waiting room past Karen, I decided the Frank Brighton of the New Florence Police business card could have been a lot of people, but, whatever some people had been telling me, definitely not Inspector Clouseau.

CHAPTER 17

I dropped by the Professor's room to show him I was all right just as they were wheeling him off for his heart pictures. This abbreviated one conversation I wasn't up for, though it gave Mendler the opportunity to grimace over another excruciating obstacle to his miracle working. As Karen drove me back to the house, it hit me there were practical ramifications to sneaking into a funeral cortege and getting one's skull bashed in, foremost the question of getting back my car. Not to worry, Karen said: The cops had driven it back to their lot at headquarters. Meaning what—a fine to retrieve it? She doubted it. I didn't, but she wasn't used to dealing with impound cops. On another front, the right knee on the only pair of pants I had was ripped from my thud on the cemetery gravel. That's what tailors were for, she said cheerily; and if they weren't up to the task, there were stores that sold jeans, slacks, even Bermuda shorts, ho, ho, ho. What about Tylenol for the headaches sure to come? I hadn't brought any with me from Brooklyn. She took her eyes off the road to look at me as if I needed a psychiatrist more than a pharmacist. I just didn't want to sponge off her, I said, so why not drop me at the first drug store we passed. "You're not quite getting it, are you?" she asked. "*Any* step you take out of this car on your own will be dropping you. You need to lie down and stay down until you get tired of the soap operas and reruns and Claudette Colbert movies on Turner Classic. By that time, I should be back from the library and we'll think about supper."

She stayed in her annoyingly buoyant mood until we reached her street and approached the Lockman house. The crime scene tape around the shuttered garage wasn't the usual yellow, but the same kind of dramatic red as on the street litter baskets; I sniffed another Walter Labine profit center. There was no sign of anyone inside the house, and Karen's face grew more pinched at the transparent thought that there would always be one less person there even when Mrs. Lockman was around. She reverted to edginess as she settled me on her couch, put some water and Tylenol on the coffee table, and reminded me how the TV zapper worked and what the refrigerator looked like. We were both relieved when she closed the front door behind her to return to the library.

What was there to do in a strange house with hours to spare? I knew the answer even as I went through the TV preliminaries. She was right about the soap operas and reruns, close on Claudette Colbert (it was Irene Dunne). I needed a nap, but I also didn't want to risk too long a doze and squander all the exploration possibilities before Karen came home. What did I expect to find without going through her drawers and closets (there was a limit even to my snooping)? I didn't have a clue, but like most everything else in the last 24 hours I had an unnerving hunch *it* would tell me. What was *it*? Brighton had called it falling into things, and had said it flippantly, but there was something to that idea that didn't feel completely off. Not an accident, exactly; more like coincidences that needed me in the middle. Whatever else was going on, *I* didn't feel like some accidental piece.

I heard the roar of the crowd as I struggled off the couch. Emperors had established vast realms with my grit, philosophers had become required reading in colleges by analyzing my kind of visionary personality. I settled for not falling over the coffee table and wobbling successfully toward Karen's bedroom at the end of the hall. The room almost wasted my stumbling achievement by knocking me over with its aggressive mix of sachets, perfumes, and musty clothes and shoes strewn around. Smell had never belonged so much to the five senses. I wasn't interested in the drawers that would reveal vibrators or old checks on New Jersey banks proving the Missus had extorted even more money than

Antonacci had back in the day. Whatever I was looking for was already in front of me: in the unmade bed, in how one pillow was halfway down the side (because she had twisted herself into that position during the night?), in the upside-down Venetian blind slats at the top she hadn't noticed or didn't give a damn about.

Swaying in the hallway, one ear alert to the danger of the hostess having second thoughts about stranding her guest for the afternoon, I landed on a concept: *adult teenager*. She had been a married woman for years, she had a visibly important job, she had scrambled through some pretty thick thorn bushes to get to where she was now, but the room wasn't as old as she was, had none of her experience. There was no dominant color or theme, just random dresses, pillow cases, a bedcover, shoes, wall prints, and a carpet that had appealed to her at a given moment. Karen Noon didn't identify Karen Noon in specific objects, in much of a physical way at all. It was probably dumb luck she had put together the sweater, skirt, and boots she was wearing so stylishly that day. She was preoccupied with the spirit of the Karen Noon trapped in her bedroom. She was comfortable materially, but she couldn't wait to run away from Mommy and Daddy to catch up with her elusive Real Self outside somewhere.

I had to grab the frame of the bedroom door. I was beginning to spook myself with my little flights of whimsy. Or was I just experiencing another symptom from the smash on my noggin? I had heard stories about mugging victims turning into different people after getting whacked too hard. What I couldn't recall was if any of those stories had had a happy ending.

The closed door between the main bedroom and the bathroom was for an orderly little study. At least it looked orderly after I negotiated the darkness to the window and opened the blinds. Here there was no real smell at all, not from the cherry wood bookcases, from the old paperbacks in them, or from the magazines piled in a straw basket next to the desk. There wasn't much to please the other senses, either, unless one's taste ran to Bargain Dollar prints for the walls and a row of CDs that seemed to have come from the Tower Record bargain bins. You wanted to hear Bach played by the Sioux Falls Symphony Orchestra or the forty-fifth anthologizing of Rolling Stones hits, you were in business. Other than that, zip. You wanted to sit down and swap stories with the lady at the desk? Forget it unless you were ready to steal her desk chair, the only seat in the room. Everything deferred to the computer and it said Personal Functional.

Which meant I shouldn't have been surprised to see that the printouts stacked next to the computer were about the Pulsar Institute.

I sat at the desk and flipped through what she had found. She had mentioned tracing Pulsar on the Internet back to the mid-nineties, and she hadn't lied. The oldest Google find was from 1995, concerning a Pulsar survey carried out in an Oregon town called Sinclair. The context there hadn't been a most admired citizen, but what had been called the Best Samaritan. The winner had been a school bus driver named Ralph Pugliesi. Not only had Ralph been driving handicapped kids to special schools for more than 20 years, but he had been anteing up for lunches for kids who had mislaid theirs, donating crutches to families that couldn't afford them, and leading the charge against politicians bent on closing the special schools. If Ralph Pugliesi hadn't existed, the Pulsar Institute would have been forced to invent him.

Proving what?

Nothing as nefarious as Karen believed about a parking lot hit-and-run and a homicide ineptly disguised as a suicide. Another poll in the Michigan town Bliss had been after the Most Underrated Institution. The most votes there had gone to something called the State Demographic Bureau—one group of survey professionals congratulating another one. That might have been incestuous on some tedious level, but other than that it was more asinine than ominous. There was no blood dripping, either, from the other poll findings Karen had downloaded regarding one-horse towns in Ohio, Wyoming, and New Hampshire. If there were any hackles to be raised over Pulsar's activities, it was over how the government had apparently been funding so much idiocy. What all the surveys boiled down to were the kind of crap personality tests that came with every Sunday newspaper magazine. The only other common element was that they had all been conducted in small towns like New Florence. I should have been thankful. Brooklyn appeared safe from one plague, anyway.

I sat with the printouts on my lap for a few minutes. I had a feeling I was missing something, but then I immediately had another feeling it might have been the piece of my brain that had ended up under a nightstick. I had never thought of myself as an interior decorator, but I couldn't believe that before buying them Karen had really looked at the dismal racing prints she had put on the walls between the bookcases. The next time I saw a horse jumping a fence into a field of clover, I promised myself, I would get a picture of it and send it to her; if nothing else, she could have an original on the theme. Where the hell was the woman's taste?

Then it occurred to me what was missing. As statistically elaborate as some of the Pulsar findings on individual polls were, none of them spelled out what the institute itself was. There were references to government-financed this and public agency that, but no specific cabinet department or, failing that, the chief agency funder. Was that suspicious? Admittedly, there was a Washington address, even telephone, fax, and email numbers, but they could have been for some back room of a Chinese takeout joint. It might not have been suspicious in the criminal way Alan Lockman's death was suspicious, but it wasn't anything to like, either.

I went through the papers again, this time paying more attention to the names cited. For starters, there was no Pauline Shepherd, making her either excessively modest in the past or a recent hire. The most frequent name was that of a Michael Zev, whom I pictured as bald with a thick goatee and wearing one of those *Star Trek* tunics. Michael Zev, I thought, would have hired the lineman doing security out at the Mochi factory annex.

The lineman so paranoid about my passing the place twice.

The lineman who might have been Leo's twin.

The lineman who, like Leo, would have had the strength to hoist Alan Lockman up over a garage beam.

It was such a marvelous train of thought that I suddenly found myself with a clear choice: go back to the living room couch for the nap I needed or do something stupid. And there was always time later for a nap.

CHAPTER 18

Weathermen would have said it was a gray fall day, but my head felt brutally exposed to the sun. Stepping down from Karen's doorway, I tested the sidewalk under my feet trying not to look like I was testing it. Just one car passing or one head in any of the windows, I promised myself, would be the signal to return inside. But the closer I got to the Lockman house, the more plausible it sounded that I could shoo away any nosy passerby by saying I was curious to see the place where that poor copyboy had hanged himself. By the time I was brushing up against the red tape, I was ready to argue it was odd I was alone, that people from New Florence hadn't been standing around the whole day to gawk at the Lockman garage.

What Brighton's people could have missed I had no idea. But he didn't have to be the clod Karen said he was to have overlooked something. I didn't have enough fingers and toes to count the number of times I hadn't noticed something at a Long Island crime scene until a second or even third visit. This one might have required more visits than that. The runneled access from the sidewalk to the garage door had been swept clean. There wasn't a scrap of paper anywhere. About the only thing at all on the path were gray pebbles of excess clay showing where the techs had taken impressions of footprints. The footprints themselves were all but invisible from where I was standing.

Since the tape prevented me from getting close to the garage door, let alone get inside, I had to concentrate on the killer's arrival and departure. There was no back door or window into the attached house, so that meant a direct approach from the street. I couldn't see anyone breaking in during the afternoon to lie in wait for hours. Even less likely was a break-in during or after dinner hour with all the returned commuters adding to the potential eye-witnesses. Also into the scratch column went the possibility that the killer had waited for Lockman in a parked car on the street. Even in blasé Brooklyn someone sitting behind the wheel under a house for any extended time was sure to prompt a call to 911.

Leaving what? One thing: The killer had followed Lockman home from the *Reporter* and had hit on some reasonable excuse for getting out of his car and approaching the kid as he had been stowing his bike in the garage. Street directions, how to find some fictitious resident in the area—it could have been anything. Or, almost. Since the killer also had to get inside the garage for a few minutes without raising suspicions in anyone who happened to be peeking out a window, he would have had to justify his stop with a garage type of excuse. The bike itself? Why not? He had seen Lockman tooling around, had always wanted a bike exactly like that, just wanted to know where the kid had bought it and whether it was as good as advertised. Lockman wouldn't have passed up the chance to show off the bike, would have invited the killer into the garage to point out its features.

It was hardly steel-tight. There were still too many minutes to account for in the garage without some third party noticing something, if only the killer's car. On the other hand, sight seemed like the only sense in play. If the killer was at all proficient, he wouldn't have made a sound in the garage or, more important, let Lockman make any. Nobody would have run to a window because of something *heard*. And a quick, expert chop would not only have silenced Lockman, but fit a broken neck from a rope.

Sort of.

There were only two houses across the street that had a direct view of the garage. At the moment there was no sign of life inside either, although one had a battered green Toyota Corolla in the garage entrance. A Brighton raised exponentially to moron level would have asked them all the basic questions, so little was to be gained by doing it again.

I hoped.

I gave a last look to the ground within the cordon before having to admit I should have already been curled up on my couch. Unlike the garage path, the lawn that stretched from the runnel over to the front of the house seemed not to have been vacuumed. There were no gum wrappers or cigarette butts, but the yellowed grass appeared to have been untouched by police hands. Why was I so cocky about that? Because if it had been processed as thoroughly as the garage path, there wouldn't have been such a marked tilt by the grass toward the street, as in someone trampling over it after leaving the garage. Since the stuff was so dead, it couldn't have been bent in such a direction by the wind. A heavy foot had to have come down directly on it.

Karen might have said it was Brighton's foot, but I thought it was the killer's foot. If the killer had any brains, he wouldn't have taken the chance of picking up something on his shoes inside the garage, then making a nice picture of his foot size on the concrete of the garage entrance. Walking on the grass would have solved that problem.

I was happy with that conclusion.

For a second and a half, anyway.

Why was I crediting the killer with brains? Lucky he might have been to get in and out of the garage without being seen. But smart? If he was so smart, why hadn't he made the suicide look more convincing? Why hadn't he at least disguised his work enough to dissuade me from coming out in the nippy afternoon air when I should have been on Karen Noon's couch?

I had no answer to that question. I didn't even suspect that I should have had an answer.

CHAPTER 19

My nap lasted the rest of the Irene Dunne movie and all the way to the last shot of Lee Marvin and Burt Lancaster riding away from the camera in *The Professionals*. My instant wooziness felt like yet another state of consciousness, but it came without a headache and didn't stop me from getting over to the telephone, deciphering the number of the hospital in my notebook, and punching up the news on the Professor. I expected a lecture for calling late, but Mendler was so high on himself for doing an angioplasty he was dangerously close to cordial. Somewhere in the middle of his crowing he got it out that the Professor had been perfectly agreeable to the procedure and to remaining under his superior care at the hospital for "another day or two." I kept my temper as I asked if that wasn't a bad sign (weren't patients released after stent insertions fairly fast?), and he kept his cheer by telling me I would make a lousy heart specialist since the first rule of dealing with a carotid artery stenosis was that every patient posed a different problem, especially when it came to stent rejection. The Professor had said I was a private detective of some sort? Obviously, I hadn't done too much work in the medical malpractice field.

Since Mendler wasn't in the immediate vicinity, I had to put the receiver back down in its cradle instead of down his throat. But he was also a given in irritation. What was lapping him was the Professor and his sudden agreeableness. The old man was so dedicated to paying off some phantom debt to Karen that he had let Mendler stick wires into his gut and up through his arteries so both of us would have to stay around. He could have taught the lineman and Leo something about staging a suicide!

I dropped down on Karen's lounge chair. I would have groaned if somebody had been there to hear it and pat me on the head. I blamed my sleep for the loony thought. Where the hell had that epiphany about Alan Lockman come from? Even going up to the garage Leo and the lineman had been only a garbage idea. A homicide, yes; the Pulsar Institute, what sense? Coming back to the house, I had put the couch cushion under my cheek wondering about Karen's fixation on Pulsar, closed my eyes on Irene Dunne's scolding, and woken up a couple of hours later sure Karen had been right. What Messenger of Truth had invaded my dreams? Maybe Joe Carroll didn't have to get out of New Florence, but I sure as hell did.

It took me two rings to realize the noise was the telephone, not bees making honey in my head. I didn't know who Karen screened, but the caller couldn't have been anybody important if he didn't know she was at work. The alternative that the call was for me didn't figure. The only person phoning me at Karen's would have been the Professor and him I had already sent into the next world by exploding his stents.

I answered anyway. It was Father Sewell. He wanted to know how I was. I thought it was nice of him to ask until it dawned on me his question wasn't only personal. "Of course, you're part of the story," he said. "A pretty big part of it. How about if I send one of my kids around to talk to you?"

"What's the official line on how I got socked?"

There was a hesitation; he didn't seem to do anything anymore without looking over his shoulder. "One of the New Florence Society people mixed you up for a Page mourner," he finally said. "Fortunately, the police were on hand to apprehend the lowlife and rush you to the hospital. And we know that isn't the truth, don't we?"

I pretended not to hear the question. It wasn't that I distrusted Sewell exactly, but I'd had more than one awkward run-in with tape recorders and reporters. I really didn't need to see the kind of suspicions I had mentioned to Brighton about the late-arriving squad car on the front page of the *Reporter*. "And this official version, it came from Brighton?"

"No, not directly."

"Funny, Jimmy. I had a little chat with him at the hospital today and he didn't strike me as the bum of the month."

"I told you that."

"Yeah, but so where does that take on him come from?"

"People who need to blame other people for things."

It might not have been the wrong answer, but it would have sounded more convincing without the defensive tone. "Yeah, maybe."

Another silence. Then: "What it still comes back to is that we have only their version. You okay with that? I've got some other reports about a cop slugging you from behind."

That I wouldn't have minded hearing on a tape recorder. "From where? Who told you that?"

Immediate retreat. "Nothing we can confirm yet."

"Even unconfirmed. Somebody from this Society?"

"C'mon, Paul. You know I can't tell you something we're not ready to stand behind as fact."

No, I didn't know that. I had never heard that rule from Sewell or any other reporter. Nor, for all my mouthing off to Brighton, did I know why any cop would have wanted me at the end of his nightstick. None of them knew me well enough to hate me yet.

"Back to the original question: You okay with the official police version in tomorrow's paper?"

Maybe it was just because my loafers were off, but I had the feeling of being so stuck in glops of local politics that any move in any direction at all would only make things worse. "How about for today's edition you say you couldn't reach me, I'm resting up? Then if I have something sensational to say, I can say it to you tomorrow?"

"*Will* you have something sensational to say tomorrow?"

"C'mon, Jimmy. You know how I work."

He apparently did—which made one of us. "By the way, Denise would love you over for supper."

It was the second time he had said that, and I thought of sending Kommandant Mendler over as me to see if Denise of so many years ago would know the difference. "Please thank her. But I'm not really up for it tonight . . ."

"No, no, not tonight. I'm sorry, I didn't mean that. Not tonight. I've got a full plate. No way to get out of it. I mean before you leave."

Someone not knowing Father Sewell might have thought his sudden panic meant tonight was his weekly S&M session with Cassandra from the *Reporter*'s accounting department. "Sure. Before I leave."

I hung up trying to put a face on Cassandra, but couldn't get past her black net stockings. That was reason enough to zap off the TV and those drab 1930s print dresses. Back in Brooklyn, my watch reminded me, it would have been time for a cocktail at the Green Fox. But I wasn't in Brooklyn and I didn't think Karen would appreciate finding me sprawled out on the living room floor and the remains of a beer can seeping into her rug. I was deciding whether my head and the Tylenol could handle a coffee when a key turned in the front door. It wasn't Karen, but Veronica. "I'm on a mercy mission," she said brightly, her orange blossoms immediately flooding the room. "To make sure you're still alive."

Who would have guessed I had acquired so much taste, but I flinched at the crack with the door still open, so close to the Lockman house. "I'm fine. You don't have to fuss."

"What fuss? A half-hour away from Mister Gruber complaining that Mrs. Cleveland wrinkled up the Lost and Found classifieds in the *Reporter* is a half-hour added to my life."

I might not have realized it before she wafted in, but I had needed nothing so much as Veronica Pell's brisk command of the late afternoon. She made me responsible for nothing but watching her invade the kitchen and reheat the coffee I had left from breakfast. Was coffee the best thing for me in my condition? She didn't know. What condition was I in? If it was one of wanting coffee, go back to the couch, sit down, and stop worrying.

I went back to the couch, sat down, and stopped worrying. "This is supposed to be your opportunity," she said when she brought in two mugs and a container of milk on a tray and set them down on the coffee table. "Don't blow it."

"Opportunity for what?"

She bustled back to the kitchen for the silex, plastic ringlets clacking on her wrists. "Oh, c'mon. Karen knows I have a big mouth and you have a lot of questions about her she doesn't feel like answering personally. There's no other reason she'd stay alone in the library with goofball Dobson. You want to hear about Dobson? I'll tell you about Dobson."

"No, I don't want to hear about Dobson."

"Good. She's convinced the Pulsar people have everything to do with the deaths of Page and the kid next door."

"I got that much."

She returned with the coffee and took the lounge chair across the table. I knew why she reminded me of an earthy aunt; my Aunt Mildred had created the same impression of always moving sideways while she moved up and down, embracing one and all. "And you write it off because of Hoboken," she said, extending her arms so expansively I thought she was going to smash the TV set with the silex.

"It's tempting."

"Drown that in milk if you think you're going to collapse. Oh, it's more than tempting, Finley. She's a whack job. She's holed up here doling out last year's best sellers to senior citizens who still like to feel 'with it'—or whatever Chinese novel was 'with it' last year according to the *New York Times* Book Review. Empty room after empty room down an infinite corridor. She's got so many empty spaces in her mind she fills it with the first junk handy. *Voila*! Pulsar!"

"Are you making a case for her or against her?"

She put the silex down on a pot handle and gave me a harder stare. "I'm not making a case at all. I'm her friend trying to make sure you don't accuse her of things she's not guilty of. And right now, I'd say she's tired of trying to get past the prejudices you've brought to the table, so I'm here as Florence Nightingale. Like I say, an opportunity."

I wasn't in the mood for being chastised; I thought the whack at the cemetery had paid me up full in that category. "Okay, good friend. Why weren't you good enough for her? Why did she have to reach out for the Professor after so long?"

She thought about being offended by my tone, but then reminded herself she was the one who had introduced my 'opportunity.' "I think he's the only living person she feels owes her in some way," she said.

"I wouldn't push that, Veronica."

"Because you think he's just acting out some psychodrama about his daughter? Karen told me, by the way. I can't tell you how sorry I am."

With or without milk, the coffee went to my head like a first Marlboro after a month. "*By the way* isn't usually how I think of it."

She kept her eyes on my shaking hand as I put the mug back on the table. "Oafish of me," she said. "Now I owe you a second apology. But as long as we're there, that's what it's all about, Finley. People being sorry to one another over and over again. You've only been here a day or so, but you must've noticed by now that's New Florence's chief industry."

"You were talking about what Joe thinks he owes Karen."

"Yes, and I was giving you some instant sociology so you'd have a minute to calm down. Over your snit at me? Ready to listen again?"

She was right. My anger had risen even faster than it still sometimes did against the old man. "Go ahead."

"Joe introduced Karen to Antonacci."

He seemed to have mislaid that detail. "So? That doesn't make him responsible for what happened after."

She looked at me incredulously. "But you didn't know that?"

"I know she was his student and he didn't like Antonacci. But they went down the aisle together anyway."

She nodded; in two or three seconds her look had gone from one of speaking to an equal to one of having to teach a child the Dewey Decimal System. "Yes, she was his student, and he apparently thought a brilliant one. But, according to Karen, someone he also thought impractical in the ways of the world. That bothered Joe a great deal since she was doing her thesis for him on Lucrezia Borgia . . ."

I heard it coming. I didn't know exactly what it was, but it had the pure tumbling boulder sound of Joe Carroll crushing what was underneath.

". . . He had a little social at his house, and one of the people he invited was Andy Antonacci. He was a political science graduate student at the time. Didn't know Joe from more than a nod in the campus cafeteria. But he showed up at the party and met Karen there. Joe went out of his way to talk them up to one another. Are you following me here, Finley?"

The boulder finally came rolling into the clearing, bringing with it the headache I had avoided since waking up. The only line of defense still standing was the old man's ridiculous remark about the part in Antonacci's hair. "He told me he didn't like the guy from the start."

She could see that. "Probably true," she said, sipping her coffee. "I looked up the family after Karen told me the story the first time. I couldn't find much to like about him, either. He was a caricature of the ne'er-do-well son of a bloated, corrupt politician. Shy Andy who never contradicted his father in public, who threatened to punch out one of his father's opponents for calling him a crook, who marched next to him in ethnic parades to say all Italians were Verdi or Pavarotti. Of course, you had an occasional drunk driving episode, but sympathetic judges and cops took care of them."

"You're telling me Joe deliberately threw this guy at Karen?"

She didn't flinch. "How can you be an expert on a piece of work like Lucrezia Borgia if you think politics is just pulling a lever every few years? "There was something off about it, but not off enough to doubt the truth at the core. In Joe Carroll's academic world anybody could have stood at the front of a classroom to dispense lectures, hand out assignments, and give grades. But why should sciences like chemistry and physics have exclusive rights to campus labs? Why couldn't his own students be white rats and black rats if the experiment gave them a better understanding of their subject? Why couldn't Karen Noon be thrown at Andy Antonacci if that gave her a better grasp of older swindlers and cutthroats like the Borgias? What was the worst that could happen? In the long run a night in the sheets with the real political McCoy would give her greater insights into her project, wouldn't it?

And maybe give the old man a thrill or two?

"Do you hear what you're saying?"

"Why don't you sound as shocked as you want to be?"

"Because it's bullshit, Veronica."

She shrugged to her mug and swayed her crossed knee: up and down, left and right again. That body trick would always overshadow the softening skin around her mouth and under her eyes; it was her, while getting older was anybody. "No, he didn't throw them into bed together," she relented. "That they managed on their own when they discovered they didn't need your Professor to like each other. Don't forget, we're talking about two people here who weren't exactly models of self-confidence. What they couldn't find in themselves, they suddenly found in each other. Joe hadn't counted on that. He'd just wanted her to get her blouse cuffs dirty by brushing up against real politics. When Karen first told him she was marrying Antonacci, he turned a dozen shades of white. Tried to talk her out of it. That's what cost him an invitation to the wedding. He mentioned none of this to you?"

I thought about our little truth talk in the hamburger joint on the drive up. It turned out to have even less truth in it than my kitchen session with Karen. "Only in his own way."

"I see."

I didn't have the strength to push myself up from the couch and away from her severe look, and it had nothing to do with my headache. I had toppled into another Paul Finley Amateur Night and it was only for me to accept the loving cup graciously. God help me if I'd ever had such an intrusive idea as the Professor using his brilliant student in some proxy sex game with the sleaze from Jersey. I would have been barred from future Amateur Nights with that kind of thinking.

"The rest was her life and he stayed away from it."

"Until she thought she had this famous debt."

She shrugged. "I didn't give her the audience she needed. I tried, but she could read right through me. I don't believe in many things, Finley. At times I think I mainly root for things to fail. Writers, politicians, the latest flavor of the month in *People* magazine, sports teams. They were riding high, but now look at them! Ha, ha, ha. I get far too much enjoyment out of that sometimes. I'd see a shrink about it, but then I'd be rooting for that to fail, too, so why waste the money? I really would have liked being the ear Karen needed, but I couldn't. She was simply too . . . closed into it all. She scared the bejesus out of me, especially after the Randy Page thing. I had never thought of her before as a conspiracy nut, but it was like listening to one of those 'X-Files' people. I'm too old for that kind of crap, Finley. There are enough people on this planet trying to make me a bitter old prune. I don't need to hear about them coming down from other stars, too. She had nobody else but Joe."

"Jimmy Sewell seems to agree with a lot of what she thinks."

I immediately lost my role as confidant; again, she had to teach the Dewey Decimal System. "Whatever people like Jimmy Sewell think," she said, landing on every syllable of every word, "is for Jimmy Sewell to know and for the rest of us human beings to guess at. Before there were apple carts not to be upset, there was Jimmy Sewell."

I started to mention Brighton, but stopped myself. I could have grabbed the White Pages next to the telephone and gone through every name in the book, and nothing would have changed. Karen was convinced Pulsar had something to do with the deaths of Page and Lockman. She had had nobody else to enlist for that idea but the Professor. The Professor owed her because he wanted to believe he owed her and for once she could be the one taking advantage of his possessiveness. And the woman sitting in front of me was very much in love with Karen Noon.

She shook her bracelets at the ceiling with a smile; a medicine woman casting a spell. "Don't let that headache go to your head," she said. "You're not the competition, just the latest excuse."

CHAPTER 20

I took a shower after Veronica left. I was giving the day a second chance to wake up with me and I was expecting better results the second time around. Conks on the head, angioplasty stents, too little information on Alan Lockman, too much about Joe Carroll—all of that had ridden off into the sunset with Lee Marvin and Burt Lancaster. I saw a clear road stretching ahead of me for the rest of my time in New Florence. One, I would pick up Karen at the library and take her out for the dinner she had coming as our hostess. Two, somewhere over the next 24 (not 48) hours, I would abduct the Professor from the hospital, bundle him into the car, and start back to the city. Number three would be squeezed in somewhere between numbers one and two—I would come up with some pretext for taking another spin out to the Mochi works for a closer look at Pulsar. Karen would have expected it, the Professor would have expected it, Veronica would have expected it, and, thanks to them, I would have expected it, too.

The first agenda item was checked off when I called the library and Karen said she would be happy to go to dinner if I felt up for it. Since Veronica had to have returned by then, I took the yes as a sign that the coffee klatch in the living room hadn't gotten me tossed into the same basket as Sewell, Brighton, and the Pulsar Institute. The lilt in her voice said she might even enjoy herself. But then she reminded me I was standing in her living room in only a towel. "Do you think you'll embarrass me with your ripped pants or do you want to know where to get jeans or something?"

I didn't think that oversight said too much for my action plan, but like all great generals I improvised to get the address of the nearest department store. I should have guessed it was a Labine's.

After the library, I called the hospital to see how my favorite patient was doing. The woman who answered described him as "stable," then made him sound better than that by offering to pass me through to the phone he had gotten installed. I told her that wasn't necessary. The next time the old man wanted to tell tales about his relationship with Karen Noon, I wanted to be dug in and ready for the unexpurgated version.

Having tallied one win and one draw, I decided to go for the loss for balancing everything out by calling Mrs. Chalian. Mrs. Chalian was my Bay Ridge apartment house neighbor who had her profound suspicions about what I did for a living, but was even more disapproving of the Chinese menus I left in the hall in front of my door. To make up for that, I sometimes asked her son Jeffrey for help with computer problems—a challenge that he looked forward to since it broke up his long afternoons in his bedroom zapping enemies from other constellations and that his mother welcomed because she could say Jeffrey had spent at least part of one afternoon away from his play station. If the bulldog-faced Mrs. Chalian and I agreed on anything, it was in the assumption that 17-year-old Jeffrey would still be on the same schedule when he was 30.

Our other point of contact was in her willingness—reluctant as it was—to collect special deliveries for me when I was away. When she came on the phone, I was prepared to hear there had been no registered letter with a check owed to me by a Park Slope lawyer for a malpractice case; after all, I had my date with Karen and I had avoided the Professor, so I was due a loss. What I wasn't prepared for was Mrs. Chalian's breathless description of an assault on her and Jeffrey. "Two women, Mr. Finley! They both looked like wrestlers and they had these fur collars with the face of the animal!"

"I'm not following, Mrs. Chalian," I said, to put it mildly.

"They said they were the wife and sister of a Mister . . . What was the name, Jeffrey? I wrote it down there." The mumbling in the background seemed to be Jeffrey having trouble reading something besides a casualty count of aliens. "Yes, a Mister Richard Lowe."

"I have no idea who that is."

"They said you did. You attacked Mister Lowe in Prospect Park when he was there with his brother-in-law. Jeffrey, what was the brother-in-law's name? You said you wrote it down."

Jeffrey wasn't in the mood for that kind of accusation, and the two of them started going at it. Once again, I had to see George Oswald's point: If the moose had been Bob Nelson's brother-in-law, there was far less likelihood the scene in the park would be forgotten. "So these women," I said, interrupting the building crisis in the Chalian household. "What was it they wanted from me?"

"I just told you, Mr. Finley," Mrs. Chalian came back tartly. "They came to beat you up and they could have done it, too. Big, screeching women, Mr. Finley. And they had all these airs about being women of high society with their animals hanging around their shoulders. Who even wears those things anymore? You get people coming up to you and throwing cans of paint at you. You ask me, it's not worth it just to flaunt your money. The one who was married to this Lowe said her husband would have to lose days of work and she was going to sue you. But before she did that, she wanted the satisfaction of breaking . . . I wrote it down here."

She went away again to decipher some note about promised mayhem. As long as I was four hours away from it, I couldn't wait for her to return with the gory details. It seemed like such a cleaner threat than some of the swamp fumes that had been circulating around me.

CHAPTER 21

Antonio Varela, as his license identified him, thought it was funny I needed a cab to go two blocks, and wasn't at all impressed at the hole in my pants I showed him. "Unless you got a date," he shrugged.

"I do."

"Then you need pants."

Since I was already blowing the following week's budget by buying the pants, I threw in a few more weeks by telling him to wait outside the store for me. He looked skeptically over at the four show windows with elaborate domestic scenes of a mannequin Mom baking a pie in the kitchen and a mannequin Dad working on a lathe in the basement, then came back to me. "You're better off with an upfront price, friend. You'll be in there at least 20 minutes. Guaranteed."

I was counting on 10 minutes max—the right rack, the right size, the right color, and the right credit card. And cabbies who lobbied for fixed rates were usually just prejudiced against the small numbers on their meters. But there was something about Antonio Varela's call-my-bluff expression that said he truly wanted to show mercy to the out-of-towner. "How much of an upfront price?"

"Another stop after this?"

"One."

"Twenty-five."

It wasn't the deal of the century, but I made the right move agreeing. The store proved to be even deeper than it was wide, snaking back through one department after another until I was walking through an endless sweet-smelling F train. There were two conspicuous differences, though: F trains didn't have the same delirious Muzak that had been playing in the hospital emergency room and they certainly had more passengers than Labine's had customers. I told myself it was the hour—most commuters hadn't come home yet and housewives were fixing supper. But I would have bought that argument faster if there had been, say, three or four customers cruising the department for women's clothes instead of the single spike-haired teenager whose pout said she had been sentenced to the skirt racks instead of to Devil's Island. The scene was the same in the luggage, infant, and children's departments: a stray customer, salespeople looking grateful to smile at anybody at all but not daring to push their luck by asking if they could be of assistance. For Labine even to break even he would have had to be paying his help strictly on commission. Nothing about the over lighted, overstocked emptiness said the powerhouse who had gotten a square named after him and who had his insurance office building guarded like a nuclear arsenal.

With no lines to worry about, I made record time grabbing some black jeans ideal for either Burger King or Buckingham Palace and slapping them on in the fitting room. Since I seemed to be her first customer in a circle or two of the clock, I couldn't have made the saleswoman tagged as MARGE happier if I had given her the rest of the week off with pay. She did everything but come up with a fur-lined plastic tote for my ripped pants, and her cooing after me to drop in again the next time I was in town stirred resentful looks in every salesperson along the gauntlet back to the door.

Antonio Varela had a shrug for everything so he didn't know what I'd found so odd about Labine's. "You got Christmas in a couple of months," he said. "You always get crowds then."

"But the place isn't open only for Christmas! And how many Labine stores are there? I saw another one . . ."

"Just the two," he said shortly. "Why worry about Labine? He goes broke, somebody else takes over the stores and you pay *them* too much for what five-year-olds are sewing in India. It's always the same bullshit, friend. Where to now?"

Antonio Varela had seen too many movies and TV shows about New York City hacks: He wanted the fixed fare, his tip, *and* my resume. As soon as I told him our next stop was police headquarters, he found three different ways to ask why an out-of-towner needed a New Florence cop. I finally told him just to shut him up—and he had a big laugh telling me the impound lot had closed at three o'clock. He timed that bulletin for turning a corner into one of those winged glass buildings to be found at any airport; but instead of Delta Airlines, it said NEW FLORENCE POLICE HEADQUARTERS. "Wanna go in anyway?" he asked, slowing down to a crawl but not committing himself to a full stop.

The rain decided me. I could have gone in for more shadow-boxing with Brighton about how I had ended up on the ground in front of the cemetery, but that might have meant coming out again and having to search for another Antonio Varela in the middle of a monsoon. As soon as the first big drops slashed the windshield, I figured I was better off looking at a few picture books in the library while waiting for Karen. My friend Antonio said no problem, he would include that as part of the flat rate.

"See our American Idol contest?"

I followed his nod to a *Reporter* poster wrapped around a lamppost; it was announcing the Community Day festivities after the Pulsar poll winner had been announced. "Who'd you vote for?"

His shoulders practically touched his ears. "Like that matters?"

"Saying it's a phony?"

"Phony like they're gonna make up the winner? No, you get caught too easy doing something like that. But you don't think the heavyweights around here don't have their employees spending all day cutting ballots out of the paper and voting for them?"

"Isn't that what this kid Page was saying?"

He glanced up at his mirror for a better look at the outsider who had heard of Randy Page. "Know about that, huh?"

"More than you know."

"What'd you hear?"

"Nothing. Just that it's a big story around here."

He dropped his eyes back to the road; I really didn't need to fill him in on that part of my resume. "Yeah," he nodded. "And the story stinks."

That made it unanimous, and I probably should have let it go there. "These police investigations can be slow at times," I said anyway. "Doesn't always mean they're hiding something."

Antonio Varela shrugged: He might consider that possibility when he came back in his next life as a fire hydrant.

"You don't think so?"

"Why not? I'm always ready to be surprised. Here's the library."

I handed him three tens and he barely glanced at them; he had already assumed that would be what I gave him. Then, as the rain began coming down seriously, he had another thought over his front seat. "Don't matter to you because you don't live here, friend," he said, "but want to know what I really think? I think we're out of surprises around here."

It was one of those rare moments when the right answer occurred to me instantly—not walking down the stairs later, as the French liked to say, but staring back at his heavy eyes then and there while he held the three tens in his hand. The most obvious of answers, really: "Don't tell that to Alan Lockman's mother." But I didn't say it. I even welcomed getting away from Antonio Varela and hurrying through the rain up the steps of the library. Was there some French expression that was the exact opposite of the one about staircase wit? If not, I wanted to take a patent out on one.

CHAPTER 22

Pull enough stakeouts and you become an ace at reading the front pages of newspapers. I don't mean the prominent stories there, but the coleslaw at the top in tiny lettering—the copyright date, the weather forecast, the company slogan, that kind of thing. On a freezing Valley Stream street at four o'clock in the morning after finishing even the crossword puzzle for dummies, that information amounted to a second newspaper. In the case of the New Florence *Reporter*, I decided the paper's founder, one Gerald Steiner, had been a man with dynastic ambitions: Why else a heraldry crest with two crossed broadswords? And if I hadn't been poring over that front page at the library's reading table, how would I have known that the paper had been called the *Valley Reporter* from its founding in 1892 until 1992 when, at the roundest of round ages of 100, it had abandoned the valley? I would have bet whatever was left on my credit card that the Labines had bought the paper in 1992.

Front pages could also be good for mental launchings into areas outside the paper itself. Back in Long Island they had gotten me thinking about how I might have made a mistake switching to Major Cases or how I could tactfully suggest to Jennifer that both of us needed a little gym work. Watching Karen stamp the last of the day's books being brought up to her desk, my missile landed where I had first seen Alan Lockman—a few yards away at the microfilm machine. He couldn't have been looking through old issues of his own paper since they would have been available to him in his office. So what paper had he been looking through and taking notes on? And why? According to Sewell, the kid had been obsessed by the Pulsar vote, so was it so wild an idea he had been researching something on earlier Pulsar polls?

Karen looked marvelously solemn as she nodded to the elderly man's excited reasons for checking out the book he was taking. She was also reminding me over the old guy's head that Alan Lockman could have looked up the earlier Pulsar polls on a home computer the way she had. So what did that leave? What could Lockman have found in an old newspaper or magazine that he couldn't have found on the Internet? Did anything like that still exist anywhere on the globe?

The old guy finally moved on with his book, and Karen nodded she was almost ready. She proved it by reaching under the desk and killing all the lights on the reading tables. I thought about protesting I hadn't finished analyzing Gerald Steiner's broadswords, but then the string bean with the black-framed glasses who had to be the Dobson Veronica had mentioned came out from the back. He had his coat on, on his way home, down to his last duty of making sure the microfilm machines had all been turned off. Maybe it was the association of losing propositions, but the sight of Dobson prompted a thought about Finley Investigations that might have explained Alan Lockman's need for the machines. Every once in a while, finances had prevented me from going to the online version of a periodical because I wasn't a paid subscriber. Would thirty bucks a year have broken the bank? No, but why start tossing thirty here to the *Slumlord Weekly* and thirty there to the *Malpractice Monthly* when I had needed them for merely one detail stemming from one case? However wrapped up the kid had been in Pulsar, he wouldn't have had the money for that kind of expense, either. Therefore, back to basics at the library.

I got over to the front desk before the idea boiled out on me. Karen had glossed her lips during her last trip to the back and her eyelashes might have also been darker than when I had come in from the rain. Anyone would have thought she wanted to impress a date. "One minute," she said, clacking keys to close out her computer screen for the day.

Dobson gave me one last chance to keep quiet by keying off
the main lights from an entrance switch, saying goodnight, and
taking a foldable umbrella out of his pocket as he pushed through
the door. The big room dropped into a creepy silence with only
Karen's hooded desk lamp and computer screen breaking the
darkness. I knew sharing my inspiration with her risked steering
the rest of the evening in the wrong direction, but I also knew Alan
Lockman's mother wouldn't have minded in the least if we ended
up glued to the microfilm machines the whole night instead of
going out to dinner. "When people come in and ask to see some
old newspaper reels, do you record the request there?"

My voice couldn't have echoed more if I had been standing in
the Grand Canyon. I needn't have worried about waking her curiosity; she started as if it had only been nodding anyway. "Alan?"

"Yesterday."

She swiveled fully into the screen and went directly to a site.
All the energy she had been holding in reserve while being polite
to the old man was suddenly sharpening her face. "An academic
journal," she reported after a moment. "*Planning Society.*"

"What's that?"

"What it sounds like. I don't think I've looked at it since my
first day here. But some of the regulars spend all day with it."

"And that's what Lockman was looking at yesterday?" She
nodded, watching me for something more. "I don't know. It's just
that he was really into it when I saw him."

She looked back at the screen pensively. "You know, I hope,
you won't have my full attention over the filet mignon unless I
look it up. He asked for three reels. The last two years plus 1992."

"Do I have a choice?"

"No. Hold on a second."

She got up and hurried off into the shadows to the reels
cabinet along the back wall. I felt smart and conscientious and
wouldn't have yelled if Dobson came back in and smashed his
umbrella over my head.

She returned with three bulky reel boxes that could have
taken us through breakfast. "You look at one and I'll look at one,"
she said, seeing my face. "The first one finished gets to look at the

one from 1992 as a reward. We don't have to go through all the issues page by page. If the table of contents doesn't say Pulsar or something like it, on to the next issue."

Once I remembered how to thread the microfilm, her plan was even less onerous than she had made it sound. *Planning Society* turned out to be a quarterly so there were only three tables of contents to scan. Better yet, the articles ran on forever, making for only six of them in each issue. Nothing about topics like "Merging with the Rain Forests" and "The Skyscraper as Vertical Mall" said Pulsar or Alan Lockman to me.

As fast as I had spooled through my reel, Karen was already clicking the 1992 issue onto her machine as I cleared mine. Was there a significance to the fact that 1992 had also been the year the *Valley Reporter* had become simply the *Reporter*? That seemed unlikely. Pulsar had been operating from coast to coast, the newspaper had been a strictly local affair.

"The aqueducts in Rome, New York's bridges, the Mississippi and its history of floods, the Aswan Dam . . ."

She thought I wanted a full recital of what she read, and I pretended I did all the way through Hong Kong ferries and Helsinki boulevards. The lower her shoulders slumped, the sorrier I was that I had bothered her with my inspiration. I found myself rooting for her to discover an extra, seventh article that would make her search worthwhile. Finally, though, there was nothing left to do but shrug to one another better luck next time and click off the machines again. She didn't say a word as she closed what still needed closing (but punishing the reels for disappointing her by leaving them out of their boxes near the machines). She didn't even seem to notice when I handed her half of the library's copy of the *Reporter* for covering her head to run down the steps through the pelting rain to her Focus. The run seemed to revive her. Once behind the wheel, she examined her hair in the rearview mirror as if she had swum through the Atlantic. "Jesus!"

"What, Jesus? We ran ten yards."

"You see hair. I see strands."

I laughed, and looked away from her to belt myself in. When I raised my head again, she was staring at me. "Thank you," she smiled.

"For what?"

"For thinking about it."

"You haven't left me much choice there, either."

The second smile was more of a wince, and she could discharge it with the emergency brake. "I just hope this place I have in mind won't close because of the rain. It's out of town and at the mercy of the weather more than most places. Very rustic. Up for rustic?"

I was up for rustic. The road she took pointed to the paper mill place Stanton and other towns to the north. She glanced expectantly at every lighted building that loomed up out of the rainy gloom. "How often you been here?"

"Never," she said, making it sound like a brazen admission. "But I've driven past it, and it looks different. Moody, very moody. We don't have many moody places in New Florence."

"Could've fooled me."

"Different mood."

Being alone with her, being *personally* alone with her, seemed to entitle me to a dozen questions. I didn't know why "How come Lucrezia Borgia?" came out on top.

"Why else? She was a total fantasy for me. She was powerful, she was a scheming murderess, she was a fabulous patron of the arts, she was a slut who screwed her father and brother. Or maybe she was none of those things and had a false reputation because of biased historians."

"And what did you decide?"

"What do you think?"

The answer could have been delivered by the tsunami building up outside the car; it certainly *felt* unavoidable. "I think you went for the on-the-one-hand, on-the-other-hand verdict. That's what attracted you to her in the first place. You could play with all those alluring sex and power fantasy things one minute, then with all those petty scholarship things the next. As long as they all left you in a safe middle."

The nub of her chin tightened, giving her that toothache look again. If her eyes had had the final say, she would have ripped the tsunami in front of us in half. "Get that from Joe?" she asked after a moment.

It was my turn to burn. "No, I didn't get it from Joe."

We splashed along through rotten roadwork. A good-sized building with lights approached on the right, but she dismissed it as a candidate without bothering to look at it. "The middle can be a very exciting place," she said. "Did you know that?"

"Sure. Like being a traffic cop in Times Square. You love all the shapes and sizes, but you warn them to keep moving."

"Not just that," she shook her head. "The middle's exciting because it lets you survive. Because whatever you don't see today you have a chance to see tomorrow. It all suddenly doesn't disappear because you stick a gun in your mouth and blow your brains out."

I wasn't supposed to have a reply to that; the Professor's generation would have said no gentleman should. But since when had I been going around disguised as a gentleman? "Antonacci gave you one side of your box. Who were the dullards who gave you the other side?"

"Nobody's that deliberate."

"Maybe not starting out. But when you had to think about the ones who were throwing you a rope, reassuring you you weren't just the Hoboken wife with too many extra microwaves in the closet?"

We had made progress in 24 hours; instead of pressing a button to eject me from the car, she diverted a smile to her speedometer. "We should be getting close."

"Me, too?"

She straightened her back to elongate her arms on the wheel. She was amused by a joke I hadn't told. "Everybody was the other side of the box," she said. "Parents, friends, even the books I read. Joe, too. He wouldn't have liked to think so, but him, too. Andy needed me. Wanted me, loved me, but also needed me. I was the only person who didn't come to him packaged and approved by his father. That was *very* exciting, made me dangerous in my own way. When he sat down to eat, it was for our food at our table.

When we made love, there was nobody else in his world. There couldn't be. He would have forfeited his exclusivity to the only person who gave it to him."

"You've given a lot of thought to this."

"I've had a lot of time to give a lot of thought to it."

"Right."

"Anything else?"

Again, I knew a gentleman would have kept his mouth shut. "How come you didn't have kids?"

She smiled as though I hadn't missed a predictable stop-off yet. "The Karen answer is that I could never get through that fourth month."

"I'm sorry."

"Me, too. But there's the Lucrezia answer, too. Don't you know how she died? In childbirth. So maybe you're right, Detective Finley. Maybe I just wanted to stay in that safe middle . . . There it is."

CHAPTER 23

She hadn't been kidding about the rustic, at least as far as the name was concerned. What was called simply the Rustic Inn was recessed a good distance from the roadway and surrounded by a grove of scrawny, leafless trees, suggesting it had been there before the asphalt workers had come. Given the bleak surroundings of power lines and shapeless patches of withered grass, most of what might still be regarded as rustic was in the log cabin look of the building's two floors. Muskets wouldn't have looked out of place at the windows for keeping away the Redcoats. There were a good dozen cars in the parking lot being washed down by the storm, and to judge by what I could catch a glimpse of through the small windows, their drivers were more interested in the second-floor bedrooms than in the ground-floor dining room. Aside from a huge fireplace, the restaurant's motif seemed to be the same one as in the New Florence places I'd seen—unused red napkins.

"For those who can afford more than a Holiday Inn," she said.

"Assuming they're going to be traveling anywhere near here."

"Not everybody has your prejudices."

Since we didn't have life preservers in the trunk, she concentrated her search for a parking spot near the restaurant door. But then I saw a car that made me not want to go in at all. "Keep going."

"What . . .?"

"Don't park. Go around again."

I heard her bewilderment as she did another mopish turn, but I was busier trying to recall if I had committed to memory any of Jimmy Sewell's license plate. Or were there so many platinum Lexuses in New Florence that I was being silly? "I think that's Sewell's car."

She idled down and peered out through her wipers to take in the Lexus. She wasn't ecstatic, but she didn't see the evening crumbling apart, either. "Damn. But that doesn't mean we have to sit with him, does it?"

"That may not be the problem."

"What's that mean?"

I told her about the clumsy way he had clarified his invitation to a home-cooked meal because he had things "on his plate." I didn't expect her to laugh. "You mean the upstanding editor is cheating on his wife?"

I should have found it as funny as she did, but I didn't. The thought of Cassandra and the weekly S&M session had been titillating because it had been ludicrous, or should have been. The universe made me dizzy whenever my idle notions brushed against reality.

"Well, we can't sit out here all night. Besides, you don't know who he's in there with. Did you see him at a table?"

"No."

"So?" So took that moment to open the restaurant door and, holding her raincoat out over her head, scamper as fast as she could on heels to the tan Murano two cars down from the entrance. Pauline Shepherd, eyeglasses hanging fashionably on a chain over her chest, swore once, swore twice, then finally got her key to open the car door. She came out with a string overnight bag, then locked up again. I didn't think the bag was filled with *Reporter* ballots for Pulsar.

"You know her?"

"She was exchanging code signals with Sewell when I was in his office yesterday. I thought it was for Friday. I'm not good at code."

"So what do you care?"

"She works with Pulsar."

Karen's interest instantly leaped over her bemusement. She didn't know whether to make another quick tour of the lot for a better look before Shepherd got back inside or sacrifice her eyes to permanent strain through the spattered back window. Shepherd took the choice away from her by racing to the door twice as fast as she had come running out. In the seconds the door was opened I could make out only a hotel-type registration desk.

"Well, I guess our editor should rank pretty high in the poll."

I shook my head. I would have been surprised if the Jimmy Sewell I knew appeared anywhere on the Pulsar list. "You don't know how weird that is in there. We're seeing Billy Graham burning bibles, the pope down on his knees shooting craps, and Donald Trump telling the truth."

"Because Jimmy Sewell is a saint."

"I know the guy! At least I thought I did. He goes to an R-rated movie, he thinks he's walked on the wild side!"

She addressed her grunt to the windshield wipers. "You're cute when you're naive, know that?"

I repressed a reply that she had been cute herself when she had been talking about how exclusive Antonacci had made her in bed. In a larger sense, she was right about me. If I had been a client making his case to me, I would have said I had needed Sewell to be Father Sewell. And how many others from the old days on the Island had I sentenced to permanent immobility so I would know where they would be if I ever went back?

"What do you want to do?"

I seemed to have learned only one answer to that question. "An old sergeant named Bailey used to say, when in doubt, push ahead. It's actually pretty shitty advice, but at least I can blame him if things go wrong."

"So let's blame him. I'm hungry and I've invested too much creative thought into this place to go back for a hamburger."

"They're not going to be happy to see us."

"And I wasn't happy to see him outside the Lockmans' last night."

She found a slot two spaces away from Pauline Shepherd's. She took it with the confidence of having seen it all along.

CHAPTER 24

Some gatherings cry out for a master of ceremonies—somebody to smooth over all the conversational lags with patter that drives everything forward to the next lag. If the emcee is polished, he'll toss in a joke every once in a while about his own role, winning more points from those who would have been left babbling without him.

Michael Zev had more professional polish than a standup comic at a celebrity roast. From the second Karen and I walked into the restaurant and Sewell looked up from his table as though we had arrived just in time with his stroke, Zev was the expansive castle baron welcoming wayfarers to his home. Our timing couldn't have been better because they had just started eating, too, so weren't we all blessed! He wouldn't hear of us taking a separate table away from the room's snug fireplace, he wouldn't think about letting us order one of the cheaper wines on the menu when he only had to request another bottle of the Rothschild Something, and he wouldn't live with himself if he didn't steer us toward the venison he had already sampled at the Rustic Inn on two earlier occasions. He knew what was good for us and what we wanted even if we didn't know.

I took my cue from Karen: When she didn't resist despite the chips weighing down both her shoulders, I had no easy excuse for contrariness, either. Through it all, chewing his food, drinking his wine, and assuming the pose of a thinking man, Sewell tossed out sickly half-smiles, as if to say both of us had ended up as victims of all the evening's torrential downpours so make the best of it. I had no reason not to smile back at him: The wine and venison beat Tylenol and coffee and, besides, I had been born friendly and non-judgmental, hadn't I?

Shepherd? She had lost her glasses from the parking lot, but not the blue eyes from Sewell's office that performed the neat trick of dismissing whatever she focused on. She x-rayed Karen's outfit, tried not to be obvious about weighing it against what I was wearing, then got distracted looking at her own caramel wrist on her fork. I got the feeling she was in more of a supporting role for the evening than she had counted on. Zev might not have been a surprise third for an intimate little dinner with Sewell, but he hadn't been the reason she had chosen a silk gray blouse that showed her taste for lacy black bras. I hadn't seen a mole perched so high on a milky breast since an old French movie about Marie Antoinette.

I gave myself a C on Zev. He wasn't wearing a *Star Trek* tunic and he wasn't bald, but he did have a thick goatee to go with his rolling baritone. It was easy to imagine him once dreaming of being an opera star, but he also could have been the drug store pharmacist who had been stuffed into his white coat. To hear his odyssey through restaurants around the country, he was lucky he could still find a tent to fit him. Kansas City beef? Forget it. The best sirloins were to be had at a place he knew in Davenport, Iowa. Catfish? Where else but one or two places he knew on the Mississippi Bayou? Cheesecake? Yes, he had to join the consensus and give the nod to Junior's in Brooklyn. Wine cellars? He had been spoiled rotten by one in Scottsdale, Arizona. "You wouldn't believe it, Mr. Finley, but you walk in and you find a good six or seven rooms. The ceiling of every room is a straw shelf with hundreds of bottles. You have the Italian Room, the French Room, the California Room, the Chilean Room. Maybe you should write to them and suggest a Long Island Room."

It was an emcee tactic I knew I could get to despise with a little practice: a biographical fact reprocessed two minutes later for making the monologue sound personal. "Buy me a vineyard and I might."

Zev thought that was funnier than it was. Keeping her fork moving from her plate to her mouth, Karen kept saying the venison was tastier than it was. I was beginning to detect a theme. "What Mr. Finley is too polite to say, Michael," Shepherd slipped in, "is that he is more interested in your work than your gourmand tour of the country."

Zev didn't need the nudge, and reached for his glass with an iron smile. "Translation: Pauline thinks I talk too much. And rather than expose you to that about Pulsar, why don't you come around tomorrow and see for yourself what we're up to?"

I hadn't expected it to be that easy; in the back of my mind I had been counting on a shrewd combination of blackmail and begging with Sewell the next morning. "Thank you. I was thinking of doing just that, but didn't know how to wangle an invitation."

"Well, now you've wangled."

It seemed like too big an opening to leave completely for the next day. "I was driving past there yesterday. What I can't figure out is why you need so much space for counting the ballots I saw in the *Reporter*."

Sewell laughed a been-there-done-that laugh, but Karen paused with her fork. "I was wondering that, too."

Shepherd tried not to make her smile seem too condescending, failed, then took in Karen as if only she had raised the question. "I'll give you the short version," she said. "You may not believe this, but public opinion polls aren't god. They do nothing more than collect the views of specific people at given moments. Poll the same people on the same question at a different moment and you're likely to end up with a different result. Today's Most Admired Citizen probably won't be next month's."

"So what good are the polls?"

"You mean aside from giving Michael and me a paycheck?"

Sewell chuckled. Zev had heard it before. Karen was waiting with more visible patience to hear anything at all she hadn't heard before. And Shepherd used the break in eye contact to come back to me instead of to Karen. "Partly because of what I just said," she resumed huskily. "They have value because they measure the fact that people have had a change of mind about something.

Keep that word *measure* in mind, Mr. Finley. Everything is in the measuring. The value of a statistical survey isn't in any given response or discernible trend, but in the measures, it provides for how truly volatile our society is. Government, private corporations, educational institutions—they all want to stay ahead of the curve. They want to know you better, more than you probably want them to know you. They want to anticipate. They have to. Anticipating is the lifeblood of government, business, and education. Of course, none of us likes the idea of being predictable. We like it even less to think we're conditionable. But like it or not, we are. The question is in what direction, under what influence. And that gets us to the central paradox. Our best shield against abuses by us or Pulsar's less imaginative brethren? Believe it or not, the measuring itself."

It was a tossup who was prouder of her—Zev because she had shown why she belonged on his staff or Sewell because he could tell himself he was enchanted by the right woman. What they both could have been proud of, as well, was how she had avoided answering the question about needing all the space out at the Mochi annex.

Even Karen had forgotten that minor detail. "So you're saying these polls are just one abstraction on top of another?" she asked.

Shepherd took a second to turn her attention back to the flintier tone across the table. "I don't think the people we study regard themselves as abstractions. Do you consider yourself an abstraction, Karen?"

I didn't miss it, and neither had Karen: I was Mr. Finley, she was Karen. "I certainly wouldn't if I were Randy Page, I suppose."

Sewell shot me a look of panic: Had I been talking out of class about his doubts? "Yes, that tragedy," Zev grumbled. "Anything new on that front, Jim? Some development today, perhaps?"

Sewell took me down into his plate with him. I had never been cut up like a piece of venison before. "There was a disturbance at the funeral this morning," he said somberly. "A few arrests."

"The police assaulted Paul."

I didn't recall having cleared that press release with Karen, but she reached for her bread so sassily I knew she wouldn't have

enjoyed the moment as much if I had. Zev was appalled. Shepherd was titillated. Sewell didn't like his scoops being given away
for free. Worst of all, I was hamstrung. If I said anything mealy-
mouthed, hinting that maybe Karen was running down the field
with a ball she hadn't caught yet, I would be worthy of my plastic
table companions. "Good whack, too," I had to say, bowing the
back of my head toward Shepherd. "The nightsticks up here have
some heft to them. They really don't like outsiders up here. But
I guess you people at Pulsar have discovered that for yourself."

What was it they used to say about the Marx Brothers—they
always left the other characters in their movies *consternated*?
Karen was blissfully consternated and looked ready for another
bottle of the Rothschild Something. Zev couldn't deny my implication quickly enough; no, on the contrary, Pulsar had never sensed
the least hostility. Shepherd was trying to decide if I had been
vulgar by aiming my head at her. And Sewell remained stuck on
the mundane, asking again if I had any concrete evidence about
the cops that he could put into a story. I thought about reminding
him he had been the one to pass along the story about a cop being my assailant, but wasn't there something anti-constitutional
about informing on an informer's informer? He himself had told
me that.

"I promised you'd be the first I'd tell."

"Minus me, of course," my new rabbity friend from the library
said. "Just so he can have a backup in case one of his quotes gets
lost."

Sewell looked at both of us with more of that disconcerted
thing. He seemed to fish back to the old days on the Island to be
sure he didn't have a hanging debt with me. "But seriously, Paul,
if you have any proof at all, you should tell me. They've already
arraigned somebody for it. The son of the head of the New Florence Society."

Karen lost her bounciness instantly. "Russell Dvorak?"

Sewell nodded. "Said he clubbed Paul from behind with his
placard. I think the charge is second-degree assault."

It took me a moment to remember where I had heard the
name Dvorak before—the radio plug for the holy roller. By then

Shepherd was fully zeroed in on Karen's red face. "You seem to know him."

"Of course, she knows him," Zev said promptly, but not sounding all that solicitous. "Everybody knows everybody in a small community."

It was more of that white rat-black rat stuff and both lab experts were staring at Karen to see how she would run through their maze. "His father's a minister and a real lunatic," she said, making it sound like she was alone with me in her kitchen again. "Anything that says the earth is flat, he's for it. But Russell's not like that."

Then her stare dropped even from my face, and it wasn't to go back to the plate she remembered. If Pulsar had happened to New Florence a few months earlier, I was sure, she would have gone to Russell Dvorak—Russell Dvorak, *Junior*—instead of Joe Carroll. "Wears a camouflage jacket, kind of husky?"

"Yes," she nodded.

"Well, he's not the one who slugged me."

"The police think he is," Sewell said.

"I don't care what they think. I didn't see who did it, but when I was bopped, this Dvorak was yards in front of me, charging down at the motorcade with his flat earth friends."

It made for an awkward silence. Even Karen didn't seem to know if she was grateful or not for the information. Then Zev rearranged his bulk in his chair and laughed. "Reminds me of the story of the five kings," he said.

"What's that?" Sewell asked dutifully.

"The five kings met to discuss problems in their realms. For several days they carved up countries and peoples among themselves to avoid potential sources of friction. Then they noticed that one of the women serving them their usual gargantuan meal had tears in her eyes. What's bothering you, one of them said to her. Oh, nothing, your highness, she said, it's just that I got word my son was drowned while he was out fishing this morning. And the woman went on serving their meal. And the kings sat there in silence not knowing what to say to the servant. They could dispose and predispose the fates of millions, but they were humbled before the natural fate of one individual. They couldn't wait for her to get out of the goddamn banquet room! Only when she did could they get back to eating and dividing up the world!"

I didn't know whether he made it up on the spot or not. One way or another, it belonged in the masters of ceremonies handbook.

CHAPTER 25

Russell Dvorak had been a decompression chamber. She didn't use those words, but that was what it came down to. He had been familiar to her because he had grown up kicking at pebbles in the shadow of an extravagant father; he had been new to her because, instead of the highways and dirt roads of New Jersey politics, he had drawn her into mesh screens, squeegees, and the other secrets of silk screen printmaking. She hadn't really thought of it as a romance, more like two people enjoying each other's laziness for a couple of months. Then one day the minister-father had shown up at the library, ostensibly to return a book on serigraphy Russell had taken out but mainly to get a look at the librarian who had been eating into his son's time around the family church and at the New Florence Society. The meeting had been bumpy, especially after it had become clear Russell had agreed to sending his father around with the book. After that the silk screen printer had all but run at the sight of her on the street.

"A silk screen painter? Up here? Sounds like a humming market."

"When what you really want to ask is . . ."

"How do you get mixed up with people like this?"

"You mean like you?"

She rolled over on me so abruptly I thought she was going to mash my balls through the mattress. Inches away, the last of her talc fading into her sweat, she was doubly naked—not only without her clothes, but without her contacts. I couldn't help wondering if Pauline Shepherd would have focused as intently in the same position.

"What?"

"Nothing."

"Bullshit, Finley."

"A moment of comparative shopping."

"How sweet!" Her teeth came down on my bicep so hard I knew they could have come down even harder if she didn't want to be just playing. "Don't tell me it's that Pulsar bitch."

"No. Zev."

"It was!"

"She has a weird way of looking at people."

"Yeah. Like why are you cluttering up my line of vision?"

"Something like that."

"Her and Sewell? You were on drugs."

"Don't tell him that."

"Sorry to disappoint you, but not you, either."

"And you know this because . . .?"

She thumped down on my kidneys and smiled with endless pity for my ignorance. "Because I know the women who hang around the movers and shakers. I've met the Befores and I've met the Afters. The Befores have this little tingle that maybe they can have gooseflesh seven days a week if they learn to do things right. The Afters are resigned to making do with what they've learned, maybe a tiny adventure here and there to spice up their fantasies while they're sugaring the kids' Cheerios. Your Lara Croft isn't a Before and she isn't an After. She's all Now because she doesn't see herself as ever being somebody else's chattel. The only one at that table she would even think of going down on is Zev, and that's only because he's Pulsar for the moment and if she has to, she'll indulge his superior title as a temporary trial. Didn't you ever learn the priorities of tomb raiders?"

"I kind of liked that beauty mark on her boob."

"You can get them at any theatrical supplies store."

"You had a chance to push her on some things but you didn't."

She preferred acknowledging it to my pillow. "Too much obscenity," she nodded, more regret in her voice. "All that food and wine on one hand, Alan Lockman on the other. Mister Convivial and his five kings on the right, all this creeping around about Randy Page on the left. I told myself self-righteousness in that setting would be the obscenest thing of all." She dropped her eyes back down to me. "Crazy?"

Any reply to her earnestness would have been short of the mark. "The trouble with not believing you're paranoid about these people is it means someone ought to be doing something about them."

She smiled, and lifted her breasts closer to my mouth. "You may kiss them for your awareness. No beauty marks, but they're pretty nice anyway."

She was right.

"You should see Brighton about Russell."

"I intended to. You didn't have to bribe me."

"Just to be sure."

There were nasty bed habits to be discouraged the second they appeared. One—which I had already stupidly allowed once—was sprawling over me and tapping down on my instep with her toenails, a kind of pensive rumba with only skin—mine—to lose. "You don't stop that, I'm going to roll you back on your ass."

"Hurt, does it?"

"I just noticed something."

"That's good for a private detective, isn't it?"

"Ever since you picked me up at the hospital this morning, you've been audible. What happened to that whisper thing?"

"Maybe you've just gotten used to me."

"No."

"Why not?"

"That would imply I'm not a great seducer, just another Russell Dvorak collapsing into bed with you at your level."

She looked smarter, harder—and vaguely hurt. "Hate to break it to you, Finley, but you didn't seduce me. That was the venison, the wine, and, 'Oh, where did all those other people go? Only Finley's left? Oh, okay. May as well. It's still early and I have to get out of these damp clothes anyway.'"

"Thank you."

Her mouth was an endorsement for Crest: It *did* have layers of freshness, even after an hour or more. She felt like half her size when she was standing away from me—still lanky and angular, but between her thin shoulders and waist only a sample of herself. "Should be time enough now," she whispered very audibly, her right hand all knuckle as she reached down between our stomachs to put me back into her.

Her timing was right.

CHAPTER 26

I didn't know if I dreamed it or it really happened. I opened my eyes into the darkness of Karen's bedroom. I was on my back and she was coiled into my side, her small nose somehow looking more asleep than the rest of her peaceful face. What had woken me was a muffled cry. Not a shout cry, but a weeping cry. It had come from the other side of the bedroom wall, but also from behind other walls further down the street. From the Lockman house? Yes, and I knew it was Alan Lockman's mother. I wanted to get up. But to do what? What use would I have been knocking on her door? The only important thing was that the woman sobs lowlier, not awaken Karen and stir up more of that useless consternation.

And then I fell back into the darkness.

CHAPTER 27

Karen dropped me off at police headquarters on her way to work. She waited till I was getting out of the car to ask the question I had been pushing away since both of us had gotten up—was I still intent on pulling the Professor out of the hospital and starting back to New York sometime during the day? She asked it as neutrally as possible but I thought I trumped her with a glowing "Let's see how things go this morning." She whipped away from the curb before she had to say how she hoped the things went.

Captain Frank Brighton's office was on the second floor. I knew he ranked because the lobby directory named only him and his superior, Chief Anthony Lama, individually; every other office was merely the name of the given squad. Inside the street door was a combination Manhattan office building lobby and station house booking desk: The sergeant on duty was as much a security man clearing visitors to the elevators as a tour boss. I had the feeling they didn't like it when collars stood around in cuffs too long in full view of the street while names and crimes were being recorded. Bad for the building's image.

It took five minutes for the calls to go upstairs and back down again. I was told to wait on a bench out of view of the entrance until somebody came to fetch me. That gave me time to study the Wanted posters and department circulars under glass and to conclude that the New Florence police's worst problem since the 2006 jail escape of a conman named Federico Alou had been a bowling league loss to the Fire Department. Given all their free time, I wondered whether I could interest them in two Amazons in fur collars running around Brooklyn after me. I also decided the sergeant was right for his job: a barker like any deskman in a Brooklyn station house, but also old enough to fit the retirement profile for an office building security man. Both times he glanced at me while talking on the phone I sensed he was reading my mind.

The fetcher was a surprise: the black uniform who had hauled me from the cemetery to the hospital. His name was Dwayne Arlett, he still didn't have eyebrows to speak of, and he was glad about a lot of things—that I had recovered from the "bump" on my head, that I had come down to recover my car, and that I had thought to stop off to see Brighton because the captain had been looking forward to seeing me again, too. From Arlett's point of view, it was all serendipity; from mine, it was like the day in high school we had been choosing up sides for touch football and Mickey Sears had just happened to notice Reggie Swan, the best player in the class, wandering across the yard as he was due to make his last pick. I wondered whose hair oils a lab would have found on Arlett's nightstick.

"You assigned personally to Brighton?" I asked in the elevator.

He acted dazzled by the question. "Why would you say that?"

"Just making conversation."

He shook his head: The world never stopped making him wonder. I shook mine back: The world had the same effect on me.

Brighton had a corner office with an impressive oak door; no bullpen democracy where he was concerned. But he also sat at his desk so gingerly he seemed to be expecting an imminent order to vacate the premises. Even his jacket buttons were closed as he worked at signing a small sheaf of papers in front of him. "Thanks, Dwayne," he said, dismissing Arlett without raising his eyes. "Already on your feet, Finley? The big city makes them tough."

There was a copy of the *Reporter* on the desk; it was folded down to the front-page photograph of Russell Dvorak. "It wasn't him."

"What's that?"

"Russell Dvorak. He wasn't the one who slugged me."

He finally paused in his scribbling, glanced at the newspaper, then up at me. "We have witnesses who say it was."

"Your witnesses are wrong."

He gave me a how-really-intoxicated-are-you second look, then tossed his pen on the papers still to be signed, and sat back. Not only was his jacket still buttoned, but it was a little short in the sleeves. "And you're ready to swear to this?"

"Absolutely. Dvorak was yards in front of me when I got hit. Who're your witnesses? Page's friends?"

"I didn't say that."

"Then I guess it was cops. Like Arlett."

He swallowed patiently. "Officer Arlett is a highly decorated officer."

I didn't doubt it: bowling leagues could bring out the best in a man. To judge by the pictures on the cabinet under the window behind the desk and the plaques and framed certificates blanketing the walls, Brighton had done well in that department, too. A couple of the pictures showed the skinhead from the church steps I had decided was the town dogcatcher; in full braid he looked more like the police chief the board downstairs had called Anthony Lama.

"Dvorak was disturbing the peace," he insisted.

"But not my part of the peace. So I'd really appreciate it if you'd drop that charge against him."

Brighton hesitated over his next crack, then decided to go with it. "This wouldn't be a personal appeal from a third party, would it?"

It was a small town, as Zev had noted: Everybody knew everybody. "It has nothing to do with Ms. Noon," I said, not up for his games. "You want me to tell your district attorney in person, tell me where I'll find him and I'll go down there right now before your little mistake embarrasses lots of people. From what I hear, Dvorak's got a father who likes bringing the word to the spiritually bewildered."

He smiled, then did something I hadn't seen anybody do in days: He took out a new pack of one of those Indian reservation cigarette brands and a Bic lighter. "Close the door and sit down," he said, alarmingly friendly.

I didn't see any reason not to; he was the one who was going to be arrested for breaking smoking ordinances, not me. When

I turned back from the door, he was removing a glass ashtray from a side drawer. Before he closed the drawer again, I made out a tape recorder that looked keyed to preserve his sexiest office conversations.

I shook my head to his cigarette offer and took the chair farther from the ashtray. I didn't need temptations lingering in my nose longer than necessary. And just in case I had missed some finger action while I had been closing the door, why be clearer than I had to be for the recorder?

"Karen Noon seems to think these Pulsar people are body snatchers or something and we're helping them cover up their alien conspiracy."

Karen had never mentioned calling or sending an email to Brighton, and I hoped that was just her forgetfulness. I really didn't like the idea she had been under surveillance, even the loose kind. "All I came down here for was to clear the air on Dvorak and get my car from the pound."

"Sure," he said, savoring his first inhale of the day. "And that's all we're talking about right now." He paused until he was satisfied the office was reeking of smoke and his ground rules. "I'll give her this much: I've been very busy since Pulsar came to town. What do you think?"

"It's your town."

"And I can have it?"

"I don't know where you're going, Captain."

He liked the second inhale as much as the first. "Okay, so Pulsar's collecting all these votes to reduce us to lines on their electronic graphs. If we vote for Mayor McCorkle, we're in one category. If we vote for that ball-breaker Page or this church lady Sewell thinks is another Mother Teresa, we end up in another category. None of it gives me a warm, fuzzy feeling, but they're here, City Hall is happy they're here, Walter Labine is so happy they're here he gives them his paper for their little voting game. Bottom line? We're all happy they're here."

"Then you have no problem."

"Me, no. But your Ms. Noon seems to have one. And Sewell's been clearing his throat a lot lately. Considering he works for

Labine, that makes a public official like myself wonder if I should be as happy as I am they're here. As somebody wandering through the universe seeking the truth of it all, what would you do in my place, Finley?"

I laughed, but he kept staring. And waiting for a serious answer. "What do you want me to say? Do it by the numbers."

"Such as?"

"You've had two mysterious deaths lately as opposed to . . .?"

"We average 3.4 homicides annually," he nodded. "Just a mini-fraction of the suicides we get, but why dwell on that? One homicide will be a guy who drank too much and didn't like what his wife gave him for supper. Another will be a guy who drank too much and didn't like the color of the skin of the driver who dented his fender. Number three will be someone who drank enough to smother or shoot or poison a husband or wife dying of cancer. The .4—that could be a drug deal, mugging, robbery, name it. In short, we're usually on the civilized end of the state's annual homicide statistics and that's a credit to Chief Lama and the dedicated men and women under him. So no question that Page and Lockman so close together makes for some meditation. You don't have to be a bored librarian with a hard-on for Pulsar to admit that much."

I told myself he wouldn't have been much of a cop if he hadn't known about Antonacci's suicide. That didn't quite put me at ease about the surveillance possibility, especially with the recorder in his desk suggesting bad habits, but it *was* the past. "You keep trying to dump it on Karen. Because that's easier than going too deep into your meditation?"

"No," he said promptly. "Because I have only two things connecting Page and the copyboy. One, they were both male Caucasians. Two, they're both dead. Give me a third thing."

"Because you're really open to it."

"Because I'm asking."

I believed him. "The *Reporter*."

"What about it?"

"Like it hasn't already occurred to you! The poll it was running for Pulsar. Page apparently made it nightly listening. The kid was in charge of the ballots in the office."

"In other words, Karen Noon again."

The amiability suddenly made sense. The tactful headwaiter—and that was what Brighton still made me think of—avoided a messy scene over accommodating a would-be patron by having the patron himself note that every table was occupied. I warned myself not to be impressed by somebody who didn't even know how to buy a suit jacket that fit. "But you're not so sure of your ground. Otherwise, why would we be having this little brainstorming session?"

For a second he was on the verge of doing or saying something besides sticking his cigarette back in his mouth. "I just think it might make everybody's life a little easier if you passed my sentiments along to your hostess," he recovered. "I don't need her to tell me Alan Lockman didn't hang himself. And I don't need you trampling a crime scene because you think you know more about homicide investigations than I do."

Obviously, I hadn't looked closely enough at the house across the street where the green Corolla had been parked. "Then at least let people know you're opening drawers and looking inside. A little public relations never crippled an investigation."

"Where you come from."

"Where I come from."

He looked at the end of his cigarette more critically; his high had receded. "Anything else?"

I surprised myself with an actual thought. "The Lockman kid seemed real anal about those ballots."

"Always back to Pulsar."

"I'll bet he was keeping his own little count somewhere. Maybe at his office desk, maybe in his bedroom."

"So? They're publishing the results this weekend."

I had an image of not just Brighton, but Antonio Varela scoffing at me. "Be nice to know they tallied with what Lockman said."

"You're not serious."

"There's a cab driver in town who agrees with you. But sometimes we get too sophisticated for our own good. Crude can work, Captain."

"Sure. An institute operating around the country will compromise its reputation by throwing a few extra votes Walter Labine's way."

"As long as we're speculating, that's another thing—its reputation. You look them up?"

Of all the balls being lobbed back and forth, that should have been one of the most harmless. But his face reddened and he couldn't dash his cigarette out fast enough. "Of course. Very legitimate."

"I'm sure. But for who? The Agriculture Department? The Kennedy Center for the Performing Arts?"

Suddenly he couldn't reach fast enough for a business card on a desk rack of them. "Bring this down to Impound," he said, writing something on the back. "If they try to charge you anything, tell them to call me."

I reached over for the card, and could have sworn he held it back an inch or two until I had to stand to collect it. "Thanks," I had to say.

With the card in my hand he relaxed again, even unbuttoning his jacket as he sat back in his chair. "Miss police work?"

"Not this morning."

He smiled reflectively. "Everything's a tradeoff, Finley, believe me. We get our 3.4 homicides up here, nothing at all like the *agita* a big city cop has. On the other hand, we're still small beans to the outside world. Captain Frank Brighton of New Florence, New York calls up the FBI or some other agency, he's on Hold for a half-hour. You city cops get to know everybody within a couple of years on the job. You have to reach out for information, you go to the old Rolodex. Everything's a tradeoff."

I started to remind him that I hadn't had the kind of access he was talking about in years, that I was a private investigator. But before I could get a word out, he picked up his pen and dropped his eyes back to the papers he had been working on when I had walked on. The last thing he wanted to hear, apparently, was that I was no longer a cop. "See you around," he said. "And if it doesn't make you *persona non grata* with her, say hello to Karen. No coded message intended."

CHAPTER 28

I hadn't heard anything *but* coded messages from him. By the time I
had liberated my car, convinced myself I could manage with the
broken handle until I got back to the city, and was on my way
out to the Mochi plant, I thought I had decoded at least half of
one. Brighton wanted *me* to check out Pulsar. In fact, the more
I looked back on it, the more that seemed like the reason for the
whole exercise in his office. But that was the easy half of the
deciphering. The harder half was why. So he was left waiting on
Hold for a half-hour. He should have gotten used to that calling
his electric company. No matter how low on the list New Florence
ranked for strategic urban centers, he was still a cop who had the
right to expect cooperation from the FBI or whomever. What was
he playing at?

I found Sloan Avenue and my landmarks from the first day.
The baby carriages were out in force around the supermarket,
but the high school kids were apparently back in their classroom
cells. There was no one standing in front of the Tebaldi Funeral
Home; the place didn't even look open. Randy Page was in the
ground and Tebaldi's was just another storefront. I had never met
Page, probably would have lunged for the radio dial to get rid of
him if I'd ever tripped across him, but I could have done without
such a fast transition from town event to yesterday's news.

I returned to Brighton for more scintillating thoughts. His
evasiveness had to be either because he was reluctant to have
his name known to the people he would be asking about Pulsar

or because he didn't want it known locally he was asking. I had hardly taken a blood oath with the Feds who might have been able to give him his information; the less they knew about my existence, the healthier the Republic, and I had the case files back in Brooklyn to prove it. But after two days in New Florence the second alternative felt more plausible: Captain Frank Brighton, no Clouseau but a man worried about protecting his pension, didn't want the wrong people, whoever they were, knowing he had been checking on Pulsar.

Was I just beginning to feel a little claustrophobic in a town where everybody not only knew everybody else, but also what everybody else was doing? I didn't think so. Two prime exhibits, Ladies and Gentlemen of the Jury. Number One: Brighton's knowledge of Karen's feelings toward him and Pulsar. Granted this one would prove worthless if Karen told me she had been sending him dirty emails, but she hadn't told me that yet. And then Number Two: Sewell's phone call to me the day before. A cop might have slugged me, he had said. Where had he gotten that from? He couldn't say, he was bound by those nonexistent confidentiality vows. His most likely source? Who else but Brighton, right after he had visited me in the hospital and I had flown that same trial balloon with him? Brighton the cop Sewell seemed to go out of his way to apologize for. Brighton the cop who was apparently an important source for the *Reporter* and its executive editor. Brighton the cop who had his rank and his smarts, but apparently not much of a grip on either one.

I gave up. The political infighting I had sensed with Sewell during our telephone conversation was punching bag against punching bag. Every contact made a sound, but nobody got hurt because, when all was said and done, real human beings weren't involved.

Except for Alan Lockman.

Except for Randy Page.

Except for the bandage on the head of Paul Finley.

The road sign promising 1.5 miles to the Mochi works was still where it should have been. Small favors.

CHAPTER 29

Zev had said to drop by at ten. I was a quarter-hour early, but they should have had the bunting up by then anyway. As I turned down the narrow, beaten up track to the annex entrance, the lineman darted into his booth for confirmation that a visitor was expected. I didn't take that as a good sign since he had probably made a notation of it less than an hour before. A second bad sign was that he immediately stepped back out of the booth and gave me one of those French *gendarme* palm-up stop signs that begged for a heavier foot on the gas pedal. Had Zev's invitation gotten lost in a hangover from too much Rothschild?

"Paul Finley. Mister Zev is expecting me."

He cured me right away of the idea he was a moron; more accurately, he was a *hostile* moron. "Not yet he isn't," he said, grimacing to read the time on his watch. "You're 12 minutes early."

Up close, he wasn't that much of a twin to Leo. Leo had folds in his neck, a snout for a nose, and was in his late thirties. The lineman had folds in his neck, a snout for a nose, and was about 10 years younger. "So what? I'm going to sit here for 12 minutes or you're going back to that phone to call Zev and tell him his guest is a little early?"

"You can't sit there for 12 minutes. You're blocking access."

Five out of ten times I would have murmured something to keep our fruitful dialogue going. Maybe three times I would have backed up and taken a spin up to the picnic benches before coming back to be exactly on time. The ninth time I would have just sat there looking baffled. But I was at the tenth time, right after my little chat with Brighton, and I was getting pissed at the number of people who seemed to have detected a key on my back. "Look, Otto . . . That your name, Otto?"

He heard an insult but didn't know where. "Hal."

"Okay, Hal. How about I go off to the left here and park? By the time I close, it'll be almost exactly ten o'clock."

Who knew how long it was going to take him to process that idea? Just furrowing his eyebrows over it seemed time enough for one of Mochi's machines across the way in the main building to turn out another set of drapes. But then Zev himself stepped out from behind the heavy front door. "It's okay, Hal," he called. "Park over there, Paul."

For the longest moment, long enough for Zev to wonder if he had been heard, the lineman stayed planted in front of the car. Even when he ordered his pier pile legs to move away, he was waiting for Zev to cancel his order and reinstate a red alert security level. I didn't know what the guy had for breakfast, but I didn't rule out something from a lab vial.

"Hal takes his job gravely," my affable host said after I had parked and rejoined him at the door. "We told him people might be snooping and now he thinks everybody's a snooper. Come in, come in."

I had an awkward thought. The last time by, Hal had not only seen me drive by twice, but had written down some of my license plate. A suspicious person might have concluded that this information had been passed along to Zev and Zev had known more about me than the telephone company while he had been charming us all at the Rustic Inn with his tales of five kings. But who was a suspicious person?

I had walked through more than one factory door over the years but I hadn't realized what they had all had in common until I followed Zev inside. What they had all had in common was a smell—of what was being produced, of machine oil, maybe only of dust or of the sweaty workers. The air we entered, on the other hand, gave off nothing, absolutely nothing. We might as well have stepped into a vacuum.

"We were lucky to find this place," Zev said. "You usually have a choice between a facility in the middle of town where you get . . ."

"Snoopers?"

The fat man laughed, and on his feet, he was very much that more than the gregarious host from the night before. We had taken merely a few steps, and already his breathing was louder than it should have been. "Out here we have both the space and relative privacy."

His short arm swept over two rows of a score of computer operators seated in front of screens with the intensity of Atlantic City slots players; some wore headphones for musical accompaniment, all of them looked mesmerized by what they were pulling up, magnifying, miniaturizing, and turning everywhichway. The work stations were an island on a wide floor otherwise dominated by the canvas covers that had been thrown over Mochi's hulking machines. Two iron-railed walkways hung in the air—the first cutting the floor in half over the biggest canvas lumps and the second in the back leading to several office doors on an aerie level. "They tell me in his later years Mochi himself patrolled up there in his wheelchair," Zev said, following my eye to the nearer walkway. "Make sure nobody below was sleeping on the job. The offices in the back were for the accountants."

On cue, Leo emerged from the corner door on the far walkway and waddled toward a middle door and went inside. Leo looked to have many talents, but accountant wasn't among them. I really couldn't locate him and Hal in the great scheme of Pulsar things. If I had sought the privacy Zev claimed was so important, would I have had such conspicuous brutes around? All they did was advertise for suspicion. And to what end? A retired school guard who needed a few bucks to supplement his pension could have done Hal's job. And how many times had Leo been called upon to heft the ballot box from the *Reporter*?

I was so confused for answers I almost missed Zev's introduction of the skinny carrot top he wanted me to meet at the first computer. There was a bakery full of colorful pie charts on the guy's screen. "Ben's assignment is the ratings of city officials. Explain what you're up to, Ben."

Ben started talking just in time to head off Zev's labored breathing from working itself up to full-blown wheezing. "Well, as Mike has probably told you," he said with a giddy enthusiasm, "each theater of study is an ongoing data addition to the theaters we've already studied elsewhere in the country. Here, for example, we have the showings of the leading elected official in the towns Pulsar has already visited. With the daily tallying we get from New Florence, we can compare Mayor McCorkle's standing with his electorate *vis-a-vis* that of the other mayors and their equivalents."

"Why don't you just wait until you get the final number?"

Ben couldn't have been happier for the question; even Zev smiled at me as a dope. "That would seem like the easiest thing to do, wouldn't it? But if you do that, you miss the *in-moto* fluctuations."

"The what?"

Ben had to remind himself he was talking to an imbecile. "You get curious flows of votes sometimes," he said more slowly. "Let's say no one takes the survey too seriously at first. But then somebody in the mayor's office hears one conversation too many at the coffee shop about what Pulsar is doing, so he suggests that maybe the mayor should pay more attention to it. This can lead to an eleventh-hour roundup of the mayor's supporters who then begin flooding the newspaper with votes for him."

I wished Antonio Varela had been there. "Okay, they wake up late. But what does that tell you about anything?"

Ben hesitated, but Zev's nod gave him the permission to continue. "Keep in mind we're speaking only hypothetically here because that's not necessarily a trend we've detected in New Florence. But what it might be indicative of is an administration slow to have a sense of its electorate, that once elected, reacts rather than leads."

"Or it might mean they didn't take Pulsar seriously until some idiot aide thought of a new way to earn his salary."

Zev's booming laugh shorted Ben's look of rejection. "And that's why we move on to work station two," he said, taking my arm and leading me to a buxom blonde working at the next screen, this one filled with text. Her name was Belinda and her specialty was the second question on the ballot—the one about why the respondent admired his selection. If she had been surrounded by tourist posters, Belinda's exuberance might have been for the snorkeling and scuba diving to be had in the Bahamas. "This is really the fun question," she assured me in a semi-squeal, "because you can tell so much about the person answering it even in a few words. If they just say something like 'he's honest' or 'I agree with the things he says,' you can surmise they haven't spent too many hours on the question. They're like Garbo—they just want to be left alone."

"And what does that tell you presidential elections don't?"

Belinda laughed heartily for herself, Zev, and everybody else on the eastern seaboard. "Not much when you think about it," she said. "But they *did* fill out the ballot and they had no Constitutional sense of obligation to do so. Maybe they're people extremely reserved with opinions in social situations but who still take every discreet opportunity to make those opinions known. And isn't that alone an interesting contradiction?"

"*Maybe* they are?"

Zev had recovered enough breath to step forward. "None of us take an oath to turn off our speculations when we come to work for Pulsar, Paul," he smiled. "If I were Belinda and I had to stare at this screen all day, I'd write a science-fiction novel every hour."

"And you could, too!" Belinda gushed.

Zev had learned to take his staff's compliments in stride, but he made a show of discomfort for his guest. "The primary point is that the motivation cited by the respondent says as much about his values as those he wants to believe are personified by the individual he's chosen. Ergo, that tells us about him even as he's telling us about his hero."

"That much I get."

Belinda looked happy for me, but Zev seemed disappointed I had grasped the idea. "So your question . . ."

"Why is any of it what you people call hard data? All I'm hearing is a lot of speculation and guesswork wrapped up in the obvious. Right?"

There was more of an edge in Zev's chuckle, but he had to admit I was smiling and trying to be polite. Or not. "Well, it's a good thing we don't depend on you for funding, Paul."

"I'm just trying to understand."

With Belinda's anxious eyes on him, he didn't have all that much room to doubt me. "What Belinda's analysis does," he said evenly, "is plug into Ben's hypothesis about the standing of civic leaders. What exactly is the flow of communication between the town and officials? Do people get elected because they're viewed as the same as the voter or different from him? Because they are seen as reflecting a voter's principles or because they've become a habit for lazy people? All these researchers behind you are deconstructing another aspect of that question. You can't take any of the conclusions we reach about individual questions separately. They're useful only insofar as they contribute to the whole."

"Like those kids with the shining eyes."

He looked as baffled as Belinda. "Kids?"

"The old movie, *Village of the Damned*. The kids have to feed into one another to get a really good explosion in some enemy's brain."

Belinda tittered, but Zev didn't. It felt like the moment to get away from questioning Pulsar's right to existence. Besides, there were other diversions. "Sounds like a lot of focus on the mayor. Does anybody else have a chance to come out on top?"

Belinda started to clarify, but Zev cut her off crisply. "Don't get the wrong impression. You just happened to drop in on us when we were dealing with elected officials. Everyone who receives a vote is profiled in comparison to others occupying a similar standing in other communities. If you'd come by yesterday afternoon, for instance, you would have seen Belinda and everyone else analyzing the local impact of a religious leader like the Reverend Dvorak. Sorry, but you're stuck with the politicos."

Belinda went back to her happy laughter as Zev reached for my arm to lead me on to the next computer. The nail in my chest said that, physically pushed as he was, he intended walking me down the entire gauntlet. As an overkill tactic, it ranked up there with the Professor collapsing in the library. "But what about the actual vote tallying?" I asked, as the young Japanese in the third seat turned around to greet me. "That's what everybody outside Pulsar is really interested in, isn't it?"

Zev dropped his hand from my arm and the Japanese tried to put a friendly face on being ignored. "And what?" Zev grinned. "We should tell you the count so you can have a scoop for Jim Sewell?"

"Not that so much . . ."

"The counting is still going on. Not even I know where things stand now. Pauline is very protective of her turf. All she'll tell me is that the response has been tremendous both at the *Reporter* and the post office. I'm waiting like everyone else for her to feed final data to our programs."

His eye drifted up toward the office doors on the second walkway, and I obeyed his lead. I tried picturing Leo in the room he had entered working a calculator to assign one vote to McCorkle, one to Labine, and one to the supermarket checkout guy. I couldn't manage it. "But if I wanted to place a bet on the winner, you could tell me when I'd be wasting my money, right?"

We all laughed, including the Japanese I hadn't yet met and Belinda from somewhere behind Zev's girth. It wasn't the most useless crack I had ever made. If I hadn't made it, I might not have noticed that in the upper left-hand corners of the two computers closest to me—the Japanese's and Belinda's—there was an identical screen title consisting of the plus and minus signs separated by an ampersand. I thought about asking why that name had been chosen for their program, but at bottom I really didn't care and I was already committed to enough of that kind of jabber with the Japanese taking his turn to explain what his graph lines meant. None of them seemed to forecast a faster way to the door.

CHAPTER 30

On my way back to town, I thought about calling a press conference to discuss my fact-finding mission to Pulsar. It would have saved me the bother of repeating myself with Karen, the Professor, Sewell, and anybody else who was interested and it would have saved the third or fourth listener a bored, clipped version of things. Then again, there wasn't all that much for a first listener to hear, either. I had been had and I knew I had been had—full stop. But not even that would have made for great listening since I didn't know exactly how. Had Zev, Ben, Belinda, and the rest of the happy elves just waited until my car had disappeared down the road, then gotten rid of their computer screens to go back to the donkey baseball game they had been using Mochi's plant for? All I was sure of was they couldn't have been serious about the gobbledygook they had laid on me.

Ugly dampness or not, I lowered my window completely. Big foul air felt cleaner than small foul air. Were they all in on it or were the Bens and Belindas too busy swooning over Zev to question what he had them doing? I couldn't guess, but either way it was another case of split pea soup. Once upon a time, my parents had lived across the street from a tatty grocery store that had sold nothing but withered lettuce and cans of Campbell's Split Pea Soup. There had been more of that soup on the shelves of that grocery than in the Campbell's factory, and the cans that hadn't been covered in thick dust had looked like they had been run over by a tank. As for the two guys who ran the place, they had looked offended every time somebody walked in the door for a to- mato. Did I think the store was a front for something, my parents' neighbor Mr. Burns had wondered one day. Duh! Yes, I had said to Mr. Burns. I didn't know if for gambling, prostitution, or coun- terfeiting, but a front it definitely was and, when all was said and done, not an especially subtle one. (It had been for gambling, as a police raid finally revealed.) The lettuce might have been a little fresher and the front men made more of an effort to act interested in customers, but other than that the Pulsar Institute was very much in the business of selling Campbell's Split Pea Soup.

Which made my first priority after leaving the factory easy. Brighton or no Brighton, Zev's three-card monte game had sup- plied all the irritation I needed to make a call about his funding. What made it doubly galling was that the charade had slipped so easily into my intentions to visit the premises even if I hadn't run into him at the Rustic Inn and gotten his personal invitation to drop by. When all was said and done, in fact, I didn't need Brighton, the Professor, or Karen turning a key on my back, I was the most advanced robot you could have—moving autonomously, no one-step-at-a-time directional commands required once the program had been installed.

Regardless of the fantasies of New Florence police captains about the vast networking resources of big city cops, I had one possible source of help and one only. Bobby Rosen had been with the federal prosecutor's office since the early 1990s, back when I had been with the Nassau Department. For reasons I had never fully understood, he had been mostly amused by my regular bang- ups with his office, the FBI, and the other Long Island badges that answered first to Washington. He had kept his smile even after the Bushies had started moving their people in to replace the Clintonites, but then the Homeland Security *uber*-badges had come along and it had become difficult even for Bobby Rosen to believe he still had a purpose getting up in the morning and going to the office. The last I had heard, more than a year ago, he had been stuck in some basement office alphabetizing cold case files.

In short, Bobby Rosen fell considerably shy of being the attorney-general. But he was all I had for getting some harder information on Pulsar.

I decided against making the call to Mineola from Karen's phone. I might have been right or I might have been wrong about Brighton's job anxieties; the overriding thing was I was beginning to feel my instincts were good only for being ignored. If I had been Hawkeye tracking game through the woods, I would have been trampled to death by a raccoon two days ago. The one public phone I remembered seeing was near Tebaldi's funeral home, so I stayed on Sloan Avenue until I reached it.

The phone was there and it worked. Odder still, I had no trouble ferreting out the number for Rosen's office or getting the operator to accept my credit card number. I was just about to declare an extra New Year's Eve when Rosen's drone came on. What had slipped my mind in my gratitude for thinking of him was his addiction to parsing every word he heard for puns and *double entendres*. It was a tic that attached a running meter to every conversation with him.

"Finley, Finley. I remember the name but not the birthday card."

"How's it going, Bobby?"

"I'm sure *it* is several lengths ahead of me by now. But you still have time to bet on me to place."

I knew I had to play for a bit, so I did. His affectation had been bad enough when he had been a senior investigator in major cases, but with little to do except find out if a suspected forger from 1976 was still alive, he had raised the third-ear small talk to Andean heights. New Florence? Why would anyone want to visit a place called New Florence before visiting Old Florence? Come to think of it, he had once made the opposite mistake by crossing the country to see Old Faithful only to realize belatedly that he had never seen New Faithful. Etcetera. Etcetera.

A woman dragging a month of groceries up the street started at the expression on my face. Her shopping cart prevented her from running up the block in fright, but she seemed to consider it, and that was sign enough to get to the point of my call. "Give me a second here, Bobby. There's something I've got to ask you."

The other thing I had forgotten about him: When he sensed he was going too far, he could stop on a dime. "Go ahead."

"The Pulsar Institute. Ring any bells?"

"Ring one."

I told him the nutshell version I remembered from one of Karen's printouts, then moved on to the New Florence operation. Rosen said nothing. I couldn't help thinking I was the first person in ages to ask him something besides the time.

"You sure they have any government backing at all?" he asked after I'd finished. "Could be a private thing. Or maybe one of these pseudo-churches. Those people are everywhere lately."

"No, there's all these allusions to public agencies. A corporation or a church would get a commercial in somewhere. No commercials."

"That you see."

"That I see."

He liked himself for that correction, and fell silent again. When he came back a moment later, he had the Internet with him. "Busy little bees," he murmured. "Buzzing all over the country, looks like. What do you have as a common denominator to all these places?"

"I don't," I had to admit. "They're small towns, but even the poll question is different in each case."

"Not always. I see another Most Admired Citizen here, two . . ."

"Okay, Bobby. I didn't look that far."

"I know this one in Nebraska. Spent a week there one afternoon."

"They stopped telling that one before vaudeville died."

"Don't let the folks in Fleming, Nebraska know it. They probably still go to vaudeville. They sure as hell don't have a local TV station."

"Okay, they have no TV station. But I need a little more."

"Client?"

If you left out the retainer part, I thought. "Yeah."

There was another silence, then: "What makes me think this is going to get complicated, Finley?"

"That'd be an answer in itself, wouldn't it?"

He whipped his sinuses together for what resembled a laugh. "And you'll throw my retirement party where?"

The sidewalk down the street was filling up with kids coming out of the school for their lunch break. A lot of them were heading toward me, toward a luncheonette up a couple of doors from the funeral home. "If you sense anything like that . . ."

"I know. That'll be an answer. What's your cell number?"

If New Florence hadn't been good for anything else, it had given me a break from that question. "I don't have a cell."

"Jesus Christ! You're a PI and you don't have a cell??!!"

"If it's that important, people will call back."

"Give me the prize, Finley. I must be the millionth customer you've used that answer with."

He was only a few hundred thousand off. "How about I call you back at this hour tomorrow?"

"No," he said more sharply. "How about you call your machine tomorrow and you'll hear whatever I have to say? You'll still be up there in Remodeled Florence, yes?"

I really didn't have to commit to staying in New Florence for that question; I could have always picked up his message from my apartment, too. But the picture that popped into my head was of reaching Riverdale with the Professor and banging the steering wheel in frustration that I had been in too much of a hurry to get back home. "Yeah, I should still be here."

"Talk to you."

If there was anything faster than fiber optics, it was Bobby Rosen disconnecting me. I didn't want to think it was because some boss had walked into his office.

The first ranks of the hamburger-and-fries brigade were trooping past on the way to the luncheonette. The girls still sprang along from their heels, the boys still hunched their shoulders like extras in some 1930s gangster movie. It was life-affirming to see that, tattoos and iPods aside, not all that much had changed since my days at Andrew Jackson High.

And that would have been the extent of that day's encounter with the teenage generation if one of the kids close to the building line hadn't made an exaggerated turn of his shoulders against the wind to light a cigarette. Except there was no wind and he didn't have a cigarette. What he did have was the face that had been in the front seat of the Audi behind me out at the cemetery.

Most people who had known me as a cop would have said I was pretty good at the job—maybe not Hall of Fame caliber, but an all-star more than once. What I had never excelled at, though, was reflexes, a flaw that almost proved fatal once. The neurons between my eyes and brain had always refused to rush their decisions, and that was all there was to it. Now again, I stood adding up one and one a few dozen times while the kid stretched out his distance down the block. It wasn't until he was walking tall again, faking interest in what the jocks next to him were saying and warning himself not to peek back over his shoulder, that it occurred to me why I wanted to talk to him. Russell Dvorak hadn't belted me, but somebody had, and there was no way the kid couldn't have seen who that had been.

I let him go. With so many kids around there was no way to corner him smoothly. I knew where I could find him anyway.

I toted that rationalization back to the car and watched him go into the luncheonette without once turning around. Dread or balls? I could have asked myself the same about not wanting to hear what he could tell me.

Then I got tired of just talking to myself.

CHAPTER 31

The luncheonette hadn't seen the memo about what eateries in New Florence were to be called; instead of merely Luncheonette, it had the name Barney's. It also had a real, living Barney in a big-shouldered, sad-faced guy in a black peak cap who was spending his golden years sitting in a raised wheelchair behind a register next to the entrance. The door seemed to have been measured to the inch for not swatting him in the face whenever a customer came in or went out. Barney had never learned to trust the measurement: Every time a customer passed through without leaving behind more than a breeze, he instinctively grabbed at the arms of his chair and shook his head at the close call. Given the bags under his eyes and the gray hair matted over his ears, I figured he had been doing that for 182 years.

Maybe he preferred it to the arena atmosphere of his booths. The animal house made me feel guilty. It was so much like the Silver Diner down from Andrew Jackson High at lunch hour that I knew my friends and I had frozen civilization where we had found it. The years since then had only been ageing. Why just pick up a catsup squeezer for a burger when it could do double duty for squirting a trash mouth? If you were going to slide into a booth next to Janet with the big rack and the blonde pigtails, why not keep nudging her further and further into the corner so at least an elbow could get a cheap feel? And if none of that had your name on it, there was always shouting across booths to rip the asshole home room teacher, ask if the asshole English teacher had sobered up in time for class, or ask if somebody had the asshole biology teacher's notes from the last class. How could anyone not feel sentimental about the halcyon years?

One way was to be down to a sip from finishing my coffee and not really wanting to order a second, not with all the promise that held for inflating the dull knot in my head into a full-fledged head-ache. But what choice did I have with Audi Boy refusing to get up and go into the bathroom? I would have settled for one of the two jocks with him to leave for a few minutes to give me some booth room, but nobody at all was stirring. All three of them had gone through jumbo sodas that would have forced the Professor to rent a urinal by the minute, but they were young, the future of the na-tion, and clearly unimpaired in the bladder category. And that was without counting the greasy stuff they had been shoving into their mouths in between snickers and guffaws and all those other de-pressing teenage sounds. I told myself to keep confident Audi Boy would overcome his present phase. Gaunt and loose-limbed as he was, I could see him one day running for president or heading an automobile distributorship, whichever paid more. Just as long as he did something about the crooked smile thing on his lips that might have its appeal for the girls in the booth behind him but that otherwise threatened to stick with him like a scar. I wished him well in all his pursuits—starting with a run to the john.

Trust in what the Greek plays the Professor had given me for my last birthday called a *deus ex machina.* The mousy counter-woman didn't appreciate my taking up a stool at lunch hour for only a coffee, but she had been tolerating me because I wasn't still breaking in my voice and asking how much she'd had lately. Then she went one better by calling out from the middle of the counter if I wanted a refill. As soon as I nodded and she headed down toward me with the carafe, Audi Boy stopped pretending not to see me at the counter and slumped back in his booth seat with a despondent exhale. His bad news was I wasn't running out before I had talked to him. The fact that he didn't say anything to his companions, wanted to keep me his little secret, seemed to rule them out as the backseat passengers who had shared his cemetery adventure.

Being as upbeat as I was, I was down to counting the seconds when he would give up and either go into the back or come directly over to me for the conversation he didn't want to have. I could see that kind of moral fiber in him even across the luncheonette: a realist. I was so sure of his imminent move that I considered taking off my jacket and draping it over the empty stool next to me as a reservation claim. But then Barney spoiled everything by clutching his chair arms again and letting Dwayne Arlett saunter in like a sheriff monitoring a saloon on his nightly rounds.

The uniform had little effect on the general noise, but it did too much for Audi Boy and me. The kid couldn't drop his eyes to his fries fast enough, and the red streaks running up to his sideburns weren't because of some dirty joke one of the jocks was telling. I told myself I was doing him a favor by not continuing to stare over at him, but then I always told myself a lot of crap. For sure, Arlett wasn't buying it.

"Hey, Mr. Finley! Get your car okay?"

Arlett was smiling, I was smiling, the guy down at Impound was probably still smiling to get rid of my wreck. "No problem."

"Good, good. Sometimes those guys can get cranky."

I considered asking him what had happened to his eyebrows, but thought that might get complicated. "No cranky."

"Great. Enjoy your lunch."

Everything was payback: That was the same line I had gotten into the habit of thinking was droll in another life when I had spotted a bum named Dutch working on his pint of plunk around Valley Stream.

Except Arlett had interest in mind. "Listen up, everybody!"

He tucked his thumbs into his belt and spread his legs with more authority as one pocket of the place after another fell quiet and turned toward the door. Barney frowned and the counterman and my waitress looked annoyed, but I knew they didn't count. Audi Boy knew it, too: He started making designs with the fries on his plate.

"As you know, we had an incident at the Randy Page burial yesterday. A lot of people got hurt, others got arrested. Some of those who got arrested may not have deserved it, but we can only go by what people tell us. Now if any of you or any of your friends witnessed something you think would be material to our investigation, I would really urge you to come down to the police station after school today and tell us what you know. The smallest thing might be helpful. Let us figure out how. It goes without saying that anything you tell us will be held in the strictest of confidence. I thank you all for your attention. Have a great lunch and a great afternoon in school."

I was a second or two behind, but when Arlett paused to wink at me on his way out, I knew I should have expected it. The New Florence Police Department wasn't going to leave any stone unturned in finding out who had really whacked Paul Finley, visitor from New York. Least of all were they going to leave undisturbed the stones the visitor from New York himself was about to upturn.

The Audi Boy stared across the luncheonette at me. Now he was so scared he didn't show the least bit of fright.

I was mad. I hadn't needn't the refill at all.

CHAPTER 32

"You were the one in such a hurry to get out of here!"

"When did I say that?"

"Okay, I'm hard of hearing, too."

I hadn't intended exciting the old man. As unshaven as a cactus and wrapped in a frayed blue robe in the hospital room chair, he looked like he wouldn't have made it back to the bed on his own power. But now that he had found space to be contrary, he was going to occupy it without mercy. "Well, whatever you thought, I've changed my mind," I said, lowering the volume and hoping he would follow my lead. "You look like you could use another 24 hours here."

"Back to your medical degree."

"Okay. There's also something I have to look into."

I caught the glint in his eye, but he was interested in more than an I-told-you-so. "So look into it. I can take the bus home."

The bluff wasn't the point; why he felt the need to stage his little drama, that's what I wanted to know. "You were the one who asked me to nose around, remember? There was even talk of a retainer."

He dropped his glance back down to the crossword puzzle book in his lap. It was one of those books for novices in which every answer was B A T, but he eyed it warily, as if it had already proven too much for him. "And you were so gracious saying yes."

"I think I was just trying to point out a couple of realities."

"And now you've discovered new ones?"

"Like you said before, there's nothing I have to run back to. And there'd be a little something empty about getting out of here without knowing who clocked me."

"Right. You always finish what you start." So I was being a hypocrite. So I would have liked another night with Karen. If I hadn't been that hypocrite, I wouldn't have seen the phone on the bed table for anything but a phone. But what it actually was, I realized, was the reason for the latest big turn. "Karen call this morning?"

"She was nice enough to do that, yes. I told her what I told you: I'm feeling much better and Mendler says I can leave when I want. Besides, it isn't right we keep imposing on her."

The satisfaction and the sulking made for an odd cocktail, but I knew it was called sex. "You know, Joe, I can go into any bar these days and they don't card me. Same with Karen."

"Good for you."

"And here's another flash: It has nothing to do with you."

He wanted to raise his head from the pencil, but decided that would be giving me too much. "If I knew what you were talking about, maybe I'd be able to contribute something to the conversation. What do they call those damn lizards they're always asking about in these things?"

It sneaked up on me, but I *did* want him contributing something. Just how many snide airs was an outsider entitled to? I hadn't made it work with New Florence and he shouldn't have been able to make it work with me. I felt like I was picking up a plunger and pushing it into a toilet, but I knew I had to do it. He started to object, then dropped his head back on his chest and gazed at the blank boxes on his lap. I knew exactly where to start—with the word *again*, back when I had been sure his complex about Karen had really been about Jennifer. Once I had latched on to that, the rest came easy. The *again* hadn't involved Jennifer at all, it had always been about Karen—first with Antonacci, now with me. And all the time he had been stroking his chin sagely to see how we would respond to his stimuli. But then Karen had called and spoiled everything. She was more alive and younger than an old man with a heart condition in a hospital. She had hinted at too much, maybe if only in the tone of her voice, and he had been thrown back to Antonacci and that glorious fiasco of an experiment.

He said nothing for a moment, then laughed; humorlessly. "Like I should care what you two do?"

"If I was in a good mood, I'd say sure, you don't want me to end up like Antonacci. But I'm not in a good mood."

I didn't know anymore what he respected and what he didn't. I had probably deluded myself I ever had. "You feel used? You wanted me to ask permission for something."

"You're not listening, Joe."

"Sure, I am. You just don't know what you're saying." He had enough strength to lean forward and toss the puzzle book and pencil on the bed. He smiled in self-congratulation as he sat back again. The puzzle book was on the bed, but he was still back to the safety of words. Nobody had ever beaten Joe Carroll on that turf. "Think I'm that decrepit? If I'd gotten through that little talk the other night, I was going to look into this Pulsar thing myself. You don't set up that kind of operation for so long without running into a hundred people I could call for information. Universities. Associations. Institutions."

It was a fact, and an irksome one; he had far more Bobby Rosens tucked into some address book than I did. But he had also fixed it so that I was the one who had to call Bobby Rosen. "Too bad you bowed out at the critical juncture and I'm the one who had to ask for the favor."

He came alert. "Yeah? Who?"

"What difference does it make?"

He shook his head, but the alarm lingered in his eyes. "That might not have been wise. This clout on the head you got . . ."

"Because I was getting close to something? The only thing I was close to was the second limo in the funeral procession."

"Probably," he said, frowning into the light from the window.

I knew what he was doing: Putting Finley back in the box marked Finley Investigations. It was more spacious than the one with Karen Noon and his fantasies about her. And that was okay with me. You could feel self-righteous only so long comparing dicks with 75-year-old men. "What?"

"Nothing."

"Which nothing?"

He shrugged. "Just a thought."

The old bastard couldn't see anything outside but a dirty sliver of gray cloud bringing more rain, but I knew he was back to sending me business. "And that thought's what?"

"I was just thinking about why you hit people. The most obvious reason is to discourage them from whatever they're doing."

"Yeah?"

He looked back at me with more taunt than alarm in his fish eyes. "But every so often, when somebody gets hit, he gets *encouraged*. Sometimes that's the whole purpose of it."

"What are you raving about?"

"The converted Finley, what else?" he smiled too knowingly. "Sure seems to have worked in your case."

"I don't know what the hell you're talking about."

I didn't listen to whatever he answered. He had been too removed from things for 48 hours to give me the confirmation I needed. He hadn't even met Brighton or Dwayne Arlett.

"You don't look as mystified as you should, son-in-law."

I tried concentrating on the cloud he had found so mesmerizing. I told myself I should feel ahead of the game just not hearing him repeat his threat to check himself out and take a bus back to New York. Besides, I felt owned enough without throwing in the son-in-law thing.

CHAPTER 33

Give this to my instincts: They hadn't been *completely* dulled since we had sailed into New Florence. About John Mendler, M.D., for instance, they had been right from our first meeting in the hospital corridor. I really couldn't see the two of us ever kicking back over a few brews and swapping yarns about great Buffalo Bills touchdowns. Okay, he wasn't the only heart specialist with an ego bigger than his savings account. And unlike some of the prizes I'd dealt with in malpractice cases, he had been scrupulous enough to focus his vanity on his patient, making sure the Professor couldn't taint his reputation because of a hasty diagnosis here or a wrong incision there. Maybe he even liked Shredded Wheat as much as I did. But all that on the plus side, he was still a prick, and nothing out of his mouth could have brightened my day. He was the last person I wanted to see while I was waiting for the elevator after leaving the Professor's room.

"Have a minute, Mr. Finley?"

The old man had looked weak and haggard, and Mendler was too polite by half. I suddenly had a hot flash that all the jabber about checking out had been a decoy. "I just saw him," I said, keeping the evil eye away by getting in first. "He's a little rocky."

He seemed to need a second to recall what patient I was talking about. "Oh, that's nothing unusual," he finally shrugged, flapping his white coat from inside the pockets. "He's had a major procedure and he's not a young man. You mind? There's someone I'd like you to meet."

So much for Joe Carroll and his new heart balloon on Mendler's list of urgent concerns. I could have choked the fuck even as I was exhaling. He was already heading back around the corridor bend from where he had appeared, assuming I would be trailing after him. Why not? I was running out of pout ammunition, and most of the day still lay ahead of me. But I had expected a sexier destination than the nurse's station. How could anyone discuss something interesting with patients scraping by on walkers and visitors wandering around matching room numbers to scraps of paper in their hands? There was even somebody hanging over the station desk ready to eavesdrop.

But not exactly. The eavesdropper in waiting was Russell Dvorak, Sr., the radio preacher, and Mendler introduced us holding his nose. I was about to start feeling a fraction of a percent better about the egomaniac when he patted Dvorak on the shoulder as he passed behind him to say something to one of the nurses. It was *my* half of the introduction the bastard considered an unpleasant obligation!

It took a hot spasm or two to concentrate on Dvorak. He was a dwarfish man pushing 70 who had more bushels of orange hair on his head than anyone his age should have had and made me think of my children's book drawing of Rumpelstiltskin. He also had a nose like an eagle's beak and tight, rheumy eyes that seemed to picture everyone as field mice about to become prey. I didn't see much of Russell Dvorak, Jr. in him, and that was probably too bad for Junior. I felt like diving for my hole in the barn when he extended his bony hand. "I am sure you have heard my name," he said in a whine that would have left him third behind both George Oswald and Bob Nelson for the Cyclones job. "Certainly, you know my son's."

Having done his distasteful duty, Mendler was full of muttered orders for the nurse who looked like she had learned her trade at Attica. A second woman with a bad auburn dye over her black roots just stared up at me and Dvorak as an unscheduled entertainment on her shift. It was such a wholesome group I wondered if I had stumbled into an impromptu meeting of the New Florence Society. I was also tempted to skip the part about telling Brighton Dvorak Junior had to be released. But I couldn't do it. Fathers were still fathers and even one like Dvorak deserved better than the front-page photo on the *Reporter* stuffed into his raincoat pocket. "Your son wasn't the one who assaulted me. I told the police that this morning."

The floor fell silent all the way down to a TV soap commercial at the far end of the hall. Mendler interrupted his whispering with the warden to give me the first look of surprise I'd earned from him. The warden studied me with new curiosity. The nurse who had expected to be entertained frowned at me for being a spoilsport. And Russell Senior came close to looking human. He found it hard to believe I could be trusted more than the paper in his pocket. "You're telling me the truth?"

"Call Captain Brighton if you want. Okay, guys? Can I go now?"

The Reverend recovered first—like Charles Bronson deciding not to blow away another crack dealer in the alley. "Then I have no quarrel with you, Mr. Finley. The millipedes of the soul are to be found elsewhere."

He meant it, so I did, too. "Maybe next time Russell will go after the millipedes instead of trying to stop parents from burying their son."

Dvorak's recovery was complete; he got back to flexing his talons. "You speak as a parent, Mr. Finley? If you don't, your observation is without value. If yes, I worry about the moral direction of your children."

The last time I had belted someone, he had been twice if not three times the size of Dvorak, it had cost me a bad knee for the rest of the day, and it had led to fur-collared Furies chasing around Brooklyn after me. Only Rumpelstiltskin's size seemed like an argument for not giving the nurses someone to work on. But then Mendler finally found his voice. "Let it go, Russ. The main thing is they'll drop the accusation against Russell."

I didn't know why *Russ* had to be the one to let anything go, but I also felt the moment pass. I went back to the elevators wondering if Mendler had stuck some New Florence Society literature inside the Professor's stent. I liked the idea. It consolidated my attitude toward Mendler and would have infuriated the old man.

"John says you're a private investigator."

I noticed what I hadn't back at the nurse's station: For somebody so committed to the straight, the narrow, and the even narrower than that, Dvorak dressed like a bum. The collar edges of his black raincoat looked turned up not because of haste getting out of the house that morning but because they had taken on that shape after being neglected a long time. The blue work shirt under the coat looked clean, but also frayed enough for the white cotton to peek out from the collar. But best of all were the sneakers that had let him creep up on me at the elevator: Old-fashioned Keds with sloppily tied laces that were as black as the shoes themselves. "I guess we all have a calling, Reverend."

"Being disrespectful isn't a very inspired one," he shot back. "Are you planning on being here awhile?"

"Why? Want to hire me?"

He didn't laugh; he probably hadn't since he had been born the first time, but he was still supposed to have laughed. "You strike me as an honest man, Mr. Finley," he said instead. "That's not much in the present state of the world, but it's better than nothing."

"We do what we can do."

"Not always."

I had a picture of Junior bringing a report card home to Senior and being grounded for three years. "You really should have this conversation with your medical buddy back there."

The elevator did its part by opening its door, but Dvorak came right in with me. "John Mendler happens to be one of the few people in New Florence who doesn't shop for his morals in a department store."

"Then Labine's should be doing more business."

"Excuse me?"

"Never mind. What do you want, Reverend?"

For once the hospital lobby looked like a hospital lobby. There were real people around—two receptionists, a maintenance man vacuuming the carpet, some visitors taking a minute before facing the wrecks upstairs and others getting over the wrecks they had just seen. There were even a couple of kids skidding on the patch of floor not covered by the carpet and delighted with their scuffmarks. Best of all, no Muzak! "What every one of these people wants," he said, lowering his voice but dogging me to the glass door entrance. "Health for themselves, their loved ones, and their neighbors."

"Who can say no?"

He swung around to stand between me and the electric eye working the door, defying me to walk through him. The smell of brimstone grew sharper. "But there's health and there's health, Mr. Finley. And the fact is, there's an evil in this town. And I think you know what it is. You seem to have toppled into its company the last couple of days."

Even showing nothing showed him too much. Was he talking about Karen, the Siren who had brought his son down? I couldn't believe it. Not even Neanderthals like him said those things.

"You shouldn't let them flatter you so easily, Mr. Finley."

I got my wind back. At least he was talking about Pulsar, and that immediately opened two possibilities. The first was that one of the crows I had spotted overhead going back and forth out to the Mochi annex had been a secret member of the New Florence Society; there certainly hadn't been any tailing traffic on Sloan Avenue. The second was the Rustic Inn. Did one of the waiters donate his tips to Dvorak? "You following me around the tourist sights, Reverend?"

"It's a small town," he said placidly.

"You mean this was Paradise before Pulsar arrived?"

He finally found something funny. "At least we agree on what evil I'm referring to," he smiled grimly. "And no, they aren't the only problem we have. But they have become an overt part of it with their bogus science and their plebiscite passions. The tawdry is always tantalizing, especially to those with a weakness for it."

I saw my rescue in a Chinese string bean who finished locking up his car and started for the entrance. But then, instead of coming all the way up to trigger the door, he stopped to finish off the cigarette he had going. "Sounds like a sermon your listeners will like. Have to go now. Nice meeting you."

He didn't budge. "I know what they're after, Mr. Finley," he said, studying me for a reaction. "And I think your . . . friend Miss Noon does, too. She may not know she knows, but she does."

Two years before Jennifer's accident, I'd had another bad patch on Major Cases. For months my ready answer to everything on the job had been to push, punch, and pummel. I hadn't actually *done* it most of the time, but the impulse had been there almost daily. Like it had been lately.

"I really think you should move, Dvorak."

He might have been wrapped up inside his zealotry, but he also cared about his radio public. A peek at the people sitting behind us told him to back down a little. "Instead of being wined and dined by these charlatans," he said, standing aside, "you might ask your friend about that poll that brought so much tragic remorse to her husband. The obvious can sometimes be too obvious for us to see it."

"Deep."

I almost got the Chinese guy's cigarette butt in my face for hurrying through the door so fast. I didn't know why I was in such a rush. I was just running from aggravation to aggravation. Just when I had needed a cheap shot against Dvorak, my mind had gone blank. What French staircase was going to explain that to me? I was feeling frustrated enough to cross the entire length of the parking lot to the squad car in the far corner to ask Dwayne Arlett if he had any *bon mot* to suggest.

CHAPTER 34

I drove to the library slowly enough to keep Arlett fully in my rear-view mirror. You had to respect a show-me tail for what it was. I certainly didn't want to be responsible for the ever-solicitous Dwayne having to go back to Brighton and admit he had lost me between two fire hydrants. That wasn't likely to get him another ribbon of honor.

Why Brighton felt it necessary to flaunt the flag was another matter. Barney's luncheonette might have been because Arlett had been keeping an eye on Audi Boy rather than on me and I had just stumbled into his radar. But not the hospital. And why hadn't there been any sign of my browless friend during the ride out to Pulsar? Because the nervous Captain Brighton already had that covered in some way I had missed? It was a puzzlement, as the King of Siam had once said.

Karen and I missed each other between the library and the hospital. I went to give her the answer to the question she had asked dropping me off, but she had already gotten it inside the Professor's request for some books on local history. I doubted that was how she wanted to get it, and not only because she had to run a mercy errand.

Veronica gave me one of her jaded aunt looks when I said I would wait for the head librarian to come back. She seemed on the verge of further instruction on social behavior when her phone rang. That left me alone with a platoon of old timers reading magazines, the doofus Dobson doing as much dropping as reshelving, and Arlett presumably waiting outside to report on what Harlequin romances I checked out. It also left me back with Rumpelstiltskin and his two homily themes—Karen knew more than she realized about Pulsar and all that stuff about what was supposedly too obvious to notice. Why credit any of it? The answer sprang to mind far too readily: *Because aside from Karen, Dvorak was the only one who didn't seem to worry about stepping on official toes in saying what he believed.*

And there was something else: He had been 2-for-2 in pressing my buttons. Karen and I had been flying over a lot of white space on Pulsar and Antonacci and I had been warming to not filling it in. Why spoil a good time by acting like a private investigator? And the obviousness thing, that clicked into items I had been lazily writing off as oversights, idiocies, or curiosities from a parallel universe. The Lockman crime scene, for example. How louder could the killer have been about trumpeting his handiwork? The garage door high enough for passersby to see the kid hanging. The expert job on the rope knot. And then there was what Sewell had said about the butts and the roach in the parking lot after Page had been run over. Coincidence? Any philosopher, including a private detective, who believed in that much coincidence had a Burger King counter job in his future.

Dobson dropped another book; worse than dropped it, caught it between his stomach and the shelf so that he managed to wrinkle a wad of pages before he had control of it again. Veronica had said the kid was a spazz so that was the way I had looked at him both times I had seen him. Because of Karen, I'd had the same low thoughts about Brighton the night of the Lockman killing. Veronica and Karen might have been right and they might have been wrong, but the bottom line was that, as an outsider, I had been leaning more than usual on second party opinions about third parties. That too was a good way of one day having to ask customers if they wanted fries on the side.

The library had three computers for public use. A woman in a 1940s-type turban was using one for looking at photographs of the Grand Canyon and a hunchbacked skeleton with more years on him than the Grand Canyon was using the second one for what looked to be results from European soccer games. I logged on to the third one and, after a glance up at the desk to make sure Karen wasn't striding back in, typed in Andy Antonacci's name. The uneasiness of being a sneak slowed Google down to the speed of my Model T Compaq at home. But the thrills couldn't be denied forever: As Veronica had already discovered, there turned out to be quite a few Andrew Antonacci entries. The first three were about his suicide, and they stole from one another in referring to the Pulsar poll and the reporter who had dug out the incriminating letters, memos, and other papers that Andy, apparently not the brightest bulb in Hoboken's harbor lights, had kept laying around. Malfeasance in office, bribery, mob associations—it was a happy sprint through some of the penal code's greatest hits. It also added up to nothing the Professor and Karen hadn't already told me. What had I been hoping for? A personal appearance by Zev at the funeral?

After the suicide accounts came earlier items about Antonacci as a politician—positive stories when he had opened a homeless shelter, negative stories when he had been named in an extortion investigation into his father, more positive stories about leading a campaign to have Hoboken build a memorial to three firemen, more negative stories about how he had a bad habit of fueling himself as much as his car before hitting Jersey's highway system, so-what stories about endorsing this mayor and that gubernatorial candidate. Two of the stories were accompanied by the same photo of Antonacci looking like a high school senior slicked up for his prom. He didn't look like me in the least.

And so?

I sat back to take in the Grand Canyon on the screen next door. I'd had similar feelings of profound achievement going through Karen's printouts on Pulsar and the *Planning Society* issues Lockman had been researching. What had been obvious about any of that?

The rickety hunchback grunted for the benefit of the whole library and snapped off his screen. The Grand Canyon lady wasn't amused. The old guy went off so disgusted you would have thought he hadn't covered the spread on Real Madrid. The mind wandered. Was there some place in New Florence where I could have put down a bet on a Spanish soccer team? Maybe I should have gone outside and asked Arlett. The redhead at the coffee bar? She certainly had the personality of a bookie. What about my cabbie friend Antonio Varela? He couldn't have negotiated *that* many fixed rates every week. Or maybe there was a shop-pe on some side street I had missed that specialized in European sports gambling. Every town had places like that. Every town had its Labine's, its libraries, its Rustic Inns, its police stations, its newspapers . . . Willy nilly, by decree or by custom, every town had its *plan*! Sometimes the patterns were even worth studying in a periodical like *Planning Society*!

There was a minority movement in my brain to give in to giddiness. I thought that was premature and told it so. Just because the dentist slapped a mask over your mouth and opened his gas tank didn't mean you were going to be happy. Besides, why alert Arlett to movement in my brain? He might have charged in to slap the cuffs on. I scribbled some words in my notebook to stop from looking over at the microfilm machines; they were marvelously undecipherable even to me. I felt more professional about myself looking up again at the microfilm machines. More than merely obvious, they were jeering at me in their obviousness. They were hiding in plain sight. And behind them were the *Planning Society* issues Karen and I had scanned. They were hiding in plain sight, too, because Lockman hadn't been digging into them to find specific references to Pulsar, but to get a better idea of what territory a magazine called *Planning Society* covered. Why scratch after depth when visibility said it all?

How did I know? I could have come up with tons of reasons with a few months thought, but they would have all come back to Alan Lockman—eager but not terribly equipped Alan Lockman. I knew next to nothing about the kid, but the little I did—his motorcycle, his counting of the *Reporter* ballots, his reluctance to hand the envelope of ballots to Leo, his absolute snubbing of Shepherd—had been big, had been out there. He hadn't been a Rhodes scholar. He had been a dork not even up to the level of Ben and Belinda, hadn't had their training in sophisticated rationalizations and so probably would have ended up running the classifieds at the *Reporter* instead of working for a glib maestro like Zev. But unlike someone I could have named, he also would have taken one look at Zev's slot machines and let loose with a big *bullshit!* He had been a kid!

I had no excuse for even thinking of watering up. In my worst days I hadn't been Alan Lockman, so forget that unconscious identification stuff. I hadn't exchanged word one with the asshole. I couldn't remember a single person with a motorcycle I'd ever particularly liked. Cut out that sequence with Steve McQueen from *The Great Escape* and my life would have been richer if motorcycles had never been invented. But despite all that I had an overwhelming urge to shriek at the whim that had decided Alan Lockman had to go. *That* was what was obvious—the sense of monotonous caprice that infested everything in New Florence from its useless candle shop-pes to department stores that would have been more profitable as corner Mom and Pop outlets. Karen had been right about the ooze and Dvorak had been even more right about the obviousness—and that was before Brighton and Arlett had signed on with their show-me tail. Did Rumpelstiltskin realize he himself was a proof of what he had said with his creepy Jesus freak act? Why should he have? I hadn't. I might as well have been standing on 34th Street at the entrance of the Empire State Building and wondering what made it such a special skyscraper. If George Oswald had been doing the play-by-play, he would have reminded me that field position was everything and that I had been in the wrong one.

I looked at the clock over the circulation desk; it seemed more reliable than my watch. If Karen hadn't stopped off somewhere for lunch, she must have gotten trapped by one of the Professor's monologues. Either way, I wasn't in the mood to sit around looking at a hundred more angles of old rocks along the Colorado River.

CHAPTER 35

There was no sign of Arlett when I left the library, but I made up for it when I strolled into the Labine Building. With Sewell the praetorian guard had barely been on good behavior; with me it practically ordered a strip search. While the concierge type called upstairs and battled his suspicion that a terrorist had answered in the name of the *Reporter* switchboard, the two guys with the epaulets passed my driver's license back and forth as if touch would give away how phony it was. Meanwhile, the guard with the gun kept his eyes glued on my hands to make sure they didn't reach for the Uzi under my jacket. All four of them looked dejected when the voice on the phone said I could go up. One of the epaulets got a piece back by banging the elevator floor button for me, just in case I had explosives under my fingernails.

A few hours made a big difference at the *Reporter*. This time the people in the cubicles acted genuinely busy on their phones and computers; one guy was even losing his temper with somebody about "if there's been an official complaint or not." As the Professor had said, I hadn't noticed any of that energy in the finished paper, but maybe I was too jaded by the flamboyant con-men the *Daily News* revealed every day.

Father Sewell looked harassed, too. He threw me a why-you-now nod from behind his desk without interrupting a lecture to two of his acolytes. One of them, a spindly brunette with bangs and anxious eyes who had to be named Betty Lou, was holding a red-white-and-blue poster with the words COMMUNITY DAY

splashed across it in star-shaped lettering. The way she was holding it away from her body said she had been given the heavy
lifting by the beard next to her and didn't appreciate the assignment. "It's great, guys," Sewell said, sounding like he was review-
ing some movie he hadn't seen, "and sure, the more people who
look at it between now and Sunday, the better for us. But did you
bother checking the weather forecast? No, you didn't. But I did,
and plenty of rain is coming. Hang these posters today and they'll
be dishrags by Sunday. Then what?" The beard started to say
then what, but Sewell cut him off with a slice of his hand. "I know.
They can run off a thousand more of them. But who's going to pay
for that? You got some special Community Day budget nobody's
told me about? Believe me, Artie, everybody will have a chance
to see your work Sunday. But for now, I don't want these things
being hung. Saturday is time enough."

Artie and Betty Lou trooped out without further protest. I was
about to watch how long it would take her to slam the poster back
into the beard's gut, but Sewell let out a sigh directed at me. "I
know you're walking in here with solutions, not problems, right,
Paul?"

"What problems? I'm a tourist."

He didn't object to my taking a chair, but thought about it.
"What I'm secretly hoping—between you, me, and this stapler?
Labine finishes so low in the poll he's embarrassed and calls off
Community Day. Of course, you repeat that to anybody, I'll call
you a liar."

"Already cleared my memory of it."

"Good. So now you should be able to see who really walloped
you out at the cemetery."

There were two ways to answer. The first was to tell him my
suspicions about Arlett and precipitate a crisis between him and
his buddy Brighton. The second was to decide he wasn't truly
counting on getting a straight answer so I could feel all right about
moving on to the topic I had come to discuss. "Alan Lockman," I
said, not surprising myself.

I was right; he shrugged like a good sport. "I talked to Brighton a half-hour ago. Nothing new."

"Meaning nothing new in his *homicide* investigation?"

We had traveled a whole 40 seconds without his executive jumpiness; the 41st was the bitch. "I told you Brighton isn't a fool. They're just not ready to announce anything yet."

"You mean something that might make Mrs. Lockman feel marginally better about what happened."

"Why should they if they have nothing concrete? But are they buying a suicide tale? Hardly."

"I think you just said *why should they*. Funny, but I remember a lot of conversations where I was the one saying that and you were hell-bent on pointing out it was their responsibility to do it. Something about the public's right to know, wasn't it?"

He pressed the wattle between his fingers and searched the ceiling for spiders. I could imagine him measuring his throat and other things on a regular basis. "All right," he said, "I'll tell you what you have no business knowing. Maybe you'll stop thinking of me as a hack gone to seed."

"Did I say that?"

It was his turn to ignore facetiousness. "Frank Brighton is a very good cop. There're a lot of people who would like to see him police chief instead of the one we have."

"Lama, is it?"

"Anthony Lama. Thirty seconds with Tony and you know he cheated on his first-grade test to get into second grade. But he's loyal to people like the mayor and people like the mayor appreciate dolts more doltish than they are. They especially appreciate them when they don't have dark stains in their pasts. Like with under-aged girls."

"Brighton?"

He rolled back from his desk with the help of a knee, got up, and limped over to close the door. I didn't know if the new melancholy in his voice was for Brighton or for having to hobble around since his accident. "From what I've been told, something happened soon after he joined the Force. Got caught up in his new macho uniform or something. I don't have all the details, but Brighton was old enough to know better. Lama knows about it and McCorkle knows about it, and every time there's some stirring about maybe telling Tony it's time to retire, Brighton gets the message he should be satisfied with his corner office. Otherwise, who knows what tales could be warmed over?"

"Scrumptious. But what's that got to do with calling Lockman's killing what it is?"

"Didn't you hear me? Brighton's learned the hard way not to get ahead of himself. My bet? He'll put off as long as possible calling it murder so he can have the killer in hand when he makes the announcement."

"Great. Does he have a suspect?" He went over to the window with a shrug. It was another half-answer I was supposed to value as inside information. "So Mrs. Lockman's likely to celebrate New Year's Eve still thinking she may have some blame for raising a suicide."

"For Christ sake, Finley."

Some interrogators I've met over the years have been of the view that the more the subject squirmed, the more a direct assault was called for. I've always been of the opposite opinion, that the more the subject squirmed, the more he should be given the opportunity to appease an interrogator some other way. He didn't want to confess to mass murder? Back off and let him tell you how you could get your hands on good season tickets for the Rangers. He would be so grateful for the change of subject you would be set up at the Garden and he would be even more vulnerable when you doubled back to get what you really wanted to get from him. "Lockman struck me as a kind of secretive kid," I said. "Am I off base on that?"

Don't ever let anyone tell you relief can't be disguised as suspicion. He looked around at me lacking only the tiniest ingredient more to be glad I had come to keep him company. "Not the greatest mixer," he nodded tentatively. "That's why I made him the ballot keeper. When he wasn't talking about that damn bike of his, he didn't have much to say at all. I couldn't see him staying in the business very long."

It felt good to have at least one of my highs from the library shared by the real world. "So he didn't have close friends around here."

He was convinced he was smelling more than a change of topic, but as hard as he strained through his glasses he couldn't identify it. "I never noticed anybody, male or female. If the Great Counter in the Sky added it all up, I'd say he spent more time talking to me than anyone else."

"Really?"

"Don't look so surprised. Some people can learn things from me."

"But you mean just small talk?"

He nodded. "Yeah. Any excuse at all, really. I guess he missed having an old man. I heard more about his bike than anyone."

"And other things."

"I know that sound, Finley. There were no other things that stick out. Tell you the truth, it made me edgy sometimes. Like when you were here and I told him to give those ballots to Grue-some Leo. If I hadn't been here, I think he'd still be holding on to them. What can I tell you? I have my own kids. One family is enough."

"And there was nobody else around here he felt that way about."

"Nope. Sometimes after work the staff goes down to that bar where I ran into you the other day, but not Lockman. He always went home. Now you going to tell me where you're going with all this?"

I couldn't help picturing the microfilm machines again and, behind them, *Planning Society.* "A tourist's curiosity."

"Really," he said, returning to his chair. "And this tourist, what ideas has he come up with?"

"One more question first?"

"I get the feeling you're not going to come back to mine."

"The scuttlebutt, the gab around the water cooler, the bullshit down at the redhead's saloon—how much of it has been about what Pulsar might *really* be up to with its little questionnaire?"

"What're you talking about?"

"C'mon, Jimmy. I was out there today. I saw their setup. They've got enough hardware to blast a satellite into orbit. Zev himself admits this admirable citizen thing is just a pretext for some other mumbo-jumbo."

If I hadn't seen him panting over Shepherd, I might have thought he was offended for the Pulsar Institute. "What's the mystery? They have what you call their mumbo-jumbo objectives and we have ours. We get a few more sales and Community Day from it, they get their statistics. One day the votes that went for Margaret Despina will be a number on a chart in some academic quarterly establishing that the people in the Northeast believe more strongly than those in the Southwest that four is more than three. Our public education dollars at work!"

"Who the hell is Margaret . . .? Oh. The church lady?"

"You going to enlighten me?"

It was a stupid thing, granted. Any business having to do with the public—newspaper, restaurant, shoemaker—is going to have photos and plaques on the wall showing the boss with cops for being the best example of this or annual recipient of that. In a place as small as New Florence, there probably wasn't a hot dog stand that didn't have showoff crap of the owner shaking hands with Brighton or Lama for working together to bring the town law and order franks. But the photos behind the desk immortalizing Sewell with the two chief cops made me hold my tongue. I hadn't come up in the elevator distrusting him. He had never made a secret of his regular chats with Brighton. When all was said and done, what was there to distrust him about? But my ferret was warning me that if I said another word, I would get chomped in the gut.

"What else have I got to do waiting for the old man to be fit for the trip back?" I said, standing. "I play mind games. What-if games. I haven't been in a library so much since I was working up to ask Kathy Lewin to be my date at the junior hop."

He didn't believe me and I was supposed to know he didn't. My reward was his sly smile. "Looks like the same reason now."

Kathy Lewin had never given me the time of day, and she had worked after school in her father's bakery, not at the library, but he still seemed to have a point. "Don't be obnoxious."

He agreed not to be, then waited till I had my hand on his doorknob. "Brighton says you had a useful talk this morning."

"Glad he thought so."

"Don't abuse my reference. I told him you knew your way around the block. You might stagger and trip over the sidewalk a few times, alienate everyone you came across, but you'd eventually turn the corner."

"Oh, yeah? When did you tell him that?"

"I don't know. Is that important?"

"Probably not."

Probably not, I thought as I walked back through the newsroom. As long as I didn't want to know who had suggested to Brighton that having a loose cannon stick around town for an extra day or two might have its advantages for a cop living in a glass house.

CHAPTER 36

I wanted a bigger favor from Karen than books on local history. I not only needed an introduction to Alan Lockman's mother, I needed Karen to get me permission to invade the kid's bedroom for a few minutes. I had a hunch there might be more there than tallies of ballots Lockman had been keeping on his own; if Brighton had found the time to take me up on my wisdom, he would have already looked into that, anyway. More important, the bedroom had to be where the kid had kept his computer for communicating with all the people he apparently hadn't at the paper.

I created what I hoped was a pretty-please mood. I bought a good bottle of Pinot Grigio and slipped it into the refrigerator so it would be chilled perfectly when the lady of the house walked in the door from work. On the way to raising her wine glass to her lips, she could stop off to sample the wedge of taleggio and wheat thins I set out on the living room coffee table. I cleaned the breakfast plates off the kitchen table and took the garbage out. Just in case she wanted to hold an inspection, I even bagged the socks and underwear from the day before that I had left scattered over the guest room. How could anyone resist helping me out for such a teensy-weensy thing as an introduction to a neighbor? That minor business of having to learn indirectly from the Professor that we were sticking around for another day? She was hardly going to make a big deal out of that once she saw that the breakfast table had been cleared. Nobody was *that* small.

And she wasn't. When she came through the door, she could have been mistaken for cordial, especially when she saw the cheese. When she dropped her bag on the couch to focus on the mail she had picked up outside, she was clearly more aggravated by a bill in her hand than by me. When she tossed the mail on the couch and asked how I had spent the day, she was obviously too stressed by the thought she had left her bedroom window open all day to stick around to hear what I answered. So what if she took forever to get out of her heels and dress and come back out barefoot in jeans and a denim shirt? It wasn't as if the wine I had poured had been in danger of turning to vinegar waiting for her.

Right. She wasn't going to be small about my cavalier manners as guest, lover, and all the minefields in between, but she wasn't going to be a benevolent goddess about it, either. Then, just as I was accepting that as a judicious compromise and getting her endorsement of the wine and taleggio, she dropped down on the couch and made sure I wouldn't have to be entrusted with any more announcements. "Joe says he wants to go tomorrow," she said. "He asked if you could grab his stuff and drop by the hospital around eight. He wants to get an early start."

I gave it a big "oh" because that seemed to cover it. She thought so, too, because she nodded to some spirit of vengeance somewhere behind me, then said again how much she liked the wine. "I don't know why the hell he's in such a hurry," I grumbled for the record. "What's he got waiting for him back in Garden City?"

"Well, he's certainly not going to have the greatest memories of New Florence," she said airily, picking up her mail for a more thorough look. "In his place I'd want to get away, too."

It was as good an opening as any. "What he really feels miserable about is not helping you the way you hoped."

"That was stupid," she shrugged. "I don't know what I was hoping."

"To find out what Pulsar is up to."

There was the briefest flash of irritation, but then she put her feet up on the cushion in front of her to form a perfect palisade of toes and knees between me and what her face was showing.

"I think Veronica's right," she said from her side of the wall. "It's time for me to get on with my life."

Sergeant Bailey made one of his predictable entrances, but I didn't want him or his half-assed philosophies between us. *I* wanted to push and I wanted to push for *me*. So I told her about running into Dvorak at the hospital. She gave it a theatrical shiver, but without lowering her knees or taking her eyes away from Visa's latest invitations to happiness. Only with the punchline did she look up from the mail to acknowledge I might be saying something having to do with her. "*I might know something I don't know*—what does that mean?"

"The Reverend doesn't seem like the mystical type. So I was thinking he was referring to something evident, at least to people not close to what happened to Antonacci." It was the hard part, but what the hell? I had already taken out the garbage once on the day. "You said your husband got all those pats on the back. A luncheon or something."

"Yes."

"But there had to be plenty of people annoyed by that result."

"I told you. The more Andy thought about it . . ."

"Right, the arrogance thing. You said that. I'm talking about before, when the results were first announced."

"What about it?"

If I wasn't mistaken, the new grinding I heard was the drawbridge of a castle being pulled up while the guest slapped around in the moat. "He'd already been linked to unsavory episodes. There was an investigation of his father, for example. A drunk driving thing . . ."

"I don't know what you're getting at, Paul."

Paul wouldn't have minded being Casper so he wouldn't have had to answer to that chilly version of his name. "It's like the people who voted for him were asking for trouble."

I finally earned precedence over Citigroup. She grabbed the envelopes on her lap and tossed them to the far end of the couch. She dropped her feet back down under the coffee table and took me in with the forbearance she had strewn around the table at the Rustic Inn. "Maybe I'm just woozy after the library, but I'm not following you."

"Some people liked Antonacci, some people liked him less. He had those who supported him, but he'd never be taken for the people's choice. Fair?" Sliding her thumbs more comfortably into the belt loops of her jeans seemed as good as a yes. "So for him to come out on top of a poll like this, his supporters had to be organized and get those ballots in."

"You saying they stuffed the ballot box?"

Was I saying that? I didn't think so. Not even Antonio Varela believed that. "No. It was the same newspaper deal as the *Reporter*, right?"

"The Hoboken *Journal*."

"And the margin he won by?"

"Those aren't details I've really . . ."

"Okay, I'm sorry. What I'm trying to get at is whether the people who placed second and third, his political opponents, for example, whether they attacked the results. They couldn't have been too happy."

That much she was willing to remember. "No, they weren't. In fact, I'm pretty sure they opened a lot of doors for that reporter." She unclasped one thumb long enough to reach over for another sip of wine. "But so what? Andy didn't deny what came out. He couldn't. Facts were facts."

That was more philosophical than I could have been in her position. But then I hadn't gone to bed with the six thousand facets of the question every night for years. Sometimes the philosophical attitude came after the fatigue, not vice versa. "I understand all that. Just . . ."

"Just what, Paul?" she asked sharply, clattering her glass back down. "I don't know what all these questions are for. Maybe we should think about ordering in Chinese or a pizza or something."

I went for it before she jumped up in search of menus. "The most obvious thing about that poll, Karen, what I think Dvorak was getting at, is the simplest thing of all—*Antonacci should have never won it!*"

Maybe she didn't want Chinese or Italian that badly anyway, but I preferred thinking I had given her a perspective she hadn't considered even in her most miserable moments. What else could she have possibly been telling me by swaying her legs slowly back and forth and staring off at some spot in the middle of the living room? "People voted for him for the city council, for the assembly," she protested anyway. "He always had backers."

"The city council and the assembly aren't the same as the so-called most honest politician. How many of these loyal party machine people of his who voted for him for a public office might have felt free even to vote for themselves on something like this poll? The whole thing was anonymous, wasn't it? Just like up here? They wouldn't feel the same obligation to him as in a public election. And sure as hell, they knew he might have been a lot of things, but honest? They'd seen him in action."

That felt like the worst of it out; it wasn't since I still had to ask the favor for seeing Mrs. Lockman, but for a passing moment I felt a pressure lessen around my chest. "But you're suggesting they fixed the results," she said. "And why would they do that? They didn't know Andy. He didn't know them. That makes no sense at all, Paul."

No, it didn't. But it still felt closer to some wiggling truth than the idea of anonymous Hoboken *Journal* readers filling out their ballots for Honest Andy. Since I couldn't say anything more coherent to her in that area, though, I moved on to the favor I needed. I had the fleeting idea of being clever for the implication that getting into Alan Lockman's computer might also shed some light on a suicide in New Jersey. "I think someone put it into Lockman's head that Pulsar was doing something more ambitious than conducting a poll about admirable citizens," I plowed on. "Since that doesn't seem to have been anyone at the paper . . ."

To her credit she remained skeptical. "But you never talked to him! How do you know what he thought about what Pulsar was doing?"

"He was looking into a magazine he wouldn't normally look into."

"You're suddenly an expert on his reading habits?"

"Then you tell me. You knew him a little."

"No, I didn't."

"A little, I said. Was *Planning Society* what Alan Lockman would've picked up after the *Dirt Bike Monthly*?"

"I couldn't answer that."

"If you had to guess."

Even as she was conceding a shrug, it dawned on me I'd had this conversation before: back with Zev and his minions at Pulsar. Give or take a few million dollars in rental space, employees, and computers, it was the same random speculation. "So we go back to who put the bug in his ear about looking into *Planning Society*. Not anyone at the paper. Not his neighbor Ms. Noon. Maybe the bartender at the night clubs he patronized every night or the wild girls he went out with? I don't think so. Call me biased when it comes to introverted guys like Alan Lockman, but I'd bet his greatest relationships were with people he knew through his e-mails."

"That's an awfully long reach."

"I know people who've made longer ones."

That she didn't want to be reminded of, at least while I was still on probation with her. But I knew she was going to do what I asked, and as soon as I did, "long reach" seemed to be giving me the best of it. Why couldn't Lockman have been drawn to *Planning Society* by a David Letterman joke on TV or some remark by his mother over dinner? I had no idea why not and I wasn't going to spend seconds uselessly encouraging that kind of possibility. It seemed like enough of a waste of energy that she had to get up from the couch and tramp out to the kitchen for the telephone directory to get the number of someone only a couple of houses away.

CHAPTER 37

Although every floor and table lamp was turned on, the Lockman living room made my vision bleary. The bland showroom furniture and bare walls and table surfaces didn't help, and neither did the heavy hand that had sprayed around a sickly strawberry scent. But more than anything it was how all the lights seemed to operate weakly and independently of each other instead of blending into a single brightness. It was a model setting for easy-chair depression. TV set or no TV set, I couldn't imagine Alan Lockman playing much in the room as he was growing up. At least I hoped he hadn't.

I had seen Barbara Lockman before only from a distance, looking into her window from the front of her house the night of the hanging. Up close, her wide dark face and bun of raven hair were more Latina than Lockman, and the Indian-faced couple sitting stiffly with her, introduced as her brother and sister-in-law, might have flown up from Mexico City. Neither visitor had skipped a meal in ages and accented Barbara Lockman's lax thinness even more. If she hadn't eaten much since her son's death, she had missed less than most people. There was an austerity about her that spited her broad face and that had long preceded the mess out in the garage.

For the brother Martin , we were the locals who had done nothing to prevent his nephew's sorry end and who were now compounding matters by interrupting a family's moment of peace. Who could argue with him? But Barbara Lockman gave off none of that resentment. On the contrary, thanks to whatever Karen had said to her on the phone, she searched my face as some last hope for refuting what the town had come to believe about her son. "Karen says you're a policeman. From New York."

Karen got to the *former* part before I had to make the correction. Barbara Lockman nodded that she had already understood that but didn't think it made much difference. "What do you think you'll find on Alan's computer? Something that'll say what happened?"

"That's what they all say they're looking for," Martin piped up truculently from his perch on the hassock. "How long you going to let them keep going in and out of his room?"

Nine out of ten times and despite his impeccable English, I thought, Martin would have done his hissing in Spanish, courtesy be damned. But he was as exasperated about Alan's death as his sister and wanted me and Karen to underline that in our copybooks. The mother smiled wanly at me to say she understood, too. "Until we have an explanation that makes sense, Martin," she said, speaking deliberately to me and not turning back to the hassock, "I don't care how many go and come."

It fell to the sister-in-law to mutter something in Spanish, and Martin didn't like it. He jumped up from the hassock and went stomping out toward some wall in the hall to kick.

"My brother loved Alan very much," Barbara Lockman smiled apologetically. "He refuses to accept this idea of suicide."

I played back what Sewell had told me about Brighton's two-step political strategy of announcing murder only when he had the murderer in custody. I played it back, then threw out the tape. "The police know it isn't suicide, too, Mrs. Lockman. They're just being obtuse about admitting it. Won't look good on their resumes or something."

"You know this for a fact?"

As usual, I had gone too far. She grabbed me by both elbows for further confirmation of what amounted to the most miserable consolation prize anyone could ever give her. And even that little she wouldn't have had, I realized, if she called Brighton in the morning and heard him hide behind another non-committal answer. But then Karen came to my rescue. "Everybody has known it as a fact since it happened, Barbara," she said firmly. "Sometimes people get caught up in their self-importance and forget others are counting on them to be honest."

I parsed that observation all the way down the hall behind Barbara Lockman to Alan's room. Karen didn't like Brighton, I reasoned, so that was why she had rushed to get in her dig. Or Karen didn't like Finley for treating her as a one-night stand so that was why she wasn't going to pass up the opportunity to re-mind us all of the evils of self-importance. Then Barbara Lock-man opened the last door on the hall, reached in to snap on the light, and the sight of the bedroom shut me up.

It should have been a lot of things—an ancillary crime scene, a place of investigative interest, a location containing a computer requiring police examination. But it was none of those things; it was just a kid's bedroom—a *dead* kid's bedroom. The posters on the walls were mostly the bikes and dirt races I had cracked wise about to Karen. Except for one leathered blonde hanging off a Harley, there were no tits and ass, but what kid living alone with his mother *would* have splashed that around? I assumed that kind of stuff was socked away in the DVDs that filled two entire shelves of the largest bookcase. The other two shelves below were devoted to CDs, leaving those antiquated book things to a small bookcase under the window and to the window sill itself. I didn't see Alan Lockman going into crisis if the next hurricane blew all over Mark Twain.

"That's the computer."

Barbara Lockman said it just to say it, taking advantage of the chance to use her voice in the room again. I walked over to the thing gingerly. What had seemed like an inspiration the last couple of hours was beginning to sag back to earth. The computer itself might not have been more sophisticated than my Model T at home, but it looked like it was simply because it wasn't mine. And then there were all the dragons waiting for me once I sat down. How about a password to get to the e-mails? How about the possibility that the kid had erased anything of interest—or, just about the same thing, that Brighton had already taken what

I wanted? Compared to those delightful prospects, the thought that I might have been wrong from the start, that there was nothing to discover in the first place, seemed like a minor obstacle. Practical sweats had precedence.

"He was very involved with his motorcycle," Barbara Lockman said to Karen behind me, drawing her attention to the posters. "My husband Charles also loved motorcycles. Do you like them, Karen?"

I flinched to ward off hearing the story about Alan Lockman driving her down to the library one morning; no way that wasn't going to push the mother closer to the edge. But Karen said no, joked about having enough trouble with her car. It was good karma because just then my eye fell on a scratch sheet scotch taped to the back of the desk; the first combination of numbers and letters looked like a computer password.

"He left that there for me," Barbara Lockman said, suddenly standing behind my shoulder. "I can never remember that password when I want to contact my brother or sister."

I typed in the password instead of dwelling on the idea of her coming and going into the kid's bedroom whenever she needed to send an e-mail. In Alan's place I would have made a computer for her my first big Mother's Day gift. In her place I would have used my connections at the insurance company to get a good deal from Labine's department store. Why had they both waited for me to come along with those ideas?

"It might be better, Barbara, if we leave Paul alone for a few minutes. We'll get out of your hair faster."

"Oh, of course. I just wanted to show you where it was."

I closed my ears until the two of them were gone. Karen had once again stepped in at the right time, but I didn't want to hear the price for it in Barbara Lockman's dithering over what she shouldn't have been dithering over. It was her house and her son's room and computer, for Christ sake! She didn't owe explanations to Karen, me, or the man in the moon. It was like Veronica had said: People in New Florence were always apologizing to one another for the wrong things.

The password was my first triumph, the un-erased e-mails in the inbox my second. There were nine of them, all sent the day Lockman had been killed. Which meant either the kid had been meticulous about getting rid of his correspondence every evening or he hadn't received a single message the day before. I went with the former, and did him a belated favor in the next world by deleting the three pieces of Viagara spam. It was also good to see that Doctor Nybala Douri of the Central Nigerian Bank was offering Lockman the same 17 million dollars in exchange for his bank account number that he had been offering me for a couple of years. I had always felt guilty about having been singled out for that windfall with so many homeless people living on the streets.

Once I'd gotten rid of Doctor Douri, I was down to five messages. The first and third were from an ANBEL who wanted to know why Lockman hadn't been in their chat room lately. The second was from SIMONJ who had some question about pistons he assumed Lockman could answer. I would have spent so much time just trying to translate SIMONJ's question into English I wouldn't have had time for ANBEL in the chat room, either. The fourth message was from JIMBOR who had been to a motorcycle race and went on about it so long I felt mud being splattered on my face. The last one was from the BIGH who wanted to know if Lockman had "thought any more about what we said last time or are u still into all that conspiracy shit u like?"

Not being Edison or Pasteur, I didn't shout "Eureka!" after reading the message from BIGH. For one thing, I didn't know what I had discovered; for all I knew, the "conspiracy shit" might have been about some third party cutting them out of their weekend grass stash. For another, I didn't want Barbara Lockman hearing me and running back in with more of those intimidating hopes in her eyes. But shout or no shout, I had the first feeling in ages that I knew how to do more than annoy people or be annoyed by them. The Professor might regret it yet that he had made that foolish offer to pay me for poking around.

I took down the e-mail addresses of BIGH and—just in case— of ANBEL, SIMONJ, and JIMBOR for another time and another computer. Then I moved over to the Sent prompt on the off-chance that Lockman had already replied to BIGH and could point me closer to the importance of *Planning Society* for him. The Sent box was empty. I told myself the consolation prize was having further confirmation that Lockman had been a creature of habit—dealing with his e-mails after he returned from work in the evening and starting each new day with a clean cyber slate. I really wasn't in the mood for consolation prizes.

Just for the hell of it, I went into the offline files. Finding one labeled PULSAR would have been too much to expect, and I got what I expected. What I hadn't anticipated were what must have been a hundred files named after authors. Hemingway, Roth, Faulkner, Balzac, Tolstoy—they were all there on the screen like one of those full-page ads for morocco-bound Great Literature at only $49.99 a month. Then there were other names of people I dimly recognized as the authors of those lose-a-hundred-pounds-green-the-earth-and-make-a-million best sellers. For what? I opened the Hemingway and found a long page of quotes and page citations from *The Sun Also Rises*. Just to be sure my first impression was correct, I then opened Tolstoy and found similar quotes and page numbers from *War and Peace*. JJ turned out to be a marine biologist who had listed the danger signs for the survival of orcas.

I looked over at the small case of books under the window. Alan Lockman didn't have more books because he had read them (probably from the library), copied out lines, and then returned them. This said two things to me. One, Alan Lockman hadn't been the book-illiterate I seemed to have had an interest in believing he was, but had been one of those self-improvement types that saw accumulation as a shortcut to understanding. Two, I had been right to read him as too anal merely to count the *Reporter* ballots in the office and then forget about them when he came home. As I had said to Brighton, he had to have kept a tabulation somewhere.

But that somewhere wasn't among the files labeled with the names of authors. I opened a few more just in case he had decided to stick the numbers under some joke name I would get only after hours of profound reflection. Nothing. The only one that gave me pause was an empty file labeled CB, initials instead of the name. I took that to mean that, anal or not, Lockman hadn't been able to delude himself he would ever need the poetry of Charles Baudelaire for quoting around the newsroom or bike shop.

Then the X at the top of the screen reminded me of what I was overlooking. I went back to icon that got me into the computer's list of recent deletions. My quarry was at the very top of the list, slugged BALLOTS. It had been excised at two minutes after noon that day, presumably after being printed out. I understood what brother Martin had meant about cops coming and going into the bedroom. Brighton had taken me up on my tip, after all.

The trouble was, I didn't know if that was good or bad.

CHAPTER 38

Barbara Lockman identified SIMONJ and JIMBOR as two of her son's high school friends equally passionate about motorcycles. BIGH she had never heard of, and I decided to hold back ANBEL just in case her chat room was on some XXX website. Only later did I start thinking it odd that a woman desperate for answers about her son's death and familiar with his computer had not contacted his last correspondents on her own.

We got out of the house without deflating quite all the hopes we had stirred walking in, although brother Martin looked ready to pop me for not coming up with more than I had. The sister-in-law just nodded goodnight to us from her sentinel's post on the couch, and I had the feeling she was going to be the one presiding over the Lockman family council as soon as the front door clicked closed.

Back at Karen's, BIGH whipped out his credentials as a diplomatic mediator. She wouldn't hear of anything but contacting him immediately about the "conspiracy," and that preempted at least temporarily all thoughts, calculations, and talk about whether for my last night in town she would go to her bed, I would go to mine, we would both go to one of them, or any combination thereof. She didn't want to hear my objections that BIGH might not get our message for days, that he might at that very moment be devouring a platter of cheese on vacation in Wisconsin. Why upset Barbara Lockman the way we had if we weren't going to follow up on what we had found, she wanted to know.

Because she hadn't thought to provide a second chair for her study, she had to pace back and forth with her arms folded across her chest while I sat down at the computer and tried to emphasize to BIGH that we would like him to get back to us as soon as he received our message, preferably using the telephone number I was supplying. The beep signaling the message's departure for who-knew-where didn't brake her pacing. With only the desk lamp shining, she kept moving in and out of shadows, and not all of them seemed to belong to BIGH. One second she looked like a captain on the bridge of a destroyer waiting for the depth charge to reach its target, the next like a frail woman who might have come into her thinness more genetically than Barbara Lockman but who had still starved some kind of vital substance inside. And that was just fine with me. Since somewhere inside the Social Security bureaucracy someone was already inching my number closer to monthly checks, I could no longer deny a lengthy pattern of being attracted to women with what were called issues. Medea and Lady Macbeth and Bonnie Parker—they had always gotten more of a rise out of me than *Sports Illustrated* swimsuit models. Watching Karen move fluidly back and forth, her jeans hanging off her hip bones like they had grown there, I told myself she was a mature, conflicted woman with a sweet face who would never confuse a two-night stand with a one-night stand.

"Mind telling me what attracted you to those horses?"

She needed a second to remember who else was in the room with her, then another to zero in on the prints. At least she stopped parading over all her misgivings. "You don't like horses?"

"I love horses. And I bet I could press a key here and find a zillion prints of them. But those things are pretty bottom of the barrel."

"If you do say so yourself."

"If I do say so myself."

She nodded at the closer print. "They were a major part of my dowry," she said, trying to sound amused at herself. "They came with me from my bedroom wall from my parents' house. My horses, my body, and my starry eyes. I guess I didn't have much taste in those days."

"And you keep them because . . .?"

She turned back to me as if looking at another horse; or at least part of one. "I can't count on my body and starry eyes forever, can I?"

At that moment, close to rearing back under her twinkling gaze, I knew what I was going to do. Being under the same roof with her was no longer a challenge, picking up the Professor in the morning no longer a deadline. It was really very simple once I had made up my mind to do it: drive the old man home and unload the tangled urges he had ridden into town on, then come back to New Florence by myself and see through with her whatever had to be seen through. Eight or nine hours both ways? Why had that seemed like such a forbidding trek? Some nights I spent that much time watching *Law and Order* reruns.

A dozen phones seemed to ring on all sides of me. Actually, it was only one on the desk and the muffled extension out in the kitchen. I picked up the receiver before a second ring. I didn't look up at Karen until I was sure BIGH wasn't eating cheese in Wisconsin. By then she had gotten over my forwardness about grabbing for her phone.

His name was Harold Geis, he worked a compactor at a Sanitation Department plant, and he thought it was kind of fun talking to a private detective for the first time in his life. He sounded older than Alan Lockman, but not by that much. I had last met Harold Geis in the upper stands at Citi Field screeching down at million-dollar ballplayers who struck out in the clutch. He was the sort who never needed to smoke because he had been born with enough catarrh in his lungs to see him through his 70-odd years and never needed to worry about clothes as long as sports teams sold T-shirts and sweatpants. Whoever his wife would someday be, she would match him arm flab for arm flab. The one thing I couldn't figure out, especially after he said he didn't know motorcycles from mules, was how he had become a correspondent with Alan Lockman. Agile as I was, I came up with the solution to that one by asking him.

"The radio show."

"Radio show?"

"Randy Page. You know."

I found myself swinging the desk chair around from where Karen was watching intently. I had the searing feeling of being jealous of her for having been right all along about the Pulsar web. What else could a schmuck in my position do than at least postpone her I-told-you-sos for another few minutes? "Right. That radio show."

"Page was doing this riff a couple of weeks back on the killin' of Kennedy. You know, the old President?"

"Heard of him."

"So he's goin' on about how it was a conspiracy that nobody's had the balls to talk about even today, then he opens the phones for listeners to call in. I call in and give him my two cents worth."

"What two cents was that, Harold?"

The laughter was a cackle. "Whattya, kiddin' me? It's all bullshit, that's what. They got the guy in Dallas or Houston or wherever the hell it was, end of story. Oswald was his name."

"I still don't see how that got you to Alan."

A lower, more pensive cackle. "Funny how they're all dead, ain't it? Lockman, Page, Kennedy, and Oswald. Even the guy who shot Oswald, I think he's gone, too. Maybe they're comin' after me next. Whattya think?"

I was supposed to laugh at that one, so I did. He didn't sound like the kind of guy who could believe too long in his own sense of humor. "So you must've been at the Page funeral," I said to fill in a space.

Wrong way to fill a space. "Bein' funny? Guy ran his mouth and nothin' good ever came out of it."

"But you listened to him anyway."

"Why not? It's a free country."

Karen hurried out of the room toward the extension in the kitchen. I presumed I had missed some arm waving to let her in on what Geis and I were talking about. "You were about to say how you and Lockman got hooked up. How did that happen?"

Maybe it was just a chauvinistic moment, but I couldn't help thinking that anybody back in the city would have held up by now, asked me if there was any money to be earned answering my questions. But Harold Geis just sounded happy to have somebody filling in for Randy Page in helping him through the night. "He called the station right after me, said *I* was the one full of shit," he laughed. "Started talkin' about all these books that said there had to be a conspiracy against Kennedy. I didn't know what the hell he was talkin' about half the time, but he was really wound up about it. Page loves it all. He asks if anybody else has an opinion, but nobody else calls so he tells me to call again. Right there over the air! 'Hey, c'mon, Harold, what do you think of what Alan said about you?' Just like that. He was like a pig rollin' in shit. So I call again. Me and Lockman, we end up doin' most of his show for him! Back and forth. He does something with his switchboard so we end up havin' a direct head-to-head three-way. Wish I had a job like that. I'm not sayin' I want to be run over by a car, but if all I gotta do is let other people do the talkin', hey, who wouldn't want a paycheck for that?"

I made a note to myself never to say anything compromising on the phone with Karen and an extension around. If I hadn't been listening for it, I might have missed her picking up the receiver in the kitchen. "But you two were in contact after Page's show," I tried again.

"Oh, yeah. When we were off the air for a commercial, Lockman asks me for my phone number. I don't know why he wanted to keep in touch. We didn't agree on diddly. Maybe he was lonely or something. That was the first thing that came into my head when I read about him hangin' himself. Page gets in the middle, says it's station policy or FCC rules or something that he can't allow that. It's okay, though, he says, if we want to swap e-mail addresses. What the hell's the difference? What're they worried about—some heavy breather? Those guys can get off on a computer, too."

"Probably. But what I'm really curious about, Harold, is this last message you sent, something about a conspiracy. Were you just referring to this debate of yours about Kennedy?"

"Kennedy, King, Abe Lincoln. Who remembers? Everything was a conspiracy to him. The government, that was another favorite. How they had all our Social Security numbers and credit card numbers and that shit. I told him so what. If he hasn't done anything wrong, it's on them to buy more file cabinets for all their useless shit about him. He didn't think so. Know what I think? I think he was so lonely he needed at least an enemy. He couldn't find one, so that's why he put that noose around his neck."

"It's a thought."

"Fuckin' right. He was even draggin' his mother into it."

I let Karen suck in her breath for both of us. "His mother?"

"Yeah. We're goin' back and forth last week about how everything's on some big board in the CIA. One of these electronic things coverin' the wall, you know? Whoops, there goes the Big H out his front door, so the green lights on the CIA board start goin' crazy. Like the way they follow trains. Beep, beep, beep—across Lake Street, Sloan Avenue. They follow me all the way to work. You know."

"What's that got to do with his mother?"

"Hang on. I tell him he's full of shit, no such thing exists. And he says his mother don't even work for the government, but even she can tell you about the people livin' in places like New Florence because of some charts in her office. I think she works for an insurance company."

"You mean actuary tables?"

"I don't know what they're called. I tell him, yeah, sure, as long as the people got a policy with the company. He says no. Even the people who don't have policies, they're on the chart too because that's info the salesman buggin' you on the phone at supper time needs to have."

Karen hadn't said what Barbara Lockman did at Labine's insurance company and I had never had a reason to ask. But how far was an insurance firm's demographic research from *Planning Society*?

"Did he ever mention the Pulsar Institute?"

Karen's interruption rattled me as much as Geis. "Hey, who's this?"

"Mr. Finley's assistant. Did Alan mention the Pulsar Institute?"

"Hey, this is good! Like that night on the radio!"

"Did he ever mention Pulsar, Harold?"

Even Geis picked up the steelier tone. "The ones with the poll?" he asked more soberly. "No, I don't think so."

I didn't know why she had expected it to be so easy, but she immediately fell silent again. "What about a magazine called *Planning Society*?" I asked. "He talk about that?"

"What's that? One of those things with the debutantes?"

I didn't know why I had expected it to be so easy, either.

A few seconds later, I hung up and Harold Geis was officially Dead-End Harold Geis. I sat at the desk nursing my wounds. The TV hucksters pitching debt consolidation told me to be positive at such moments, so I tried to be positive. It might not have been a David Letterman gag that had sent Alan Lockman to the microfilm reels, but it had been his mother and I had entertained that notion too, hadn't I? Didn't that entitle me to extra credit? So what if she had mentioned her demographics job at Labine's to her son years ago or if they had talked about it religiously every evening at the supper table? I hadn't *completely* wasted my thoughts for the last two days on *Planning Society*.

Had I?

Karen was standing in the doorway. I hadn't heard her come back in from the kitchen, which made it unanimous for all the senses controlled by my brain. She gave me a full shrug and hapless smile, one of those things Charlie Chaplin had done while holding both ends of a cane in front of him. That was just the way of the world sometimes, the gesture said.

"Barbara Lockman knows more than she's let on," I insisted.

She had heard denial before. "Like what?"

"I don't know."

"It was her son, Paul."

"I know that."

I got away from the computer screen before I sent BIGH another e-mail telling him to go fuck himself. I was in such a wonderful mood that the cheap prints of the horses didn't look so bad upon closer examination. "The thing I was saying before?" she said. "About letting it go and getting on with my life? I think you . . ."

"I'm bringing Joe home tomorrow," I cut her off. "He's been grossing me out with all these vibes about you. I'm also getting bored blaming him for not thinking clearly about all this shit up here. What I'm saying is that I'll be back tomorrow night so don't rent out your guest room. There's too much of the half-assed about this place and I want to know why. Not just for you, but for me. I want to know what happened to that kid down the street. I want to know what the mother is afraid to say and if it's just because that short fuse of a brother is around. I want to know who smacked me and why. I want to know why one second Brighton has a uniformed tail on me and the next second there's nobody. I want to know what that creepy preacher was after chasing me down to the hospital lobby and I want to know what game Pulsar's up to. If I put that last, it's only because right now everything else I mentioned is irritating me more."

She didn't answer for a second. But then, sliding over to turn off her computer: "Plus you want to know who's the most admired citizen."

The desk lamp was hers, and now I must have been the one in all the shadows. "I still don't know if you're right about Pulsar," I said. "I mean, I know they're up to something besides that questionnaire, but I don't know what it has to do with you, me, Antonacci, Randy Page, or Lockman. What I do know is that a lot of people, including you, have been working to make it my business, so why not?"

"You mean like doing a thesis on Lucrezia Borgia?"

"What's that mean?"

She came out from the light. "It's seductive, but it's also safe. Safer than what you have going on back in New York."

I defied my brain to summon up a single image of George Oswald. It got the message and backed down. I felt like a vampire sinking into her hot, talc-smelling neck. Off to the side of my head, I thought, she was staring valiantly off into the near distance. Not the innocent fawn I had been trying to see her as since arriving. Something more regal. Like a swan.

CHAPTER 39

General MacArthur had nothing on me. He had returned only once, I had three returns in front of me—taking the Professor back to Garden City, going back to New Florence, then back again to Brooklyn. Put that way, it sounded a lot more exhausting than it had pledging to Karen I would make a quick turnaround. Or maybe what was really exhausting was having to be in the car all morning with the old man and not telling him I had promised to go back. That command decision I'd made on my way over to the hospital. Why thicken the air in the car all the way down to New York?

For the first hour or so, my discretion paid for itself ten times over. We might as well have squirted the car with Cheer before setting off. He had many wise and witty things to say about Mendler, the nurses, and the administrative staff at the New Florence Medical Center. Then there were the inspirational lessons to be drawn from having a sputtering heart, from experiencing the blessings of old age, and from obeying the laws covering seat belts. For background I had a medley of radio stations breaking up commercials for the state lottery with a rap version of "Mister Sandman" and some endless one-note dirge on a soprano sax, up to then my favorite musical instrument. I passed a sign pointing to New Baltimore, and was surprised it didn't turn out to be the scene of the crash. I had even worked out the headline for *Newsday*'s obituary page: JOSEPH CARROLL RUNS OUT OF HISTORY. And in smaller letters: So Does His Chauffeur.

One thing ticking him off I could understand was his interrupted talk on the Spanish Lady. He didn't mention it explicitly
except as the first act to his medical drama, but it clearly weighed
on him as much as anything else he hadn't delivered for Karen.
Given the alternatives, I liked thinking it was the main reason
he kept squirming around in his seat like a cow that hadn't been
milked in the morning—a poetic image that occurred to me when
we went by a field with a herd of fat white-and-black things nibbling on what looked like grass. I didn't mind relieving him; it was
much better than having to dwell on present-day corpses.

"So what was going to be the punchline of your talk?"

That got me a snort. "You mean like in a joke?"

"Right."

He gave his seat belt another tug, but there was no drop-dead
spit and I knew I had hit on a topic that would cover conversation
for a few miles. "What I saw," he grumbled, "place looks like it's
still got the flu."

"What'd you see? You were in a hospital bed!"

"I saw, I saw. No wonder Mochi liked it so much . . . Mochi.
Meucci's brother-in-law."

"Yeah, I know."

"I did some reading up on him. Sounded like a zombie catcher
happy to find a whole town of them. When he showed up, there
was a motion in front of the town council to burn the whole place
down to stop the spread of the disease. The only reason it didn't
pass was they couldn't get enough people to show up for a council
meeting. Everybody stayed indoors. When they went out, they
had their faces covered like burn victims."

"What the hell was he doing up here anyway?"

He nodded approvingly at the question. "Karen's books said
he was a drifter along the eastern seaboard. Had suspicious luck
at craps and cards."

"A hustler?"

"Sounds like it. But if your name was Mochi in those days,
you were suspected of a lot of things. First day in town, he almost
got arrested as a labor organizer. Then somebody pointed out
that if you wanted to start labor trouble somewhere, Pinewood

wasn't exactly a prime target. About the only things around were a couple of small timber processors and a plant for making towels. The towel place was where Mochi set up his factory."

"And all this taught you . . .?"

He exhaled loudly through his bottom teeth. "That it took an outsider to get the measure of the place. The locals were so busy sealing their windows and feeling sorry for themselves they couldn't see straight."

"I think it's called fear and panic, Joe."

"You use your dictionary, I'll use mine. Mochi sizes it up, sees his chance, and launches his American dream with the money he's pocketed from the suckers on his travels."

"Nothing all that new there."

"No. Just a reminder."

"Of what?"

"He wasn't sick and he didn't know any of the people falling over. He had no emotional investment."

I didn't know what that answered, and the stare he fixed ahead of him didn't look ready to volunteer clues. Was I supposed to have been paranoid enough to play it back as a criticism, a warning, or another of those negative things people didn't like believing they had heard from former fathers-in-law? Lucky that I wasn't. "Yeah? So?"

"You listening, or what? The guy had a Frankenstein complex. He was going to build something up from everybody else's discards."

"Maybe to impress his sister so he wouldn't have to keep hearing Meucci, Meucci, telephone, telephone."

"Forget I said anything."

"Is it that loony? If I had a sister married to somebody like Meucci, I wouldn't be too eager for holidays with the family, either. 'You'll never guess who we talked to on the phone yesterday, Claudio! The ants under the sink! Every day that brilliant husband of mine adds more and more wire!'"

"Finished?"

"All right. Tell me about the Frankenstein complex."

He was too bent on talking about it to be dissuaded by an idiot audience. "Both books say he walked around town the first week itemizing all the decay in the place. The restaurants closed because nobody wanted to eat somewhere where there were other people, and that's without counting the fears of food being touched by a cook or a waiter. The streets were all torn up, horse shit everywhere. Nobody picked up the garbage except the cats and dogs. Kids were hanging around in front of saloons because the schools were shut. The ones that weren't hoping they could tap a keg were playing on the coffins the undertakers had piled up outside their funeral parlors. Some traffic lights worked, some didn't. And hanging over it all was this shit smell from a swamp just outside of town."

I remembered the swamp near the Mochi factory and realized who had used those mysterious picnic tables: Anybody at all in New Florence without a nose. Some questions just weren't going to get fabulous answers. "Why fabrics? He have background in that?"

I had finally said something funny. "They got it into their heads the epidemic was being spread by cloth. Killer microbes attaching themselves to the sheets and curtains. So they either washed everything a dozen times a day or burned it. Mochi notices how there's not a curtain on a window in town and gets his great idea. He tells them they've taken the first step, now it's time to manufacture their own curtains free of any contact with disease. I don't know how he convinced them they could do that without using their hands, but I wasn't there. He tells them he knows a supplier who can ship in the raw materials and—here's the miracle of miracles—the supplier lives in Montreal, out of harm's way!"

"They fell for that?"

"Why not? He really did have a crony in Montreal. And he was the one putting up the money, not them. It didn't hurt that by the time the first shipments came in from Canada, the epidemic was over. Gone as fast as it had come. And when the sun rose and the birds started chirping again, they looked around and behold, they saw they'd trashed a good part of their economy but, hallelujah, Claudio Mochi was there with their future!"

A moron in a green VW about 100 yards ahead couldn't make up his mind about his favorite lane; I shared his pain. "But you didn't know any of this the night you were going to give your talk."

"No," he said, instantly dropping back down into his hospital gloom. "Just as well I didn't shoot my mouth off that night."

"Why? What did knowing about Mochi change?"

He shook his head; suddenly he was more interested in the VW than I was. A reluctant Joe Carroll threw me off track. It could have been only one or two things—he didn't want to hurt somebody's feelings or he had to admit having miscalculated something—and neither was standard Joe Carroll issue. "The pandemic could've been the best thing ever to happen to that place," he finally said. "They could've taken a deep look at how close they'd come to the edge of the abyss and maybe drawn a moral or two from it. But no. Years later they were still fighting over whether they should rename the town for Mochi, if they should let Jews live on Sloan Avenue, and if the town council wasn't pushing it with two black nurses at the hospital. The hottest issue at the high schools was if the biology classes should refer to sex. That clown newspaper of theirs was all in favor of banning not just D.H. Lawrence, but anybody who used a four-letter word stronger than *darn*."

"It's called America, Joe."

"They were given a test and they failed it."

"Excuse me?"

"You heard me."

I thought he was joking because that was usually what I thought when a 75-year-old cynic started sounding like the Reverend Dvorak. Or was I taking that word *test* down the wrong lane? The Professor *was* the Professor, after all; nothing all that shocking about someone his age viewing the world as a classroom that either passed or failed his exams.

"You don't think so, Finley?"

"Historically, maybe."

"Pardon me. I forgot the astrological point of view."

"C'mon, Joe. They had a bad time, but they got over it, whether it was because of Mochi or striking oil in the swamps. They didn't turn into a Utopia? Bulletin: Not too many other places managed that in the 20th century, either. They've probably always had the same ratio of creeps and cretins as Garden City. You hand out marks to your Long Island neighbors yet?"

"Garden City has creeps and cretins, but it also has too many radical factors. Commuters to the city. Just the TV stations in the metro area."

"Meaning . . .?"

"It's not contained enough. You want to fleece a place like Pinewood the way Mochi did, you want to know all the perimeters. You want to *see* them all. You want to be king, you better have all the keys to the castle."

He was spooking me, and not just with the thought that the operation had taken more out of him than he had realized or that Mendler had fucked up with his medicine. There was also something eerily familiar about what he was saying. Then I remembered what it was: Bobby Rosen had also made a big deal out of the fact that Pulsar's earlier projects had been in places without TV stations. Yeah? And so?

"For Christ sake, Finley!"

I caught my lead foot with whole inches to spare. The VW jerk was practically through my windshield. Call it my second stroke of magic that I remembered to glance into the rearview mirror. For reasons having nothing to do with me, the closest thing behind was an SUV a quarter-mile back.

I got over to the right lane, half-wishing the VW would also go there and give me a second shot at the son of a bitch. But he kept going, and I mainly felt free to sweat.

"You okay?"

"No, Joe, I'm not okay."

He nodded at a reasonable observation. "My driving instructor told me never to think while I was behind the wheel," he said after another moment. "I had that pearl of wisdom printed out and put on the wall of my first classroom. I thought it made a wonderful sardonic point. Then one day I walked into the classroom, looked at it, and realized I didn't know what I was getting at putting it up there. So I pulled it down and threw it away."

He was chattering, I was calming down, and the VW was getting so far ahead it would have had time to destroy half of New York before we got there. "Your driving instructor? He must've known Mochi."

The Professor nodded; he was comfortable with predictable cracks. "We all have our tests, Finley," he said. "Don't screw up yours."

CHAPTER 40

I dropped off the old man at his house in Garden City, picked up a few groceries for him, then went on to Brooklyn. I didn't mention going back upstate. Part of me rationalized he was a divine seer into all things so had already figured it out for himself. When that didn't take, I told myself it was none of his business. By the time I found a parking space two doors down from my building in Bay Ridge, I didn't know why the hell I had ever agreed to go back to New Florence to begin with.

With Mrs. Chalian left in charge of our corner of the fourth floor, there wasn't a single circular from a car service or Chinese restaurant in the hall. Thanks to the soap opera blaring from her apartment, I could tiptoe into mine without one of her usual who-goes-there challenges. So much for the day's sterling accomplishments. Hushing the door closed behind me, I saw that none of those reality makeover shows had taken advantage of my absence to redo my apartment; the place looked as much like a high-class Salvation Army showroom as it ever had. They hadn't even opened a window to disperse the fried egg smell from my last breakfast.

Habit took me directly to my sock drawer in the bedroom to make sure my Smith & Wesson .38 was where it should have been. It looked annoyed for the disturbance. At least my message machine was glad to see me. The flashing red buttons were absolutely jovial as I commanded them to do their thing and collapsed on the couch with the garbage that had been filling up my mailbox. How could I have doubted George Oswald would be first, and from only an hour before? Whatever else the Brooklyn Cyclones could be accused of, it wasn't haste in picking their announcers. According to Oswald, they still hadn't sent him the contract committing him to their broadcasts. He, for one, had every suspicion why. Even as he was screaming at me on the phone, he knew, they were playing back the tape Bob Nelson had sent them and consulting with their lawyers about what constituted a verbal agreement. What was I going to do about it besides spend his money? I had no idea.

The second message was from Mrs. Richard Lowe, one of the fur-covered banshees Mrs. Chalian had warned me about. Exposed to a voice like Mrs. Lowe's, my mother would have called her a fish wife. Wrong. This was a serious whale mouth. Goddamn me, I was going to regret ever walking into Prospect Park and assaulting her husband and ruining the lives of their family. Goddamn me, a person like me should get run over by a bus. The cops already knew about me, and so did her lawyer. Goddamn me.

I took a better look at the trash on my lap. Mastercard and Mobil had never been so welcome. There were no more formalized threats from Mrs. Lowe. The only official looking envelope was from a law firm that threw work my way every few months. I forgot about Mrs. Lowe to see if they had remembered how critical I was to their business. They had. The mission this time—if I chose to accept it—was an eye-ear-throat guy named Habib Golub who had trouble distinguishing cancerous and non-cancerous thyroid conditions. I accepted the mission. The only downside was that Golub had his office in Park Slope, which was always one of the bitchiest places in Brooklyn to find a parking space.

Mrs. Lowe was still goddamning me when the phone rang. I told her to add it to her list of grievances as I got up to snap off the machine and pick up the receiver. A second too late, I realized I was being rash. The whole point of the machine had been to screen calls from the Mrs. Lowes of the world, but now here I was making it part of the problem instead of the solution. Was that irony or just stupidity?

"A very lifelike machine, Finley. You should market it."

I was back in New Florence so fast I didn't know why Walt Whitman, John Roebling, and the Brooklyn Dodgers had ever bothered. "Bobby?"

Rosen played it over for possibilities; he was disappointed to find so little. "Yes. Not your stereotypical London copper, but still carrying a badge for special occasions."

"How many times have you used that one?"

A sigh. "Unfortunately, the second part is truer every day. But that's not why I rang up, is it, old boy?"

"I hope not."

He dropped the British accent before I had to ask him to. "The short conjecture to your question is DOD."

"Department of Defense??!!"

"Or the first three letters of Dodsworth."

"What do you mean *conjecture*?"

"Exactly," he said, sounding like he was holding his nose against a sneeze. "There are tracks through congressional budgets, but they never quite lead to a clearing in the woods."

"You mean stuck under some Miscellany heading?"

He reopened his nose for a snide laugh. "Miscellany is a category for your tax form. Of course, you might have something roughly equivalent. Say an Emergency Contingency Fund, known to insiders as the ECF. Not to be confused with anything the European Community and that lot is up to. But people varnish their self-importance by standing around in hallways and whispering about ECFs."

"Okay, okay. Got it."

"I thought you might."

"What else?"

"I would've thought that enough for free favors."

And it probably would have been, I thought, if I paused to digest what he had said. But as long as I had him on the line, why waste time thinking? That could come later when Pentagon cops were breaking down my door. "You found something else, too. I can tell."

There was a pause while something like a bus passed him. Whatever else he had found, he preferred talking about it from the street. "Mainly that the cellphone generation has left us very few pay phones," he said. "Remember: If they ask who called from this number, it was . . . hold on . . . Richie who says Jan Gives Blowjobs to Everyone on Long Island Sound . . . Or at least everyone but Richie, it seems."

"C'mon, Bobby. What else?"

"The DOD thing was your normal two-step through public records. What you really owe me for is the curiosity that Pulsar's turnover rate of employees would make McDonald's envious. Except for one or two people with titles, they appear to re-staff for every one of their little studies. Mostly from graduate schools and computer institutes selling some in-the-field education angle. The exceptions are . . ."

"Michael Zev and Pauline Shepherd."

"Two for two, I think. Zev, definitely. He seems to be the first among equals. Has a lot of capital letters after his name. I didn't realize there were degrees in half the things he has them for. Maybe I should go back to the university and explore the alphabet more carefully."

"Bobby?"

"Patience. This is my credit card. The Shepherd woman seems to have just joined two projects ago. She has almost as many degrees as Zev, all of them in the snoop sciences and all from the Ivy League. Before her there was somebody named Matthew Vickers who had his name attached to as many of these projects as Zev did. Vickers died of a stroke six months ago. If Shepherd is his replacement, yes, she's another long-termer."

Ben, Belinda, and the other computer jockeys made more sense in that light. Whatever Zev had told them they were doing wouldn't have held up more than once. How it could have held up even that long was between them and their geek god. "You're invaluable, Bobby."

Wrong compliment. "Which to you means what—I have no value that can be reciprocated? Never mind. As I pointed out last time, there is no constant in the questions asked for these so-called studies. Most this, Best that. But the towns themselves . . ."

"Don't have local TV stations."

"You remember!"

"Somebody else noticed that, too."

Second mistake. "Then why call me?"

The nice part of suspending thinking was that I didn't have
to recall exactly what the Professor had said and what I had gone
off on a tangent about. "He said the importance of no TV stations
was that it made the towns more local, more self-contained."

"I think that's pretty obvious. You build a box with blocks, you
don't want extra blocks left over."

"But New Florence has a radio station. A small one, but a station. And I'd bet most of these other places did, too."

"Not the same thing. Most local radio stations have a range
that in our mysterious electronic universe covers Main Street,
Jeb's farmhouse outside of town, and some fishing village in
northern Manitoba. In between those hits there's little but static.
It's an entirely different dynamic from television. Come by some
day and I'll explain it to you. I've been studying up on it. One of
these inventions, for instance, has pictures, too!"

The slam of Mrs. Chalian's door sounded like Jeffrey going
off on his daily outing—down to the mailbox. "But what about
computers? Nothing is that closed in anymore."

He hadn't quite worked up his gag lines for that. "You'd have
to ask Zev. Evidently, he doesn't consider that a disruptive factor.
Or maybe he's just pretending it doesn't exist so his subsidies
keep coming. Never underestimate that factor, Finley. The first
business of poll taking, no matter who underwrites it, is staying
in the poll taking business."

"Zev is more than a grant conman."

"Why? Because you never ran across his kind before? That's
what conning is all about, isn't it?"

"And the DOD doesn't know it?"

"Don't get me started."

"Okay, that was stupid."

"Yes, it was."

I was stumped. He was the Answer Man and I should have
had a dozen things to ask while I had him available. But all I was
left with was: "What's your opinion, Bobby?"

"After our last little chat, I looked into New Florence. You seem to have two bodies recently. That your interest?"

"Could be."

"Oops. Curiosity encounters client confidentiality."

"No, it's not that. It's just that I don't know what the connection is, but I'm positive there is one. What do *you* think they're doing?"

I couldn't have complained if he ended the conversation right there. But he didn't. He thought about it for what seemed like an entire stoplight behind him. Then: "I see a lot of money and a lot of organization. What I don't see is anything published for all this effort except these specific poll results—at least nothing for public consumption. You hardly need a Zev or Shepherd for that. Their parents didn't put them through a dozen universities so they would end up doing market research questionnaires. Overall, it's what you might call an incomplete picture. If I were you, I'd be rooting for that con game for a grant."

Which seemed to be where the Professor had started with Karen that day in the Italian restaurant. Believing that would also mean a lot of effort without anything to show for it. "Failing that?"

His sigh said he could have done without the question. "In the golden age when my credentials meant something, if I was confident of persuading my bosses and a judge there were sufficient grounds for a subpoena, I would visit Pulsar's offices. But even back then there was always a *sine qua non.* You may recall it—it's called suspected criminal activity. Is that what you're claiming on the basis of what I've told you? If you are, you've been out of Major Cases longer than you think."

"All I'm saying is that there are too many coincidences. A talk show host and a copyboy both crossed paths with Pulsar . . ." It sounded so stupid I wanted to slam down the receiver before Rosen beat me to it. What I really should have been doing was calling back George Oswald and sticking to what I could foul up on my own.

"Finley?"

"Yeah, yeah, I hear you."

Pause. Then: "An old London copper's gut?"

"It's your credit card, Bobby."

"Your instinct is right. These people are up to more than pop-ularity polls. But whatever it is, it's not something that's going to get bogged down in these two bodies I read about. Self-important people are addicts. They need their daily dose. A copyboy and a talk show host with a few dozen listeners really don't strike me as the kind of VIPs that would keep a Michael Zev's engine running. What I think you have are two sets of problems that you're fixed on connecting. Keep them separate and maybe you'll earn those millions you charge those idiots who hire you."

"Appreciate it, Bobby."

"Reflect on that sentiment and you'll see how glib you are. I'll send you a list of restaurants I'd accept as payment."

CHAPTER 41

With Rosen signing off, the red lights on my message machine resumed their pestering. I didn't want to hear from them. More George Oswald hysteria or more business from hysterics I hadn't met yet both came down to aggravation. What I really needed was that miraculous concept I had heard so much about after Jennifer's accident—*closure*. Mindy Castellani, our next-door neighbor at the time, had been the first to use the word. Sometimes I wondered if she had invented it because after Mindy everyone I had seen for months had suddenly wanted me to have closure, at first as something too soon to expect, then as something they were sure I would have imminently, then as something I was evidently resisting and should have had a long time ago. But hearing Jeffrey Chalian stomping down the hall back to his apartment, pissed off some new Invasion Earth game hadn't arrived in the mail, I warmed to the idea of any version at all of shutting down, closing up, sealing from top to toe. Clean it out, burn it away—*some*thing had to end. And since I still hadn't made all that much headway with Jennifer and Susan, let alone with Pulsar and New Florence, only one prominent target remained.

It took three calls in three voices to Flatbush Gladys to make sure all the principals were on the premises and would still be there in a couple of hours. She was suspicious of my Bobby Rosen British accent on the last call (why the hell would anyone from London want to talk to Lou Pastore?), but I got off the phone without giving away the store. For the next half-hour I went the way I needed to go—by rote. I stuffed my overnight bag with a little bit of optimism and a little bit of pessimism, tossed in my .38 because I didn't want it sitting alone in my sock drawer overnight again, grabbed two tangerines for lunch, then went downstairs and gassed up the car. I thought about stopping off at Vesuvio for an estimate on the door handle, but decided to postpone that depression. I had made it down from New Florence with the metal hanging on, and saw no reason not to repeat the trick.

The DOD kicked in on the Belt Parkway. Why the Department of Defense should have any interest in New Florence or any of the earlier New Florences was another of those puzzlements to fox the King of Siam. Was there some connection to the praetorian guard Labine had stationed in the lobby of his building—maybe a nuclear silo beneath Father Sewell and the *Reporter*? What about all those people who deserted the town during the day for that paper mill in Stanton? Was there really such a place or did those commuters get up every morning and go off to work on secret military satellite hardware behind the Rustic Inn? Had even Karen seen the inside of the paper mill she took so much for granted?

Okay, the Belt didn't inspire helpful thoughts. Neither did tangerines with more pits than fruit. But on that subject how helpful had Bobby Rosen been? Couldn't he have been wrong? When you lined up all the government agencies side by side, didn't the DOD make the *least* sense for being connected to Pulsar? The Interior Department could have bullshitted Pulsar was really testing New Florence's attitudes toward the town's three Native Americans, the Labor Department that Zev had moved into Mochi's plant to do an inspection of historical working conditions. But the Department of Defense? What did ICBMs have in common with Randy Page? Was a puzzlement, was a puzzlement.

There were more painful tortures than looking for a parking space within helicopter distance of the Empire State Building, but none occurred to me. Already stranded in blown-budget land, I made straight for one of those Midtown lots with the subliminal neon flashing PARK HERE, SUCKERS. The elevator ride up to WBOV was once again a scramble for ideas that might come out resembling a plan. Some skyscrapers simply weren't high enough to give people time to think.

Gladys showed no sign of recognition when I asked to see Oswald. With a pencil between her fingers she swept me off to one of the chairs in the waiting area, then dropped her attention back into her ears at what somebody was saying, crooning, or screeching through her headphones. The Madison Avenue magazines were still on the table and were still not being read—this time by a pair of sales reps who looked like they had dropped by to be executed. He kept tapping his gleaming black loafers to some foxtrot he couldn't keep timed even in his mind, she kept tugging at the hem of her navy-blue skirt and then gazing up at the wall clock to make sure it hadn't seen her crotch. Both looked very annoyed when George Oswald came out from the back first.

Mister Potato Head wasn't happy to see me at his place of business and even less so when I brushed off his attempt to lead me through the glass doors back out into the hall with the elevators. I lost track of his glares and grimaces as I went up to Gladys and told her Bob Nelson was also expecting me. Oswald tittered I was a jokester if there ever had been one, but I assured Gladys I wasn't. She earned her first *mensch* points by suspending her confusion for a longer look at Oswald behind me, realizing she liked seeing him flailing around, and then pressing one of her console buttons and calling inside for Nelson.

"What are you playing at, Finley?"

There were obvious answers to that one, mostly having to do with my midlife career choice and the riffraff it had brought me, but I preferred making Oswald notice how his sweaty blustering had sharpened the interest of the two sales reps in us. "Discuss it here or somewhere more private?"

"Mr. Nelson will be right out," Gladys said gaily as Oswald got it into gear to lead me out of the reception area.

"Thank you, Gladys. While you're at it, see if Lou Pastore's around. Could you do that for me?"

"He's expecting you, too?"

"How'd you guess? You're a love."

"And you're no Brit."

What else was there to do but to submit to her knowing smile with the deepest of court bows? I could tell she liked me.

Oswald gave it barely three feet out of sight of the reception area into WBOV's Hall of Fame photo corridor before whirling back on me. Even his doughboy cheeks were trembling. "You're insane!"

"I was thinking more like conscientious. I took your money for advertised services. So now I'm settling up."

Who knew if he was so rattled he wanted to throw thousands more at me just to get rid of me? I never found out. Just as he might have been about to reach for his wallet and shovel more big bills at me he caught sight of Nelson approaching from the far end of the corridor. "Hey, Bobby!" I beat him to it. "Good to see you! Lou around?"

Nelson needed a few steps before his vision cleared. He didn't like seeing me, either, and being with Oswald solidified that reaction. His look of distaste was uglier than the mole over his ear; TV stardom was definitely not in his future. "What's this all about?" he asked, on the verge of running back to his closing prices. "You invite him here, George?"

"What it's about, Bobby, is I'm suing you and your brother-in-law for assault and your sister for harassment. Or maybe you want to talk about it?"

He and his mole stood frozen as I tried the door Pastore had come through on my last visit. The other side was an anteroom to another door that said STUDIO 3. The STUDIO 3 sign was unlit. Not that I would have been crushed by walking in on the middle of some health or financial guru telling radioland what was good for it, but I really didn't need to tap my seeping energy for side skirmishes. Wasted worry. Better than empty, who should be cluttering up the small spaces between microphones and monitors on STUDIO 3's table with a greasy looking hero and a can of Tab? None other than the last of the Maquis Gang, Lou Pastore!

"What the fuck is . . .?"

"Relax, Lou. We're having a summit meeting, and Bobby and George insisted you be part of it."

"Call Security, Lou."

Pastore took in Nelson as if he had bitten down on a hot pepper. "I'm your gofer? Call yourself."

In the seconds of awkward silence that followed, all three of them looked at me as though I had grown a Pinkerton uniform and a paunch. I took that as a vote of confidence they wanted to hear me out. "Good," I said, making sure there was nobody on the other side of the glass in the dark control room. "The short of it, guys, is that I'm having an existential crisis having to deal with you three. Plus your extended family, of course, Bobby. And what we're going to do is make a peace agreement here right now that either makes all four of us happy or just me. In other words, one way or the other I'm walking out of here happy."

Pastore was beginning to be amused. "You can talk to these two all you want, but I'm having lunch."

I didn't know what the station's policy was on Tab on the rugs, but it felt good knocking the can off the table and getting more serious attention from Pastore's bug spots of eyes. "No, Lou, you're actually fasting for a few minutes here. But I would suggest you deduct the price of that soda from the money you give back to Bobby."

"What money?"

"The money you're going to return to him when he gives you back your tapes of George's little comedy show."

Pastore's doubt said he had taken me more seriously when I had been trying to nail him to the Maquis Gang. "I'm not giving him shit."

"Tell him why he's wrong, Bobby."

Nelson wanted to believe in Pastore's bravado so he could borrow a piece of it for himself, but just dropping heavily into one of the interview chairs at the table gave that hope a serious shaking from his ass to his brain. "I don't know what either one of you is talking about."

That was the wrong answer for Oswald. I let him rant, mainly because the three creeps together suddenly grazed something in my memory from New Florence. Mister Potato Head, the Moleman, and the Sleaze—any one of them could have been Batman's next archenemy. But that wasn't what the tickle was about. I pictured the McCorkle group assembled on the church steps for Randy Page's funeral, but that hadn't been it, either. For all their official smugness, they hadn't been quite grotesque enough.

I told myself it would come later and reintroduced myself to my fans. Nelson had found Oswald's raving good for a smirk, Pastore bad for his digestion. All the indignation was Oswald's, and why not? Between his comic routines and the check he had written to me, he had laid out the most. That seemed worth a bit of favoritism. "You're going to get the big prize out of this, George. You're going to get your job with the Cyclones."

With time to think about it, Oswald might have remembered it wasn't my job to hand out. He might have also just broken down and blubbered in gratitude. As it was, he could only hang his mush face in the air waiting for me to splatter it with a lemon meringue pie. "Seriously?"

"Absolutely. Because Bobby—or Mr. Nelson, as he prefers—is going to be a great sport about it all."

Oswald couldn't believe his luck. He turned to Nelson to see all the grace he had somehow missed over the years, and looked disappointed not to find it. "You're a self-deluded man, Finley," Nelson said. "Do you really think I'm going to let an amateur rob me of what I have coming?"

"Sure. Because if you don't, all kinds of legal things are going to happen. We're going to hear from Mindy Castellani about your brother-in-law in Prospect Park . . ."

"Who the hell is Mindy Castellani?"

I hoped that if she was still in her old house, Mindy Castellani would approve of my reach for closure. "A nanny in the park that morning who saw Richard Lowe come over to me with his bad intentions."

"Oh, you mean the Richard Lowe who ended up at the hospital because of what *you* did?"

"And that's the great thing, Bobby, because not only did Mindy see our little tussle, but she's also ready to testify that as she was wheeling her baby carriage toward us, she saw you giving Lowe the signal to come after me. How's that sound?"

"You're full of crap. There was no Mindy Castellani."

"You know there was, Bobby. Tallish, blue overcoat, brown gloves? Yellow checked blanket on the baby in the carriage? And guess what I do for a living? I spend most of my time tracking down the Mindy Castellanis of the world. When they walk babies in the same place at the same time every day, know what it is?"

"A walk in the park!"

Oswald loved himself for his little joke. Pastore thought it was pretty funny, too. Nelson looked miffed—but also one too many details past disdaining the possibility he had overlooked Mindy Castellani. "Whatever you provoked in Dick . . ."

"Fine. We'll tell the precinct cops what I provoked."

Nelson knew better than to look at Oswald for sympathy. "I'll admit I was a little overwrought that morning. Dick was a Marine instructor for a long time, not used to subtlety. I agreed with him that maybe he should be allowed to leave an impression on you and Oswald. I shouldn't have agreed with him. I'll give you that much."

I could see why Nelson might sound authoritative giving out stock quotations. "So it was his fault, not yours?"

"I didn't say that."

"Sounds like it to me," Pastore chirped.

They nattered back and forth another couple of times. For a second I thought I had what they reminded me of in New Florence, but then the feeling slithered away again. I got back to cases. "Then there's my neighbor, Bobby. A Mrs. Chalian. You should talk to your sister and her friend about it. They harassed Mrs. Chalian and Mrs. Chalian doesn't like being harassed, especially by people who wear dead animals."

"That was none of my doing! Harriet gets things . . ." He stopped himself before he gave away her blood type, too. "None of my doing," he mumbled again.

"Nothing's any of your doing, and that's great. You'll have a spotless record when you apply for your next announcing job and I'll be able to say it couldn't have been you if I hear anything about our pal George here not being hired by the Cyclones because of his tasteless ideas of humor."

Naturally, Mister Potato Head heard only the parts he wanted to hear. "Exactly!" he crowed. "And the same goes for you, Lou."

"Actually not, George. Lou is going to have more to worry about than his fingerprints on studio tapes."

Pastore didn't notice he was squeezing his sandwich so hard that an anchovy was sliding out from the bread. "Like what?"

"C'mon. You don't want us sharing about our first meeting."

"Ancient history."

"No, not really. See, my friends out in Mineola have never been all that satisfied about the way they rounded up that French underground group. They still have that story in the drawer marked Incomplete."

"You're bluffing, Finley."

About that there was no question. But I had also been bluffing about something else lately, and *that* was what Batman's archenemies were trying to remind me of. They just weren't trying hard enough.

"I don't think he is," Oswald, wrong as ever, said for me.

"Listen to my client, guys. He knows when I'm serious. That's why he's going to be sure I get those three cancelled checks within a month."

Oswald looked ready to blubber again, but without gratitude this time. "What cancelled checks?"

"The ones you're going to write to three charities of your choice. One is going to be about women, the second one about the handicapped, the third one about Filipinos. I don't know—the Association of Manila Veterans Who Helped Win World War II? I'll leave those choices up to you. But I'd say three checks for five hundred each would be nice. Fifteen hundred, double what you paid me. I think that's an appropriate figure. And then when your bank sends you a record the checks have been deposited, you can make copies for me. What, six weeks at most? After that I stop being indifferent again to your career. Go, Cyclones!"

Closure, it turned out, meant only what it said—the end. It didn't mean savoring a sense of achievement or even relishing a petty retaliation. It meant getting out of Studio 3 with a begrudging nod from Oswald, a red-faced stare at his fingernails from

Nelson, and a hateful glare from Pastore. It meant moving away so far so quickly from the three jerks that I scotched an afterthought in the hallway of going back to remind Nelson that I didn't want to hear from the Lowe family again, either. Ends were ends.

The sales reps were gone from the reception area, replaced by a lawyer type in a pin-striped gray suit and a layer cake of a big head. Gladys threw me a wink, but had to look away again to her board before she saw me reciprocate. I thought about asking her what sense the ad magazines made, but had to admit that as much as we had fallen in love, she was unlikely to enlighten me. I was a romantic, not a dreamer. If I owed my epiphany to anything, it wasn't to Gladys, but to the ambrosia of building detergent fumes that almost knocked me out waiting for the elevator. It was really a muddle of an awareness—on one level the seemingly appropriate actually being inappropriate, on another level the three grotesques probably at that very moment engaged in a group hug in Studio 3. And squatting atop both levels were the charmers Hal and Leo, who not only didn't belong, but who were advertising they didn't.

CHAPTER 42

Thanks to two leisurely coffee stops along the way, it was almost nine when I turned into Karen's block. Maybe it was because of what Rosen had told me about the DOD, but the uniform slate houses with their bleary front room lights and square dark lawns made me think of where officers and their families lived on military bases. I still couldn't salute the idea.

During the day Brighton had gotten the crime scene tape removed from the Lockman garage. I couldn't see that doing much to return Mrs. Lockman to a normal world, but then what would? In the meantime, the implication was that the cops had gotten all they were going to get from the garage. I hoped Brighton was right.

What I wasn't counting on was that I would have the chance to ask him in person so soon.

I had kept my key, but it seemed polite to ring Karen's bell. When she opened the door, she gave me a full color chart of reactions. She was happy to see me, she was relieved to see me, and she was awkward about seeing me. The awkwardness was sitting on her couch in a gray suit and red tie. At least his jacket was unbuttoned this time.

"Captain Brighton is here," she said, as in "Heads up, but too late, he's already seen you."

Brighton nodded without standing. He was used to treating any seat at all as his office desk chair from which he received and dismissed callers. He also looked like he had lost a bet with

himself in seeing me again. I had the rum thought that his condescension toward Karen was more of that masked lust I had just
dropped off in Garden City.

"They're investigating Alan's death as a homicide," she
announced.

"That's nice. Tell Mrs. Lockman?"

"As a matter of fact," he said stonily. "Karen says this isn't
news to either one of you."

Or to anybody else on the globe, I thought. But I kept my
mouth shut as I took the lounger. I wouldn't have minded another
coffee to keep my nerves at their jangled best, but that would
have opened the door to offering a cup to Brighton, too. Karen
might have been acting less openly hostile toward him than she
had at the hospital, but why push the amenities?

"Mind telling me how you reached that conclusion so fast?"

To make sure I understood we weren't having another infor-
mal chat as in his office or the ER, he played cute by taking out
a notebook, putting it on his knee, and clicking open a pen. "And
in return you'll tell me why you've had Arlett trailing around after
me?"

It was the Claude Rains moment from *Casablanca*: He was
shocked, shocked! "You're the one who told me it wasn't the
Dvorak kid who hit you. Which means whoever did is still walking around. Officer Arlett was just making sure you didn't run
into him again. In my jurisdiction, Finley, your enemies aren't
just yours."

"I didn't expect to find enemies in Barney's luncheonette."

"Meaning you had your guard down. But what about Lockman? Why so sure he wasn't a suicide? You knew him?"

Some drills acquired venerability by being dragged out for one
and all occasions; others were just a pain in the ass. "Like I'm
sure Jimmy Sewell told you, I was in the same room with the kid
once. We never exchanged a word, not even hello."

"But you also ran into him in the library, I hear."

Karen parked herself gingerly at the other end of the couch;
she acted like she had violated a trust between us. She had—by
tying her hair in a ponytail. It tightened her face too severely and

gave her too much forehead, to say nothing about what it did for her soft eyes. "Saw him from a distance. Again, we didn't get to say hello."

He made a note of the bread and milk he had to buy on the way home, and it reminded me of something I had overlooked: Lockman had also been writing that afternoon in front of the microfilm machines. Obviously, he *had* found something in *Planning Society*, and most likely in that 1992 issue he seemed to have dug especially deep for.

"So you're saying it's just professional intuition."

Intuition, schmintuition. There were two ways I could have gone. The first was to throw him out, but it wasn't my house and even though Karen might second the motion, we would still lose precious seconds of our stately indignation in front of him while having to come to an agreement. The second option was simpler. "How about we do this, Frank? You stop your bullshit and we really compare notes. Believe me, taking the broomstick out of your ass will make you feel much more comfortable."

This time I liked her marbles-in-the-mouth look; it was damming up what they called guffaws. Brighton wasn't nearly as enthusiastic, he even seemed irritated. I was the mold on his long, stale day. But at least he clicked his pen closed. "You mean more about how Pulsar is up to dark things . . . You're not accusing them of killing Lockman, are you?"

I could feel her willing the words out of me across the coffee table. If we had been alone, I would have given them to her. But for a third person, especially Brighton, I too needed to separate Hoboken from New Florence. "We both have a lot of pieces. I'm not sure we'll have a whole jigsaw if we put them together, but I do know we'll never find out if we insist on keeping the pieces we have for ourselves."

He didn't have to turn to Karen to feel the challenge in her stare, it was all but boring through his cheek. He nodded. "Okay," he said, slipping his notebook back into his pocket. "You start. Give me one of your pieces."

Why not? He was the home team. I saw no reason not to begin with the biggie, and I knew what I must have looked like when

Rosen had told me about the Defense Department because it sucked the color out of Karen. If I listened more carefully, I probably would have heard old walls covering up Andy Antonacci collapsing somewhere inside her. But I didn't listen all that carefully because Brighton wasn't quite as dismayed as he should have been. I suddenly knew why he hadn't want to make any calls in his own name. Whether from his own industry or from somebody like Chief Lama, he had already smelled the military. "That's what you wanted me to find out for you, isn't it? What you didn't want to do yourself?"

He wasn't going to dignify the accusation. "Whatever this source of yours told you, it's ridiculous. He's wrong."

"No, he isn't," I said, wanting to be half as convinced as I sounded. "There must be something military up here."

"Absolutely nothing."

Karen was shaking her head, too; she wasn't helping. "Maybe some kind of chemical or biological thing masquerading . . .?"

"No. N O."

Why get hung up on the negativity of the English language? Wasn't he just worried about how Rosen's information might further compromise him with the local politicians who had been shaving his nerves about his taste for underage girls? Of course he was. That was why he was drumming his long fingers so anxiously on the couch rest. It was just too bad for me I could see how both things could be true—he was worried *and* there was nothing military near New Florence. "Your turn," I retreated.

It took him so long to decide what to throw into the pot I thought he was just going to forget our deal, get up, and leave. "You were right about Lockman's unofficial tallies," he said finally. "He was keeping track of his daily counts on his computer."

"And Mrs. Lockman told you I was in his room and saw what you printed out and deleted. You're not trying, Frank."

The original part was harder for him. "I talked to Sewell for a few minutes before coming out here. He got Pulsar's final results this evening. They're not the same as Lockman's. In fact, he practically gagged when I told him how the kid had the thing turning out."

I didn't need to hear that; it threatened my respect for the intelligence of cabbies like Antonio Varela. "Who did Sewell say won?"

"That's their golden secret until tomorrow's paper."

That, on the other hand, I needed to hear twice. "You showed him yours and he didn't show you his?"

"He made a pretty good point."

"What was that?"

He shrugged. "Who knows how complete Lockman's count was? Did he start counting from the first day? From the second? And so what, anyway? You have the post office votes, too."

"But you said he gagged when you told him."

"He sure didn't like it. But in his place, I wouldn't be happy having even different partial results turning up somewhere else. He admitted himself he really didn't know the overall total of votes. Maybe there were a few hundred from the post office, maybe a few thousand."

There were cartoon characters that couldn't have sputtered more than I did. "Am I missing something here? It's a homicide investigation!"

He blinked for an answer, and I realized I'd once again been looking at things upside-down. The scene between Sewell and Brighton outside the Lockman house, Sewell's criticisms and backhanded defenses of Brighton, the conversations with Brighton that Sewell had relayed to me—I had assumed they belonged to the normal give-and-take of a newspaperman's relationship with a cop who was good every once in a while for a colorful tidbit. But Father Sewell was not a reporter working for *Newsday* anymore; as a right hand of Walter Labine, he was part of the establishment that was keeping Brighton in hives and sleeping pills. Who knew when the *Reporter* would have to remind its readers of what Officer Frank had once done in his spanking new uniform?

"Your turn."

I didn't know which of us resented the other more for my attack of nostalgia for how things had once worked on the Island. It was probably a tie. "Ever eat any of Denise Sewell's grub, Frank?"

She was mystified, but he wasn't. "Yeah," he said icily. "They have a big thing in their garden every Fourth of July."

"Got it. Corn on the cob and Mayor McCorkle. Hot dogs and Walter Labine. Happy Independence Day."

"What are you talking about, Paul?"

"Your turn," Brighton repeated.

He was right: I needed to keep my macho in my pants. Stiffing him as much as Sewell had wasn't going to do anything for Mrs. Lockman, no matter how half-assed his investigation was. "Whoever did Lockman wasn't the kind who got sand kicked in his face at the beach. Took some strength to do that noose, and in what—less than a minute?" He nodded. "The kind of strength those two wrestlers hanging around Pulsar have."

He stopped nodding. "That's a joke, right?"

Saying it out loud wasn't the same as thinking it for highway trees, I had to admit that much. "There must be a dozen retired cops or bank guards around who could've used a few bucks to sit in that booth out at the annex. And Leo wasn't hired just to carry the ballot box."

I recognized Brighton's twitch; he wanted a cigarette, but didn't want to ask Karen permission. Instead, he did something like laugh. "Now they're killers? You've had a long day, Finley."

Even Karen looked more unsure about having me back; she was silently imploring me to make more sense. "They're out there like neon signs. What are the signs advertising, Frank? *Don't you kids even think of breaking in here to steal our computers?*"

"Why not? They're funded by the Feds. Maybe not the Pentagon, but *any* government agency is protective of its property."

"Right. And Leo's an accountant."

He shook his head in wonder, and this time didn't mind looking over at Karen for support. "You can't believe this, too."

She didn't know herself. It had been one thing blaming Pulsar for her husband's suicide, much the same suspecting Pulsar was *somehow* mixed up in what had happened to Page and Lockman, but altogether different to picture the Leos and Hals actually using their hands for killing. "I think if you rule out things before you've even started investigating," she said with just enough iron covering her doubt, "the investigation isn't likely to be very complete. Don't you think, Captain?"

I should have been thankful for the support, but loyalty had never appealed to me as much as agreement. "That gets us to Page, doesn't it?"

Brighton shook his head. "So far I've told you a fact and you've given me more of this science-fiction fantasy about Pulsar. This what you mean by putting the jigsaw together?"

"You can't still believe that was an accident," she prodded.

"Why not? You have conflicting evidence?"

I didn't know why I was hesitating; I didn't owe anything to Walter Labine's right-hand man. "I know what you found in that parking lot, Frank. The driver was waiting for Page to come out."

It had the effect it should have had: He didn't need the lamp on the end table next to him to bring out his unhealthy color. "Who told you that?"

"Guess. Nothing on the cigarette butts? From the Red Bull can? From the tire treads? Nobody out walking a dog or driving by noticed the car waiting? You buy Red Bull, you buy it in a store, right?"

In his place I might have shoved the coffee table into my shins or shot me through the eyes or obliterated my presence from the planet in some other vengeful way. But he didn't do any of those things. He just sat and stared at something behind my left shoulder, registering some passing car outside, then just receded into a quizzical expression saying maybe he should have been satisfied to have gotten so far on so little. Karen was so alarmed by his silence she was on the verge of reaching over and shaking his arm when he finally came out of it. "The editor seems to have told you quite a lot," he said dully. "All of it?"

I didn't owe him anything, either, but I nodded.

All news was bad news, and for a second he looked ready to accept the purity of it. "From what I hear from the same flap-mouth, you've had your balls in a wringer a couple of times, too. How did you get them out?" He immediately waved off the question. "No, don't tell me. I don't really care. The fact is, I'm used to this place. I could've moved years ago, probably should have. But those doors are closed now and I don't waste time worrying about what's behind them. This is it, and if that means eating crow every once in a while, too bad for me."

I didn't want his confessions and I didn't like the doubts growing on Karen's face about her opinion of him. She had been right the first time. He might have been only half-alive, but that was still a half more than Randy Page was. "Somebody told you to go slow on what you found with Page?"

He shook his head: I needed a keeper for understanding so little. "You still don't get it, do you? You don't have to be told things. You got ears? Then listen to what the air's saying."

"But why?"

"Why what?"

"Because there was always the *chance* it had something to do with what Page had been saying on the radio about Pulsar," she said firmly.

It took Brighton a second to catch up with her, but then he nodded. It was probably the first time the two of them had ever agreed about anything. "She's right. They all wanted Pulsar. The last thing they want it connected to is a felony homicide."

"Too bad. But I'm still back with my why. What is this damn survey supposed to be doing for this place? Will it help Barney sell more burgers? Give Labine capital for opening another department store?"

He whipped out his cigarette so fast he seemed afraid of thinking too long about doing it. "Do you mind?" he asked Karen, already searching for his lighter. "I can stand near the window."

She should have been gleeful about telling him to take his habit out to the street; instead, she reached over to the drawer in the end table next to her and pulled out a green plastic Cinzano ashtray for him. He put it on his lap, and was already breathing easier before his first drag. "What Pulsar's giving them," he said, "is recognition."

"Who the hell in Buffalo or Dubuque gives a damn about New Florence's Most Admired Citizen?"

"Nobody gives a damn about that but the one accepting the plaque," he said, the nicotine restoring some of his self-assurance. "I'm talking about recognition for the whole town. *We exist.* Pulsar has pulled us out of the hat of tens of thousands of towns in this country and decided we are worth its attention. They passed over us for the next Olympics, for the newest NBA franchise, and even for those Nielsen ratings people, but we got Pulsar. *We're worthy.* Don't you get it?"

"No."

He sighed before my obtuseness. "Right. By the numbers."

"When in doubt."

"Okay. By the numbers. We have suggestive evidence from the parking lot. We have dozens of cranks who have phoned, emailed, and snail mailed Page over the last couple of years wishing him the state he's in right now. You met some of them at the cemetery. And that's all without getting into a girlfriend he dropped for another one, the brother of the first girlfriend, and a couple of people he pissed off on the air because they were bigger idiots than his usual callers. You tell me, numbers man: How much investigative plodding is that? Weeks, you think? Maybe a few months?"

"Let's say until the day after Pulsar folds its tent and leaves."

No, he didn't want to say that. "Open your ears, Finley. Nobody from Pulsar wrote a threatening letter or made one of those threatening calls. Or should we keep them around for the hell of it until we land on a suspect?"

"You might start with background checks on Leo and Hal."

He spat a laugh through his smoke. "Why bother? You already told me who they are. SAC generals!"

She pushed herself back into her corner of the couch. It was supposed to have something to do with his cigarette smoke, but I knew it had more to do with being able to drop her eyes naturally so as not to show her disappointment with my end of the ping-pong match. "So if it's not Pulsar," I said, trying to salvage something, "where have your leads taken you so far?"

"What do you think? You've seen the father and son."

I had forgotten Dwayne Arlett had picked me up from the hospital. "The Reverend Dvorak is a creep, but he seems to worry a lot about public reaction to what he does. He even left the cemetery protest to his son."

His smile was almost blissful. "Welcome to New Florence, Finley." He started to stub out his cigarette, then looked at his watch and decided instead to take the rest of his smoke out to the street. "It's getting late," he said, standing. "I should go."

I didn't like the way the Dvoraks had been left hanging as the answer to something. "Whatever you want to believe, there's no substitute for getting into that annex and seeing what they're really up to."

"I thought you did that yesterday."

"I mean a real look. Without their p.r. bullshit."

"Sounds like you're talking about breaking in. I don't think that would be very smart. All kinds of laws against that kind of thing. And that's without counting these two killers of yours."

I had said it a thousand other ways, so why not directly? "You're not much of a cop, are you, Brighton?"

He might have been back to wanting to strangle me or he might have just been reflecting the glare from the end table lamp. "I think you've made it pretty clear I'm not up to your downstate standard. But I wouldn't break any windows out at the annex, if I were you. You don't have a key to get in, you don't belong in there." He looked at the ash building on his cigarette, then over at Karen apologetically. "Sorry about this. Good Night."

She didn't even nod as she followed his quick steps to the door. He had become irrelevant to her before he was gone. "You were awfully nasty to him," she said.

"He seems used to it. Too used to it."

We both waited until we were sure the engine starting up outside was Brighton's. It was her signal to pull herself off the couch and gather up the ashtray for cleaning. "You once accused me of looking at all this through Andy," she said. "Who are you looking at it through?"

She didn't want an answer. She was already out in the kitchen when I had to admit to myself it wasn't her.

CHAPTER 43

She didn't know what to make of it, and either did I. The first call, from Veronica, got her to reach out from under the covers to her cellphone on the night table. That got her awake and hopping around the bedroom to find her underwear and something she could throw over her to go out to the lawn for the newspaper. The second call, from somebody named Lenore, had her yes-yessing to what she had already heard from Veronica. She thanked Lenore not all that thankfully, hung up, and grabbed a white terrycloth half-bathrobe thing that left plenty of black panties to see. She ran out the door tying the sash and asking if she was decent. She really didn't want my opinion, which was a multiple-choice answer anyway.

When she finished swearing her way out through the living room and slamming doors, she reappeared with the paper. She seemed to have already run through half a dozen cracks to the question mark on my face. I thought I got the seventh answer when she handed me the *Reporter* and said, "Guess who the eighth most admired citizen in New Florence is."

I guessed before I took in the front page. And yes, I should have been just that—admiring. But her bafflement was also good for concentrating instead on the DVORAK MOST ADMIRED headline. Since the only pictures were of Labine, McCorkle, and Page, I needed a second to figure out which Dvorak they were talking about. Call it a victory for older, responsible dipshits over the younger, irresponsible kind that it turned out to be the Reverend, not the silkscreen painter opposed to unholy burials.

"It's crazy!" she said, coming back into the bed. She couldn't have been out on the lawn for more than a few seconds, but her legs and feet were icicles. "224 people voted for me!"

"Or you used those free library copies of the paper to make a lot of extra ballots for yourself."

"I'm serious, Paul. It's ridiculous."

It was, but not because of her name in the eighth slot on the Top Thirty list slathered over the front page. To begin with, there were people I had never heard of, so what better grounds for disqualification? Then there were the ones I had and shouldn't have been seeing on any such list. Every local Babbit, from the mayor McCorkle to the police chief Lama, had made the cut. If they had an office in City Hall, chaired a community committee, or traveled regularly to Albany for business, they were on the list. Who wasn't, on the other hand, was Sewell's Mother Teresa; an administrator from the New Florence Medical Center, but not the charity worker Margaret Despina. And how many other worthies like her must there have been—grass dealers who sold below street prices, construction workers who didn't wolf-whistle, bartenders who bought back regularly? I wondered if by not running Dvorak's photo, Sewell had been exacting payment for all those omissions.

"You really think it might have been somebody from the library doing what you said?"

"What?"

"Making a whole lot of copies because I talked to him once about the books he was checking out?"

"No, I don't."

"You mean it?"

"I mean it."

And I did—sort of. But what I also couldn't shake was the thought that we were staring at something we had already talked about regarding Antonacci: *He shouldn't have won.* And were there really that many people in New Florence who lit candles in their homes at night to the likes of Dvorak, Labine, and Lama? Same conclusion: *They shouldn't have won.* But I wasn't going to say that, not with her working up to believing in my reassurances about her own finish. She wanted to be serious. She wanted me to be serious. But when all was said and done, she really didn't mind standing behind only seven others as the sovereign of New Florence, either. "It may say eighth," she purred, "but I'm really first when you think about it. The ones ahead of me are natives. I'm an outsider."

Which reminded me that there was no mention of the Mochi heir on the list. "What's his name?"

"Lawrence," she said, repositioning her legs under the covers to make sure her chill went straight to my nervous system. "You saw him the other night at the lecture."

"I did?"

"He always wears an ascot, looks like a fop and likes looking that way. Hilariously vain about his hair."

"*That's* Lawrence Mochi??!!"

"He prefers Lorenzo. Veronica says he blames the factory for not being a great artist."

"They're buddies?"

"Veronica hasn't given you her lecture yet about how she likes failures? Lorenzo is made to order. But forget about that. Russell Dvorak and the New Florence Society? They're a joke, Paul! The only people who admire him are his disciples!"

I didn't break the news to her that this included the world's greatest heart surgeon. On my third read-through I also noticed that not only had the wrong people won, but that there was something immaculately grubby about the list. If some local cynic like Antonio Valera had drawn it up, he couldn't have done a better job than Pulsar had done. Even Page lost his luster as a ballbreaker by being in the middle of so many hacks. The town librarian aside, who could have admired any of them? It was a lineup that should have had neighbors taking long second looks at neighbors and then pulling out of town before the disease got them, too.

Just like when the flu had hit town in 1918.

Before Claudio Mochi had arrived.

She hung her chin on my shoulder to take another look at the rankings. Her Prell shampoo was still as strong as it had been when she had come out of the shower last night. "Weird Sewell isn't there," she crooned. "Okay, he's not editing the *Times,* but aren't you supposed to admire editors?"

"He probably recused himself."

"Labine didn't, and it's his paper!"

"You don't know Father Sewell. This way he kills two birds with one stone—he's objective and he can think he would've won if he hadn't taken himself out of the running."

"That sounds doubly sleazy."

"It is." Even her ear was cold. "That's why it turns him on."

"No Brighton, either."

"So they got one right. Not even Pulsar's perfect."

Or so I wanted to believe.

CHAPTER 44

Since it was Saturday, Karen didn't have to open the library until noon. That seemed a little backwards to me, but who was I to criticize what superior budget minds had decreed? It took three more congratulatory calls for her to turn off her phone and a little longer than that for both of us to stop being distracted by the fourth, fifth, and sixth ones that couldn't get through. Only when we somberly committed ourselves to playing did we remember that we had nowhere better to go outside each other.

As had been becoming a habit, she went off to work with a question I could have done without. *What was I going to do with the day?* Start it over so I could again watch her running around looking for her panties, was one answer. Sit around with Big Ben tolling in my skull wondering why I couldn't have just as easily invited her down to Brooklyn, was another. There had been a purpose in coming back, that much I recalled. I was going to help her help Mrs. Lockman. Or something. And I was going to do that because I didn't like strangers being murdered and nobody doing anything about it. Except that even Brighton seemed to have begun doing something about it. So what was I going to do with the day?

I got into the car with a host of choices. For instance, I could have gone to a supermarket and gotten the ingredients for the one and only supper I was good at preparing—chicken paprika. Or I could have gone down to taunt Sewell about the missing Margaret Despina and gotten his opinion on why all the people who shouldn't have won had. Or I could have looked up the Reverend Dvorak for an updated opinion on the evil he identified with Pulsar. Or I could have meditated on Karen's question about whose eyes I was seeing Pulsar's fieldwork through. None of those choices promised to be as entertaining as the Mets at the end of June, but the season was over, and you settled for what you could. And when in doubt about delicious alternatives, as a more imaginative Sergeant Bailey might have said, do the wise thing and choose them all.

Early Saturday afternoons in a New Florence supermarket were like early Saturday afternoons in any supermarket in the country—too late. The only chicken breasts left looked like discarded lab specimens. I was considering taking a package anyway when somebody tapped me on the arm. I turned into Zev's geeks, Ben and Belinda. They were happy to see me. How was I doing? Still skeptical about what they were up to out at the annex? What did I think of the poll results?

The happy talk rolled on as I tried to make sense of the cart bulging with groceries that stood between us. "I thought you were finished out there," I finally got in. "You look like you're shopping for a week."

Belinda explained through her usual gushings. There was the B team, and they would indeed be packed and gone by the end of the weekend. But the A team—she and Ben and a couple of others—were still needed for monitoring immediate responses to the results. "You can't say we're not thorough," she beamed.

"The thought never crossed my mind. But at what, exactly?"

They were glad to see I was still a big kidder. Ben gave me the address of the bed and breakfast where he, Belinda, and the other A team members were boarding and invited me to the chili they were making that night for the landlady and the other roomers. As they wheeled off in search of the spices section, I didn't know what was more dubious—the chicken breasts staring up at me from the freezer or the idea that Ben and Belinda were involved in a DOD conspiracy that had claimed two lives.

The hammers and saws were hard at work in Labine Plaza. Betty Lou, the girl with the bangs I'd seen in Sewell's office, was directing two high school students on ladders on how to stretch out a COMMUNITY DAY banner over a wooden board. Other kids were lining up folding chairs before what I assumed would eventually be a stage. I thought it was funny they were arranging the chairs before getting to the speaking platform; like Karen's library hours, the priorities seemed a little backward. But tell that to the two tots holding their father's hands as they watched the banner being adjusted. They were as fascinated as kittens taking in a rolling ball of yarn. I didn't like the thought that, again, it was just me seeing things backwards.

At least Sewell was in the funereal mood I expected him to be. In fact, the whole *Reporter* office was blanketed in gloom, a little like my Fifth Avenue OTB was if a glue factory fugitive at Delaware Park had blindsided all the touts. "This isn't a good time, Paul," he said, celebrating the weekend by not wearing a tie with his white dress shirt. "Every aunt and uncle in town wants to know why Nephew Joey didn't make the list, Labine's on my ass about Community Day, and there's a little thing called the Sunday paper I have to get out."

It was my third visit to his office and the second time in a row he had acted less than thrilled to see me. I wondered what Ben and Belinda would have made of that trend. "Anything new on Lockman?" I asked anyway.

I caught the look before he dropped his eyes back down to whatever he was searching for in a bottom drawer. He had undoubtedly already heard about Brighton's visit to Karen; that was the kind of thing power networking was supposed to be good for. Which left him wondering why I should be playing him. "Nothing. Why don't you talk to Brighton?"

Judge Finley saw no reason to ease the defendant's conscience. "Those poll results seem to have gone over big with your people outside."

He came back up from the drawer with a new box of scotch tape; he hadn't heard an answer to his question and had switched over to Wily Sewell. "I haven't been jumping up and down, either," he said, tossing the old tape roll from the dispenser. "Between us hard cases, I'd thought a little better of New Florence than that."

"You mean Margaret Despina . . ."

"Not just her. I'm turning out a daily paper here, for Christ sake! Makes me wonder for who . . ." He didn't need his letter opener to slit a line across the new tape roll, and that cheered him up. "Ah, never mind. In case you haven't noticed, I'm snarling at the world today."

"Why? You can only double-check so much."

"Double-check . . .?"

"What all you newspaper editors do, isn't it? Your sportswriter comes back from Yankee Stadium with the day's score, but you don't even run that without glancing at AP or getting confirmation somewhere else."

"Pulsar signed off on those results," he said stiffly.

"You mean like advertisers sign off on their claims?"

"So what? I telephone Zev to bring in all the ballots so I can have somebody here recount them?"

"Delicate, I know. There's probably even some federal law against demanding to see the ones sent to the post office."

He knew he should have thrown me out, but he had a gene that said never do what was obvious. "You're insinuating something, but I'm not quite sure what it is."

"What else? Somebody like Pauline Shepherd hands me something and says it's god's truth, who am I to say no?"

He reddened all the way down to his doubly exposed wattles. But he also recognized an escape hatch when he saw one. "Have to admit she's the whole package," he said leadenly. "What we used to fantasize about in eighth grade. You too, right?"

I nodded to be locker room friendly. It had actually been sixth grade.

"And okay, you're right."

"About what?"

"What you said about signing off on an ad. Pulsar was the next best thing—a circulation booster. I've never thought of it as hard news. The only people who do are the ones who made the top of the list. Pulsar says that's what the standings are, that's what they are. I don't test every Ford we run an ad for, I don't feel a need to have somebody outside recount the ballots. Does that lower me in your eyes? Sorry."

"Not for me to say."

"That's right, Paul. It isn't."

We might have sat there the rest of the afternoon trying to make our stares mean more than they did if one of the cubicle people from outside hadn't stuck his head in the door. "Somebody threw a Molotov cocktail at Dvorak's church," he all but panted. "Pretty good fire going."

There was something to be said for Sewell's automatic instinct to start to jump up and get out to cover personally what he was being told. But then he remembered who he had become and subsided again. "You and Slattery, Rudy," he said. "Call if you need more."

The one called Rudy went ripping back outside and yelled across the room for whoever Slattery was. I didn't know what Sewell was seeing in the scotch tape dispenser he was contemplating. "This is the kind of shit I warned Labine about," he muttered.

It was a good thing I didn't run a newspaper. My headline wouldn't have been about a Molotov cocktail, it would have been something along the lines of FATHER SEWELL SAYS SHIT!

CHAPTER 45

Rudy hadn't been told the half of it. Miles away from the entrance of the Labine Building, the dark furls climbing the horizon wouldn't have been confused for a factory smokestack; mere blocks away, they were like Mister Clean's evil brother whipping up a black tornado. Even the praetorian guards had abandoned the lobby to go outside to wonder at the thickening cloud over the rooftops. Taking it as an omen that I had toyed with visiting Dvorak anyway, I left my car where it was and headed over by foot. Karen had wondered what I was going to do with my day? She had her answer: watch New Florence burn to the ground. With every few yards I picked up another curiosity-seeker hotfooting it in my direction. Those who weren't walking stood in the middle of the sidewalks gazing off at the unexpected weekend diversion. By the time I got to the scene two blocks behind Labine Plaza I felt like a pilgrim.

I also felt in need of my handkerchief against the acrid soot thickening the air. Dozens of people had been corralled behind a police line halfway up the street from the fire and they had reached the same conclusion. I felt accepted joining the general stupidity—30 or 40 adults standing where they didn't have to so they could cover up their faces to absorb toxic fumes slowly, not hastily. The football coach in front of me was sneezing and tearing, but the best cough went to a fat woman to my left; she knew what mucus was really about. Rudy from the *Reporter*, as penned in as everybody else, was coming up for air only to ask what people thought of the smoke. The Professor would have called it an Alien Moment: An ET flying by and wondering why the earthlings were doing the inane thing they were doing.

The church was a converted movie house squeezed between a pair of two-story red brick buildings that had probably been cold-water tenements in a pre-gentrification existence. A sign on the pool table rack of a marquee proclaimed the New Florence Redemption Mission, Russell Dvorak, Pastor. Whoever had tossed the explosive must have opened the door to do it because what must have once been a glass entrance had long been replaced by an ugly plywood front; the only windows now, columns of serrated, tinted glass on either side of the door, were still intact. The firemen who weren't backing off from the continuous plume of charcoal pouring through the entrance were busy wetting down the adjacent buildings. Dvorak himself was of two minds about that strategy—first imploring the firemen with the hoses to throw more water on what appeared to be his home to the left of the church, then dashing frantically over to a fire chief to demand more commitment to the hall. In his sneakers and shabby clothes, he still made me think of Rumpelstiltskin, but his orange hair looked a little less flaming so near the real thing. The chief kept nodding at him as if to say he had listened to pests before and wasn't going to let this one distract him from Rulebook Action Plan 10X45 any more than the ones in the past had.

Dwayne Arlett was patrolling the crowd corral, but he was too adrift on his own thoughts to see me. He looked positively spiritual—or like someone who had offered up his arsonist handiwork to a New Florence power greater than he was. Of course, it was a ridiculous idea. An eavesdropper on my thoughts might have thought I had something personal against the man. I had taken the bandage off my head that morning to find little more damage than an ugly patch of scalp. By now I should have graduated to being cavalier about how the mess had happened, chalked it up to life's daily misadventures, right? No, I wasn't quite there yet. Fire or no fire, I still relished the idea of having that high school kid from Barney's confirm what I would have given odds on and ramming Arlett's nightstick up his ass, preferably with Brighton and

Sewell watching. I would leave it up to Sewell to explain to them that this too was a lesson to be learned from a visiting authority.

Which was not the same thing as turning into a visiting cinder. The whoosh came so loud and fast under the marquee it seemed to go screaming behind me. One second, there was smoke spiraling through the main door, but more tiredly, showing gaps of yellowish wisps; the next, thunderheads were charging out into the street and cracking the hard glass columns flanking the door. Whatever salvation oils had been stored inside the New Florence Redemption Mission sputtered and exploded one after another, the vibrations knocking the firemen near the entrance off their feet. Two people desperate to get further up the street before the marquee came tumbling down pounded my shoulder one-two, and for some reason I thought of it as an achievement to stand my ground, to dare a third person to charge me. Rumpelstiltskin and the chief went down together, but out of harm's way. Arlett and another uniform were too slow. The poisonous funnel covered them so completely I didn't know why they bothered struggling. Even their yelling seemed extravagant.

I was so frozen taking in the firemen dragging Arlett and the other cop along the sidewalk that the gorilla hands from behind already had me up out of the gutter before I realized where I was being hurtled. I lost more seconds dodging the metal tip of the laundromat window's border and another concussion. When I finally regained my balance, I saw my savior was a bruiser in a sandy crewcut and a greasy blue jumpsuit. The last time I'd seen Russell Dvorak, Junior he had been wearing a camouflage jacket and guarding the next world against unwanted corpses. Did that mean he saw me in the same light as he had Randy Page? He stood tipsily in the center of the street, fists clenched in frustration there was nobody else to spin out of danger, sizing up the smoke itself as an alternative target. I couldn't help thinking of Tom Elligott, an Islip fireman who had specialized in starting fast food franchise fires so he could be a double hero—saving people from the flames and from their high-cholesterol diets. It was an unworthy thought. Junior was just being grateful I'd forced

Brighton to drop the assault charges against him. Nothing more than that.

The explosions from inside the church hall had opened fire holes all over the wooden entrance. There had to be half a dozen firemen or cops or EMT people crawling away from the smoke. Two EMTs were hovering over Arlett and the other cop. Dvorak Senior had gotten to his feet but, the laces on one of his sneakers slapping the sidewalk, hadn't a clue about where to go, and the chief was too engrossed in recovering his white cap from the ground to tell him. The braying of another arriving engine somehow sucked more hope out of everything.

I slid down to the ground in the doorway of the laundromat. A tide of exhaustion didn't exactly overwhelm me, but I let it think it had. The slim difference didn't seem worth fighting about. I told myself the whirring of the machines inside the laundromat was normality. That idea might have taken better if an Indian woman in a gold-and-purple sari at the folding table just inside the window wasn't methodically arranging her clothes as if everything *was* normal! I counted to ten before she even raised her heavily lined eyes to look out to see what was happening on the street. I made a mental note to write to Zev to inform him of my data-collecting instincts in the most trying circumstances; just in case Finley Investigations ever went under.

Junior Dvorak moved out of my sightline, and I didn't feel like raising myself to see his next rescue victim. For somebody who had to be in his thirties, he had lousy teenage skin and the kind of half-mustache that was still waiting for a clinching argument that he had reached puberty. I could have done without the image of Karen going down on him. Thankfully, the first VIP on the scene chose that moment to arrive—the billiard ball police chief Lama. Credit him for driving his own car; fail him for just about everything else. First, he left his white Mercedes in the middle of the street, making it harder for any other engines that would be needed to get close to the fire. Then he came out from behind the wheel and stood conspicuously annoyed that nobody was acknowledging his arrival. When a cop finally ran up to him and began jabbering, he didn't look all that mollified.

I wondered how Lama and the gang were going to keep Pulsar away from the firebombing, too. Could they really hope to persuade anyone the attack and publication of the poll results were just a coincidence? Sewell had warned them, hadn't he? One and one made . . .

I aggravated some bone in my back by sitting up too abruptly. I told it to go to hell. One and one were a plus. As in that Plus and Minus business I had seen on Pulsar's computers. But I hadn't seen it anywhere else, not in all the stories about Pulsar in the *Reporter* and on the Internet. Rosen hadn't mentioned it, either. And where was the minus anyway in a survey toting up votes for an admired citizen?

My Indian friend inside had no idea whatsoever: She was too busy folding children's clothes. Getting right down to it, the only people who could have answered that question were the Pulsar people, and specifically Zev and Shepherd. Why did I think they wouldn't be enthusiastic for the question?

Another engine came trundling down the street where I had been standing and gawking. The writing on the side said it came from Stanton, home of the paper mill. If I wanted to know if the mill was a front for ICBMs, maybe being made by pod people just pretending to be citizens of New Florence, I would have to get inside and look. By the same token, if I wanted to know more about Plus and Minus, I would have to get inside Mochi's annex for a more thorough look.

The Indian woman practically took the paint off the laundromat floor scraping a metal folding chair up to the table and flopping down in it. She looked totally defeated by the children's socks in her hands. Was it just that one sock was missing or that she had somehow picked up an extra one in the washing machine? She should have been paying more attention.

Like I should have been.

The kids in the oversized helmets wasted no time unfurling the hoses from the new engine and pulling them down the street to the church. One of them almost knocked over Rudy, now apparently hot for details about how to turn on water against a fire. One imbecile's criticism of another. I couldn't believe I had missed it for so many hours. Just like he had asked me to call Bobby Rosen, Brighton had left another heavy invitation in Karen's apartment before leaving. He didn't *say* it exactly and he could always deny he had. He wouldn't have been Frank Brighton otherwise. But he had told me as clearly as he could how to find out about Plus and Minus. I couldn't just break in. That was against the law. What I had to do, he had said logically enough, was find somebody with a key to the place.

CHAPTER 46

Saturday afternoons weren't weekday afternoons, so the redhead's bar was transformed from my first visit. I hadn't seen as many lumberjack shirts since Marshal Matt Dillon had brought order to a logger camp. No surprise it was a Bud crowd, probably a weekly reward for having driven junior to the morning soccer game or the wife to the shopping mall. Except that this Saturday the talk wasn't about scoring goals or buying juice glasses, but about Molotov cocktails. They had seen the fire, they were sorry for Dvorak, they wondered who had started it, they weren't sorry for Dvorak, they hoped the burned cops came through, they didn't give a damn about Dvorak one way or the other, they had to agree Dvorak had already had a pretty full Saturday, first winning the poll and then being attacked. Crazy world sometimes, wasn't it?

I agreed with all of it and none of it. I had enough opinions without others barking theirs over beer steins. Who knew how fragile mine might turn out to be if exposed to others?

"We better get something here at the bar," Veronica said, "or he'll sit there worrying about us sticking him for the drinks."

I tried not to stare at the booth where Lawrence (Lorenzo) Mochi was once again in residence with his brandy. After my selling job at the library on Karen and Veronica, I didn't need a misinterpreted look spoiling everything before I got to open my mouth. "Beer?"

She nodded just as the redhead strolled up and gave me the fisheye. It was a warning not to test her patience by ordering coffee again. When I pointed to the Bud Lite tap and flashed her two fingers, she begrudgingly admitted I was fit for citizenship and went for the beers.

"I'm not guaranteeing anything, Finley."

"Never occurred to me."

"Good. Then give me a couple of minutes. You bring over the beers when I call you over."

"*Ja wohl.*"

She gave me a look of long-suffering, repositioned the bag on her shoulder, and took one of her spry bounds away from the bar. Like most of my ideas, enlisting Veronica's help to get Mochi's key for the annex was at its best when it was fermenting in my skull. Actually, going over to the back booth and acting delighted to see him sitting there demanded a commitment by her that tainted the purity of my inspiration.

I belonged in a monastery cell atop a cliff on a deserted island.

The redhead clunked down two overflowing mugs in front of me. "Five dollars," she demanded. "Each."

"Starting a fund to rebuild Dvorak's church?"

Too many conversational circles on both sides of me fell silent. No question I could have handled her hustle a little more deftly. "But hey, it's a worthy cause," I said, practical joker that I was laying down a ten. "Don't let me slow it down."

She wasn't sure the bill excused the sarcasm, but then upon ample judicial review decided it was neither here nor there. She grabbed the ten without a thank you and all but paraded it to the register down the bar. "Don't let old Dorothy bother you," the lumberjack shirt at my elbow said lowly as the all-clear was given to the people around me. "She does that to everybody now and then."

"How does old Dorothy keep her customers?"

"Buys back more than most."

Which amounted to a plus and a minus cancelling each other out, I thought, seeing that Veronica had landed and was rattling on with Mochi. He wore the same white linen jacket and ascot, had the same hilarious comb-over. The major difference was a book instead of the *Reporter*. I could understand why he wouldn't have wanted to dwell on that day's paper.

"You want to be careful what you say about Dvorak, though."

I turned into a head of thick black hair lowered away from me. Only through the bar mirror could I tell he was Mister Suburban—candid blue eyes, flat face, frameless glasses. I wouldn't have been surprised to find him managing the home tools department in one of Labine's stores. "Why? He's got spies in here?"

He had the decency to laugh before he threw his beer into his mouth. "Just a thought," he said nonchalantly.

"Where're those beers, Paul?"

Mochi followed Veronica's wave over to me and immediately showed second thoughts about having been sociable with her. But it was too late for both of us, so I went over, beers flying and dripping in the wind. Up close, he looked even more doughy sickly, and it took a second to see (as Veronica had told me) he had just had his 32nd birthday. If there was nothing wrong with him physically (as she had said), it probably annoyed him. The Lorenzo Mochis I had known had spent years wheedling hypochondriac invitations to the ICU before finally keeling over for real. At the very least he had copied a few of them in assuming fashionable black could apply to fingernails as well as clothes.

Veronica intimidated him. As I sat down, she was teasing him about his absence from the Pulsar list, and he could work up only a timid smile to her "You should have gotten your employees to vote for you." The tactic of getting directly to the reason for our beers made me uneasy. Left to my own devices, I would have sidled up to him—smooth, suave, and subtle—and asked why he was reading the latest book about the building of the Panama Canal. How many times was the damn thing going to be built despite yellow fever mosquitos? But I could have saved myself the fretting. When he finally stopped chewing his lower lip to go for his brandy, he returned her edge twice over. "They wouldn't have voted for my great-grandfather," he said in an oddly cracked voice, "and him they owed. The only thing I've been presiding over is pink slips. I wouldn't have voted for me, either."

"Things that bad?"

He had to remind himself Veronica was vouching for me. "A couple of years ago," he said, affecting the blasé raconteur, "I had to ask myself which would be worse: Wal-Mart coming to me and saying they wanted to put in a big order and me having to tell them I didn't have the facilities for it or Wal-Mart never showing up at all and me having to lay off more people. Thank god Wal-Mart never came calling. If I'd had to turn down a big order because I wasn't prepared for it, it would have been more my fault."

His zinger would have had them rolling in the aisles in some comedy club for manic depressives, which meant I was up for a smile. I had to look again into that parable about the one-eyed man in the kingdom of the blind.

"You're not convincing me, Lorenzo," she pressed. "Maybe even 28th or 29th, but you expected to be in there somewhere."

"I didn't see you listed, either."

"All my votes went to Karen. They confuse us all the time."

"Of course."

There was hissy and sissy, grumpy and pouty, and I had locked myself into it for the greater good. But that didn't mean I wanted them running down the virtues and vices of everyone listed in the paper, either. "How did these people ever pick your place for setting up their operation?"

He shrugged. "Why not? The annex has been laying empty for years. Just in case some idiot comes along one day and wants to buy the machinery, I send my maintenance people in every fall and spring to make sure it hasn't rusted away. It wasn't going full capacity even when my father was running things. He should have dismantled it and sold it off decades ago. But no, he'd never do anything that might slight the Mochi name. What Claudio founded, let no man put asunder."

"Who did the renting? Michael Zev?"

"Yes. Why?"

"Just wondering why he needed so much space for a few computers. Did he mention why?"

"Your friend asks a lot of questions, Ronnie."

She blushed, though I didn't know if it was because she didn't want me knowing she was Ronnie to some people or because Ronnie had been an earlier, more rambunctious life. "Because he's leading up to asking you a very big favor, sweetheart."

Deer in headlights felt more comfortable than I did in front of their stereo bemusement. I wanted to believe she was still playing it cleverly and not in some anti-Finley key, so that's what I believed. I didn't have much choice. "There's something in there I'd like to check," I said to him. "And if I could do it without telling them, so much the better. You have a key, Veronica said she knew you, so I thought I'd ask."

I had matched her frankness, so she swiveled back to his face for his answer. No wonder she had agreed to help: There wasn't any big tennis tournament nearby, so she was going to make do with us as entertainment. And that made her less surprised than me when he sized me up a third or fourth time, then tittered at what he saw. "What something?"

"A computer program."

He nodded as though he should have expected that answer. "So like an extra maintenance check after the midnight hour."

"Right."

"And your interest in this program is what?"

I wouldn't have minded the bar mirror closer to see how much of a straight face I was able to keep. "Maybe a couple of murders."

We were twins: He was counting on not showing much of anything, too. "Page and this copyboy from the newspaper? You mean them?"

"Yes."

He looked at Veronica for the punchline, but she just smiled. "I didn't even know those people were murdered."

"But you guessed right, sweetheart."

"Who else has died lately? The paper says . . ."

"They'll catch up with the news one of these days."

He might not have believed me, but he understood her curt nod. He retreated to a world-weary sigh he hadn't earned and thought about taking another sip of brandy. But the glass inside his dirty fingers talked him out of it. He needed another second to think. I wasn't surprised when it was about him, not Randy Page, Alan Lockman, or even Pulsar. "Do you believe in the skipping generations thing, Finley? How you're more like your grandfather than your father? I do. That's why I never wanted to be involved with the factory. I was like my grandfather Joseph. He hated the idea of living in New Florence and having to talk about curtains his whole life. Joined the Army to get out of here as soon as he could. Too bad for him he got a leg blown off in Germany and ended up having to come back here to live, anyway. But that wasn't his intention. He just got screwed by fate."

"So?"

"So I relate to that. My father never did, but I always have. Skipped a generation, see? It's Joseph to me, just like it was Claudio to my father."

"So you've been screwed by fate, too? That what you're saying?"

"I'm still here, aren't I?"

"But you still have your legs. How has fate screwed you?"

"Tell him, Ronnie."

"I haven't the slightest idea, sweetheart."

"Sure you do. Same way you've ended up its victim. We've both let the familiar choke the life out of us."

"If you say so."

"I live so. And so do you."

She hadn't bargained for that part of the conversation, and welcomed her beer. He was waiting for some applause from me for having embarrassed her. "It's the truth, Finley."

"But you still have both legs."

"Saying I'm a coward?"

I was, but it seemed smarter to get the key first, then run down the street before turning around to wave my ears and stick out my tongue at him. "I'm saying your property may be being used as a front that people with more serious IDs than mine could be dropping in any day now to investigate. I'd think you'd be interested in knowing that."

Even before he brightened, I sensed what was coming. He'd had time to think about the Lorenzo Mochi angle—the one that would make it unnecessary to worry about other people, especially the dead kind. "You mean something unfamiliar may happen to me?"

"I don't think that's my point."

"But of course it is! Publicity, Finley! Maybe I *can* get rid of that machinery. And who knows, maybe even sell off the main building! Then nobody around here can say it was my fault Mochi went out of business."

I didn't have a stick so I couldn't poke him. "But they might be able to say you've abetted a few felonies."

The more I went on, the funnier he thought I was. "Ronnie says you're a policeman or were a policeman or something. Well, Present or Past Policeman, Pulsar gave me a check, I gave them a key. End of story."

"But why not do more than that? Something really admirable. What nobody else on that list has had the nerve to do."

"You're wasting your time appealing to Lorenzo's nobility, Paul. Tell him he's wasting his time, Lorenzo."

He knew a double-teaming when he heard it, but he was still leery of having missed something. "Your friend doesn't seem to know much about New Florence realities. The town council voted unanimously to bring Pulsar here, Finley. And guess whose hand went up the fastest? They thought they were getting god knows what, but I *knew* I was getting the rent."

"So they didn't owe you a spot on their Top Thirty list. You were already taken care of."

"You're saying the results were fixed?"

"Put it this way: How many other town council members didn't make the list published this morning?"

I wouldn't have minded knowing the answer to that one myself. It was my make-or-break bluff, and his big swallow of brandy said I had survived to fight another day.

"Labine swinging his shillelagh again?"

His laugh was mostly a sneer. "Shillelagh!"

"The impression an outsider could have."

"He's going out of business faster than I am. And he's tumbling down from a higher hill, I'm happy to say. For the tumbling part, anyway."

"I know. I've been to his department store."

"There you go."

"There I go."

He strummed his black bugs on the table, staring in my direction but seeing the drinkers at the bar more clearly. And Walter Labine was in his head even more clearly than they were. "I hate the man," he announced.

"I got that much."

"He's even living in my house. Did you know that?"

"Because you sold it to him, Lorenzo," Veronica added.

"So what? I didn't need it. Too big for a poet."

I could see the Labine conversation bringing us all to the edge of a cliff I didn't need. "You write poetry, do you?"

He laughed through my clumsiness, but how could he object to having himself instead of Labine at the center of the conversation? "Free form. Inspired by Baudelaire."

I remembered the CB on Lockman's computer. "You should have talked to Alan Lockman. He wasn't quite convinced."

Mochi said something else while I realized I wasn't quite convinced, either. Alan Lockman and Baudelaire? It made no sense at all. There had to be another author with the initials CB I was forgetting.

"I would've bet on that holy roller Dvorak winning," Mochi said, seeing my attention had strayed from his aesthetics.

"I thought he was a minority around here."

"A loud minority. In a town that studies its navel and wonders if maybe he doesn't have a point with all his fire and brimstone. Take it from a student of self-loathing, Finley, that the Reverend presses more buttons than those in the New Florence Society. I could've predicted the firebombing, too. No one likes being outed that flagrantly."

"But you got distracted by what? The Panama Canal?"

He put his head back against his side of the booth. He didn't like me and he had new reasons to distrust Veronica, but when all was said and done, we were helping him pass the time more originally than any old construction project for joining the Atlantic and the Pacific. "You're really serious about this, aren't you?"

She left it for me to nod.

"And you really think something's wrong out there."

"Yes."

He dropped his eyes obviously to his almost-empty glass, and I turned back to the bar to get the redhead's attention for another brandy for her favorite regular. "I really don't want to be helpful," he said, sharing a joke with his glass. "I'm sure Ronnie's told you we have some of our best times together cackling away at how the sludge always finds its bottom."

"Yeah, she's mentioned it."

Veronica could have done without the reminder. "Just for a couple of hours, Lorenzo. We'll return the key tomorrow morning."

How could optimism come out as pessimism? It did at that moment. My optimism was the vibe he had made up his mind to say yes. Vindication, jealousy, sport—whatever the latest whim in Lorenzo Mochi's existence, it told me to be optimistic. But I was also so certain of it that Veronica's added appeal to reasonable practicalities threatened to sabotage his decision. And the eerie part of it was that he seemed to know what I was thinking. "Where you putting your money, Finley?" he smiled gloatingly.

"I think you'll do what you want. We've already entertained you with our little request and that could get you through every afternoon here for the next week. That might be enough for you."

The redhead deposited his refill on the table with the subtlety of dropping a sledgehammer between us. "Thank you, Dorothy," he said. "You won't have to put this one on the tab."

Dorothy grumbled something and went off again. He was waiting for me to make a crack about her, but I sipped some beer instead. He nodded in approval. "You should've been born up here, Finley," he said. "You adapt very quickly. Or did you have a head start?"

"On what?"

"Getting what you want by whining for it. Or maybe not getting it but still whining. It's all in the whining, right?"

Who could disagree?

CHAPTER 47

There wasn't one key, there were three—one for the padlock on the front gate, one for the outer door of the annex, and one for an auxiliary door right inside the entrance I hadn't noticed during my visit. Any one of them was hefty enough to have freed the Man in the Iron Mask. Only with them weighing down my hand did the scope of the latest Finley production fully dawn on me. And Karen was only too ready to help with the dawning, especially with my overcooked rigatoni already straining tact at her kitchen table. "I think it's crazy," she said. "If all this is so hush-hush, why wouldn't Zev install his own locks? One of those code pad things we have at the library? What's to stop Lorenzo from sneaking in to look around?"

Half-day or not, the library had left her in a brittle mood. For sure, the furtive glee at finishing eighth in the poll had petered out during the day. "If he's met the man, he knows curiosity isn't Lorenzo's bag. And that's assuming Lorenzo even knows how to turn on a computer."

She consulted the ceiling to see if it had heard what she had. Maybe it was only because I had deprived her of Veronica's assistance for an hour. Or maybe it was because she hadn't yet straightened out her reaction to an invitation to join Walter Labine and the other poll leaders for a brunch before Community Day ceremonies. Whatever the reason, she had definitely developed grave doubts about my infallibility during our afternoon apart. "But you're so good at computers, you can sail in, bypass any security system locking them down, pull a password out of the air, and find out everything you need to know about this Plus and Minus business."

I could hear Jeffrey Chalian chortling along with her. But when there was no reasonable rebuttal, one pettiness of mind deserved another. So I focused on how fluorescent lighting did nothing for the skin, particularly at the end of a work day. It took all my suavity not to point out the zit that had blossomed through the matted perspiration on her forehead.

"And even before you get that far! You don't think he keeps one of those gorillas out there at night? Didn't Zev himself tell you that was why he kept them around?"

"So what? We just sit around and give ourselves reasons for doing nothing? Keep going. There're probably millions more."

"I'm just saying . . ."

"Yes, I know. You should've been at Little Big Horn. 'Hey, look, George, there're a few thousand of them up on that hill, too!'"

"It's not funny, Paul."Of course, it wasn't funny. She hadn't even gotten to where I was dithering about where to leave my car. As far down the road as the picnic tables so I could add two hikes to the night's activities? Maybe right in front of the gate so a Hal or Leo on the premises couldn't miss me? *Funny* would have been spending the rest of the afternoon with Mochi at the redhead's saloon dissecting the character flaws of every drinker at the bar. Lorenzo had been up for it, too; it seemed to be a pastime when he was on the town with Veronica. But that wasn't why I had dragged Veronica out of the library to get the key and wasn't why I had to give the annex a shot. "Where were all these objections when I was at the library this afternoon?"

"They were there. I just never imagined he'd give you the key."

"Got you. Let him drown. It'll teach him how to swim next time."

"That isn't what I mean."

"Then let's leave it up to the lies."

"What lies?"

"Whatever the case, whoever the suspect," Professor Finley of Crime Investigations 101 informed her, "the lies usually decide everything. If the suspect persuades you to go chasing after them, you're lost, gone, *kaput*. But that's also the suspect's riskiest bet. If you discover he's lying, he's the one who's gone because the lie's always his last defense. If Pulsar's been lying about what it's really been doing here and we find out what that lie is, we may make some headway."

There were no cheers from her side of the table. Just the opposite, she looked frighteningly clinical, as if studying me as an old manuscript. "You sound like you almost believe that."

That was about right. "Yeah. Almost."

"And the possibility hasn't occurred to you they've been secretive just to make their lives easier? Why try explaining something the upstate rubes won't be sophisticated enough to grasp?"

"That's reassuring."

"No, it isn't. But is it the criminal lying you're talking about? Does it have anything to do with Alan or Randy Page?"

"You meet a lawyer today?"

Fluorescent lighting could also exaggerate the marble in people's eyes. Worse than an old manuscript, she seemed to identify me as a forgery of some kind. "I just don't trust straight lines."

"Even if Antonacci is at the end of one?"

"If you mean Andy, I told you I was over that," she said with yet more edge. "Maybe the rest of this has just been an excuse."

"For what?"

"For us."

No more doubt, I had missed a chunk of her afternoon while off being clever with Mochi. "What are you saying, Karen?"

"You're being willful. I don't trust willful."

"Straight lines. Being willful . . ."

"They come down to the same no good."

"Because?"

She glanced down at her plate, but she had given up on being evasive about that, too. "It's not important."

"Then don't make it sound like it is."

"And if you don't like me so much for telling you?"

It was the first one I had gotten right since turning on the water for the pasta. "I'll take that chance."

"Right."

"I mean it."

She had to brush off a last doubt. But she had been thinking too much about what she was about to say to let it get away. "Sometimes, if you really work at it, you can turn the truth into a lie," she said, daring me to deny it. "Is that part of your experience, too?"

"We're talking about . . . Andy, I guess."

"Yes, we're talking about Andy."

"I'm not following."

"He didn't break, but I did. Why should he have? Those newspaper stories weren't telling him anything he didn't know. I was the one learning everything. He was even resigned to what you said the other day—all that legal bargaining for some farm for white-collar embezzlers. The only thing he didn't do was buy me my Christmas presents and tell me to keep them in the closet until the holidays."

"But you didn't let him get away with that."

She sat back with her glass, very aware of how much wine she had left and where the bottle was sitting on the table. "No, I didn't. I would have made Joe proud."

"What's Joe got to do with it?"

My ferrets heard the unpleasant coming, what I really hadn't wanted to know since our first conversation at the same table. "He wouldn't listen to me when I told him we were through," she said. "He kept repeating I was disappointed in him, so of course leaving him would be a natural reaction. He understood completely. And god knew, he didn't want me staying around just to play the loyal wife for the media. Some of his people wanted that, but not him. He'd seen enough of those scenes at press conferences and he never wanted to have to think of me as one of those lectern zombies. The only thing he asked was I give it some time, not act hastily."

"But you did."

"Not what he expected, but yes."

Her chilling tone made me feel as if I had been part of whatever she had done in Hoboken. "What did you do?"

She was long past thinking it was funny, so her mouth wrinkled on its own. "I put down all the embarrassments—that's what one of his friends called them—I put down all his embarrassments on a chart. Then I made another chart of all the embarrassments that involved his father or one of his father's friends. Like the graphs I made for Joe when I was doing a paper. And one night I set them on the dining room table with his favorite poached salmon. He didn't know what they meant until I went through them for him, showed him how all the lines and arrows intersected. What it came down to, he saw, was that he hadn't even been corrupt on his own. He was still Daddy's little boy going off to jail. He had never been anything else. Least of all for me." She sipped her wine. "I'd never felt so spiteful in my life. But it was . . . You know what it was? *Cleansing!* And he looked at me like he had never seen me before. He would have settled for the lectern zombie at that moment. Anything but the creature in front of him. He got up and went out to the garage. I didn't think about it at first. I was still trying to accept what I had done. Then I realized he wasn't making any noise. I ran outside. He was just standing against the fender of the car watching an ice cream truck ringing its chimes as it went down the street. I could feel his satisfaction practically through the back of his neck. He knew I'd run out there thinking that maybe he had gone into the garage to . . . well, what I *did* think. I couldn't believe I'd thought something like that, and so naturally! It was like having Novocain in my brain. I knew it was me, but it was also me removed from me. I went back inside the house before he turned back to see my face. I didn't look at him again that night and he was gone early the next morning. To his office. Where he did what he did."

She sat with a tic of a smile, waiting for me to pronounce some judgment that would prove once and for all I was irrelevant to her. I didn't dare think anything but the need to keep my mind a blank. Convicts served shorter life sentences before she finally got tired of waiting for me. "So I really don't believe too much in what you think you're going to accomplish by discovering one of your lies," she said, reaching for the bottle before she had finished what was in her glass. "You want to go out there because that's what you expect from yourself, excuse me if I skip the pompoms."

"So we'll sit paralyzed because we've done nasty things."

"If you want to put it that way."

"That's the way you're putting it, Karen."

"I just don't like futility! This isn't one of your malpractice cases! Pulsar is bigger than that. Let them leave town the same way they came in."

"Little late for that. Take a walk down to Dvorak's church."

She had one friend and one friend only in the room—the ceiling. "Like some people around here haven't been looking for an excuse for years to throw that bomb."

"Well, the *Reporter* got around to providing it today."

She had no answer except to fold her arms over her breasts. The way she held herself together over her pleated white blouse with her chin cocked toward the ceiling light bothered me more than what we were arguing or not arguing about. She might have almost been posing for a camera. And with that thought I was suddenly sure there was a third person with us. It seemed like the only explanation for the testiness that wanted to confess the past and the low self-esteem that insisted on being hostile. "Did you run into somebody today you could have done without?"

"Why would you say that?"

"Somebody had to invite you to this brunch."

"Labine's secretary. On the phone."

There was too much of a whiff of relief in her answer. I was close, but only that, so she didn't have to say. I knew those mind games, and the silent part was usually a threat. That was the third party at the table.

"Don't be ridiculous," she said to the idea.

"I'm right, aren't I?"

"Are you ever wrong?"

"Someone dropped by the library today. Who? Brighton?"

No, Brighton wasn't in her eyes. But I was close again.

"Mister Billiard Ball? Lama?"

She came down from the ceiling for her wine; not for me, for the wine. "He saw you at the fire," she said to her glass. "He wondered whether you being there had anything to do with the cemetery."

"What are you talking about?"

"Well, Russell was accused of . . ."

"And I was the one who told Brighton . . ."

"I reminded him of that, but he wasn't impressed. He said he saw the two of you together. He just wanted to warn me how people could jump to conclusions about you denying he'd attacked you."

"We weren't *together*, Karen! The guy threw me out of the way of the fire! I didn't say a word to him!"

She hadn't heard that detail before, and was impressed. "I was sure it was something like that . . ."

"And you listened to this bullshit? Even for a second?"

She raised her eyes as if she had lost a bet with herself. "I know them, Paul. They'd detain you until they got tired of the charade."

"Detain me for what? My god, Karen, listen to yourself."

"They don't want anything spoiling their Community Day."

"Again, a little late."

"Not if they have an outsider to blame the fire on," she said, jutting her jaw at me. "Even for just 24 hours."

I didn't know who I was looking at. Somebody afraid. Somebody protecting something. Somebody trying to ignore both things. "Then they fucking well better knock on the door right now."

"I talked him out of it," she said evenly.

"How did you manage that?"

"By reminding him I'm supposed to be on that stage tomorrow, too."

"He didn't need you to remind him. That's why . . ." The sense of the Top Thirty list died in my throat. Would she have even finished 108th if we hadn't run into Zev and Shepherd at the Rustic Inn?

"That's why what, Paul?"

"Why he dropped by the library in the first place," I scrambled.

She searched my face for the better answer. She seemed just as glad she didn't find it. "Obviously."

It wasn't a knock at the door. It was the front doorbell.

CHAPTER 48

Brighton had lost a lot in 24 hours—his attention to dressing stiffly, his observance of the social niceties as a visitor, and his routine dread of cracking the eggshells lining his path. Let alone ahead of Karen, his wild eyes seemed to come through the kitchen door ahead of the rest of his own body. Before I had a chance to warn him off about the charade Lama had hinted about at the library, he told me what else he had lost. "Arlett is dead and I've got another officer on life support. You were with Mochi this afternoon. Did he give you what you were after?"

I didn't need Karen's scowl to know not to marvel at his information resources. Charging bulls weren't detoured by flattery. "Yes."

"Then let's use them."

I glanced at the wall clock to see it was only a few minutes after nine. I didn't give a damn about the time; if Ben and Belinda were having their chili party and the B team was on its way out of town, the annex was going to have or not have the same Zevs, Leos, and Hals around at nine as it was going to have at midnight. But I needed a second to slot a Brighton with his tie knot halfway down his chest into my file cabinet. "I've just been out there," he said to hurry me along. "No sign of anybody inside."

Karen slipped into the kitchen and went over to the sink for a wine glass. When it came to Brighton, all the chainsaw objections she had made to me about going out to the annex were an invitation for partying. "You should think about this, Captain," she said. "Have some wine."

He ignored her. "I'm assuming you know a little about the hardware you saw out there," he said. "If not, just give me those keys."

"Paul doesn't . . ."

I threw her a glare, but it was too late. He recognized the 800-pound gorilla standing between us right away. "Jesus, don't tell me he was counting on you to work the computers!"

She seemed to have considered the possibility. How come I hadn't gotten around to mentioning that part? I had an excuse somewhere; I just couldn't remember where. "Sensitive as ever, Frank."

"Look, hotshot. You may be right about all this or you may not be. But right now, I owe it to Arlett's widow and two daughters to find out one way or the other. You coming or not?"

She stood against the sink wagging the wine glass with a bratty look on her face. If she was thinking the same thing I was, the little foray to the annex had just gained official police protection. "Sounds like the two of you together couldn't get a screen up," she said, all but batting her eyelashes. "Or maybe they just keep everything on paper."

Brighton knew the answer to that as well as I did. Give or take a nano, he spent a second of regret for his high-handedness with her. "I'm a little bent out of shape right now, Karen. I've got two likely homicide investigations going everywhere and nowhere. I've got an arson investigation with a third and probably fourth homicide. If I was the chief of police, I'd be pounding my desk for results, too. So I'm sorry if I said anything to insult you. It's just not front and center in my head right now. But in the meantime, I'd welcome any help you can give me."

I looked away from her. In her place I would have taken anything less than groveling on the floor from me as gloating and I didn't want any wrong reads from her. Brighton was right: We did need her to access the computers to see what Plus and Minus was about. Naturally, she chose that moment to fall back into her whispering. It took a sigh of relief from Brighton for me to get that she was hurrying out of the kitchen to get her coat, not to go hold the front door open for him on his way out.

"I'm sorry about Arlett," I said.

He nodded and pivoted out of the kitchen after her. I really had nothing to add anyway.

Nobody said anything, but we all seemed to agree one car would have compromised somebody and three would have brought too much attention. At least that appeared to be the reason Brighton pulled away from the house in his blue Impala without offering us a ride and Karen clicked open the passenger door for me in her Focus. I might have devoted a few minutes of learned resentment to that spill-out, pointing out that I had more experience than both combined behind the wheel, if the arrogances in the air didn't amount to a pretty insignificant fare for their company. Had it really been only ten minutes ago that she had been on the verge of putting my bag on the sidewalk if I had gone through with using Mochi's keys? I might have almost felt grateful to Brighton if that road hadn't immediately led me to thoughts of Dwayne Arlett and the nightstick he was presumably taking to the next world with him.

There was nothing to say on the ride over to Sloan Avenue so we didn't say it. She had Brighton's tail lights ahead of her by the same half-block as we approached the factory as she had had on her own street. As George Oswald would get around to saying one day next season, all the players asked from the umpires was consistency.

The only light on in the annex was a night light over the entrance. I had seen stronger bulbs in broom closets. The security booth was more closed than a New York subway token booth and the windows saw nothing. On the other hand, there was a car at the end of the parking area. It was an old, dusty green Olds from the 1980s, maybe out of commission since being left there by Lorenzo's father, but it was still a car. Brighton didn't take any chances, slowing as he neared the front gate but continuing. It took him the rest of the wire fence and then another hundred yards to slow down to a complete stop. He was out from behind the wheel and coming back to us as Karen rolled down to her own stop. The only annex windows facing us, barred office squares apparently off the catwalk where I had seen Leo, were dark.

"We'll take care of the cars," he said to me. "You go see if those keys are going to get us inside."

"What about that Olds parked there?"

"It's been there for years."

"You know that for a fact?"

"I don't know anything yet for a fact, Finley. What about you?"

Sometimes I felt like life's noncommissioned officer. That might not have been the road to glory, but I had to admit a bunny rabbit snugness about having Brighton take such confident charge. In the grand scheme of things some people were generals and some were sergeants, and that was all there was to it. Men like Brighton would have illustrious careers and get elected president, I would have the respect of my men.

As soon as I found some.

I took it as a reward for my innate humility that the padlock key actually worked. I might have appreciated the snap still more if it didn't start the chain down a clattering slide that would have aroused generations of Mochis from their graves. I stopped the slide at no more cost than a flap of skin off the heel of my left hand. My reward for not howling was that the gate didn't squeak when I nudged it ajar.

"That took some doing," Karen said behind me.

I hadn't heard her boots over the gravel, and that didn't seem like a positive development. "How much faster was I supposed to be?"

She didn't know—either what I was talking about or what she was talking about. The break in her voice said her bluff in coming along had caught up with her. "Brighton said leave the door open for him."

Just when she should have gone to inaudible, she sounded like she was talking through a loudspeaker. As we made our way down the entry path toward the door, I wondered if that was part of her agreement with Lama—since she couldn't talk me out of sneaking into the annex, she would come along and speak loud enough for Zev and Leo to hear us and have time to erase all the computer evidence inside. Could I put that kind of double-dealing past someone who had finished eighth as an admired citizen? There was a reason seven other people were considered more admirable.

She went back to murmuring her surprise at the absence of a code pad on the front door. I might have been just as elated about it if what she had said back in the kitchen about changing locks hadn't made so much sense. Telling myself the old Olds wasn't parked ominously but was just parked, I turned Mochi's second key. It too worked. It began to feel too easy. Since when had I begun trusting people with hair combs like Lorenzo's?

The inside vestibule door was the easiest of the three. In the paranoia that was quickly wrapping me within its coils that also made it the most suspicious. Standing on the factory floor, taking in the left row of computer slots that had already been unplugged and covered by plastic, I reminded myself that all had ended happily for the white bwana and the others who had stumbled into King Solomon's mine. Or was I confusing that with one of those Indiana Jones things and the white bwana had in fact been dropped into a pit of scorpions for his greed?

"Plus and Minus?" she asked, deciding on the workspace where I had seen Belinda. "That what they called it?"

"They didn't call it anything," I corrected far too tensely. "It was the symbols I saw on the screens."

She gave me another odd look, then went over to Belinda's computer. Why she chose then to start tiptoeing I had no idea.

Since I was unlikely to be of any help until she cried EUREKA and I had never had the thrill before of reconnoitering a fabrics factory annex closed for years, I strolled down the Pulsar row to check out what I had missed on my first visit. The smells I hadn't encountered the last time—old oil, new dust, the drilling odor from some great rotten tooth—were waiting right past the last computer, as though Lorenzo had leased the place to Zev by the square foot, a line drawn over the concrete floor for separating the tenant from the landlord. The shrouded machinery might have been antique compared to the Pulsar hardware, but it hadn't lost its intimidating size; even silent and inert, the network of iron piping and elaborate funnels hanging in the air felt on the edge of rousing itself into a din. I wondered if my father had ever seen the machines at his plant in such a state or if they had always been going when he had turned up for work in the morning and left at night. I didn't think he would have liked seeing them the way I was.

I took it as good news that Karen's screen was illuminated, bad news that she was staring at it with a blank expression. Since I hadn't become any more helpful to her in the minute she had gotten as far as she had gotten, I ambled down to the second catwalk. There were bridges in New York that weren't as long or high, but none had so many office doors arrayed along them and demanding closer inspection. I took the metal staircase two steps at a time. In the best of all possible worlds, I would discover all the evidence the most dim-witted of prosecutors would need for tying Pulsar to Page and Lockman. At worst, I would do a lot of knob rattling.

The knob rattling it was, at least for the first two doors. The locks were so tight there wasn't even a decent rattle. I was just about to clamp my hand around the third knob when I heard a sound I shouldn't have heard—of a toilet being flushed. It came from the single door catty-cornered to the shoulder-to-shoulder offices against the back wall; once I focused on it, it looked very much like a bathroom. There was even a weak light under it. I really wouldn't have minded seeing a computer walk out. Any other possibility threatened awkwardness.

I was too far away to warn Karen without making a noise that would defeat the purpose of the warning. I leaned on the thought that the bulky machinery blocked most of the view to the front door and that Leo hadn't noticed me the day I had been standing where she was now sitting—at least I didn't think so. Bad as the odds were for a repeat performance on that score, they were still smaller than the ones against me being spotted. I was down to pleading to Baal for divine intervention as I reached for the third office doorknob. There was no reason for it to turn in my hand, not after the first two had been so adamant, but it did, and so softly I had the door open a few weeks before I realized the miracle

I had worked. I slipped inside just as whoever was in the bath-
room began coughing up enough catarrh to explode Mount Saint
Helen's. Musical expert that I was, I was sure it was Leo. Or Hal.
Or someone else capable of pitching me off the catwalk.

Whoever it was seemed to be wearing slippers as he scraped
out of the bathroom. I could have done without a spasm that I
had closed myself into where he was sleeping. At least the moon-
light through the tiny window was reassuring on that point, providing enough outline to see I had landed in a storeroom with
ceiling-high metal shelves and cardboard boxes stacked against
the walls. Better, I couldn't make out any couch or daybed. Yeti
went scraping by—scrape, scrape, scrape, down to the first door I
had tried. He had a key for it. I had been lucky by being unlucky.
Who would have guessed the ape was so distrustful of his fellow
earth creatures that he locked up even to take a leak?

The door being shut gave me permission to breathe again.
The boxes made me curious. Because Baal knew he already had
me in the hole for a couple of animal sacrifices, he threw in my
pen lighter as a courtesy, letting it work for a change. The payoff
should have been uncovering parts of a ground-to-air missile and
the stamped NF NY shorthand on the cartons looked promising—
until I realized it meant nothing more than New Florence, New
York. I could have saved myself the trouble of slitting open one of
the tops to find old red tassels for Mochi's curtains. It was just as
well I had never been married to the idea of Lorenzo as an on-the-
scene contact for the Pulsar conspirators.

I made my way back down to the factory floor more cautiously
than I had come up. Brighton was standing behind Karen and
reflecting a quieter version of her frustration with the screen. "We
heard him," he said lowly. "Thought you were going to blow it for
us."

"Thanks. Shouldn't one of us keep an eye out for him?"

"Yeah. One of us."

I left that job to Arlett's spirit and concentrated on the screen.
It was stalled at demanding a password from Karen. "I've tried
Plus and Minus written out, as symbols with the ampersand, ev-
ery variation on Pulsar and Zev I can think of," she said.

"What about DOD with Plus and Minus?"

She tried it with no better result. "You sure there weren't the signs for multiplication and division, too?"

I let that go as the question of someone too eager to square off the universe in traditional ways. Brighton, though, was beginning to look less forgiving about everything. We didn't have too many circles of the second hand left before he went back to be the bureaucrat who dropped hints for others to do what he didn't have the nerve to do.

"You're not making your case, Finley," he said on cue.

I was feeling a little scrunched myself in entertaining the idea that Ben or Belinda might have made a faster job of it than Karen. And that was a nonsense like no other. One, because Ben and Belinda wouldn't have helped us against their employer. Two, because they had the password we were searching for. And three, because . . .

"Wait a second. They've been doing these polls all over the country, right?" The two of them looked at me as if I had declared Washington the capital. "I mean, they must have tons of files by now. Tons of this Plus and Minus stuff. Right?"

"If that's what all the programs were called," she objected.

"Well, we haven't got time to think about what else they might have been called. But if they were all called Plus and Minus, they must have some subcategory for filing. Like location. That's the most obvious one. So try Plus and Minus with New Florence."

The angels started congregating on the head of the pin. Plus and Minus as words with the name of the town. Plus and Minus as symbols with the name of the town. The name of the town first. The name of the town after. The name of the town with the addition of New York first. The name of the town with the addition of New York after. And then, just as Brighton's nervous footwork seemed to be leading up to an order to strike our tent, I knew what it had to be. Baal hadn't let me come so far without the final revelation. "Try NF NY and then the symbols."

I was mesmerized as the monitor flashed a mini-biography of the mayor McCorkle. He wasn't a very attractive man in his postage stamp photo, but at that moment he was more beautiful looking than Ava Gardner had been at her peak.

"Oh, my god!"

I didn't know which deity Karen had in mind, but I was ready to find a whole flock of sheep for sacrificing. Then I saw she wasn't reacting only to my powers. The McCorkle screen was merely the first of hundreds of pages with similar breakdowns of the locals. Just to be sure, she flashed forward through some of them. The Social Security number and addresses at the top right-hand corner of each entry were the least of it.

Brighton seemed to be staring through the screen. "We can't print out this stuff," he said feebly. "It'll take forever and our friend will hear us."

"No need." Karen went back to her jazz piano, creating boxes within boxes on the screen. One final flourish, a moment to make sure it had taken, then a smile up at me. "I just sent it all to my computer at home."

Even Baal needed her help.

CHAPTER 49

The file waiting for us on Karen's computer was all you never needed to know about New Florence. With a promise to recompense her for the paper and toner, Brighton commandeered the copier to print out every single page; the program indicator said the final total would be 497. Just pulling a page here and there as they came out, I found everyone from Veronica to Barney from the luncheonette, from the funeral director Tebaldi to the MARGE (last name Castle) who had sold me my jeans at Labine's. Social Security number, address, marital status, job, schooling, financial standing, auto license, community activities, magazine subscriptions, military service, political affiliation, medical problems, arrest record—who could have ever wanted more intelligence on Milo Draper, the pharmacist of New Florence Drugs? Milo's hookers might have been missing, but not much else.

Under the copier's incessant whining the stack on Karen's desk became two piles and then three. There was a suffocating robotry to filling up the copier tray, reaching down for what it yielded, shuffling it into shape, then adding it to the desk. At least Mochi had gotten a few drapes out of that kind of monotony. The biggest diversion came when I glimpsed Brighton sneaking one of the pages from the feeder to his inside jacket pocket. I didn't have to think too long about whose thumbnail bio that was. Call it the captain's personal surcharge.

By two o'clock the junky horse prints were comedy relief. I was grateful enough they stared back at me. Both Brighton and

Karen had gone out of their way to avoid eye contact since we had started printing, and I wondered if it wasn't because we had crossed some line with me as the outsider who, for all his good intentions, would never quite understand the intrusiveness of what we had found. I was pretty sure that not even telling them my Brooklyn mailman knew how much I owed MasterCard would get me into their club. In the meantime, Brighton hovered over the copier with a fixed frown while she matched each entry with the poll names published by the *Reporter*. There were only 30 names so it shouldn't have been a mighty task, but she went at it so painstakingly she might have been translating a newly discovered gospel from the original Aramaic.

Then again, as trivial as the facts in the thumbnails might have been, there was nothing at all banal about how they had been gathered in the first place. Mailman jokes didn't cover everything. It seemed a point worth underlining to my fellow workers in despondency when I came back from my second coffee run to the kitchen. "Say three-fourths of this crap can be gotten from a public record or credit card companies or something like that. But what about the rest? The personal stuff?"

Brighton was up for his coffee refill but not for the extra guff. "There is no rest."

"Oh, no?" I pulled the sheet off the top of the third stack on the desk. Karen didn't move her eyes from her tabulating. "Eric Moss."

"A lawyer," Brighton said, unimpressed. "Civil suits. Half his clients are grateful to him, the other half thinks he could have gotten them more money. All of them usually have something to say to the *Reporter* after they've won or lost their suit."

Happily for the point I was making, that didn't cover what Pulsar knew about Eric Moss. "'*Even as a schoolboy, Moss was known for his command of the spotlight and for polarizing classmates into friends and enemies. In one noted incident classmates slipped tranquilizers into his coffee before a scheduled school debate in which he was considered the favorite.*' Something he'd brag about to the *Reporter* 20 years later?"

Brighton shrugged. "I don't know the man personally."

The next one I grabbed was also heavy on reminiscences from the halcyon days at Poly High. "*Amy went through a traumatic junior year in high school following unsupported allegations that she had contracted a venereal disease. The rumors proved false.*" That got Karen's attention. "We not only have a reporter, we have one who's on the scene long enough to put hallway clap rumors to rest."

He knew she was waiting for a reasonable explanation as much as I was. "Sounds like Lozier," he said reluctantly. "She's been the principal out there for years."

"Sounds like Lozier what?"

"She's on the town council a long time, too." Karen said through me.

Brighton nodded. My whimsical notion of Lorenzo as a local Pulsar plotter wasn't nearly as funny the second time around. "So we have two big questions here, Frank. First, why all this research into the petty details of people's lives. Second, who supplied them locally with the information they seemed to want so badly. This Lozier sounds like one candidate."

He finally accepted that the printer could do what it had to do without his vigilance. He didn't know if he wanted to pace or just sit away from the murk being spewed out page by page; the lack of a second seat in the room decided for him. "It's not just Lozier," he conceded. "Some of these details had to come from others."

"Like who?" she demanded.

She might as well have planted her boots on his corn. "Is that important?" he bristled. "We didn't take this stuff to find out some people have been closer to Pulsar than they've admitted. Okay, that's not nice. Even makes you wonder about their little poll. But what laws have been broken? It's gossip you spill over lunch and this Zev or whoever never lets anything pass without putting it in a file."

He didn't believe it, either, but that wasn't a reason to let him get away with it. "Gossip about this Amy's sex life years after the fact? C'mon, Frank. How does that just pop up in conversation between some member of the town council and Zev?"

"Okay. That's why Pulsar came to New Florence."

"Sure beginning to look like it."

He fired the same wild look at me he'd had rushing into the kitchen earlier. "Keep your eye on the ball, Finley. In case you've forgotten, none of this is why we went out there tonight. We were chasing after your homicide fantasies. See anything new on that front, do you?"

The simple answer to that was no. The less simple answer was his agitation—that of a man wishing he could still be a hundred percent skeptical of fantasies. "Maybe we just have to look more carefully."

He thrust his head away as if deliberately showing us his profile. He was worn down defending what he had known for a long time wasn't worth defending. I let it go for the moment, and so did Karen. At bottom I wasn't any more comfortable with what we were doing than he was, if for a different reason. For all our efficient copying and collating, there was still something off about it all, and I remembered the feeling out at the annex that getting in with Lorenzo's keys had been just a little too easy. At least in retrospect, so had hacking into Plus and Minus. It was as if Zev had wanted us to do what we were doing so that every whine from the copier could drop another electronic bug into the house.

But then again, I'd been drinking too much coffee.

"These are all the ones that finished in the Top Thirty," she said, picking up the pages she had been separating into a small pile.

"We know who they are," Brighton growled.

"But suppose they have more in common than that?"

"Dvorak and Randy Page? I don't think so."

I took the papers from her hand. Her look said she would have preferred Brighton taking them to acknowledge her contribution. Dvorak was on top of the set, followed by McCorkle and so on in the order the *Reporter* had said. My finger skipped trying to get at the eighth one. "Nothing you don't know," she smirked.

"*Touché.*"

She shook us both off. "Sorry. I'm just getting tired."

I was grateful for the reminder. Her face did look lined and her white blouse had lost its ironed freshness. For hours, it seemed,

I had been treating her as nothing more than a cog in Finley's Anti-Pulsar Machine; maybe the most efficient cog, but still just a cog. "Me, too," I said.

I went back to the top sheet with her blessing. Dvorak hadn't been Elmer Gantry, but he'd had his moments. Booze had apparently been his best friend in his thirties and there was more of that Amy kind of gossip and denial about Russell Junior not being his only kid. But there was almost as much on his New Florence Society as on him personally, especially on its public forays in defense of any issue acceptable to Flat Earthers. *"The Society's actions have often alienated other sectors of the New Florence community, including those who might share some of its positions but not its tactics."* Who could deny it? I'd been at both the cemetery and the fire.

Then I noticed something in the upper left corner. Directly under the program logo of +&- there was a second minus sign. At first, I thought it was some kind of printing shadow, and that seemed all the likelier when the second sheet on McCorkle also had it. Just for the hell of it I went deeper. This time I landed perfectly on Karen. But she didn't have the minus sign in the corner; it was a plus sign.

I flipped through the other admired citizens. For every Karen with a plus there were three Dvoraks with a minus. Even Brighton gave up his sulking in curiosity. "It's not men and women," he said, leaning over my shoulder with his coffee breath. "Nothing to do with marital status or the jobs they have . . ."

While he droned on with the self-evident, I looked at Karen's sheet again. What was it Dvorak had said about overlooking the most obvious thing? So what was the most obvious thing about the research I had in my hands? I closed my eyes and dared something to jump up at me first. And believe it or not, something did. The most obvious thing staring back at me when I opened my eyes again was the tiny photo of a gawkier Karen. It had to be a copy of her driver's license picture. In fact, that had to be where *all* the photos had come from.

Brighton nodded until he remembered he wasn't supposed to be all that bothered by the town's cooperation with Zev. "All right, so there's somebody down at the MV who gave them what they shouldn't have been given," he said, going back to the printer. "I get a clerk fired for accepting a few bucks under the table."

She fired her pen down on the desk before I could put the words together. "Don't you see what's in front of you, Captain? We're not talking about Zev going down there and paying fifty dollars for a few photos. These are *all* photos from their files. It took planning to collect these. A lot of overtime hours by the people blessed for their sacred mission."

He was more intimidated by her sarcasm than mine. "Okay, okay. There're serious infractions here. These are municipal files. I agree. "

She rolled her eyes at me and sat back wearily. "Moving right along, Frank," I jumped in. "If you pulled somebody aside at the MV and asked them to do a little job like this, what would they tell you? We both know. Get it cleared with Lama or somebody else who controlled their paycheck. And if they didn't tell you that straight out, they'd make a little call to cover their asses. Right or wrong?"

"Your point?"

"You know what it is. No need to make that call if that authority is the one making the request in the first place."

He slapped at his side jacket pocket, and I thought he was going to pull out his own bio sketch to see if he had ranked as a plus or a minus. But that was the wrong pocket. What he came out with were his cigarettes. "I need a break," he said, heading for the door. "Five minutes."

"Somebody may see you outside," she said.

He laughed without stopping his march from the room. "Finley's convinced me. That ship has sailed."

She waited to hear the front door opened, then leaned down behind the desk to unzipper her boots. "He may keep going to his car," she said.

I wouldn't have blamed him.

CHAPTER 50

Once the last Plus and Minus subject had been printed out, Brighton had no reason for staying. He bundled the printouts in a plastic tote like someone carting off unappetizing leftovers he intended ditching as soon as he came across a garbage can outside. But I knew he wasn't going to trash anything. Not because he didn't dearly want to get rid of Pulsar's sketches, but because, always straddling his fence, Captain Frank Brighton muttered goodbye without mentioning the program still on Karen's computer. He might not volunteer to do something awkward, but he had learned to anticipate the blackmail others could wield against him if he didn't.

My head might have hit the pillow before I fell asleep, but I couldn't swear to it. Karen was in the bathroom when I conked out and she was there again when I woke up in the morning. This time she had the shower going. The sober blue suit and blue silk blouse hanging on her closet reminded me of Labine's brunch for the poll winners. Did she dare turn her nose up at it? Probably not if she wanted to buy more books for the library.

I blinked myself into consciousness, counting on more graduated levels of it to come before having to admit I was completely awake. I hadn't noticed before how unnaturally silent it was waking up in the Noon house. Because there were no trees outside there were no birds in the trees and because there were no birds in the trees there weren't even the occasional whistles of the sparrows and jays from the back of my building in Brooklyn. For a place that was supposed to be "in the country," New Florence came up miserably short on some of the fundamentals.

I thought about the towns in Oregon, Nebraska, and elsewhere where Pulsar had pitched its tent. They were probably as obscure to the people in the big cities of those states as they were to me. But there had also been a lot of them over many years, and that meant a lot of financing, the kind that, yes, the DOD could supply. But when was big money like that ever satisfied with small projects? The next time would be the first time. Big money had big ambitions. Towns like Bliss and Fleming and New Florence had to be pilot projects for something grander. I just couldn't think of anything grander than Rumpelstiltskin as the most admired citizen.

The shower didn't sound like it was running out of water and the cellphone on the night table beckoned me to eliminate one chore before getting out from under the covers. I was hardly expecting any calls to Finley Investigations on the weekend, but why be biased against miracles? Who knew when a Trump Tower princess might hear I was the ideal investigator to get evidence against her philandering sultan of a husband? My machine knew: Never. There was only one message. From Bobby Rosen. But from a Bobby Rosen less starched than normal. Wonder of wonders, he had even left what seemed to be a personal number.

I hesitated about calling him back. I didn't really know the number was his and last time he had phoned from the street like he was informing on John Gotti. Did I want to have Karen's number recorded by someone who probably had a thousand times more bios than Pulsar?

I tried to think of a way that wasn't a too little-too late worry, but couldn't. Besides, I was responsible for whatever Rosen wanted.

He answered in the middle of the second ring. There was a splash of water in an echoing hall behind him. Sherlock guessed indoor swimming pool. "You were just about to be covered over by a towel, Finley," he said, not sounding different. "Do you feel muffled?"

"You don't usually leave your private number, Bobby."

"No, and I don't usually get interrupted during my weekly dip. But since you were willing enough to depend on my judgment, I thought I owed you a follow-up. I have to confess I wasn't as thorough as I might have been before. I'm mortal, Finley."

"Sorry to hear it."

"Yes, well, virginity has always been a relative concept. Do you think families celebrate that in Richmond and Newport News?"

"I know this is important, Bobby. Otherwise, why have me call?"

"All right, all right." Somebody seemed to have dived into the pool from the ceiling; the splash must have produced a geyser. "Ever hear of Carlisle Barracks in Pennsylvania?"

"No."

"It's where they have the Army War College."

I had to sit up. Between the shower in the bathroom and pool splashes in the phone I had a sudden pang of being about to be inundated. "Yeah?"

"Well, after our last little conversation, there was something nibbling at me. Then I remembered it was Matthew Vickers."

"Who's that?"

"Jesus, Finley. Follow the bouncing ball, will you? Vickers was the Pulsar guy who died last year, the one replaced by this Shepherd."

"Right. Okay. Got it now."

He sighed to make sure I heard how tolerant he was being. "Well, after I called you last time, I had this irritating itch of maybe having read something by this Vickers way back when. It took me the better part of Sibelius's Fifth Symphony to find it in my library, but I did. Top shelf, red cover. The book's title is *Community Responses in Times of Crisis*. I'm sure it sold at least 14 or 15 copies."

And I knew one of the possible readers. Carlisle Barracks wasn't Charles Baudelaire, but they certainly shared initials. "He didn't contribute to a magazine called *Planning Society*, did he?"

"What does that mean?"

"Never mind. Go ahead."

"If you keep interrupting the oracle, you won't know your destiny."

"Go ahead, Bobby. Please."

Another patient exhale. "The title tells you what the book's about. How people in the United States reacted after Pearl Harbor, that kind of thing. But what I thought you might also be interested to know after our little talk about Pulsar's financing is that Vickers taught for years at the Army War College, in their Strategic Studies Institute. And here's the cherry on your cake: One of the political scientists who considered him a mentor and who also taught there was Pauline Shepherd."

I didn't think it a coincidence that Karen chose that moment to turn off the shower. Everything in the universe—Alan Lockman going through *Planning Society*, the CB file that had been empty, Matthew Vickers, Pauline Shepherd, Plus and Minus—had hooked up with the clang of the shower stopper being dropped back to tub level. "You're sure about this?"

"No, I just made it up."

The patterns on the bed quilt were no help. I didn't know what to thank him for. I owed him, that much, yes. But for what? Had he just given me the last foundation block for what Pulsar had been doing in New Florence or had he driven in the last rivet of an impenetrable door to what it had been doing? I barely took in his ritual cracks about the dinners I was going to buy him. He was right. I couldn't afford the feast I owed him.

"Do you mind if I enjoy my swim now?"

"Bobby, I'm really . . ."

"I warned you before, Finley. Stick to those inept doctors you call a profession. You'll be happier and so will the folks at Carlisle Barracks. Talk to you not too soon."

And he was gone. Leaving me to imagine his dive into the pool.

CHAPTER 51

Karen had enough to think about with the brunch and the dog and pony show at Labine Plaza, so I didn't mention my call to Rosen when she came out of the bathroom. Maybe if I had, she wouldn't have filled the bedroom with the assumption I would be escorting her to the brunch to meet the other locals as admired as she was.

"Of course you're coming," she said, toying with second thoughts about the blue blouse in front of her closet mirror. "There'll be husbands and wives, lovers and other strangers. I'm sure we can fit you in under one of those categories, don't you?"

"It really isn't my thing."

"No problem. I go to brunches at Labine's every day, so I can show you how to behave. When a tall, elderly man with more white hair on his eyebrows than his big head walks up to you and extends his hand, you stretch yours out and say, 'Nice to meet you, Mr. Labine.'"

"Karen . . ."

She turned back with her frailest fawn look. The hunters had entered the forest toting their big rifles. "Please?" So we went to the brunch, and in the great tradition of tradeoffs I got to take my car and to persuade her to stick to the blue blouse. I had never met the jasmine-smelling librarian in the neat blue suit and flesh stockings next to me in the front seat before. She had never stamped a book for me in any of New York's library systems, had never broken into a factory with me, had never made love with me. She was so completely new she was daunting, and I couldn't believe I had been so self-confident about staring at her legs the evening of the Professor's half-lecture. That had been such an intrepid, younger Finley he deserved investigating of his own.

The tip-off to what was ahead came in the wide fields we hit about twenty minutes due west of town. Instead of the seedy autumn brown of the other grassy outskirts I'd seen around New Florence, green was still the dominant color. "There're only two possibilities. Either Labine's had all the grass pulled out and replaced with artificial turf or he's sold a policy to the sun and rain to make sure they tend to business year-round."

She had no opinion. She had put on her sunglasses for a reason. It was under the heading of I'm Edgy, Leave Me Alone.

I left her alone. A quaintly jagged wooden sign around a curve abruptly pointed us up a side road off the side road that had started from an original side road. The sign said LABINE and the red beret painted over the L said some mornings threatened to be longer than others. About 50 yards in, the small rise flattened out under one of those massive trees with snarled branches that terrorized kids in cartoons. Driving under the branches had probably been the scenic idea; a better one would have been to remember to take my .38 out of my overnight bag.

The house was what Bobby Rosen would have called Old Florence: short on the cliff-top needed for reinforcing obedience from the peasants below, but picture-book flamboyant eaves over two floors of burnt sienna walling. I wouldn't have walked out on any of the upper-floor balconies or tried to ring what seemed to be a real bell in the mini-campanile, not without first doubling up on Labine's insurance indemnities, but it certainly was a change from Lefrak City. "Lorenzo says he sold it to Labine."

"Claudio had it built in the Twenties. The first piece of Epcot Center."

I laughed, and she relented to grin.Of course, there was an iron gate to drive through, into a pebble-strewn parking lot. I was glad to see a dozen cars already there and hear the bubbly voices coming through the grill-covered windows on the first floor; that meant less chance of having to make conversation with Labine by asking if he was bragging about some special forces background or just liked the first letter of his name to have a hat. It was a letdown, though, to see the parking attendant was just another rent-a-slug and wasn't in livery. "We'll make a deal," she said, as the guy waved me to the only logical spot with the frenzy of guiding a jet-fighter down onto a carrier. "You won't say anything to jeopardize the library budget and I won't tell anybody how you were kicked off the NYPD for taking bribes."

"Nassau County. I was never on the NYPD."

"Well, I'll put you on it so you can be kicked off."

"Sounds good."

The party room was a huge salon done up in the kind of red wallpaper that signified nobility or cathouse. And there was a lot of it since the ceiling was high enough for a cathedral. I didn't look at the gigantic, gold-framed pictures blanketing the walls. What else could they be but portraits of redheaded women with pale faces holding apples in their lap?

There were 20 or 30 people standing around in small huddles. Most of them registered our entrance without losing a beat in their conversations. I recognized Lama, McCorkle, and Dvorak. Also, there was Dracula from the top step of the church at Randy Page's funeral, now at McCorkle's elbow to make sure Mayor Babbitt didn't say anything stupid to the two women who had cornered him. He hovered over every remark as a challenge to his alertness. Like everybody else in the room, Dracula, McCorkle, and the women were drinking something Bloody Mary red.

Or, like *almost* everybody else. Dvorak was content keeping his hands in his jacket pockets as he eyed the room warily for an outbreak of sin. He had ditched his sneakers for the occasion, sporting the kind of clunky brown Oxfords usually for sale at flea markets. He even seemed to have a white shirt that wasn't frayed at the collar. I didn't know what was odder—that New Florence's most admired citizen didn't have a single person currying favor with him or that he seemed totally recovered from staggering around in front of his burning church 24 hours earlier. If he was any more orange than usual, I couldn't detect it and I thought that said something ruthless—but nice ruthless—about his character. I was starting to worry about my prejudices where

Rumpelstiltskin came in: When he spotted Karen and me entering, he gave us a welcoming nod and I nodded back. At least in present company, I had no problem thinking of us as buddies.

"One obstacle down," Karen said lowly. "I thought sure Junior would be here with him."

"Maybe he doesn't admire his old man like others do."

People started coming at us. I knew they were people because they wanted to give me their hands and Karen insisted on giving me their names. I went along until I remembered she had already placed eighth in the poll and wasn't running for anything else, so a friendly smile should have covered it all. Mrs. Labine, a tiny, freckle-faced woman with what her hairdresser would have called a perfect gray coif, acted in the market for a little more than that, but I had a feeling she had conveyed the same thing to Mayor Babbitt so I wasn't flattered. The real question was whether she had sent the same vibes to Dvorak, who was looking more and more like somebody invited so he could understand how much of a pariah he was.

I was just about to go over to my pal Rumpelstiltskin when Karen gave me a nudge. "Our host."

She hadn't exaggerated on the eyebrows. The hulking 70ish-old who strode into the salon from an adjoining room must have had a hard time seeing through the white tufts growing over his eyes. On the other hand, I couldn't say how thin on the top he was because, as the wooden road sign should have warned, he was wearing a red beret on his medicine ball of a head. The beret had an insignia; it wasn't for the Mets.

He headed straight for us, at the expense of a giggling couple that tried to get his attention. Up close, he showed recent skin scrapings on his forehead and nose. "I'm so glad you could come, Karen," the bellowing voice said. "I take it as a positive that so many value a librarian."

She answered something becoming and introduced me. What eyes there were under the brows were bloodshot but not surprised. "Yes, I've heard your name, Mr. Finley," he said, gripping me with paws that had done more than own insurance companies and department stores. "I think it was Jim Sewell. That possible?"

"Jimmy and I go back," I said, making out the faded represen-
tation of crossed rifles and a battalion designation through the
beret's wrinkles.

"And now you're here but he isn't! Where the hell is he?"

Considering how evasive he had been with me, I shouldn't
have given a damn Father Sewell was blotting his copybook. But
somewhere in some recessive gene there was still my father's hierarchy of arrogant management always giving off a worse stench
than corrupted labor. "Maybe he's thinking about a little thing
called tomorrow's paper."

Labine wasn't buying. "It's Sunday, for Christ sake. Anybody
even read a Monday paper? Not according to my circulation
people."

It was the perfect opening for pointing out that it was supposed to be his wife's paper, not his. But why be satisfied with
aiming the dart at an outer circle? He wasn't wearing his beret to
have it ignored, was he? "So what's the significance of the beret?
Something military?"

He was used to the younger generations changing topics on
him. "I'd hate to think it was just *something* military. A lot of good
men died wearing this beret, Mr. Finley. Wore it honorably."

"Where was that?"

He clenched his jaw at the possibility he was being put on and
should not have risen to the bait. In his heart of hearts, though,
he wanted to rise to the bait until he had chomped me whole.
"Name any field of honor."

Karen's stare said not to. "What are those interesting looking
things everybody's drinking?" she asked.

He accepted her diplomacy for what it was and waved to the
room where he had come from. "Bar's back there. Ask for a Bloody
Walter. It's your basic Mary but with a little more tang for the
adventurous."

She smiled dutifully and we headed across the room. She
might not have knuckled me in the kidneys, but the ache was
there. She had smiles and hellos for the people we had missed,
including those who slid their eyes from her to me and tried to
look impassive while they wondered why she hadn't settled for

throwing a quarter in my tin cup. Just like when I'd first read the list in the *Reporter*, I had a fit of *angst* for those missing. Where was Lorenzo? And the redhead from the saloon? How could you have a party without BIGH? Most of all, where was Brighton? What was he doing at that very moment with the stuff we'd gotten from Pulsar?

One thing he wasn't doing was questioning Michael Zev and Pauline Shepherd because they were standing near the bar in the adjoining room. When was coming across those two spooks not as bad as it might have been? When one of those waiting to fill up on Bloody Walters a few yards away was my favorite heart surgeon John Mendler. Dvorak Junior might not have been there, but Rumpelstiltskin hadn't come alone, after all.

"I'd heard a rumor you left town, Paul", Zev said, rocking under his belly in a cardinal red pullover. "I'm glad to see it isn't true."

He was happy and Shepherd was elated. Otherwise, I wouldn't have seen her equestrian motif—brown jodhpurs, pea-green corduroy jacket, and brown boots. She wasn't holding a crop, but there was still an irritating aggressiveness to it all. From Hal and Leo to the clothes the two spooks paraded around in, everything was in-your-face. The two of them had probably spent the morning screening tapes of our break-in at the annex.

"So what did you think of the poll results?" Shepherd asked, a magician soliciting applause for her trick.

"I was astonished," Karen replied.

"Welcome to the club," Zev laughed, ever the baron even in someone else's castle. "I daresay everyone here feels that way to some degree. What do you think that says about us as a people? Maybe that for all our strutting through the world we're essentially modest? That we don't believe we should be accorded so much respect? Food for thought."

Mendler passed by with a Bloody Walter and a sparkling water. He had never seen me before in his life. Maybe that should have reassured me about what a professional he was, how he saw nothing but pumping organs he had to mend, but it didn't. Pricks were pricks.

"Are there always these Community Day festivities after one of your polls has been published?" Karen asked.

It came out too innocent by half. Zev's windiness had touched an old Antonacci nerve. Shepherd started to reply, but the fat man got there first. "We've had them before in a couple of places," he said. "But if you've done any research on Pulsar's history, you'll probably know that not all our surveys have had the positive tilt this one has had. In some instances, we have posed MQs that haven't had . . ."

"Watch the jargon, Michael," Shepherd said with a stiletto smile. "By MQ he means the Magnet Questions, the point of reference. In the case of New Florence, it's been the most admired citizen. Elsewhere . . ."

"Well, I'm sure they know," Zev said, regaining the lead in smiles. "If Karen is any kind of librarian, especially after finishing as high in the poll as she has, she went right to the Internet to find out what other MQs Pulsar has asked elsewhere in the country."

I was right: She was fast losing the sang-froid I was supposed to be emulating. "Why do you think I would wait so long? I checked you out as soon as you arrived in town. And I think you know why very well."

Zev nodded gravely. That meant he was being solemn. "Of course. I was being fatuous. My apologies. I'm sadly aware that not even what should be cause for celebration always ends that way. All I can say is . . ."

"One of those bloody things, Paul?"

I nodded. I wanted a drink, but I also wanted her and her beet-red ears over at the bar before Plus and Minus slipped out. They might have known about our late-night foray at the annex, but how everyone showed his cards still seemed worth something.

"Maybe I should give you one of my boots so you can have an even heartier breakfast, Michael," Shepherd said for the record.

He raised his arms theatrically and, trying to look chagrined, carried his drink past me into the main room. His heavy-handedness didn't stop her from glowing with the triumph of having rearranged the furniture to her satisfaction. "So what's the question,

Mr. Finley? The one you've been dying to ask since Jimmy's office?"

If the idea had been disorientation, it worked. "Put it that way and it's something along the lines of, 'You've never had too many self-esteem problems, have you?'"

"Should I?"

I had gone down the wise guy road with her before. Why repeat the mistake? "I ran into a couple of your people yesterday. They said they'd be staying around a few days. Something about how you don't think your work is over until you see how it takes."

"You think that extraordinary?"

"No, I suppose being responsible means . . ."

"Good."

The clumsy guy wasn't much better than the wise guy. "I guess that riding getup means you'll be around, too. Who has the horses—Labine?"

"As a matter of fact. After the ceremonies today. Do you ride?"

"No. Where'd you learn?"

"It isn't nuclear physics."

"That's what all the scientists say."

The cat was disappointed: The mouse was determined to hang around his woodwork hole. "My uncle has a farm. Blue grass of Kentucky."

"That must've been fun as a kid."

"When my parents let me visit him, yes."

"Your uncle's a breeder?"

She didn't sigh, but not because she didn't feel one coming on. "He's had several entries in the big races. Kentucky Derby, Preakness . . ."

"Wow! I'm impressed."

"Are you really?"

"What's his name? I'll watch out for it at the OTB."

She didn't want me watching out for it; she didn't want me talking to her anymore, either. And she had her excuse when Karen returned with two Bloody Walters. "I think you'll find them excessive on the lime," she said. "But they're drinkable. Excuse me."

She made a Joan Crawford exit—my favorite part of Joan Crawford movies. "Even when I've rattled her, I'm the one who feels rattled. Why do you think that is?"

Karen was back to being alone behind her sunglasses; the only thing missing was the sunglasses. "I want something bad happening to them," she said with an eerie casualness.

"Did I miss something they said?"

I didn't like how little her expression changed in withdrawing her gaze from Shepherd's back to me. "Anything they say is too much."

She kept staring until I imagined her showing Antonacci the charts she had made about his ties to his father. She knew about talking too much and she was never going to forgive herself or anyone else for it. All the coaxing and back rubs in the world weren't going to get me across that line to her.

Then the phone in her jacket pocket rang,

CHAPTER 52

She went into a deeper and deeper frown as she listened to what her caller was telling her. At first, I thought she was having a problem hearing, but there was really no competing noise from the brunch crowd; there were only a couple of people left waiting for drinks at the bar and the chattering was concentrated in the main room. As red as she had gotten with Zev, she was just as suddenly looking drained.

"Who is this?"

I knew that meant threat, and my instinct was to grab for the phone to get it out of her hand. It was a stupid reflex, and I was saved from it only because she inadvertently turned away from me. First rule: Let the victim be clear on how the victim was being victimized.

When she finally stopped listening, she stood in dismay, holding the phone open in front of her. "Who was it?"

"I don't know. I thought I recognized the voice, but I'm not sure. He warned me not to go near the plaza."

I didn't know what—or who—I expected to see, but I went over to peer into the main room. The only person holding a cellphone was one of the tea-in-the-afternoon ladies who had been chatting up McCorkle as we had come in. Mendler was ready to kick himself for making eye contact.

"Then that's what you won't do," I said, returning to her. "And right now we call Brighton."

"Why should I . . .?"

The bartenders might not have triggered the call through tele-kinesis, but I didn't need the curiosity they were throwing our way in between pours. I got her away to a barred window that looked out over a big rear lawn. "Take it seriously? How about that at-tack on Dvorak's church yesterday?" She didn't resist when I took the phone from her; what the caller had said was still settling in. "I'm calling Brighton."

She said nothing, only looked at her drink, wondered why she had thought about drinking it, and set the glass down on the window sill. She looked puzzled more than frightened. By the time the operator had given me the number for the police station and the police switchboard had put me through to Brighton, I had agreed with Shepherd about the lime and put my glass down, too.

The captain lacked a little something in the alarm department when I told him about the call. "That's not nice."

"No, it isn't, Frank."

"Did he warn something specific, like a bomb?"

"I don't know. I'll put her on . . ."

"But it's a warning, not a threat. Someone cares about Karen . . ."

A thought scampered in and out of my brain. It didn't stick around because, par for the course, Brighton was steaming me. "I'm glad you can philosophize about the distinction. In the mean-time, maybe you'd like Karen's cellphone number, see where the call came from?"

"By the numbers. Sure."

I hadn't liked the way he had left Karen's last night with his tote bag, but that had been pure energy compared to what I was hearing on the phone. If he hadn't already been something of one, I'd have thought the pod people had gotten to him during his sleep. "I feel like I'm talking to a wall, Frank. Are you taking this in, or what?"

"Oh, every word. But did I mention you're the fifth person call-ing this morning with this kind of message? On top of that I've got two groups organizing to protest this little show in the square. I'm on the verge of calling the State Police for help."

"On the verge."

"Put Karen on."

"Brighton . . .!"

"Put her on, Finley!"

She took back the phone the way she might have accepted a dirty stick. Except for her phone number, the questions Brighton had all seemed answerable by no. I couldn't tell which question was about her having some idea who the caller had been so I couldn't tell which no wasn't true. She had certainly detected something more familiar about the voice than she had said, as though her only doubt was about not having heard it trying to be anonymous before. Her library gom Dobson came to mind. Maybe shelving books was just his day job.

"We can skip the rest of this show," I said when she signed off.

"Why? The warning was about the plaza, not here. I don't know about you, but I'm hungry."

She cut off debate by going back to her willowy self and heading for the main room one precarious high-heeled step after another. The call had angered her, but also composed her in some collateral way. Granted I was prejudiced, but she really did have a lot more moves than Shepherd. And who would have ever guessed that upon first meeting the two of them?

Her timing couldn't have been better because the coiffed Mrs. Labine was just announcing brunch was on. The crowd started drifting toward a hallway. Some of them seemed to know where it led. Seeing Mrs. Labine latching on to Karen, I hung back with the reluctant part of the flow. "You were fortunate not to be injured yesterday," Dvorak said, appearing at my elbow. "So many poor souls were."

Mendler was keeping a few feet behind, looking very much like a retainer. I was beginning to wonder if Dvorak had some rare heart condition Mendler wanted to be on the spot for when the crisis came. "I didn't know I stuck out so much."

"You didn't," he said solemnly. "But my son throwing people around in the street—he was hard to miss."

"Tell him not to aim me at a window next time."

He shrugged. "Russell doesn't know his strength sometimes. That can be a gift and a flaw. But he means well."

Did I want to know what he had listed under the Gift column and what under the Flaw column? No, I didn't. "What have the cops told you about their investigation so far?"

The subject dejected him. "I prefer to believe it was an accident. But they might be right."

"Meaning they have no leads."

"Meaning I may still be right."

"There's always evil, Reverend. You're the one who told me that."

"And sometimes we can be punished for thinking ourselves immune to it," he said, practicing the same cutoff he had in the hospital lobby. "Was that fire a lesson to me? Perhaps it was. Perhaps it was a reproach not to become prideful over what the front page of yesterday's paper said. If anything, maybe I should have listened to the warning I gave you about Pulsar and been mortified by the results."

When he was blocking my path, I really didn't have the same buddy-buddy feeling toward him as I did across a room. His eyes were ablaze with a bit too much on-the-scene reporting from Hell. "So if you knew those results were trumped up, you'd have no reason to be prideful."

"What are you saying, Mr. Finley?"

Mendler was interested, too. In my place the Professor would have called my sudden urge for mischief testing a hypothesis. "You're not telling me you expected to win that poll?"

Mendler stepped forward, but Dvorak raised his hand peremptorily to freeze him. I hadn't said anything the Reverend hadn't been saying to himself and, upon reflection now, he looked crestfallen that he had argued himself out of his skepticism. "Even if what you're suggesting is true, Mr. Finley," he said measuredly, "why me?"

That answer I knew. "Because you're so immaculately wrong."

"That's enough, Finley," Mendler put in.

"Hold on, John." I hadn't missed the instant credence he had given me, and neither had Mendler. For a second he stared at the ground as if he had lost the thread of what he wanted to say. When he finally lifted his head back up, he had picked up a few more bags under his eyes. "For that to be so," he said, "I would have to be despised even more than you despise me."

"I don't know you that well, Reverend, and we can both do without the chance for me to. But no, not necessarily. Instead of thinking about who despises you, maybe you should think about who sees some entertainment value in toying with those who do. Nothing beats entertainment, right?"

He smiled glumly. "I've had occasion to preach on the topic."

"I'm sure."

I had said it better than I would have rehearsing it for a week, but I didn't feel good walking away from him. Dead horses were dead horses, even those that kept shitting on the street after taking their last breath. I liked thinking I was leaving my flogger behind me in the salon.

The brunch was in a dining room that looked out on the other 90 percent of the back lawn not visible from the room with the bar. Ducks floated by in a lake at the foot of the grass. Just about every seat at the imposing oak table that ran the length of the room had a view of the lake, and even the sideboard filling the window had been fit low so everyone eating could see the ducks. I hadn't thought of Claudio Mochi before as a man of detail, but what con man wasn't?

Most of the table places had already been taken and a waiter was hauling out tureen seconds of something. I watched Karen fill her plate with an omelet and enough greens to start a garden. She was still in Mrs. Labine's grasp and took an end seat next to the woman. Labine himself was at the other end of the table with the power collection—Zev, Shepherd, McCorkle, Lama, and Dracula. The commandant for life in his red beret, Labine seemed to be doing all the talking while the others ate. That would have been more impressive if Zev and Shepherd didn't exchange looks warning each other to remain attentive and Dracula didn't keep glancing at his watch. I had a picture of Labine still yakking away while the last mannequin in his department store was being hauled out to a garbage truck.

I filled up on the Eggs Benedict thinking about Mendler. Once I peeked above my distaste for the man, there was nothing at all plausible about the way he stuck to Dvorak. For that matter, it was just as odd that Russell Junior wasn't on hand to crow about his father's triumph.

Unless, of course, Russell Junior didn't consider the results of the Pulsar poll a triumph for the Dvorak family and the New Florence Society.

As I have said, being slow on the uptake wasn't all that rare a service provided by Finley Investigations. The hollandaise sauce went slop-sliding off my plate into the grooves between my fingers as I looked back to where Karen was nodding politely to Mrs. Labine. The guy next to me waiting to help himself to the eggs wondered if I had ever learned table manners—I could see that out of the corner of my eye just as I was sure Karen sensed I was gaping over at her. I hoped I didn't look as undressed as she did. Dobson had been the wrong doofus. The voice she had recognized on the phone was Camouflage Jacket from the cemetery and Jumpsuit from the fire, he of the silk screens and the father who ended his love affairs for him.

And why not he of the Molotov cocktail?

"Need a napkin there?"

Mr. Helpful was already handing me one. He took it for granted some questions were superfluous.

CHAPTER 53

The dining room was too far away from the parking area to hear any
car leaving. But when Dvorak and Mendler didn't come in for
their eggs I assumed at least one car had left. So Rumpelstiltskin
could climb up Junior's hair and see how lethally morose his
heir had become? The inspiration hadn't subsided with my food;
it wasn't firm enough to phone Brighton to suggest he look into
the Dvorak family for the church bombing because the orange
man had skipped brunch and Karen had acted evasive about her
caller, but it teased as your average homicidal psychodrama in
a house of zealots. Introverted Junior had grown weary of being
pulled away from his silk-screening to march in cemeteries and
had blown a fuse when told all those around him thought of his
old man as the most admirable of admirable citizens. The classic
Born Again saga of father-son conflict ending in a typical bombing and cop killing. Too bad his name was Dvorak and he was a
New Florence Touchable. Mrs. Arlett, for one, was unlikely to be
appeased by another rebirth epiphany for him.

No one outside the power circle at the end of the table seemed
to miss the Reverend. The more Labine pontificated, though, the
more he gave off the air of telling fairy tales so the children at his
knee wouldn't hear the monsters running over the roof. McCorkle
and his wife were pleading with their fascination to behave, as if
they truly hadn't heard the same anecdotes a dozen times before.
Lama was trying to look equally rapt, but, like Dracula, had been
fielding cellphone interruptions regularly; neither had thought

it prudent to turn off his gizmo in the name of courtesy. They all knew something was building outside, maybe they even connected Dvorak's departure to it, but nobody was going to be the first to sound an alarm with so much grub still to be wolfed down before heading off for Labine Plaza.

Through it all Zev burped out compliments for the chef to nobody in particular and Shepherd appeared to be counting the seconds down until the ceremonies were over and she could get outside to the Labine stables. In the right bar at the right hour and with my mind wiped clean of Randy Page and Alan Lockman, I could have adored them as a team—he playing at playing and she profoundly bored toying with a world beneath her. When you thought about it, they were only office employees trying to show themselves to be above their cubicles. At least she seemed to have kept a grip on where her desk was. If my Fourth Avenue OTB handled more than horses, I would have laid a twenty on Zev needing a few seconds to remember he was in New Florence and not in one of his other stopovers for Pulsar. Generic behavior was for generic people.

My private generic person since I had sat down was Doreen Lozier, the booming-voiced principal of the New Florence High School and a Minus on the bio sketch rating system. She might not have been as much of an outcast as Dvorak, but three different people had carried trays past after sizing up the empty chairs on either side of her. If Brighton was right and she had filled in Zev on the school's sexcapades 20 years ago, it wasn't because Zev had forced the tales out of her. Near retirement and with scraggly black hair that should have never been allowed near the dye bottle, she still had a bruiser's shoulders for wheeling any rig on the highway. The more she said her "kids were all good at bottom," the more I saw her coming to that conclusion year in and year out after half-nelsoning every member of the new class to a gym mat.

"I have to tell you, Paul, I never really wanted to live in a big city. How can you expect to educate children when you have more students than desks in every classroom?"

"In some places."

"Everywhere in New York. And believe me my sources are extremely reliable. They know what they're talking about. You should get better acquainted with your own city."

Okay, she *was* a Minus. But I still didn't know what that meant by Pulsar's standards and I had a hunch it wasn't a trivial addition to the sketches we had printed out. She hadn't earned her rating by citing her "extremely reliable" sources for saying nasty things about some Tennessee restaurant Zev liked.

"Zev tells me most people here were surprised to find themselves at the top of the Pulsar list."

She took in the table to both sides, thought about editing what was on her mind, then tittered: "Of course they'd say that. Humility is always in season. And as parents a lot of them have plenty to be humble about."

"Great stories over the years, I bet."

I didn't know if she leaned in to whisper or to get closer to her Bloody Walter. Whichever, she seemed to have applied charcoal instead of mascara to her eyes. "No names because they wouldn't mean anything to you anyway. But I counted at least four people on that list who came very close to being grandparents without knowing it."

"Wow!"

Her pride earned her another sip of Labine's lime concoction. She'd been feeling proud for quite a few slugs. "New York City doesn't have a monopoly on some things, I can assure you."

"I guess not."

"Be sure of it."

"So you yourself weren't at all surprised?"

The very thought was offensive. "Frankly, I would have been stunned if I hadn't been named. I've put a lot of years into the education system here. Is it asking so much to have a little recognition for it?"

"No, I guess not."

"Be sure of it."

The only thing I was sure of was that it was time to get Karen and take her home. But just as I caught her eye, Labine roused himself from the end of the table with a commanding crack of his chair on the floor. I was familiar with tapping glasses with a spoon and clearing one's throat into a microphone, but banging chairs into floors? What did I know? It worked: The talk up and down the table died out immediately. Only Mrs. Labine looked miffed at being cut off mid-sentence with some cadaverous guy who might have been the greeter at Tebaldi's funeral home.

"As far as this old soldier is concerned," Labine announced, "you're all welcome to sit here all day and eat me out of house and home. But in case you've forgotten, we've got other commitments." McCorkle nodded gravely. "So if you're still hungry, start thinking about doggy-bagging." He liked the chuckles that came back to him—or just liked using *doggy-bagging* for the first time in his life. "But a word to the wise," he said, stern again. "Forewarned and forearmed and all that. It's no secret there's a minority in New Florence who don't think this day should be a celebration and they'll be waiting to throw sand in our engine. But Mayor McCorkle and Chief Lama have assured me there'll be no security problem when we get down to the square . . ."

The Digger O'Dell from Tebaldi's hadn't heard about any security problem needing solution, and smiled bleakly when Mrs. Labine patted his hand. He was as ready to skip Labine Plaza as I was.

". . . The main thing is *we* celebrate the day—to demonstrate that when all the defeatists get through with their shouting and their whining, we'll still be there to remind everyone that New Florence, New York is just another name for effort and industry . . ."

Lozier beat even McCorkle to the clapping. When the rest of the table did the same, she looked around with a satisfied nod at what she had sparked. She had definitely passed her Bloody Walter quota.

". . . Now for those of you who'd feel doubly safe riding down with me, Tony Lama has thought to provide us with a couple of police vans for the trip . . ."

"Do we have to be handcuffed, too?"

Lozier frowned; she didn't think the question from the other end of the table was funny. It represented competition to her. I nodded to Karen, and she nodded back. I wanted to believe she was agreeing to go straight home.

"I do hope they have a commemorative token for the day," Lozier said, as people began rising from the table. "Something I can put on my office shelf. Do you think they will?"

"I really don't know."

She reminded herself of essentials. "Oh, that's right, you wouldn't get one anyway. Well, it's been nice talking to you."

I might have challenged her on her sincerity if I hadn't been in such a hurry to get the hell away from her and down to Karen at the end of the table. Mrs. Labine had taken her time getting to her feet; she had lingered for me. "You shouldn't choose your dining companions so randomly, Mr. Finley," she said, not all that amused. "How many illegitimate children has Doreen counted up for you? I'm sure quite a number."

"A popular topic?"

"Unfortunately. I hope to see you down at the square."

Lozier hadn't been all that sincere about being pleased to know me, and I wasn't so sure seeing me again at Labine Plaza was all that high on Mrs. Labine's list of hopes. But you collected the compliments where you could, especially when the road ahead threatened to be rougher.

"I think I know who it was," Karen said, beating me to it. "On the telephone before. I think it was Russell Dvorak."

She might or might not have needed our time apart to think about it. I didn't care. "Makes sense."

"It does?"

"The Reverend was a little more subdued than usual. Probably happens anyway when you've been burned out and people have been killed, but I think it was more. He took off without any goodbyes."

She seemed to have been hoping I had come up with a better candidate for her caller. "I see."

"The question now is if you're going in one of those police vans. Because I'm sure as hell not driving you down to this Mardi Gras."

She looked over to where Lama had stopped near the door to take another cellphone call. Now it was firm enough to share with the cops, but I didn't want it to be with Lama. He'd already had me conspiring with Junior. "Russell's really terrified of that old man," she said, her voice as glazed as her eyes. "You think it could've just welled up inside him and . . .?"

"If it did, he killed somebody. Unlike you."

"That's not what . . ."

"Yes, it is. Can we call Brighton now?"

Two ducks passed from her left to right shoulder before she nodded and once again handed me her phone.

CHAPTER 54

Two minutes away from the villa, I sensed her second-guessing herself for being too hasty in running to the sidelines when there was a platform chair waiting for her in Labine Plaza. Should we have done more than alert Brighton? Should we have just assumed all those cellphone calls to Lama had included that alert and that the other brunch guests would be all right?

"If you're feeling that left out, there's only one cure for it—go take your chair on the platform and wait to be blown up."

"But maybe if he saw me sitting there . . ."

"You don't want to get into that kind of bad conscience, Karen. I saw him yesterday. First, he blows up Dad's church, then he's the Incredible Hulk in the middle of the street saving lives. That's not what you'd call a clearly marked map. You don't sit anywhere."

"You don't know him."

"No, I just know your lousy horse sketches."

"What does that mean?"

"You keep your horses, but nothing from Russell? I mean, there must be *some* silkscreen piece you liked. Something he could've given you or that you even bought from him. Which did you want to forget about faster—Russell or the hobby he has to pass the time?"

"Screw you."

I accepted that as a reasonable compromise. Still, I didn't want her going through the next few hours restlessly, either, so I made a detour over to the library. She didn't believe I was serious asking if she had all her keys. "Like Brighton said last night," I reminded her, "first things first, and that's Alan Lockman. Run that 1992 issue of *Planning Society* through the machine again. See if there's any article in there by a Matthew Vickers. If there is, copy it."

Maybe it was my tone. I prefer thinking she too was looking for something to do besides regretting she couldn't be a bulls-eye for her ex-boyfriend. In any case, she held all the questions that rushed up to her eyes and got out to let herself into the library. I'd spent longer quarter-hours than I did waiting for her to come out again, but that had been in my former life as Benjamin Franklin. I was on the verge of getting out of the car to search for cigarette butts on the ground when a group of protesters came trooping down the street in the direction of Labine Plaza. They held their placards lazily, over their shoulders, not yet hoisted for prime time. At least trying to make out what they said distracted me from thinking about how a wild goose chase would affect Karen. When I couldn't decipher the signs, I zeroed in on the protesters themselves. They were all ages and all sexes, the solemn and those out for fun. One guy was licking an ice cream cone, the woman next to him was on a cellphone. Conclusion: They were normal people with the extra gene of not worrying about missing NFL Sunday. For my money, that made *them* the most admirable citizens in New Florence.

I guessed from the way she came down the library steps with papers sticking out of her bag that it hadn't been a wild goose chase. "How did you know?" she asked, sucking a mint as she got back in and handed me the papers. "Who is Matthew Vickers?"

The Xeroxes identified the article's author only as "a Rudolph Serge Fellow at the University of Pennsylvania," whoever the hell Rudolph Serge was or had been. The article I recalled from looking over her shoulder at the machine: how the aqueducts of Rome had stood the test of time. Nothing suspicious about that on its face so I didn't feel all that bad about not having shrieked "Aha!" the first time around.

"You going to tell me or should I go into my corner and lie down?"

"Give me a sec." I still didn't want to make announcements without being sure there was one worth making. But then I found it, midway on the fourth page, under the subtitle of Popular Responses. On occasion over the centuries, the aqueducts hadn't just been venerable marvels of urban infrastructure, they had been decrepit marvels of urban infrastructure. Floods here, stoppages there. And what needed "deeper study," according to Matthew Vickers, was how Roman neighborhoods had reacted to the problem in different ways. One blockage in a poor neighborhood had turned into a rallying point for radical politicians opposed to the monarchy. When an affluent district had been left dry two centuries later, cartoons and poetic lampoons had been the chief reaction in the opposition press. "Matthew was certainly faithful to his career track," I said, handing her back the papers and pulling away from the library. "All we ask from our umpires is consistency."

"Okay, I'll just sit here guessing."

I told her about what Rosen had said about Vickers and Shepherd at the War College. She should have crowned me for not mentioning it before, but she let that detail simmer as she clicked the mint against her teeth until we reached her street. Like every other block we had passed from the library, there were more cats prowling around than people. The desolation began making me as anxious as she was. Shouldn't we have at least joined the rest of civilization down at Labine Plaza for some cotton candy? We could always get away again before the bombs went off.

But then Baal intervened, to show me why I had been wise to skip the cotton candy. Barbara Lockman and her porcupine brother were coming out of her house and going over to the garage. Martin was carrying a dark suit on a hanger. Since it was too small for him, I knew the suit was for Alan Lockman and they were taking it to Tebaldi's for the burial. The hanger was wire, not the wooden kind I had used for Jennifer and Susan's dresses.

"I have to talk to her a second," I said, pulling over.

"About what?"

It annoyed me to have to admit it, so I didn't. If Finley Investigations had ever had the great fortune to be hired seriously for a murder case like Alan Lockman, I would have already gotten to what his mother had left out of our last conversation. What I told myself, anyway: A perfect example of how inadequacy added to fantasy could deliver a boast. In the meantime, I flattered myself that Barbara Lockman's tentative smile meant she knew it, too. "Hello, Mr. Finley. I'd have thought you and Karen would be downtown with everybody else."

The bitterness was sincerity; the trepidation in her eyes what she didn't want to talk about, especially in front of her brother. "There's something I have to ask you, Mrs. Lockman."

"I'm in sort of a hurry right now," she said, proceeding over to the passenger side of her gray Honda. "Can it wait?"

"I *know* it can," Martin put in as he opened the back door on the driver's side and put the suit inside.

"We have to go make arrangements," she said, trying to smooth over her brother's hostility. "They finally released the body."

"Just one question, please. It's important."

Her blink was astonishment that I could think anything besides her son's wake was important. Karen looked as aggravated as Martin. "If you say so. What is it?"

It had been easier thinking about it than saying it. "You and Alan talked about how your company profiled people, potential customers, right? And I imagine he was very interested in that."

The brother slammed the back door with visions of my head caught in it. But something in his bullish bearing also sagged. He seemed to have to fight himself not to look across the roof of the car to Barbara. What I was asking he had already asked.

She didn't deny it. "Yes, we spoke about it. But I don't see what that has to do . . ."

"Was it something you mentioned to him just once? Or was it a topic that kept coming up?"

"Paul . . ."

"You should leave my sister alone."

Barbara Lockman didn't need allies; what she needed was to rest her forearms on the roof of the car to get the weight off her feet. She looked beaten up all over again. "He was obsessed with it," she nodded. "I mentioned it once, ages ago, but he never forgot it."

Martin let go with a volley of Spanish. I picked up enough of it to get she had been blaming herself for her son's obsession and he didn't want to hear it anymore.

"How exactly did it come up? The first time."

She registered the brother without looking at him. "I was just talking about the office one night at supper, I guess," she said, transfixed by a jade-looking ring on her finger. "Alan always tried to listen then because he knew my husband and I had liked filling each other in on the day while we ate." Martin threw himself down behind the wheel, but kept his door open. "When I referred to the profiling Labine Insurance did, his eyes widened. He couldn't hear enough about it. I told him it was nothing unusual, it was what all insurance companies did." There was more Spanish grumbling from the car. I didn't understand it and she ignored it for me. "Alan had his things. I should have never said anything. He was . . ."

"Into conspiracy theories?"

It sounded better that way, and she acknowledged it with a smile. "You hear about a lot of people that way."

"Every day."

"Frankly, I thought he was too . . . Anyway, he didn't mention it for a while. But the last few months he brought it up several times. Wanted to know how the company got the information. I told him there was nothing special about it—the usual government records and yearbooks and things like that. He wanted to know every little detail."

Just like she didn't, I realized. If she had taken the trouble to contact BIGH and the others, as any normally curious mother in her circumstances would have, she might have discovered something implicating herself in Alan's obsessions. And somewhere in the back of her mind she knew as well as I did that those obsessions had had something to do with his death. "And especially the last couple of weeks?"

It was a TILT, and her eyes hardened immediately. "You're asking this why, Mr. Finley?"

If I mentioned Pulsar, I rationalized easily, she would have had no choice but to go careening down to Labine Plaza to confront Zev, timing her arrival for getting herself blown up. BIGH did the rest. "I hear he was on the radio recently arguing some of these theories. Kennedy, King . . ."

"That was months ago. On Randy Page's show. He told me."

"It might have been that, yes."

"You think there's some connection between Alan's death and Randy Page's, is that what you mean?"

"The thought occurred to me," I half-lied.

She looked past me to Karen. She might have been wondering if being a neighbor's friend was credentials enough for me. "The police didn't say any of this."

"Paul is just trying to make sure they haven't overlooked anything," Karen volunteered. "I asked him as a favor. We didn't mean to upset you, Barbara. I'm sorry if we have."

Martin stared into his rearview mirror, the closest thing to a lie detector handy. He didn't know what he saw, but it was good for another hiss of being pissed off.

"Everyone worries about upsetting me," Barbara Lockman said as she leaned off the roof and opened her door. "Know what I worry about, Karen? How the only joy my son seemed to have come from his motorcycle and from figuring out how everything in life was a giant conspiracy. I think I loved that bike as much as he did. It was the only thing the rest of the world—his mother included—wasn't plotting against him. If you really want to help, Mr. Finley, show me how I'm wrong to think that."

I didn't move my foot as Martin backed down the driveway. I knew he would miss it and I didn't mind him blowing my pants cuff.

CHAPTER 55

How come Alan Lockman had Googled on, while Karen and I and everyone else who wasn't Bobby Rosen had stopped? Motivation, like the cable channel hucksters ranted every morning between midnight and dawn. The kid had been addicted to taking names, the more incidental the more suspect, and putting them in his It-May-Be-Paranoia-But-Maybe-It-Isn't file. Some people collected stamps, he collected his obsession. Even Twain and Hemingway had been more important to him as entries in the Alan Lockman Dossiers than as writers who might have had something to say. Karen, on the other hand, was the last one to pursue a name like Matthew Vickers for its own sake. The Pulsar Institute didn't exist for her as specific individuals responsible for Antonacci's suicide; she had that area covered all by herself and had no intention of sharing the credit.

She still didn't. The impersonal had invaded the house—or maybe it had always been there with just the details changing from day to day. There was the Sunday paper on the coffee table reminding her in big front-page headlines how she should have been at Labine Plaza. There was the glare of the sun through the blinds warning the afternoon would be measured in milliseconds for anyone trying to wait it out. There were the suit and heels she kept on in case she decided she had been wrong to come home with me. She couldn't go through enough motions around the living room—realigning knickknacks on the bookshelf, straightening out couch cushions that didn't need straightening, sharpening the sight lines of the lounge chair on the glass stain on the coffee table. I thought of my first look at her bedroom when I had been recovering from my sock on the head, of the smells that had been hers only because her name was on the lease, not because they had to be Karen Noon. Her prim blue suit really didn't sober up much of anything.

"Are you staring at something in particular?"

"You."

"Or making a list of what you're protecting from being blown up?" She turned back wanting me to match her arid smile. She had to fight somebody, and I would have picked me, too. "Oh, c'mon. What does it come down to? 114 pounds with all those special items you see on anatomy charts? I could strip for you and remind you of what you have invested."

The idea wasn't the worst; teeth-rattling the way she said it, but not the worst. "You asked me to help."

"To be exact, several days ago I asked Joe to help. And if you recall, I scrubbed even that idea. Right now, we have screwing. Should we get back to it? I have nothing better to do for a couple of hours."

"I told you: If you want to go get blown up, go."

"You're wrong about him."

"Was it Junior on the phone or not?"

"I never said I was a hundred percent sure."

"No, you didn't."

"And the more I think about it . . ."

"You called him from the library, didn't you?"

She gave the cushion in her hand a good whack; I told myself to take it personally. "Of course, I did."

"And?"

"No answer. He's turned his phone off."

"So we'll let Brighton sort it out."

"Lovely."

She found some kind of crumb in the wedge of the couch cushion. She couldn't have looked more vindicated if she had discovered a nugget of gold, and she promptly marched it out to the kitchen trash can, her blue suit on her like an unrippled piece of her body. I thought of another suit—tan instead of blue, on Pauline Shepherd that first day at the *Reporter*. It was reminding me of something, the way a gnat reminds you of a fly. Too bad the thought kept zigzagging away.

Karen stood in the entrance of the kitchen looking in at me. She had lost her air of melodrama by going into the kitchen, but her expression said I hadn't gained anything. "I can't do this, Paul," she said.

I held out for Community Day. "We could take a drive."

"Me, no." So it wasn't Community Day. "Tell me where I've gone wrong."

She shook her head to the thought and followed her steps back inside, one unstable stride after another, until she was behind my chair. "Nowhere," she said. "It's never been Route 66, has it?"

"One mile at a time."

I felt her hands on the top of the chair, but then they were gone and she was walking over to the window next to the front door. "That should sound more enticing than it does. Why doesn't it?"

"Because you want to fuck it up."

She laughed; tactfully, but not falsely. "Maybe if you hadn't been so busy trying to save my life . . ."

"That's Russell."

She fell quiet. Whatever the hell she was looking at out on the street would be there for years, and that alone seemed like reason to stop being polite. "Don't, Karen. It's not . . ."

"What? Right?"

She wasn't looking at me and I wasn't looking at her, so a nod covered it. That seemed to release a hum in the air—the kind that only got louder by having attention paid to it. I stopped paying attention to it.

She finally got bored waiting for a car to pass and came back into my sightline to sit down on the couch. She had a squeamish smile as she rubbed her hands between her knees. "Maybe I've gone native and never realized it before," she said.

"How's that?"

She didn't know, but she had nothing to lose by floating the idea with me. If I didn't buy that one, she could always come up with something else. "When Claudio Mochi came to town with his production plans, there should have been an enormous sense of relief. Did you know things were so bad some people wanted to burn down the town?"

"So I've been told."

"Mochi interrupted that, and I don't think they've known ever since whether to be grateful or resentful."

"That was a hundred years ago."

She found a thread on her skirt; it understood her more than I did. "The air, Paul. You haven't breathed it in enough."

"I'll pass."

"What I've been saying. You haven't been infected yet."

"It's not a social phenomenon, Karen. You have nothing to do with Claudio Mochi or burning down this place. You're talking about you."

"And Barbara Lockman and Brighton and Veronica . . ."

"Yeah, right. Veronica."

"Don't tell me you've fallen for that nihilistic thing she does."

"I don't care about Veronica right now."

"You have!"

"Me? Why? Just because she and her buddy Lorenzo have turned it into a festival? Nah, not me."

"You don't know her."

"Granted. But we were talking about . . ."

Too late; she recognized a detour when she saw one. "She's told me a hundred times. When her ex took off on her, she didn't know if she hated him or was grateful he was just gone. With the result?"

Pauline Shepherd's tan suit did another flit around the room, and that suddenly felt more important than tales about Veronica Pell.

"With the result that on a very bad day she can blame herself for driving him away. You can't be grateful *and* resentful, Paul. They only make guilt when they're together. And as Veronica says, that's why everybody in this town has this itch to be sorry for things."

Whatever she was saying was supposed to have something to do with us, but I'd had enough of that kind of sociology reading about the aqueducts in Rome. There was still the empty house down the street because the owner was bringing burial clothes down to the funeral parlor. That was the ball I had to keep my eye on—the only one I was even qualified to look at.

"You're not listening to me."

I could have said there was no reason to, that she had already kicked me out of bed and that I had never known begging to get things back to where they had been. Instead, I told her what *I* was interested in: "I've been making a specialty of reading things upside-down ever since I got here. Like Brighton and Sewell. I think I've been doing the same with Sewell and Shepherd."

She hadn't thought of me as offensive since our first conversation in the kitchen and she couldn't give in to it now, either. They were her rules, and she couldn't ditch them because I was playing by them, too. "A way of saying he *hasn't* been panting for her?"

"The first day in his office I thought they were talking in code about getting together. But for what, meeting at the Rustic Inn with Zev along as chaperone? I don't think so. They'd already been together and that's what they were being coy about."

"So? The pope does shoot craps every once in a while."

"Maybe. That's more like what he would have been titillated by. Something naughty they'd *already* pulled off. Their little secret together. Don't forget the Pulsar people have gotten around. Somebody even put up with Doreen Lozier for a glass of wine. These people did their research. How could you be that thorough and skip the editor of the town newspaper?"

"I'm happy. Sewell and Shepherd got together."

"Where a newsman like Jimmy asks as many questions as he answers. And where Shepherd has to drop something about her great mentor Vickers."

"She doesn't *have* to do anything."

Another time it might have been fascinating discovering why she insisted on thinking she was envious of Shepherd. But not then. "Anybody on the *Reporter* could have kept a running tally of those votes as they came in. It didn't have to be Lockman. And even if the secret counter had Dvorak last, who could prove it? Nobody was interested enough to recheck the overall vote count. That was the beauty of the option of sending votes directly to the post office. They could be cited to contradict anything about the votes sent to the newspaper. So it wasn't the results in themselves that made Lockman troublesome. It was the results *plus* Vickers."

Only her bafflement seemed to keep her interested. "Who I never heard of until this afternoon and who's long past caring about Plus and Minus."

"Who Lockman had been looking up as a specialist on popular reactions to social crises and who he connected to the poll. We found that one article in *Planning Society*. How many others did he find?"

"I think you're talking about Alan Lockman. The Alan Lockman his own mother just came close to saying needed a shrink."

"That Alan Lockman. Who didn't talk to BIGH about Vickers and Pulsar, who talked about them to the person he considered his second father. And his second father . . . Well, tit for tat when you're searching for tidbits to disguise just wanting to jump somebody's bones."

It was more than one full circle, and she smiled to her knees to resist saying it. "You're his friend," she said. "I guess you're the one to ask him."

I nodded. My heartburn from sipping Labine's damn Bloody Walter reminded me I had no other reason for sticking around.

CHAPTER 56

Did a prison guard worry *about being at fault if the inmates broke out after he had knocked off for the day and gone home to supper?*

The best thing about the question was Karen couldn't hear it. If she could have, she would have already been tearing out of the house and heading down to Labine Plaza.

The second-best thing was that I trusted her not to do that, that she realized staying away from the square was about her, not us.

I had to look into why feeling like Galahad seemed like the obvious alternative to failing at Lancelot.

The usual Sunday afternoon coma was settling over the streets I took to the center. An elderly couple poked along the sidewalk on what looked like a daily constitutional. A skel with tattoos up to his Adam's apple was catching a smoke outside a hole-in-the-wall bar. A cabbie was waiting in front of an Andy Hardy house for his passenger. Two teenagers sat on a stoop in earnest young love talk. I saw people through windows but nobody else outside. It was New Florence's version of a curfew: You could go out, but only down to the plaza to cheer on the local admirables. I turned on the local radio station to see if they were doing live coverage, but Walter Labine's clout apparently extended just so far: The gabber was one of the Oklahoma silo DJ's trying to sound like he was broadcasting from every neighborhood in the country.

It started changing only near Sloan. Store-keepers had moved their wares out to the sidewalks for impulse buying—candles, brass plates, a flea market rack of winter jackets and pants. Those going past kept going past, more intent on reaching the screechy band swelling nearby. It might have been a high school band, heavy on the trumpets and light on anything else musical, but Doreen Lozier's contribution to the festivities was more of a lure than discounted corduroys.

I might have gone on filing my report for Chelsea Barracks if a black Cherokee Laredo hadn't started nosing out from the curb. The driver looked miffed I was there to replace him so greedily, but his two little girls in the back with their cotton candy thought I was funny. I did, too. I was still taking it too much for granted that I would find Sewell in the square and that what I had to ask him would lead somewhere. There were just so many stumbles you could get away with by pretending to be Nijinsky at his most avant-garde.

I didn't notice the cop until I finished locking up. Aside from his gray Hitler mustache, he wasn't all that noticeable. Backed up against the glass door of a real estate office, he was closer in age to the Professor than to me and was wearing a heavy Bills windbreaker over a faded uniform shirt and holster. Brighton had apparently vetoed the state police idea in favor of herding together every cop in the vicinity on and off duty, active or retired, from a nursing home or a lunatic asylum. I wondered what Lieutenant Billy Danks in Nassau would have said about that scraping the bottom of the barrel strategy; with Danks you were entitled to the uniform or you weren't and screw the football jackets. He hadn't even tolerated auxiliaries. The old man sizing me up might have been dressed by one of the used clothes stores I had passed. And the last thing he looked ready for dealing with was a Junior Dvorak passing by with a Molotov cocktail or two in his knapsack. At least he had been detailed to the outskirts of the square.

I felt his eyes on me down the rest of the block. The band was still blaring and thumping through "Everything's Comin' Up Roses" when I turned the corner into the square and a very serious crowd. There was no parking for cars, no line between the sidewalk and gutter, no one wandering along at more than a snail's pace. The air was popcorn and hot dogs. Skip the differences in place, temperature, and my attitude, and it might have been balmy Coney Island without the rides. Every store on the street had opened for Sunday, and as long as they were selling balloons, drinks, or food that could be grilled, they were doing some business. Why one guy thought it was the perfect occasion for unloading a dinette set and an elephant foot's hassock was between him and his creditors. Betty Lou and her students had tacked up Community Day banners at every eye level around the plaza, here and there throwing in an American flag and a poster for the *Reporter*. The few empty seats were covered by the coats of the people coming back to reclaim them. A fully uniformed cop seemed to have been stationed at every fourth or fifth row, alternately to the left and right aisles. They didn't look like they were going to give a pass for too long to the coats taking up the unoccupied seats. What they seemed less concerned by, on the other hand, was the line of protesters standing behind the last row with placards saying nasty things about the Reverend Dvorak, Labine, and the Pulsar Institute. A couple of the uniforms assigned to the area couldn't have been chummier with the demonstrators. Maybe they had a point: As long as the band was huffing and puffing on old Ethel Merman ditties in front of the stage, who was going to try to compete by shouting from the rear?

Some of the brunch people on the speaking platform looked like they wouldn't have minded an egg instead of another tuba note being thrown their way. McCorkle was cupping his ear in annoyance because he couldn't hear what Dracula was telling him. Next to him in the front row, Labine, acting very much like somebody who had been counting on a hit parade of military marches, was twisting in anguish at "Everything's Comin' Up Roses." A far-too-bouncy emcee with a carnation in his lapel was moving back and forth on the stage shuffling and reshuffling his index card notes in search of the magic words that would make the band disappear. Only Lozier looked enchanted with the teenage horns, and kept turning for nods of approval from the other poll winners. A drawn-faced woman with grey curls I didn't remember from the brunch gave her the smile she wanted.

Dvorak's presence was an empty folding chair in the place of honor behind a standing mike at the center of the stage. I had a good news-bad news vision. The good was that Junior Dvorak and the lethal toys he had prepared for the day had been intercepted by the Reverend a mile away from the square. And while he was at it, Dad wanted to know why the hell his church had to be blown up; wasn't Junior pretending to be a sensitive artist enough aggravation for him to deal with? The bad was Junior's answer: setting off his toys to take care of two generations of Dvoraks once and for all.

I cast around for worthier thoughts. Walkie-talkie in hand, Brighton was standing under the stage off to the right with Lama. He was acting a little short in the deference department, snapping off monosyllabic answers with his gaze fixed on the crowd, forcing Lama to move in closer and ask him to repeat himself. The captain didn't manage it with any enthusiasm. I was convinced he really had cared about Dwayne Arlett.

I spotted Sewell in the company I might have expected—standing with Zev and Shepherd below the other side of the stage. He made for a matching piece with Brighton, nodding absently to whatever the fat man was prattling on about and scanning the crowd for something he didn't want to find. I got over to them just as the final rose came up and Lozier stood to lead loud applause for the band. Only Zev pretended to be happy to see me.

"He flits in, he flits off! We never know where he'll flit next!"

Shepherd's smile said she knew what species was good at flitting; she had swatted more than one of them in her time. "What happened to Number Eight? They'll never start until she and Number One get here."

"Right. You want to get back to the stables."

Sewell hadn't lost any of his possessiveness about her. "Oh, Pauline's told you about going riding?"

It came out so adolescently even she had to drop her eyes as she said: "I think Mr. Finley is being a detective. He sees somebody standing in jodhpurs and jumps to the conclusion I'm going riding."

Sewell might have discovered new concentrates of red if Zev hadn't intervened to ask about Karen. "Nothing an aspirin can take care of?" he asked when I gave him a headache story. "It's a shame she'll miss all this public acclaim she has coming."

I let that one go: Sometimes when you took a whack at a grapefruit, you just got spritzed in the eye. "Can we talk a second, Jimmy?" I didn't give him much choice. If we had embraced at our first meeting outside the redhead's saloon, it didn't seem all that forward to grab his elbow and steer him away from Pulsar. Zev and Shepherd didn't waste a second moving off their spots to the other side of the stage.

Sewell looked after them forlornly. He had just had his afternoon ruined, and I hadn't even gotten around to ask him where Denise and the girls were sitting. "I'm manning the command post here for my people," he said, trying not to look ornery about sliding away from my hold. "They have to see me and . . ."

"One name, okay? Matthew Vickers."

It was still early enough Sunday, so there were probably people all over New Florence at that hour who were regretting having taken that one drink extra the night before. But Jimmy Sewell hadn't been out drinking Saturday night; his hangover dated back much longer. "Vickers?"

"Part of your small talk with the horse lady a week or two ago. Material supplied by Alan Lockman."

He was coming back to me; unwillingly, but coming back. "The social scientist? Paula's guru? What about him?"

He wasn't that good an actor. A minute before he had been all but drooling over his claim on Shepherd. It was a situation Pulsar would have been the first to understand: He was an addend behind me, and that oddly worked out to making both of us minuses. "Lockman mentioned this Vickers to you and it came up in conversation with Shepherd, right?"

The answer to himself was yes, but that didn't mean I deserved it, too. "You're implying something here, friend."

What the hell? My vacation in New Florence seemed to have come down to only a few more hours anyway and *friend* also was pushing it. In fact, if called to testify, I would have to admit to feeling extremely mean-spirited. "No, I'm saying it, Jimmy. You passed along that little tidbit about Vickers to Shepherd. She was sitting at a restaurant table and paused in her chewing. Or if you hit a home run with your fantasies, maybe she pulled the sheet up over her more tightly in a motel bedroom. Either way, she asked where you'd heard about Vickers and you told her Lockman."

"You bastard!"

His anger pissed me off coming and going. Not only was he doing an inept job at dissembling, but I was the one who should have been pissed off. "No, that's you," I said, my tone worrying an apple-cheeked woman and her elderly father at the end of the row behind Sewell. "You're responsible for nothing, but somehow that also comes out as everything."

"Power of the press. Anything else?"

"Yes. You want that quote for being slugged out at the cemetery? Here it is: *It was Dwayne Arlett.* After you suggested to Brighton I should hang around while he looked into Lockman and Page. For all I know, you got Labine to suggest the same thing to him. Just in case things got a little too sticky for his big promotion day here today."

He still wasn't acting and he was still incredulous. "So I had them slug you, that what you're saying?"

"No, I didn't say that."

"Hooray for small favors.""Maybe not even Brighton said it right out. Maybe it was Arlett improvising. I don't know, and unless I start getting weird headaches and fainting spells over the next few months, I don't really give a damn about that anymore. But I do know it all started with you—for old time's sake. And I'm flattered, Jimmy. I just didn't need to be knocked out."

"You're on holiday, Finley. I'm not. I have to get back to . . ."

The woman behind cringed when I grabbed him by the arm again. The old father, who either couldn't see or who was past it on several levels, was asking what was bothering her. "Part Two. Your crush over there got very disturbed when you mentioned Vickers, so you told her how his name had come up. Then it turns out Lockman's also keeping his count of the ballots."

He processed it with a pained squint. "And this means?" The daughter patted the old man reassuringly on his leather glove; she was having second thoughts about having dragged him out. "Are you . . .? Jesus, Finley, you do need a vacation. And maybe one without some neurotic who . . ." So Galahad wasn't always up to Galahad standards. If I had to testify in front of that same jury, I might have had to admit being grateful for his hit at Karen. Since I already resented the guy, by her formula that made for the perfect guilty act in New Florence, New York, thank you, Claudio Mochi. Or almost. My hand was already in the air when I changed direction and gave him a schoolyard jab to the solar plexus rather than the face shot that had seemed so appealing. Too many people saw it and did their stunned thing anyway, but at least I could keep my sick buddy propped up on his feet. "I don't really need to hear that," I said, smiling to help along the confusion of the three or four thousand people who were staring at us and one second away from calling for a cop. "Not from you. What I do need to hear is anything useful the Dragon Lady might have said when you were talking about Vickers or Admired Citizens or even the National Horse Show. Be a help here, Jimmy. Lockman died on your watch."

He didn't want to be a help. He was concentrating on his breathing, not on the blank spaces in my puzzle. And that was the least of it. Because all stupid things flowed from stupid Finley things, the Carnation Man decided it was time for him to walk his index cards up to the mike and say how wonderful the band had been. And that was stupid because the protesters in the back immediately realized the Carnation Man didn't have a fraction of the band's volume so they broke out the chanting they had been holding back. *"Randy Page, Randy Page! Who Killed Randy Page?"* It didn't have the crescendos of "Everything's Comin' Up Roses," but it was a little easier on the ears. The chummy cops stopped being chummy. Brighton signaled to a uniformed sergeant to get more uniforms to the back, and that got half the seated crowd to turn around to see where all the blue was rushing. Something flew through the air. It was only a spool of confetti, but Lama lost my campaign contribution by instinctively raising his arms over his face.

"You better find your people, Jimmy. They'll need direction."

"Fuck you." He meant it, too. We weren't old-time colleagues from the big city anymore. As he limped back toward the skirt of the stage, still holding his chest, I had my usual after-thought about needing to apologize to everybody for everything, but this time it evaporated faster than a snowflake. Labine hurried it along by shouting down to his editor to make sure the paper got "every last name" of the troublemakers in the rear and getting an obedient nod back from his editor.

The second missile wasn't confetti; it was an orange and it landed on the stage right next to the Carnation Man. It would have taken Robert Clemente to make that kind of peg from the back of the square, not to mention a lot of cops standing with their arms crossed as the orange had sailed past them. Neither thing. The flinger was a young guy sitting halfway back to the right of the stage, and Brighton himself moved a quick five steps and, one hand still holding on to his radio, grabbed him around the throat from behind. The guy went down so fast he created a geyser of people scrambling up from their seats to get away. For at least a second Brighton looked content with life.

The second elapsed. There were too many other geysers sprouting up from the crowd, other oranges and apples cutting the air toward the stage, other decibels besides the chanting from the rear and the Carnation Man's fluttery appeals from the front. The placards in the back were a false front, at most the signals corps for the real problems scattered throughout the seating. Labine shoved the Carnation Man away to command the mike. He was back in all those places where he had worn his beret and this time he had nothing to duck but supermarket produce. He was invulnerable! "Would the authorities please control these hooligans!" he demanded. "And the rest of you folks stay seated! Don't let them ruin our day!"Mrs. Labine had apparently been listening to that command for too long back at the villa. She bolted out of her front row seat in the audience and cried up to him. "Jesus Christ, Walter, get everybody out of here!"

He ignored her. He wasn't paying too much attention to the defectors on the stage behind him, either. A uniform appeared from the back of the stage to help Dracula escort McCorkle over to a side staircase. The mortician who had been talking to Mrs. Labine at the brunch had already beaten them down the steps and the others were following suit. Only Doreen Lozier and two guys sitting in the back row weren't in that much of a hurry to leave. They might have been the most admired car salesman and most admired vet in New Florence and they didn't want their day of glory cut so short. As for Lozier, she had warned somebody of something somewhere along the way and now she was seeing all her predictions coming true. She was taking as many names as Sewell was supposed to be taking.

Then the worst thing of all happened. What could top the hundreds of people all but trampling over one another to get away from the square, some of them yanking the arms of their petrified children out of the socket? Or the cops pressing against the protesters with night sticks arcing here and there? Or some of the fruit pitchers changing their targets from the stage to the cops in the rear? Or Zev and Shepherd standing between a corner of the stage and a tree, he prizing the spectacle like a personally produced entertainment and she trying to maintain an analytic interest as she tapped out something on some electronic gizmo, glanced at the crowd, then went back to the gizmo? Only one thing could top all that, really: I needed a cigarette. Specifically, I needed one of Brighton's cigarettes. It was the most inventive idea I'd had since coming to New Florence. And I probably owed it to George Oswald and the other two WBOV stooges. And how could that *not* lead to disaster?

CHAPTER 57

Enough people had scattered that I had no problem cutting through a row of the folding chairs to get over to Brighton on the far aisle. He was trying to cuff the orange thrower he had throttled in between keeping his knee pressed down on the guy's wriggling back and barking at somebody on his radio. All I needed was for him to see me, and he did. He didn't know *why* he was seeing me, and the kid's balkiness about getting cuffed made him too steamed to ask, but that was fine with me. I wished him luck in his public order duties, checked that Zev was watching us, then wished him luck a second time. His last shot at an explanation died when he had to turn his bewilderment to the crackling radio again. Zev saw me coming, but Shepherd was still tapping away on her toy. "Brighton's office," I told the fat man.

"Excuse me?"

Shepherd looked up as though I had interrupted her in the middle of chewing. "Captain Brighton wants you out of here now," I repeated. "He says I should get you over to his office until this clears up."

She had no intention of taking orders from somebody with fewer grants than she had, but Zev played back what I'd hoped he thought he had seen between me and Brighton. "Let it go, Paula," he decided. "We don't want to get on the wrong side of the constabulary."

"So we'll wait across the street," she objected logically. "Why do we have to go to any office?"

"Because he needs a statement from you about the poll. In case you haven't noticed, they have a situation here that's going to call for a lot of investigating. Including your little survey. He wants to get that out of the way first thing to head off questions."

Zev was beguiled. "What questions?"

"Gee, I wonder. All the people's choices up on that platform."

"We've already discussed this potential scenario with Chief Lama."

I didn't doubt it; I was sure Lama had even understood every third or fourth word. "But your friend the chief doesn't face the nitty-gritty of filling out reports and filing them. That's Brighton's problem. Let the little people do their jobs, Michael. It leaves giants like us less to worry about."

He preferred being amused by me than distracted by his doubts, but she wasn't so captivated. My magic powers with women were not having a good day. "And when did you become Brighton's messenger?"

"Since his cops got busy."

It was almost too much, and she searched my face for the chink that would say so. A big moan followed by a panicked shriek went up behind me, and that didn't sound good for several people. But if she wasn't interested in what it was, I couldn't be. We were equals at being indifferent to the human condition. I finally cut her off by starting away with the assumption they would follow. For some reason they did. But we were barely clear of the speaking platform when Zev's labored breathing began covering over her boot stomp, sounding a warning we were unlikely to get out of the plaza, let alone to Brighton's office, if he had to keep hurrying. What had I been thinking—walking them all the way back and around to my car? The answer, of course, was that I hadn't really been doing much thinking at all. But just as my great idea about penning them up in Brighton's office was about to die the rapid death it had invited, we came to a social planning detail Matthew Vickers wouldn't have had to write a magazine article about: The rest of the town might have been banned from parking in the plaza, but not the VIPs. There was a half-dozen cars and police vans clustered in the northern shadow of the square, and

their engines were running. Dracula was closing McCorkle and
his wife into one car, a uniform was supervising the boarding of
a van by Lozier and others I'd seen on the stage. "Mind if we take
mine?" Shepherd asked. "Or are we under your personal arrest?"

Winks between winky people, but I wasn't up for it. In their
company even Junior Dvorak could have seemed sympathetic.
She marched over to a gray Caravan; it wasn't the car from the
Rustic Inn parking lot and that irked me. In so deep, I wanted at
least the illusion of having tracked her continuously from Chelsea
Barracks to Mochi's annex.

I got into the back to let Zev wrestle with the seat belt. As
Shepherd pulled away from the plaza curb, she gave me another
look through the rearview mirror that said she wasn't through
being suspicious. I smiled back at her. "Always get this kind of
reaction to your little projects?"

"Hardly," Zev grunted for her. "New Florence seems to be an
arsenal of short fuses. Not good."

The gizmo she had been tapping on was sticking out of her
bag between the two front seats. On a good day I would have simply snatched it and seen what she had been so busy annotating.
But it wasn't a good day and I had a hunch Ben and Belinda had
already told me what I would have found, anyway. "But you keep
going with the flow, that it? The poll, then the after-poll, then the
after-after-poll? Where do you draw the line? When do you lose
interest in New Florence altogether?"

He smiled in her direction, but she was too busy figuring out
which deserted street to take to police headquarters or what game
I was playing at or when she would ever get back out to Labine's
stables. "What makes you think there's a line?" he asked. "Even
today, years later, we keep an eye on places where we've conducted our studies."

"Me, too. I keep an eye on the Middle East crisis."

It took some effort with the strap across his belly, but he
turned halfway back to me with his best baronial condescension.
"You're a very cynical person, aren't you, Paul?"

"I never thought so, really."

"Next best thing: You always assume other people are?"

I hadn't thought of it that way before, and didn't like thinking about it then. "That would be a copout."

He turned back to the front with a satisfied nod. She glanced at him as if he had won some bet between them.

The sergeant on duty in the police headquarters lobby was my crusty friend from my first visit, and he could believe anything was true of Brighton. If he could be the only cop in New York State told he wasn't fit for a plaza assignment, why wouldn't Brighton also impose some of his hoity-toity friends on him for refuge? It was a law that assholes did asshole things. But the captain's office was something else. "Why can't you just sit over there and wait for him?"

That question I had anticipated. "Because of what we both know is going to be happening in here in a few minutes, Sarge. The whole idea is to get Mr. Zev and Ms. Shepherd away from a mob scene. You're going to have more collars to process this afternoon than you've had for a month."

He looked through the door to the street and instantly developed a bad case of dry mouth. *Month* was severe understatement, and we both knew it. But why admit to the outsider he usually had a laidback job? "Right," he said reluctantly. "But I don't have anybody to escort you upstairs, and that's how we do it here."

"I know where the office is, Sarge. And Frank knows I know. That's why I'm the escort. Radio him if you want."

Processing collars, Sarge, Frank, month, radio him—it all went into the nod that got us past him and over to the elevator. "Not a very skeptical gatekeeper," she said as we went up.

"Everybody's a little stressed today," I said, wondering who else in the elevator besides me I had in mind.

Once they entered Brighton's office and sat down, I felt a little better. They weren't being printed and lined up for mug shots exactly, but it seemed close enough until Brighton walked in to find us and plunged into his moral, professional, and other crises. However that turned out, I was first going to have my few minutes with them the way I needed to have them. We weren't having dinner at the Rustic Inn or drinking Bloody Walters at Labine's villa or staring at computer gobbledygook out at the annex; they were suspects in multiple homicides in a room where they had to answer questions. It might have been years and far to the north, but I was the one on familiar territory.

"Is there any coffee or tea?" Zev asked, squirming enough to make the wide chair look like a vise.

"I don't think anybody's been refilling the silex today."

"No, I suppose not. Too bad. A tea would be nice. How long do you think we're going to be sitting here?"

She came out of her bag with a dark green sweatband that she put around her head. It didn't do anything for her appearance, and I wondered if she wanted to have a judo bout. "What can I say?"

"Something true might be a good start," she said, looking less like a judo fighter than Geronimo.

Winky people just indulged their equals with cracks like that so that was what I did as she modeled her forehead for me. Only then did I see the perspiration glistening everywhere around the band. I slid open Brighton's top side drawer and, luckily for brilliant ideas, found the discount reservation cigarettes in the ashtray and next to the recorder. "Mind if I smoke?"

They both reared up in their chairs so comically at sight of the cigarettes I might have been Satan appearing out of a cloud of sulfur. "Very much," she said indignantly. "And I can't imagine Captain Brighton would be happy to know you're going into his desk."

"We all have our addictions, Paul," he said more smoothly. "I'm the last one to criticize in that department. But if you could abstain until we leave, I'd be grateful."

"No problem." I tucked the cigarettes back into the drawer, right next to the recorder's Play button. My pinkie did what it was supposed to do and I coughed to reassure them they were right about my addiction. Zev smiled at what he took for a sarcasm, but once stripped of the snide, Shepherd had a sense of humor about as expansive as the Reverend Dvorak's. She even preferred Brighton's academy graduation certificate on the wall to my wit. "So I guess your B Team's mostly gone by now," I said, keeping the drawer open enough not to smother the tape.

"Let's hope so," he shook his head. "The innkeepers around here seem to have learned their trade on the Barbary Coast."

"Oh, c'mon. I'll bet you could cover Hilton suites if you had to."

"From your lips to the ears of the budget gods. Where do you get such extravagant notions of our resources?"

As George Oswald would have reminded his Cyclones listeners, you couldn't get the game started until you threw the first pitch. "Since when has the Pentagon ever had cash shorts?"

I couldn't disagree with the Finley II in the back of my head who was spooked by how the two of them gaped at me. It was probably how a particularly intelligent and sensitive bug felt when it was being viewed through a microscope. On the other hand, Finley I thought their expressions were a riot: I was still a bug maybe, but one that had flown down from the lab wall to the microscope slide on its own volition, not one that had been taken out of a freezer for scheduled study.

Zev recovered first. While Shepherd seemed to be rehearsing a dozen ways of saying I had a rich fantasy life, he gave a quick review to looking perplexed, found it wanting, then just shrugged. "Since you have some background in officialdom, Paul, I'm confident you don't make an assertion like that lightly."

"Nope."

"Because you've . . ."

"Looked you up. In more detail than most people have."

"Or have the interest to."

"As you pointed out this morning, Karen has that interest. I guess I just picked up on it."

"Of course, of course." He glanced at Shepherd to remind her that was perfectly natural; elbow on the arm of her chair and her long fingers pushing into her cheek, she didn't look reassured. In fact, she looked ready to call her whole Apache war party down on me.

"So what is it exactly the DOD gets out of your fieldwork?"

She might have heard enough, but he had never met a silence he wasn't ready to dispel with jabber. "Don't read so much into it," he sighed. "It's a government department like any other. Projects begin in one direction, go off in another that doesn't really apply to the original purpose, but by then the agency appropriation is there in committed dollars and cents. Bureaucratic inertia. It can go on for years and the poor taxpayer is the victim. But in this instance, I'm not going to be the one to decry it."

"Right. You like those regular checks."

He was offended; mildly, but still offended. "Hardly just that. We have come up with some very provocative . . . let's call them social indicators. They may not be germane to the Department of Defense, but . . ."

"But they are."

"Excuse me?"

"Germane to the Department of Defense. Of course, they are. That's why you do what you do. Don't I at least rate the speech?"

"What speech would that be, Mr. Finley?" Even without her glass-cutting stare, I knew the *Mr. Finley* she had been holding to didn't disguise any subterranean cordiality.

"The speech you gave McCorkle, Labine, and whoever else you had to persuade about your project when you contacted them the first time. C'mon. I'm sure they all have a record of it somewhere. What can you say to me you haven't already said to them?"

I didn't like the harder shrewdness in Zev's eyes, but what else had I been expecting—the joke of the week? "Tell him, Paula."

"I don't think Mr. Finley . . ."

"You say it so much better than I do and we know it's never going to leave this office. Right, Paul?"

I didn't like his self-confidence. If he didn't mind telling me what I wanted to know, how important could knowing it be? "Absolutely."

"Are you sure, Michael?"

"As Paul says, absolutely."

Exactly how the hierarchy worked between the two of them held promise as a field project of my own in my next life. But for the moment it came down to him giving orders in the tone of compliments and her sitting up to cross her long legs like a classroom student called on to recite because she was extra smart. And just as I had once done in Father McGinley's Latin class, she did her best to block out those around her for the recital. "There is no enemy on this planet or any other," she said to her knee, "with a greater capacity for destroying us than we have for destroying ourselves. Loss of pride. Knee-jerk cynicism about the system. Corrosive guilt. Self-esteem so low it becomes self-contempt. Even in the age of terrorism these remain the most powerful of all weapons . . ."

I could have done without her choosing that moment to look up at me, but she didn't really see me or Zev through her glassy stare. She didn't even acknowledge the glare coming through the window behind me. Politicians on the election stump weren't more mechanical about *the speech.*

". . . When do these ailments turn contagious? Under what circumstances? Who are the carriers? How can they be resisted? In what circumstances? When does the individual react positively to threatening social or political stress? When does he respond negatively to uncertainty and confusion? Are there variables among reactions that appear similar at first glance? What are they? How do they become variables? . . ."

Zev's eyes wandered around the office. He wanted every plaque and photo he landed on to appreciate his windup toy. That seemed to answer my hierarchy question: Probably like Matthew Vickers before her, her main function was to keep him employed. And for all the rote she was giving her delivery, she was proud, too. She was the mistress of her material.

". . . Conversely, are there positive and negative constants to our behavior in stress situations? These are not merely academic curiosities. Every branch of government has an interest in the answers. Every private political and economic sector has an investment in anticipating what Plus personalities and Minus personalities would do in given conditions."

That sounded familiar. "Plus and Minus personalities?"

She was finished her part of the script. "Michael can explain that. If he thinks you're entitled to know."

"What do you think, Michael? Am I entitled to know?"

"You tell me," he said happily.

Second pitch time. "Okay. If I understand this Plus and Minus personality thing, sometimes you get people acting nobly, other times you get them behaving like swine. That's what gets them their plus and minus."

"That's the essence of it, yes," he nodded, surprised.

"But who decides who's a Plus and who's a Minus? You? Before you arrive here? Before you know the people you're rating that way?"

"We don't anticipate."

"Total objectivity."

"Precisely."

"But you must have at least an inkling going in."

He was trying to ignore how the back of his chair was pinching a fold or two of fat. "We do some preliminary research, yes."

"Sure you do. How do you even choose where to move your caravan in the middle of the night, right? But even that little research had to tell you New Florence would never be confused with Utopia."

"Your point?"

Bluffing aside, I wouldn't have minded one of Brighton's cigarettes. "Well, maybe this was a place where the Minuses offered more opportunity for study than the Pluses."

"No question it's a community that has had problems for some time. Rather a lot for its size, in fact."

"So a big day for the Minuses even before you set up."

"That wouldn't be objective."

"Right. I forgot." Neither of them looked like they knew where to get me Rangers tickets, but it felt like the moment to skate across the rink to ask anyway. "So how are Leo and Hal doing? They part of the A team still around or have you already packed them off with the rest of the B team?"

If I had been a fly under his microscope, I would have lost my wings. She, on the other hand, had already recited her Cicero and knew she wasn't going to be called on again. "Hal was a temporary hire," he said more tensely under her watch. "I think I told you that."

"And Leo?"

"Why does your curiosity sound so much like an interrogation?"

"Because Mr. Finley is trying to relive his youth," she smiled humorlessly to the foot of the desk. "He didn't make such a great success of being a policeman the first time, so he's hoping for better results now. I imagine being in this office brings it all back to him."

That shouldn't have twinged, not after so much time, but she had found a sore spot. "All I'm saying is that I'm confused."

"Really."

"Really."

"By something in particular?"

"Well, for example, we've had two killings here recently. One was supposed to look like an accident and the other was supposed to look like a suicide. But the confusing thing both times is that neither looked *that* much like what it was supposed to look like. It's like both Page and Lockman were killed by someone who wanted to see if the police would get past appearances to conduct the proper homicide investigation they should."

"Sounds terribly gratuitous," he said.

"Yes. And no amount of rationalization makes it less so."

"I can't imagine that kind of rationalization."

I really wanted to stretch a sudden heaviness out of my legs, but I didn't want either of them taking that as a cue to do the same thing and wandering over behind the desk and spotting the recorder. "Oh, they're out there. You work homicide cases, even back in the caveman days like I did, and you come across them all the time." Her grin was almost gracious. "A for instance?" He nodded. "Say we're talking about this Plus and Minus project."

"You say it."

"I'll say it. Just for fun speculation." They were supposed to have looked more nervous than they did. "Here's this radio man with a big following among the kids and he especially likes mocking this Most Admired Citizen thing of yours."

"The usual wannabe Howard Stern. For the teenagers."

"Well, his following wasn't *all* from the high schools. One way or another, you remove him from circulation and you're going to get an awful lot of antagonism. His followers smell a rat. City Hall gets uptight at their reaction. They lay patrol cars on the wake. You end up with scenes like out at the cemetery. So many acting like those Minus personalities. Chain reaction, and a perfect test of how New Florence responds to a stressful situation."

"So you're accepting this official cover-up accusation?"

"Me? I'm just the dumb cop arriving at the radio station parking lot. What do I see? Butts, soda cans, an emptied car ashtray all in one mound. Any Academy cadet would see the so-called hit-and-run driver hadn't been doing much running before Page came out of the station so the hitting could get started. No way to read the ground except that he had been waiting for Page to come out."

She was up on her boots in a bang. "I don't know about you, Michael, but I have plans for this afternoon."

"Wait, Paula. This is interesting."

"To you, maybe."

"Last I saw of Labine, he was still in the middle of the plaza."

Whatever the direct opposite of a smile was, she gave it to me with all her teeth. "I'm not riding Walter, I'm riding his horses. Coming, Michael?"

Zev knew better than to stay behind. He had smelled the air as much as she had and he also knew he had a weakness for prattling. But I sensed his decision a second before he announced it: the decision of a poker player who always has to call because, no matter how much he loses, it is better than being bluffed from the table. "I'll tell Captain Brighton everything he needs to know," he said. "You go enjoy your ride."

She was too committed to the door to change her mind. But as she walked out, she really trusted him less than she trusted me, and I thought that was almost like a declaration of love.

CHAPTER 58

What did they say about some people leaving a room and taking the air out of it with them? With Shepherd it was more like an anger being sucked out. There was just as much distrust in the way Zev was looking at me, but without her next to him it felt softer, like he was counting on me to draw out whatever attack I had planned. And of course, he would have: With Michael Zev, executive director of the Pulsar Institute, absolutely everything was for the long term. There was no rush about anything, even life or death. So I was the one who supplied the anger Shepherd had absconded with. "It's an endless game for you, isn't it?"

"You're the one acting like a ringmaster, Paul."

"Alan Lockman was murdered because he knew you were rigging the ballots sent to the paper."

Nothing. "A boy like that? I don't think so."

"Okay, he didn't have *all* the ballots. But he had enough of them, plus he knew why you were rigging them."

"I regret not knowing the lad. He sounds like somebody I could have used on my team."

It was time to go back for my Rangers tickets. "Okay, you're used to bothersome people like me. But what about Leo and Hal? They like shadow boxing, too? Do they even know what it is?"

He sat forward too aggressively. With his size there wasn't much he could do subtly, but his eyes clearly ignored his lurch to focus in on Brighton's desk drawer. "You'd have to ask them.

By the way, I was being tactful before. If you want a cigarette so badly . . ."

"No, but you can have one if you want." He gave me the second of surprise I needed by glancing at me as I opened the drawer to grab the pack. He might or might not have seen the recorder as I tossed the cigarettes to his side of the desk and closed the drawer again; he couldn't have said if it was running. "What's the matter? Think I'm taping this? I'm not Pulsar, Michael. If I wanted to record you, I'd have two machines going in the desk and another on that shelf over there. Your goddamn shoes would be the latest magnetic invention from Sony. And of course, a camera would be running through that wall plaque."

He lapsed back in his chair. He wasn't certain about what he had seen in the drawer, but I had convinced him I could be as slimy as he was. "I really don't smoke except for an occasional cigar after a good meal. I was just thinking of you."

"Good. Keep that attitude. I think Leo hanged Alan Lockman. Think you can help me with that?"

"I'm speechless."

"That wouldn't help."

He laughed. "Then you'll have to tell me how I can."

"How about a confession to Captain Brighton? Not only would you make Alan Lockman's mother and Randy Page's family feel better, but you could watch Brighton fumble with the hottest potato in his life. Don't tell me that wouldn't give you a lot of interesting data."

So maybe it wasn't the kind of tough love Shepherd had left behind for me; maybe it was something more along the lines of disdain. "What do you think you're playing at, Finley?"

"You, actually. I think I'm playing at you. I just heard this story about these two people being killed, and it makes me a little less enthusiastic as I'm serving you the roasted boar and the mead in your castle. I understand you and the other kings must cut up the Republic for the greater good, but I still can't stop thinking about these two victims. Help me out, Michael. My apron's got too many stains on it. It's distracting me."

All things considered, he mainly felt sorry for me. "One of us is out of our league here. Why don't we just leave it at that?"

It would have been nice to believe that the voices outside the window down in the street were just a couple of refugees from La-bine Plaza, but there were too many of them and they came with too many slammed car doors. Assuming the worst, that Brighton was back with the first group, I figured I had about three minutes before he heard about the favor he'd asked me to do for him and went tearing for the elevator. "No problem. But here's the way it's going to shake out. The New Florence police are about to lose their jurisdiction over the two killings. In other words, a new investigation from scratch. And one that's going to include Pulsar."

"Fascinating. And you're alerting me to this because . . .?"

He had been right about my sliminess. The answer hadn't even occurred to me until it was crawling out my mouth. "Because there's a lady in this town I like a lot and I don't want her hurt by having to relive a lot of useless pain. I don't want them finding Pulsar under all these rocks, Michael. I want New Florence up here and Hoboken down there. On the other hand, if they were to find some nitwit who thought he was trying to please his employer without his employer knowing . . ."

I finally had his complete attention—for a good three seconds of incomprehension, anyway. Since he knew nothing about people acting to protect others, I might as well have been speaking Urdu by mentioning feelings for Karen. But then he remembered the slime ball he was dealing with and his face relaxed again. "That would be quite a nitwit. How could we possibly be pleased by the violence you're suggesting? You'd have to think we had a secret agenda in one case and something to hide in the other. And neither is true."

"That's too bad."

He was chagrined for me. "What can I say?"

Sergeant Bailey, of course, would have said keep going. But what was the far side of a bluff? "Another raise," I answered myself too loudly.

"Excuse me?"

There were all kinds of voices downstairs—angry ones, commanding ones, reassuring ones. The cops were pushing and the prisoners were being pushed. "Nothing. I was hoping we could wind this thing up for Karen. Now she'll just have to add Leo to her gallery of nightmares."

He clamped his hands down on the sides of his chair; he too knew it was even money he could stand without lifting his seat with him. "Let me point out where your imagination went wrong, my friend," he said evenly. "I know my strengths and limitations. That's the key gift of a bureaucrat. And as a bureaucrat, I don't *care* how these surveys come out. All Plus, all Minus—it's the same to me. We collect more of that data you mock, turn it over to our sponsors, and then we go on to the next community. I have no collateral academic interests. I don't expect a film or a television series to be made from our work. I take no risks beyond those of the central program. You should appreciate my taste for well-paid muddling through. The only way you and I really differ is in the well-paid part."

He got to his feet without the chair, and that was what was going on in only one of the side rings. In another side ring was a raging Brighton coming through his door. Had there been that much sun down at the plaza to explain his coloring? I couldn't recall. I was too busy in the center ring feeling giddy about having worked out how the Pulsar hierarchy functioned in a practical way. The solution was really simple once you realized Alan Lockman wasn't the only one who thought *Planning Society* was an important credit.

CHAPTER 59

Everybody was fuming and apologizing, or apologizing and fuming. For a change of pace, we said there must have been a misunderstanding. Well, maybe not Brighton, he didn't say it. He thought he was entitled to his fuming because he had nothing to apologize for and he hadn't understood or misunderstood a damn thing besides the fact that I had gone too far. And at bottom maybe not Zev, either. What did he have to apologize for? If anybody had the right to fume, he did for having been abducted from Labine Plaza and brought to Brighton's office under false pretenses. There had been no misunderstanding. Harassment maybe, but no misunderstanding. Didn't believe him? Ask Paula Shepherd, who felt exactly as he did.

How could I have disagreed? Nobody had more of a right to fume than she did. Hadn't I noticed the same thing myself before she had left? She was owed apologies from the second Sewell had mentioned Matthew Vickers to her. She had hardly put together the Plus and Minus project in New Florence to have her published findings sidetracked by some nerd who couldn't pull himself away from a computer. A Minus field test was a Minus field test. Important people were waiting to read and analyze the results in *Planning Society* and other journals where Vickers had been a prestigious contributor. Just the effort in having to tell Leo to sit in his car outside the radio studio and wait for Page to come out had been exhausting for her. About that there could never have been a misunderstanding. Career credits were career credits.

Which got me back to mine. They weren't all that impressive
when you thought about it. A little I-told-you-so-but-forgot-to-
realize-the-full-extent-of-what-I'd-been-telling-you didn't go too
far when a cop already in an arresting mode was inching toward
the phone to have me added to his collection down in the lobby.
But because Zev was gone after a few *bon mots*, I was at least able
to get in my commercial about the tape recorder. Brighton pried
open the desk drawer as if it had been booby-trapped. The red
light on RECORD confirmed his fears. Even as he pressed off the
machine, he was working out his options around what he hadn't
heard and didn't want to hear.

"Have a listen, Frank. That's my get-out-of-jail card."

Staring down at the recorder seemed to cost him the sunburn
he had picked up in the plaza. He grabbed for a cigarette. "Get
out."

Why stop there? I might never see him again. "Play it right,
and it could be yours, too."

I didn't wait for his gratitude. I was already ahead of the game
finding the elevator car still in the shaft when the hall doors
parted. The door to the street still worked, too. I probably should
have savored those discoveries more for my sense of survival.
But, hey, bag of shells. The main thing was that I was on a roll.
My halfwit idea back in the square hadn't exactly brought down
the Pulsar Wall, but on the other hand it hadn't cost me more
than an extra bad thought from Brighton and a glare from my
friend the sergeant in the middle of all the lobby chaos. I was
going to be leaving town anyway. And the tape in Brighton's desk
with all its ambiguities did exist. Who knew where it would end
up before the gentry of New Florence finished blackmailing one
another? But end up somewhere it would. Not even Brighton was
scared enough to ignore leverage with the McCorkles and Lamas.
And one day New Florence's latest generation would be debating
the wisdom of changing the town's name to New Finley as a tactful alternative to delving too deeply into why the older folk were
scraping around the streets with humps like Quasimodo. And
since I wasn't Italian and they couldn't use that as an excuse
against me, that put me one up on Claudio Mochi, right?

It took a couple of centuries, but I got back to my car. The people along the way reminded me of the time a Citi Field game had been called because of rain and two minutes later the sun had broken through: I didn't know whether to be miffed or to think of the afternoon as an opportunity for unscheduled adventure. I yelled over to a young couple with that in-between expression on their faces that one less speech from McCorkle and Labine was a year added to their lives, but they didn't understand and asked me to repeat myself. That was something I never did.

I was up, then I was down, then I was up again. On a graph I would have given myself a headache. The drive back to Karen's was the down part wanting to believe in a little more up. I hadn't done anything for Barbara Lockman, or for Karen's optimism to her that I would, but we were all a little too old for my Superman complex anyway, weren't we? On my best day I was Clark Kent asking the right investigative questions for the *Daily Planet*, not the Big S. And as for Karen waiting for me to tie everything into a bundle for delivery back to Hoboken, that was her lookout. If she wanted to kick me out of her bed, she should have expected me to leave her holding a few bags as I was getting away.

Since it was my last shot to use the key, I skipped the false etiquette to let myself into the house with it. I had thought through a few moves for saying goodbye, but they were more useless than normal because Karen wasn't home. Only after I had finished looking into every room did I spot the note on the coffee table. It was a brusque reminder of something else I had left unresolved: I'M WITH RUSSELL AT THE ANNEX. COME ALONE. Of course, she was with Junior. Where else would she have been? While Brighton had been booking all the orange throwers in town, the bomb throwers had been cruising around and grabbing hostages for their last big bang. That alone made the telephone a nonstarter. And as for *numero uno*, why not go out to the annex to see what Junior had on his frazzled mind? What did he have against me? Well, if I wanted to get technical, that was a bad question. Too many answers occurred immediately. There was Karen. And there were the conversations I'd had with his old man that he might have considered too amiable. And don't forget not crashing into the laundromat window after he had tossed me toward it; that had been short-sighted of me. No, the answer was that Russell Junior had too many things against me and could very well think of me as a natural fit for his final act. For once, though, I had shown a little foresight. Not only was my .38 in my overnight bag, but I had even remembered to bring along ammunition.

Since there didn't figure to be cops prowling the streets with ticket quotas to meet, I hit the gas pedal hard over to Sloan. That almost cost a mangy Siamese, but he scooted under a parked U-Haul wagon in time. I missed the Professor. Not even the smug growl he would have given me for saying so weakened the feeling. If for nothing else, I would have liked him in the front seat nagging about the stupid thing I was doing. Well, screw him. If he hadn't drafted me into driving him to New Florence in the first place, I could have been home in Bay Ridge keeping in shape by lifting the Sunday *Times*. Who needed that old hypocrite's self-righteousness?

CHAPTER 60

The derelict of a green Olds was still in front of the annex and now had company: Parked next to it was a panel truck advertising Junior's silk screen printing business. The wine lettering surprised me. I hadn't pictured Junior Dvorak making money at his pastime. I assumed it was the truck that had given the road gate a good ram to leave it gaping open. It felt like my last warning to find a telephone and call Brighton.

I didn't see anybody at the annex windows as I got out of the car. Since I didn't know what was waiting for me inside the entrance door, I kept my weapon out of sight in the back of my belt. It hadn't made the trip all the way from Brooklyn to be confiscated right away at the end of a bazooka. I kept my hands up and in front of me as I walked through the outer door, then through the secondary one. The jolly gang—Karen, the Reverend, Mendler, and good old Leo—sat in a circle next to the remaining computers and where I had first seen Ben and Belinda. They were frozen looking but not dead: one reason to feel ahead. Another was that Karen had found the time to change out of her suit into a flannel shirt and jeans before being whisked off. She had obviously taken my sage counsel not to consider going down to the plaza where she would have been in danger.

"Sit down, Mr. Finley."

Junior was standing inside the door and holding something behind the flap of the camouflage jacket from the cemetery. He hadn't gotten any smaller or done anything about his acne since he had been throwing me at the laundromat. Worse, even in the shadows the empty eyes looked hungrier, no burning churches feeding his attention. "So what's the occasion, Russell?"

"I said sit down."

I didn't need to see what he was holding out of view. If Leo hadn't been up for rushing whatever it was, I certainly wasn't. I took the last stool in the rear of the Pulsar workspace. The only one who seemed concerned I could sit down without breaking any bones was Karen. Too late, I felt like telling her fretful eyes. If I wanted her feeling responsible for anything, it wasn't for writing invitations under threats; I had taken her up on that on my own. Now if she wanted to start taking responsibility for some of the teary Edith Piaf regret stuff after I took off for Brooklyn . . .

"John knows specialists, son," the Reverend said, apparently picking up on a plea I had interrupted. "They can help you. Tell him, John."

Mendler took his cue. Granted it wouldn't have been giving away much, but I could have been tempted to trade in my ideas about the Lockman and Page killings for an explanation of his relationship with Rumpelstiltskin. To my mind, Lockman and Page were no longer mysteries, but the bond between the surgeon and the holy roller was.

Too bad for Mendler he didn't hold the same fascination for Junior. "Shut up," the kid said tensely. And for once Mendler didn't look at all in control as he subsided in his seat behind a shrug to the old man.

"So what's the big show, Russell? You already missed one down at the square. This one going to be better?" If I had wanted everyone's disapproval, even Leo's, I got it. "Hate to break it to you, but whatever you have in mind, it'll be just another junior effort by Junior Dvorak."

"Paul, I don't think . . ."

Only Junior thought I was funny, in his own fidgety way anyway. And he could afford to. What he turned out to be holding was a detonator. An entire family of ferrets leaped into my chest to pass along the information when he brought his hand out from behind his jacket. And even as I was telling myself to stay trained on Junior, Karen gave me a wide-eyed signal to take a better look back in the direction of the walkway from which Claudio Mori had once supervised his workers. I didn't think so. What was I going to see? A plastique clump?? I had seen those wasps' nests before. The sight of another one wasn't going to do anything for my sense of wellbeing. "Think she says," I meandered forward. "Good advice for you, too. Know what you've gathered together here? The *by-products.*"

He might not have been Leo, but he wasn't the fastest tank on the battlefield, either. "The what?"

"By-products. Or like Leo's employers say, collateral elements." Leo frowned like somebody who had never heard that phrase from the leggy one who paid him. "We're not important. Get it?"

"I don't know what you're talking about."

"Sure you do. You're pissed Dad is the most beloved citizen in town, right? Jesus, now *nobody's* ever going to understand what you've had to put up with all these years! They all think he's a goddamn hero!" He gave one of those involuntary shakes of the head that said he was willing to hear more—or just that he didn't have muscle control. "Suppose I told you he didn't win it, that it was a fix?"

Mendler let out a sigh; like back at the villa, he didn't like his heroes run down. But Dvorak looked at his son willing to concede anything if the kid would stand down. "They'd fix it for *him*?" Junior said, contempt mixed with disbelief, avoiding the old man's begging gaze. "Why would they do that?"

"So you'd go on this little rampage of yours. You're a rat in a maze, Russell. We all are. Tell him, Leo."

The eunuch had picked up enough from Shepherd—not everything, but enough—to drop his eyes down to the ham hands entwined across his gut. There was even a little reddening behind his piggy ears. Junior didn't miss it. "What's Finley saying?"

Words weren't Leo's strong point. On the other hand, something about springing out of his chair and going for the detonator felt like it was stirring from his pea brain to the bristles of his shave cut, and that wasn't promising. "Don't ask him. He's a patriot. He doesn't ask too many questions when the answers might be complicated. Right, Leo?"

Leo's black eyes were as friendly as drills, but at least he lost his concentration on Junior for a second. "Know who you are, Russell? You're entertainment. All those hot pus feelings you have inside you for your old man and god knows who else, their only value is so somebody can watch you acting out like you have been the last couple of days. You were better off doing the Lord's work for the New Florence Society. At least then you could say you were being your own asshole."

It was good to remember I had the only gun in the place. If we had been in one of those states where they still executed people by firing squad, the platoon around me would have already been re-shouldering its weapons and wondering who had shot the blank. Mendler, in particular, looked like the condition of my heart was irrelevant to getting me on his operating table. "I really think you should be quiet," he said in his version of calm.

"Why? You seem to know Junior here. Before the church fire did he ever see anything through to the end?"

The Reverend didn't give him a chance to answer. "Most of us would be better off if we gave second thoughts to our actions, Mr. Finley."

"And I'm sure you've had a lifetime of second thoughts, Russ. But right now your spawn is planning bad things and you better start exercising some of that parental authority."

Junior had an unpleasant laugh—first because it was mostly cackle, second because the cackle sounded specially recruited for the demented occasion. The old man didn't like it, either. "You have to think of the other end, Russell," he said. "What awaits you? We should only incur the penance we are capable of performing. How many times have I told you that?"

Whatever number Junior gave him was probably a fraction of the truth. But their chatter about the sins to come and the penances to follow was enough of a diversion for inching my stool around for a look at the walkway. I managed it smoothly enough to see the clay clumps I hadn't wanted to see hanging down from both ends of the bridge. I also did it so clumsily I almost squeezed

Mendler into his computer. He reacted by stiffening like a priss in a steam room wondering why all the blubbery guys were gravitating toward him. He made such an indignant production out of wheeling himself away from me that we had both Dvoraks looking back at us.

"You could've just asked and I would've told you," Junior said through another involuntary ripple of his jaw. "I intend blowing this place up. It didn't have to be this place, but it's as good as any other."

"Bullshit. You don't like Pulsar's results. It *has* to be here."

"You're wrong."

"Okay, I'm wrong."

He felt sorry for me. "How can you not take me seriously?"

Since Karen wasn't going to jump in and tell him how that was a basic character flaw, I had to answer again—and before I felt my .38 getting any looser around my spine and deciding to fall on the floor. "Special talent. But let's keep our eye on the ball, Russell. What's the grand theme of your little show here? *This Is Your Life?* Your father I understand. Even Karen because god knows if you can't get approval from Daddy for your dates, it's better to blow up the world. But why Mendler? What's he done to you?"

I was the last one the doctor wanted speaking for him, but his steel eyes softened just the slightest in appeal before the hope of getting out unharmed. Then he got over the hope just as fast: He knew how he had earned the cold swagger Junior turned on him. "Tell him, Uncle John."

So there went that mystery, and I resented Junior for blabbing it away so flippantly. As Zev had said, small towns were lots of things, but mostly they were small towns.

"Tell him how Mother couldn't count on her brother, the great surgeon! But you learned humility in exchange. You accepted Jesus. As long as you have that waiting, you can screw up anything at all in this life."

"That isn't for you to judge," the old man said sternly. "John did what he could for your mother. It wasn't meant to be."

"And you forgive him."

"There was nothing to forgive . . ."

It would have made for a nice story line in *One Life to Live*, and I would have been there on my couch with a bowl of Cheerios watching it every afternoon. Except that Leo saw what I saw. The Reverend was working himself into such an orange fit that the cowed kid forgot about his finger over the button. He wasn't any faster taking in the fury leaping up from his chair and scoring a bulls-eye hit with one of his ham hands around Junior's throat. How could I have ever doubted who had killed Alan Lockman?

And why did I make the choice I did? I was drawn more to loons with bad skin than to pulp-brained hit men? The best part of the question was the flash of drunken confidence I would be around to ponder it in the ages to come. With one last doubt that I had remembered to load the damn thing, I caught my .38 as it was about to take the fall it had been threatening, made sure it was pointing in the right direction, and fired at the biggest chunk of Leo thigh I saw. The shot reverberated around the hangar as if Claudio Mochi had come back to restart his machines. The Reverend and Karen reached for their ears. Mendler just looked stunned as Leo let go of Junior and reached back for his leg before yowling and falling. The red ink blot was smaller than it might have been.

My second-guessing wasn't. Junior recovered his balance to position his finger over his button again. He could hardly breathe, but he had his priorities straight. Which was more than could have been said for me. Why did I always seem to do the things I did? My last thought on earth was going to be of Leo getting to the kid's voice box to stop him from being able to cackle again? Definitely a positive development, but, when I gave it more thought, not all that much of a souvenir for my years on the planet.

Because it had occurred to me, of course, it didn't happen. Instead, Junior had his finger and I had my weapon and we stood gaping at one another like we were waiting for Hurricane Brenda to come along and sweep us both into the nearest ocean. I didn't know why I was breathing as heavily as he was: I hadn't had Leo's hand around my throat. "Whoever breaks eye contact first to kick Leo and tell him to stop his wailing is the loser," I said, panting too much to be witty.

"You don't want to shoot me, Mr. Finley."

The *Mr.* was a lot more respectful than when Shepherd had pulled it out in Brighton's office, but that didn't seem like the issue. "And you don't want to kill Karen, your father, or your uncle."

He smiled—a smart, twisty kind of smile. "And you?"

"You saved my life yesterday."

"And maybe you just saved mine. So we're even."

When you were dealing with a corkscrew head, you had corkscrew conversations. "Those flames might have gotten me, they might not have. I'm still ahead on points."

He thought about it too seriously, then shrugged too reasonably. "So leave. You can tell everybody what happened."

"Nothing's going to happen. We're all walking out of here and dragging Leo with us before he goes into shock. Ask your uncle."

Mendler was a little slower on that cue, but as soon as he saw no real objection from Junior, he braved getting up and going over for a closer look at the spreading blood stain on the back of Leo's pants. "You didn't hit an artery," he pronounced as if actually examining the leg through Leo's groveling. "But he's not going to get any better laying here."

"For god sake, Russell," the old man said, "have you lost all sense of decency? That isn't the way you were brought up."

There were probably worse topics to wave in front of him, but I couldn't think of any. My eyes were so locked into the finger above the detonator button they were about to blur.

"You know that's true, Russell," Karen broke her silence.

I almost jumped from her voice. Both Dvoraks were annoyed to be reminded she was there. I made it unanimous as my lungs resettled on the grill in my chest. I needed him thinking he had been reared by wolves, I didn't need her reminding him his father was Rumpelstiltskin.

But she insisted. "You didn't want to hurt anybody when you burned down the church. Those policemen never entered your mind. But you can't blame your father for it. That was your fault. And this now is even worse."

I saw her bearding Antonacci over his favorite salmon with her nasty charts and graphs. Once again, candor wasn't its own reward. "What Karen is saying, Russell, is that you haven't done anything here yet."

"I told you to go."

"But you know I can't do that. I leave, and then what? I won't even have your father for an alibi when I have to drink myself to sleep to forget about what I walked away from."

There was a line, there always was. Asking him to think was one thing. But too many thoughts could have overwhelmed him and triggered the easiest solution of all—literally.

"Your rage is only with me," the old man said. "Let your uncle and these other people leave. Please, son."

If we had still been doing *One Life to Live*, he would have disarmed the detonator then and there and collapsed in tears in Rumpelstiltskin's arms. But the gleam in his eyes lasted only a second before the lights went out again. "It's too late for that."

If I had been a city sidewalk, my steam vents would have gone off up and down the block. Who could argue with him? Arlett was still dead and the other cop might still be joining him. Even years out of Nassau County, I still had to think of Junior Dvorak as a cop-killer, and that meant the accidental, the unintentional, and the gee-I-wish-I-hadn't-done-that were garbage. I didn't know if it was because some baptisms never wore off or because they did but it still felt noble to pretend they didn't, but I couldn't be allowed to think of Arlett as just another stiff. COP KILLED IN THE LINE OF DUTY was the headline and beyond that we were both wasting everybody else's time. "You're right. It *is* too late."

None of them understood, not even Karen, when I put my weapon back in my belt. But what was the point of waving it around if I had no intention of using it? "It's simple, Junior—rot is invulnerable. You're an endless excuse and there's no talking that down. You'll never be happy until you blow up whoever doubts you're Superman in bed and Picasso working on your prints. You're the best in everything that ever lived. Okay? I just said it in front of all these people. Now press your button and we'll go off to the Happy Hunting Ground to see if your old man at least got that part of it right."

He didn't know if I was bluffing, and there was divided opinion among my ferrets, too. Some of them seemed to think I was just really tired of all the bullshit streets that led to horseshit avenues. "That isn't what this is about! You don't know . . .!"

"What is it I don't know, Junior? Enlighten me. Right now, I can't get past you and your family and your New Florence Society—such neon assholes you've become perfect marks for Leo's employers. Fuck you and all the losers you wallow in. All you're good for is increasing the body count. Fuck you, fuck you, fuck you. Coming, Karen?"

She started as if she had been expecting somebody else to turn back and extend a hand to her. That didn't do much for my vanity, but what the hell? Soldiering on meant soldiering on. "No, don't look at him. He's going to do what he's going to do. You don't need his permission."

Give her the survival instinct that she didn't hesitate with another glance at the Reverend or Mendler. She probably would have done without my hand, too, if she hadn't welcomed a little help over whining Leo. Her hand was cold. I realized only then that she didn't have a jacket, that Junior had hustled her from the house without caring what she had on her back.

"Anybody else coming?"

"The doctor is going with you," the Reverend said. "Go, John."

Mendler had his half-moment. "I can't . . ."

"It'll be all right. Go."

Mendler stood up—not too confidently, but up. The kid was still making up his mind about it all when the stock car racing started outside. The first car in from the road rattled whatever piece of gate got in its way. The tires behind it scattered every piece of gravel on the approach lane. Brighton? The Army? Whoever it was clipped the wings off my high and had me feeling as nauseous as Junior looked. "Everybody on the ground!"

Karen chose the wrong moment to be tall: It felt like I had to yank her down with me by sections. But her head got out of the way in time to see Junior doing what he was told and getting under the first computer table. He was hanging on to his toy, but more protectively. It was his teddy bear, and he insisted on going to sleep with it.

CHAPTER 61

"Get them out of here, Finley!"

Why me caught in my throat. Suddenly it was quiet outside. I might have heard somebody closing a car door softly or I might have just imagined it. Who would have arrived like the Seventh Cavalry, then had second thoughts about slamming a door? The only sure sound was of a bird tweeting somewhere in the distance, probably in the marshes on the far side of the road. The blue bird of happiness?

"Dvorak!"

Count my blessings. Despite all my extortions and low opinions of him, Brighton had come riding to the rescue. Junior was holding his fire. Leo was still moaning in pain. The Prell still smelled nice in Karen's hair. Who could have asked for more in my situation?

Me. Who said it was a relief to hear Brighton's voice? And what was that bird across the road really tweeting about? The only blue bird I was familiar with was a jay, and according to the Professor it was a nasty bastard, not a happy one. In Brighton's place, wouldn't I have had a much easier life if I got rid of absolutely everybody holed up in the annex? Couldn't I have painted a bloodbath any way at all at the next town council meeting?

Which was the best answer to *why me*. He had to be afraid of my ghost haunting the rest of his days. "Brighton! It's Finley!"

There was no applause outside. The Dvoraks, father-and-son moles under their desks, were waiting for me to do more to drive away the snakes.

"Who's in there with you, Finley!"

Bobby Rosen would have called it a Need-to-Know moment. Who was the next best one after me for making him pause before giving in to ugly impulses? "John Mendler!" I decided. "The greatest heart surgeon in the state! Friend of mayors and governors!"

Mendler squinted at me from under his table as if remembering a sense of humor he had misplaced. Hard as he tried, he couldn't find it. In the meantime, there felt like there was some recalculating going on outside. "I'm coming out, Captain! I'll explain it all!"

As laugh lines went, it was one of my better ones. But I still needed an answer before I moved. "Hear me, Frank?"

I counted to three. Infinity was beckoning. "Come ahead!"

He didn't sound enthusiastic. One of my ferrets said I shouldn't have budged, but it was too late for minority views. I thought I was being clever enough by leaving Karen where she was. If I was going to be blasted walking out the door, why did she have to be? Veronica would never have been up to running the library on her own with that doofus who couldn't shelve books without mangling all the pages.

I was all the way to the secondary door before I realized what wasn't so clever. "Just laying it down, Junior," I said to his mole hole as I took out my weapon and placed it carefully on the ground. "They might get the wrong idea if I walk out with it."

He blinked but said nothing. Rumpelstiltskin and Mendler didn't even blink. Leo eyed the gun greedily—and the long crawling distance to it in frustration. I didn't look at Karen. I had enough of her adulation from the past few days to see me through.

There were three cars—Brighton's Impala and two patrol vehicles. I thought about the sergeant cursing his workload back at the station house; it was better than thinking about the barrels—two belonging to pump guns—aimed at me from behind the fenders. Brighton didn't have his weapon out; he looked commanderish. "You have four more hostages in here, Frank."

He waved me on with more of the reluctance I had heard in his voice. I figured I was alive when I reached the first patrol car and the giraffe from the cemetery, his ID tag saying EVANS, yanked me back with him and patted me down. He smelled like he had fallen into a tub of Mennen aftershave. I would have loved to have heard the instructions he had gotten from his boss. Check that: No, I wouldn't have.

Brighton wandered over as if he had already secured the prize he had really come for. "Who's in there with him?"

I didn't know how he had gotten so informed about Junior's doings, but why bother him with petty questions when I was still reassuring myself it was all positive that he was? I ran down the list of who and what was inside, saving the detonator for last. His gasps were few and far between; in fact, they were nonexistent. There was something off, and it wasn't just the Dvorak who had gotten his fingernails dirty with plastique. If I had been as cynical as the irritating bird across the road in the marshland, I might have said Brighton had already sent out condolence cards to the relatives of the hostages. "It's about his father," I said in case he had missed the dominant theme. "Junior will hold on to him, but I think you can get the others out."

"You do."

"I do."

"Then why take the others in the first place?"

"Leo was here. Mendler's his uncle and he's been with the Reverend all day. Karen . . ."

"Yeah, yeah, all right."

I might have almost accused him of discretion in front of his minions. Instead, I accused him of once again knowing too much about Karen's private life. "He's already half-agreed to release Karen and Mendler."

"What the hell is half-agreed?"

"We were walking out when you came charging in."

"And the Pulsar guy?"

I didn't miss the half-tone above his nonchalance. Had he broken down to listen to the tape of my little chat with Zev? "He's got a bullet in his leg. He'll have to be pulled out."

"You didn't mention Dvorak has a gun."

"Because he doesn't have one."

His afternoon got a little brighter. "Really, now. And how would a Pulsar employee, one of those evil people responsible for everything between Canada and Mexico, get a bullet in his leg?"

I didn't have to admit it was the Masked Avenger at work. Evans had heard what I had said about the plastique, had meditated on its implications for a few rounds of his wristwatch, and finally decided to suggest—very *sotto voce*—that it might be prudent to pull the cars back to a safer distance. Brighton was embarrassed for not having given the order first, but not all that much: Keeping himself and his men out of harm's way might have been only a minor oversight. As he watched Evans passing the word to the other uniforms, he might have been watching his eventual successor to eggshell walking on the New Florence police force.

With the uniforms backing the squad cars up to the road, he had little choice but to do the same with his own car. "How far gone is he?" he asked through his window as I walked alongside.

"He thought he knew what he wanted to do, now he's not so sure. That's going to make him harder to deal with."

He braked at the road with a snort. "Right. In the big city you like your psychos all business all the time."

"In his own mind he's not a psycho, he's a sinner. You don't talk sense and hope he catches on, you talk salvation and hope he still wants it."

"Really."

"Really."

It sounded good and must have looked good because, out from behind the wheel again, he pocketed another smart response to study the annex entrance from our more distant view. I didn't know anything about buildings as projectiles, and wished I hadn't seen all those newsreels about Atlantic City hotels being blasted to the ground. What I did know was that even backed up to the gate entrance, we weren't exactly standing in Philadelphia. If Karen hadn't still been inside, I might have run across to the marshland to join my blue bird of nastiness in a duet.

Then I had an attack of gooseflesh. Every safety on every gun around me joined in a group clack as Karen and Mendler stepped through the door. She was hugging herself against the weather, he was strutting his brilliance for having worn a sweater under his suit jacket. Instead of telling Evans to cut down the prick, I took it out on Brighton. "Skip the frisk, okay?"

"And suppose he has one of Dvorak's bombs attached to his back?"

"This isn't Baghdad!"

I was dismissed anyway. "Stop there, doctor, and take off your jacket! Then turn around very slowly!"

Mendler hadn't been so insulted since a patient had died on him, but he obeyed the order. The only lump under his sweater came from shoulders that were starting a serious curve downward. By the time he and Karen reached the cars, he had recorded the indignity for the Worst Personal Moments Chapter of his autobiography. "He wants you all gone in a minute," he said sternly. "If you stay, he won't be responsible for how many of you get hurt. He means it."

Karen nodded to confirm Mendler had heard right. She was starting to tremble, and it wasn't only because she didn't have a coat. Brighton tried to be graceful about getting out of the way as I put her in his car. She kept rubbing her arms even in the stuffy back seat. "He's crazed, Paul," she said as I was about to close the door. "He doesn't know what he's doing."

It was a ridiculous time to be jealous, so I was. And she hadn't noticed that character flaw while she had been locking lips with him? What did that say about what she had noticed about me?

I got back to Brighton before I had to answer her. He was getting a picture from Mendler on where the Dvoraks and Leo were inside the annex. "There's probably a back door he can't see from where he is," the doctor said. "You could get in that way."

"You want to pick the men to do it?" Brighton snapped. "Thanks for your help, Doctor. We'll take it from here."

Mendler looked at me in appeal, saw how useless that was, then turned back to the annex. I couldn't read what his sigh was about—the Reverend, Junior, or the reminder that his sister (a member of the respectable Mendler family!) had bred a bomber.

Having Karen out and putting her in the Impala hadn't done much for my jumpiness. The scene was shaping up as another of those situations she had described that first night in her kitchen—standing by and watching the ooze spread, knowing it had to be stopped but still doing nothing about it. My watch said Dvorak's minute and then some had elapsed. Evans had come to the same conclusion: He was watching Brighton anxiously for some action order. But the captain was keeping his own counsel, slipping from eerie to eerier. I was about to nod to Evans to get a little more pro-active, as they say, when both of us were distracted by a gleaming red Edge coming down the road from town. The driver's timing was impeccable: With a little luck he could pass the gate precisely when the annex went flying toward the road.

But he didn't pass, instead pulling up directly behind the squad cars squeezed into the gate. A uniform started over with a frantic wave to keep going, but then froze at Brighton's bark to back off. Lorenzo Mochi got out of the car. Brighton's expression said he had been expecting him.

"We've run out of that minute, Frank," I reminded him.

"Your watch is fast."

Lorenzo hurried over with what looked like a schematic for the annex. Whenever Brighton had called him had been hangover hour. He hadn't even had time to get into his Capote costume, settling for a brown leather jacket and corduroy pants. When Brighton pulled the plans out of his hands and spread them over the Impala's hood, he seemed ready to return to his Edge and get back to town. But Brighton was having none of it. "Finley and Dr. Mendler say there are two charges—about here and there. Worst case, what would that bring down?"

"How should I know? I'm no engineer!"

If Brighton bothered to look up from the schematic, he would have seen both Mendler and Evans sneaking looks at their watches, then Evans trying to be subtle about sidling over behind one of the squad cars and nodding for the doctor to follow. It must have been one of my invisible moments since he didn't give me the same heads-up. I went back to the trick that hadn't worked with the reception nurse the night Karen and I had brought the Professor to the hospital. "Not two minutes or three," I said loudly to Mendler. "He said one minute, right?"

Helpful as ever, Mendler was more concerned about joining Evans behind the squad car than playing with me. But then he relented to look again at his watch more openly and yelled over to Brighton. "Captain, you're running out of time here. You should protect yourself."

Brighton heard nothing, and his absorption with the annex plans was getting creepy. I hadn't seen so much manic concentration since Junior had been holding his finger over the detonator button. The perspiration gleaming off his sideburns wasn't especially reassuring, either. In fact, from the moment he had led his motor charge toward the annex and then abruptly gone into blockade formation, nothing at all Brighton had done had been reassuring. If it had been more than my ferrets saying it, I might have had to think he was as bent on a dead end as Junior Dvorak was.

I stopped wasting time. Who the hell else was I going to listen to if not my ferrets? They were the only ones who had come up from the city with me. I was past Brighton and Mochi and back into the car with Karen before I had to listen to any arguments. Even when I turned the key, Brighton looked more concerned about getting the schematic off the hood than having his car taken out from under him.

Karen grabbed the back of my seat. "What's the matter?"

The only answer to that was everything, most of which she should have figured out on her own. The rest was just getting down the road. As principles went, it wasn't a particularly difficult one, and credit to Evans for grasping it and waving to the other uniforms to follow me out of the gate. He even found the time to pull Mendler into his squad car with him.

Which left Brighton and Mochi staring after us.

Until there was a shot inside the annex and they both turned to it. Evans and the other cops weren't in such a hurry to get away, either.

There might not have been a countdown over the next few seconds, but I could have sworn somebody went into one.

CHAPTER 62

The annex didn't make it out to the gate. Its foundations remained rock solid under the chunky metallic geysers that erupted from the windows, then under a fiery plume of shrapnel on the roof. But if the building stood firm, everything in it seemed up for grabs in the dirty, violent burst of steel and glass. I'd never been in an earthquake so I didn't know how the shaking of the car and the loud sucking of the air around it compared to the real thing, but who needed a Pepsi taste test? It took enough to get down under the dashboard as far as I could and to yell for Karen to do the same in the back. She said something I couldn't make out. Was she thanking me for talking her out of keeping her suit on? If she had still been wearing it, she would have been ruining it on the car floor, right?

I had to come to terms with that obsession.

My nose in crusted glop that might have once been chocolate ice cream or something else a shoe could pick up, I tried not to think of how many metal groans and crashes the annex had in it. Was it a consolation Junior hadn't staged his show in the main building, twice as big as the annex? No, it wasn't. I also had an unworthy pang of a thought. I had been brought up with the usual morals, sat through the standard classroom lectures and church sermons about what was high behavior and low behavior. What else should I have instantly given thought to but the ferocious human cost of the tornado outside—how Junior and his hostages inside the annex were goners, how Brighton and some of his cops outside it might have joined them? At the very least, I should have been feeling bad I hadn't moved Brighton's car further down the road. But what suddenly activated every lobe in my brain was where *my* car was. Who had ever missed a second-hand Subaru? Susan had once discovered an ant hill in our backyard I had felt closer to. But that dingy gas guzzler had also been on more surveillance runs for Finley Investigations than anything or anyone except President Finley himself, and now it was nosed up against a building that had undoubtedly smashed it into junk with the first blast. Sometimes there really was very little reward in getting out from under a dashboard and taking in reality. However small you felt, you knew it was just a prelude to feeling punier.

The inevitable couldn't be postponed forever. The shaking stopped, then, after a few sputters from things I couldn't identify, so did the noise. The stench of smoke was like some great soldering of the air, but if that was toxic, so was every tail job I'd had in Red Hook. Even a half-second before sticking up my head, I didn't know I was about to have another Christmas morning—like the one when I had run into the living room and been dazzled to see the set of plastic cowboys and Indians I had wanted to sit under the tree. But surprise, surprise: Not only my Subaru, but the green Olds and Junior's panel truck were where they had been, glass and other debris over them but otherwise looking as much like working road blights as they had before the explosions had started.

"You okay?"

Karen was playing Hide-and-Seek in the space between the front seats. Her question said she was okay, too. That made two of us. The blast had come out of the annex with ridiculous discipline, right through the main door, leaving it and Hal's sentry post in shambles and following a straight line down to the squad cars at the gate. The more forward car had escaped with only a shattered windshield, but the one off its shoulder had been spun to the right, leaving the two uniforms who had been crouched behind it on the ground. They were both still moving—not much, but still moving—and from where I was I would have said they were just stunned. There seemed to be a reasonable number of heads coming up from behind the lead patrol car, too; certainly Evans and Mendler. They noticed the gore between me and them before I did.

Brighton was on the ground leaning over Mochi. He struggled to turn over the heir because he had only one arm for doing it, the other apparently having been swatted hard by an anvil-looking thing sitting a few feet away. I got out of the car and over to them a few feet behind Evans and Mendler. My calves took a few seconds to agree that was where I should be going. What had looked like an anvil was a metal seat from the guard booth where Hal had been stationed. Either it had caromed off Brighton's shoulder directly into Mochi's forehead or had taken the opposite route; either way, it had gotten one-and-a-half for the price of one. Mochi wasn't just unconscious under the ugly circular gash on his forehead, I had to keep my eyes glued to his leather jacket to see even minimal breathing. Nothing about his pasty face said it would ever reach the wine color of the gash again.

The mess was clear enough for Mendler not to wait for nudging to act like a doctor. As tactfully as he could, he moved Brighton's hand off Mochi and worked Lorenzo's eyes. Evans had apparently been at his share of accident scenes; he turned promptly away to radio for ambulances, sounding terse and professional. The two uniforms still on their feet were more interested in the other two on the ground. Brighton started to growl at them, but didn't have the strength. I knew what I would said in his place ("Leave them until you see what else is likely to explode on us in that factory, assholes!"), so I headed for the annex. Evans caught up to me several yards along. I didn't know why he needed his weapon drawn, but it didn't seem like the time to object to much of anything.

The soldering odor was pure concentrate on the other side of the entrance holes. Not much was recognizable in the Pulsar work area: It had been reduced to a crater with odd shards of monitor and keyboard things here and there. The near walkway had bucked all the way up to shear the ceiling and was hanging down like a ladder without rungs. One section of wall had been stripped to its beams and the blackened area around it looked like what was left from a colossal grease fire. But at first anyway, I didn't see much else. The tarp covering the machinery was ripped in some places and covered by metal fragments, but whatever was under it hadn't taken on any new outlines. The offices off the far walkway in the back seemed untouched. As disasters went, this one had fallen a little shy of the catastrophic.

If I didn't want to count the three people I had seen last time inside.

Evans hadn't worked *that* many accidents. He turned as white as Mochi when he spotted something on the floor off to the right of the widest crack in the floor. I warned my Eggs Benedict to behave as I went over for a look. A head had been smashed into gourd shape by the iron beam that had speared it. It was an orange gourd. I didn't live in New Florence so hadn't had to put up with his bullshit marches against the sun rising in the morning, but I felt a small lurch in my chest for the end of Rumpelstiltskin. His biggest mistake had been turning the fairy tale upside-down—believing others couldn't wait to climb up to the tower on *his* hair.

Clothing, body parts, charred lumps that had to be one or the other—I finally opened my eyes to them. They had been there from the second I had stepped inside, I just hadn't been in a hurry to see them. Compared to Evans, I was still an upperclassman in that school. There were enough pieces around to keep Forensics busy for weeks trying to put the Reverend, Junior, and Leo back together. I was pretty sure of the handle of my .38 next to a computer table. It didn't excite the sense of loss my Subaru had. Considering that its last act had been letting somebody else fire it, it deserved what it had gotten. And who *had* fired that shot before the explosion? Had Leo managed to crawl over to the gun during another father-son quality dialogue? Had the Reverend updated the story of Abraham sacrificing his son? If I was interested in that kind of detail, of course, I could always call from the city after Forensics had finished its reconstruction. I didn't think I would be that interested.

I went back outside for a breather. Evans didn't follow; he was too busy apologizing for almost losing it at the sight of the Reverend's head and atoning for it by showing he could still be a cop's cop. The road was filling up with rubberneckers. The mob figured to get thicker before it got thinner with all the uniforms either checking to see if their own bones were still in order or trying not to look helpless about Mochi and Brighton. Mendler had become so pessimistic about Mochi that he was paying more attention to Brighton's shoulder. All that was good for was a yelp of pain and another look of gloom from Mendler. When Brighton had enough of that diagnosis, he lifted himself to his feet and all but stumbled over to his car past Karen. He ignored whatever she said to him, opened the back door, and plopped down on the rear seat. He seemed barely aware that she followed over after him and got the cigarettes from his jacket pocket he might have spent the rest of the afternoon reaching for. At least she earned a nod of thanks for lighting the cigarette before she wandered away from him again.

Not that I was doing anything useful anyway, but the approaching siren of the first ambulance was all the excuse I needed for going over to join Brighton from the front seat. He didn't want the company and didn't think the door opened between us was enough of a separation, but I didn't want the questions teeming in my head, either.

"Renata Tromboli," he said almost in a spit.

"Who's that?"

"The woman across the street. She saw Dvorak's truck and him forcing Karen to go with him. She called me."

He meant the house with the Corolla, and I knew that wasn't all he meant. "You. Not police headquarters, but you personally."

"What else do you want, Finley?"

What else did *I* want? "She saw something the night Lockman was killed, too! You've been sitting on her all this time!"

"You forgot to show me your FBI badge."

"Fuck you, Frank. She saw Leo that night, didn't she?"

At least his shrug sent something excruciating all the way up to his neck. "Lots of people fit Leo's description. You yourself told me it might have been that other slug in the gate booth."

I was fuming—feeling like the Jerk of the Month, but mainly fuming. "And how much longer were you planning to sit on Renata Tromboli? Give me a ballpark figure. Years? Decades?"

He registered the arrival of the ambulance and the aides jumping out and seeing Mendler's commanding finger to start with Mochi. "I was putting it together, hotshot. I'm sure you remember that from the old days."

I almost blubbered that I hadn't had a Lama or a Labine to deal with. Too bad that wasn't true. It would have made my indignation so much purer. On the other hand, I *hadn't* spent every day pussyfooting around. "When did you plan on laying all this out for your betters, Frank? You know—Plus and Minus, Renata Tromboli, that little tape in your desk. Help me clear my calendar when you'll need me up here for testimony."

He risked shaking his head as he took another drag. "They must've declared a day of mourning when they got rid of you on Long Island."

"Look at that slaughterhouse in there, Frank! You've won! No more Leo, no more tricky conversations with Lama! It all gets buried with Leo and Pulsar goes on to the next town with Frank Brighton's conscience clear!"

He took another drag—one he really didn't want so fast. Another siren was approaching from town. The ambulance guys had their gurney up and were trying to be diplomatic about discouraging Mendler from helping them get Mochi on it. Lorenzo didn't look any more animated than he had before the oxygen bag had been clapped over his mouth. I knew how he felt.

"I'm taking Karen home. You can have all the statements you want in a few hours, but we've both had enough for now. You know where we are."

In his place I would have gotten my lasso and tied me to his car. But I had never been in his place, even when I had been dealing with the Nassau County versions of Lama and Labine. When I looked back at him, he smiled as if he had almost won a bet with himself, but not quite. "Yeah?"

"What else?" I realized. "The charge out here. The manual about deploying your forces for a bomber you threw away. You didn't really give a shit what happened, did you?"

"Five o'clock," he said, looking at his watch.

"You didn't trust yourself to have the guts ever to bring in Renata Tromboli, let alone use that tape. Your own men, Frank! They would've bought it with you! More Arletts. But of course, you wouldn't have had to make promises to their widows. That would've been somebody else's job."

"I don't know what you're talking about."

And in a way, he didn't. Having reached the far shore of survival, he had nothing in common with the kamikaze who had charged off the phone from Renata Tromboli willing to sink in the rot he was swimming in. That was already in the past, at worst making for another area of extortion (Evans? One of the other uniforms?) in a life of them. Some people were in bad places, Captain Frank Brighton was in New Florence, New York.

CHAPTER 63

Veronica insisted on coming by to drive us down to police headquarters to make our statements. I was glad she did. A couple of hours in the house making conversation with Karen because we thought we should have had something meaningful to say about what had happened had frayed both of us. Alone or just with Karen on the way downtown, I wouldn't have had the energy or tackiness to laugh at the sight of Sewell's elves hurrying to tear down the *Reporter*'s Community Day posters covering every lamppost and empty wall space. But for Veronica the scene was just another of the debacles that gave her a brittle reason for waking up in the morning, and I could have had my own HBO comedy special pandering to her tastelessness. The dead wouldn't have minded anyway, right?

Going on the record was even more of an empty ritual than I had expected. Brighton was being treated at the hospital for what had been diagnosed as a broken shoulder and the beady-eyed detective named Service who had been given the questions to ask had done only as much homework as would get all of us out of a rear first-floor interrogation room in a half-hour. That I could tell, not even one of his questions came out of a knowingly conspiratorial place. His menial assignment was to pad the files and ours was to supply the words for the padding. The only time Renata Tromboli's name came up was when Karen confirmed the woman was a neighbor across the street, and Leo came in for a mention only when I mentioned seeing him in Sewell's office and at the annex during my curiosity visit. (I didn't complicate everyone's life by admitting I'd also heard him prowling around during my break-in at the annex with Karen and Brighton.)

We were back out in the street so fast Veronica still had more than 20 minutes to go on the hour we had calculated as reasonable for picking us up again. With the only coffee shop in sight closed for a Sunday, we had little choice but to hang around the headquarters entrance until our ride returned.

"Going back tonight?"

"I think so."

She nodded, trying to look interested in the kid who came out of the precinct between his father and a lawyer. The father was being testy: He didn't like orange throwers in his family and seemed to like having to hire a lawyer to bail out his son even less. Karen followed them to a newer model of my Subaru parked down the street. "Jimmy Sewell won't have a problem with his front page tomorrow," she said.

I figured just the opposite. Between Labine and the other interested parties perched on his shoulders, I thought Father Sewell was going to have the biggest problem he'd had in years. But I didn't want to talk about the Community Day or Mochi annex festivals anymore. We hadn't talked about anything else in hours. When in doubt, reach out for an old reliable. "You should come down to the city sometime. See how the other half lives."

She nodded. "I was thinking of it."

"Catch the shows."

She smiled. "And the museums—don't forget them."

"You could help, you know."

"In what?"

"Giving me a hearty sendoff. Not letting me feel like I'm slinking out of town because you caught me being dishonest to you in some way."

"You asked me that already."

"I don't get a second whine?"

The empty street didn't rescue her by suddenly producing Veronica's Taurus. Then something funny occurred to her. "Accent on the *catching you* part? That what you mean?"

I hated people who said *touché*. Most had never seen a fencing match in their lives. Besides, I didn't feel like I was wearing one of those thick cushion vests; the jab *hurt*. "So some things should just be left alone."

There was no mistaking she was looking at me. I could see every glistening speck around her irises. "I think so, Paul."

If I had been as much of a conspiracy freak as Alan Lockman, I might have thought Veronica had been waiting for that answer as a signal to appear up the street. And it also seemed unnecessary for Karen to step off the sidewalk and wave down to the car. What was her goddamn hurry?

CHAPTER 64

I made it back to the city in the same time I'd made it with the Professor; it just felt twice as long. My goodbye to New Florence came a block away from Karen's when I turned on the local station in time to hear the announcement that the Reverend Dvorak's customary Sunday night prayer broadcast had been cancelled "due to a tragedy that has taken both our pastor and his son to their Maker." The grim announcer offered no more particulars, saying only that "the reasons for our mourning will become sadly clear in the hours ahead." As information went, it ranked right up there with the station break kind of "Wild Animals in the Streets—Details at Eleven," but for all I knew, the announcer hadn't even been told how Rumpelstiltskin and Junior had been transported for the meeting with their Maker. In the same spirit of believing whatever I was told, I kept the station's memorial gospel music on until the signal disappeared two towns away.

My epiphanies were few and far between on the ride. Of all the pieces of incomplete business I was leaving behind, the one that gnawed most was Barbara Lockman. I had sidestepped Karen's advice not to ring the woman's doorbell before setting out, but she hadn't been home anyway. What would I have said to her? Rip across the street to your neighbor Renata Tromboli and get the real story about what killed your son? Yes, that would have been a start. But I had felt such a reprieve from not finding her home I had been eager to accept Karen's reassurance that she would take care of it. Karen Noon wasn't Frank Brighton or Jimmy Sewell.

And she could hardly seal Leo into the back of her mind with the two women living so close.

Still, what did *take care of it* mean? Dusty attics existed because people had taken care of things. I felt better for having jotted down the address of the Lockman house.

The most interesting phone machine messages awaiting me in Brooklyn were two hang-ups twelve hours apart at nine in the morning and nine in the evening. It was easy picturing the Professor checking on his suspicion I had gone back to New Florence. That was something else that had to be taken care of, and sooner than later. In case I had forgotten, the old man also happened to be recovering from a heart operation. I called him as soon as I woke up Monday morning.

"How do you expect me to feel when they open me up and stick things inside? They're not my things, Finley. You want them, they're yours."

"Tell me what you need from the store. I'll stop off on the way."

"Think I haven't eaten since you called last?"

Five minutes of wrangling for strawberry yogurt and a container of milk didn't seem bad. And he'd been right about not waiting for my delivery services. When I picked up the yogurt and milk at the grocery store around the corner from his place, Bernie the owner showered me with all the details of Mendler's stents—sort of. "The Professor says they do a much better job upstate than around here. Says he had the best specialist on the East Coast workin' on him. Famous guy."

I hadn't been wrong about what I had shouted out to Brighton about Mendler: Even Bernie, proprietor of the B&B Food Store in Garden City, was ready to attest to the doctor's importance.

The old man was standing on his postage stamp patch of grass the real estate hustlers called a lawn. He had more color than when I had dropped him off from New Florence and was holding some kind of trowel thing and contemplating his favorite bush of hideous gigantic blue daisies. I couldn't remember the botanical name for the damn things, and didn't want to. For me they were triffids, ready to break free of their bush one night to stalk into the house to swallow him up. "They talking to you yet?"

"When they have something to say. You have something to say?"

So much for any dance plans. "New Florence has survived another epidemic. In about the same shape it did the first one."

He kept his eyes on his mutant daisies; as long as he didn't order them to sick me, I was safe. "That's nice. You build them a factory?"

"Nothing's that neat."

"Amen. You don't put that stuff in the refrigerator, it's no good to me."

I was glad to get away from the Fortitude for Putting Up with A Sneak I was supposed to appreciate. There was a hint of liniment in the air inside, but nothing to say he had been stumbling around in dire straits. The cherry and lime Jellos in the refrigerator might have been the ones I had gotten the day I had brought him home—I couldn't tell. I reminded myself nobody was as helpless or as crotchety or as anything else it was sometimes convenient to think. That was one of the drawbacks of having second people in the world breathing and thinking for themselves.

"I saw a couple of things on the Internet," he said, tramping in with the trowel he hadn't dirtied in the least. "Big explosion or something?"

I told him about Leo and the Dvoraks, and might as well have been giving him a casualty report from the Boer War. I had forgotten he hadn't met any of them. When I mentioned the bad shape I had left Lorenzo in, though, he dropped down at the kitchen table with a heavy shake of the head. "The highways and byways," he grunted. "Why I always hated genealogy."

"Meaning?"

"Genealogy. Tracing families."

"I know what the word means, Joe. What's it got to do with Mochi?"

"Same thing it has to do with anybody—nothing. All these people looking for their roots and that crap. They think they're going to find some order in their lives, but all they end up with is a generation-by-generation record of disorder. Uncle Silas got run over by his plow the day after Lee surrendered to the Union!

Great-grandmother Hester died of smallpox the same day as the *Maine* went down! Isn't that too bad! They come up with all that trivia and so what? Their family line tells them they're genetically susceptible to plows and smallpox? That's not history, Finley, that's the same thing as settling for the date they signed the Magna Carta."

"Whatever you say. I think."

"I'm talking about Meucci!"

"Oh. The telephone guy. The brother-in-law."

"Good. And look at the mess. The great-grandson gets a chair in his skull outside his factory. Meucci didn't see any of *that* coming, did he? No rhyme or reason to any of it. Man spends his whole life trying to be rational about improving communication between people, but he's helpless where his own future in-laws end up. No control over those highways and byways."

Maybe if I hadn't collected so many fuzzballs around my brain from my long Sunday in New Florence and the drive home I would have gotten faster to what he was really talking about. "Let me take a shot. The theme here is control."

It seemed awfully early in the morning for him to be dipping into the dish of sourballs on the table, but what did I know? I wasn't his dietician. "What else? Sometimes I have it, sometimes I don't. That look on your puss says you want to hear first about not having it. With Karen."

I told myself not to have any look. "Why not?"

"Why not, he says. Been burning your ass for days, but you never came right out and asked."

It was another *touché*, and I hated it as much standing in his kitchen as I had standing with Karen outside the police building. "Okay."

He nodded—maybe for having scored with me or maybe for having chosen a sourball flavor he liked. "Look at me, Finley. You see somebody old enough to have narrowed his life down to his isolated needs and pleasures, everything and everybody else extra. But back a few years when Karen Noon was still my nubile student, I had a lot more fantasies that 20-year-olds with adorable faces and endless legs could still be part of my social world.

Every time her hand touched my wrist or I sent her through a door ahead of me, we were a couple. I had more than sex with her, I had *her*. Who cared how her friends might have been looking at her oddly for hanging around with me? She never acted embarrassed with me, never sent any message except how much she liked being with me, how she even needed me."

I could still do without the picture of a naked Joe Carroll crawling over her with his droopy balls. "But then Antonacci came along."

He laughed snidely. "Moving right along. Yeah, Antonacci came along and I was furious. It was my own fault, of course. And later, thinking of it as my own fault became a consolation. If I hadn't thrown the two of them together, I told myself, she wouldn't have found anybody else, she'd still be coming to me for everything she needed. She really didn't have anything to do with anything, and god knows he didn't. The only one who was an autonomous agent was yours truly. Control, Finley. It has many temptations, many lies. It doesn't just let you say, 'Oops, screwed that one up. Time to get on to something else.' No, no. You must exploit all its variations. You should make the field as wide as you can so that whatever happens, you can say it was part of the program. People get hurt? Feelings get bruised? Just data. That's why control and possessiveness are the narcotic they are."

"And are still?"

He blinked twice before he was sure he had heard the question right. "Karen? The short answer is no. Sure, when I saw her the first time behind that library desk, some of those old vibrations came back. But *all* of them came back. The hunger, but the self-delusion, too. Maybe they're what keeled me over in the library. A warning to act my age. So I acted my age and almost died for her."

I was supposed to say anything at all to match what he was trying to be candid about. And he knew I couldn't. "Hungry? That Jello in there is starting to grow those hard edges I hate. You don't eat it, I'm throwing it out."

I went back to the refrigerator before I gave the bastard the smile he was waiting for.

"Okay," he sighed. "So much for Karen. You won't have to almost die for her. You'll have your list of good deeds and bad deeds and you'll work out which is more important. And maybe someday she'll come down to the city and you can take her to BAM."

"Fuck you."

"That's an intelligent response. What you should be asking is where do I still have control. Ask."

He was right about the dark edges of the cherry Jello. "Where do you still have control, Joe?"

He couldn't help straightening up proudly. "My network of academic fogies," he announced. "There isn't a competent one anywhere on the East Coast, in Michigan, Louisiana, or California who isn't right now making inquiries about the activities of the Pulsar Institute. Some of them already know the answers, but I pretend not to notice they're pretending and they still have to deliver their papers at the end of the term."

I remembered how he had flabbergasted me in front of the Meucci statue; this time, though, the lettering was more readable.

"Well, what did you expect me to do while you were up there playing her knight in shining armor?"

"Pulsar's bigger than I thought, Joe."

"So am I."

"Okay. So are you. But they're already financed for another dozen New Florences. How's a few calls from universities going to change that?"

"*That*? No, they won't change *that*."

"So where's the control?"

He seemed to consider picking up the trowel from the table and shifting *my* dirt. Instead, he settled for another sourball. "My colleagues won't be inquiring about *that*. They'll be inquiring about your Zevs and Shepherds and about the General So-and-So who collects all their so-called research and walks into Pentagon meetings with their numbers and his self-importance."

"And . . ."

He nodded. "And even if we kick up enough of a stink to get all this Plus and Minus stuff investigated, there'll be new Zevs and new Shepherds and new generals organizing some new Pulsar. I know all that, Finley. There's just too much of that precious data out there to leave it uncollected by somebody for somebody else's gain. I'll bet your Shepherd friend has even incorporated all your suspicions about her into her New Florence escapade. My god, man, if she's half as good as she's supposed to be, she probably even tracked you through the explosion at the annex! That's what parasites do—one continuous feed. But one life to live, okay? Me, I've got nothing better to do than run these people into Hell before I get there. There are plagues and plagues. I didn't get to say very much about the old one, and that just kind of compounds my debt to Karen. So I owe her and those people in New Florence some enlightenment about this new plague."

"If you do say so yourself."

He scrunched his face into a grimace. "How can you eat that stuff with all those hard edges?"

The answer, of course, was that once you melted the hard edges, they were even tastier than the soft parts. You just had to work at the melting.

www.ingramcontent.com/pod-product-compliance
Lightning Source LLC
Chambersburg PA
CBHW020257030726
47499CB00001B/225